THE LIST

JONAH GREENE MYSTERIES BOOK 1

GRAHAM H MILLER

Book Cover Design by ebooklaunch.com

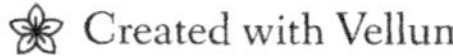
Created with Vellum

PATRICK

CHAPTER 1

AUGUST 27, 1995

The man who would be a killer waited in the dark. He had chosen his spot well, back from the path, in the shadows cast by the trees. His thoughts were occupied with two doubts. Firstly, he worried about his plan. Would anyone even walk through a park alone in the early hours of the morning?

His night had been long and fruitless – only three potential victims had presented themselves. Each time they were saved either by a passer-by, or because they were walking a dog, or simply because they looked too strong to overpower easily.

His second misgiving was that he would not be able to carry through the attempt, should a suitable victim come forward.

He checked his watch – two twenty. Should he abandon tonight? He had made arrangements. He had promised that a murder would happen before dawn. He was tired and he ached from standing still for several hours. But the thought of going back with his tail between his legs was unbearable. And possibly dangerous. He resolved to stay here as long as it took. Moving slowly, he bent his stiff knees and half sat back against the trunk of a tree.

No sooner had he achieved some level of comfort than a cackle of laughter came from the road outside the park. He straightened painfully and peered through the leaves. He could see a tiny slice of the main road. A group of young people were chatting and saying goodbye. He guessed that they had just left the local nightclub.

He tightened his grip on the bayonet and shifted his weight slightly. His hand felt sticky under the latex glove and he wished he could remove his hairnet and scratch his head. But he couldn't risk leaving a single hair.

At least it wasn't cold, he thought. It was the Sunday morning of the bank holiday weekend and the ground under his feet was like dusty rock.

Would this be the start of his journey? He still didn't know if he could transform himself into a killer.

The group on the main road fell quiet. One lone woman had chosen to walk through the park. He could hear the rest of the group getting quieter as they made their own ways home. His quarry was alone. He stepped forward and checked the other direction – deserted.

He tensed forward, like a dog straining at the leash.

She was a little over five foot and slim. She had a fashionable long blonde bob and was wearing a blue strapless dress and very little else. Over the hot dry air, he could hear her humming 'Never Forget' by Take That under her breath.

She looked so alive, so vital. Each step was a small bounce. Black heels and black clutch bag to match. White legs almost glowing in the night.

This, he would find out later, was Emma Walters. The

papers would describe her as 'a twenty-five-year-old bubbly blonde' with 'her whole life in front of her'. She 'loved the clubbing scene' and 'her many friends' were soon to be 'devastated'.

Rolling his feet so he didn't make a sound, he crept forward and crouched down.

When he saw a flash of blue between the leaves of the bush, he launched himself up and out, holding his knife out in front of him. He crashed into the woman and the force of his lunge carried them to the other side of the path.

There was a shocked expression on her face. She was level with his shoulder and just hung there, suspended.

He stepped back, withdrawing the knife and she collapsed away from him into the flowerbed. She lay there, a wounded animal, gasping for breath. In his initial attack the bayonet had stabbed her through her dress and now a dark stain slowly spread across her side.

Her killer stood over her. Had he done enough to finish the job? Would she bleed to death here in the flowerbed? No. He had promises to keep. He leant forward and pushed her harshly to the ground. Her eyes implored him. They locked onto his and begged for mercy. A single tear rolled down her cheek.

He looked away and jabbed down blindly with the bayonet. But his hand jarred as the blade struck a rib and slid sideways.

He looked back and panicked when she drew in a breath. He moved his left hand ready to stifle a scream. But she only produced a dry rattle before falling silent. Her attacker moved his feet to straddle her body, one scruffy trainer making a faint mark in the dust next to her hand, more evidence for the police.

He withdrew the knife, leant back and took a deep

breath. His victim lay on her back, completely still as shock and blood loss took hold. Each breath she fought to take made a bubbling noise in her throat. He had rehearsed this in his mind. He knew what to do.

This was the moment where he could either turn away or reach out and seize his destiny. He pushed all his misgivings from his mind. This was not a person, not a woman; this was the only obstacle between him and his future.

He placed his left hand on her breastbone. He found the ribs by touch, located a gap between them. Using his thumb as a guide, his third stroke was on target. Between the fifth and sixth ribs, angled slightly towards the centre, it went straight through the heart. The shock to her body was overwhelming. She tried to lift her head but it flopped back with soft thud onto the earth. Her hands and arms lifted off the ground and drummed a slight tattoo before everything was still.

As he waited for her to die, he looked into her eyes. He hoped to see something mystical when the light went out, but they just lost their lustre and went flat. He pressed forward with his weight, until the tip of the knife bit into the earth.

Then he stood and left the bayonet buried up to the hilt.

One life had just been extinguished and another had been changed. This was, as promised, a destiny-changing moment. So why did it feel slightly disappointing?

The killer felt a cold emptiness inside, a chill through his bones. All the details had been carefully worked out, pitfalls anticipated and avoided. He stepped back to the path and looked carefully up and down. He picked up one shiny black shoe and threw it into the bushes, to be found later in a fingertip search.

Someone in a hurry could walk past and miss her, but

any dog walker, or litter picker would probably notice the body. He nodded to himself, thinking that she was well enough concealed for his purposes. He wiped his hands on his thighs, then carefully peeled off the boiler suit he was wearing. When this was stuffed in a nearby bin, together with the scabbard for the bayonet, he removed his latex gloves and hairnet. Further into the park, he retrieved a rucksack from behind a tree and removed a plastic bag. He put the gloves and hairnet in, tied it off, turned it inside out, and tied it off a second time. Then he buried the bag at the bottom of the rucksack under some dirty underwear. He shrugged on an army surplus jacket and set off for Southend seafront.

He had a few hours to wait, so he hunkered down on a bench like a down-and-out. As he waited, he swigged from a half bottle of vodka he'd brought with him. It was originally to give him Dutch courage, but he hadn't needed it earlier. Now, it was essential.

He wondered if she wore knickers or a bra under an outfit like that. The thought of her being catalogued and inspected by pathologists and policemen was almost more unbearable than what he'd done.

No. He pushed the thought out of his mind. He took another swig of vodka. It didn't matter now, she was dead. He had moved forward. The alcohol warmed his stomach and numbed his feelings. He wasn't getting drunk, but was hardening up, pushing the unwelcome thoughts away.

He huddled up and waited, alone with his thoughts of her face, the terror, the incomprehension. The moment when she realised she was dying replayed through his mind.

Each errant thought was chased away with a sip from his bottle.

When it was time, he walked briskly to the station,

trying to banish the cold in his limbs. His timing was perfect, and he got straight onto the first train of the morning. There were hardly any other passengers and he was alone in his end of the carriage. He wondered if he'd been seen, if anyone in or around the station would remember him.

In London, he walked out of the station and into anonymity. He had breakfast at a greasy spoon without tasting his food. While he was eating, he checked over the lists he'd made in his head.

When he'd worked out his plan, he'd read a lot of books about serial killers, mostly about how they were caught. He distilled this knowledge down to one simple theory – links. If the police could uncover and prove the links between the killer and victim, then the game was up. That was why he'd dropped everything at the scene that could link him to the body. The weapon and boiler suit were only dangerous if they were found in his room, or somehow connected to him. The only items he'd taken away were those with his DNA on them – his hairnet and latex gloves. By choosing a location over a hundred miles from where he lived, he'd broken another link.

The walk to Paddington was longer than he anticipated – he wandered through the capital in a daze until he came to his station. Here, he bought a separate ticket. He didn't want a single through ticket to link his home and the murder site. By the time his train had left the suburbs, he was dozing in his seat. He arrived home before noon, bone weary. But he stuck to the plan, burning the bag containing the hairnet and gloves in a metal bin. He put the ashes with his trainers and socks into the rubbish, the rest of his clothes in the washing machine. While the machine hummed and sloshed around, he fell into bed and straight to sleep.

His sleep was fitful, the idea of links rattling around in his head. He tried, in his dreams, to count all the connections between himself and his victim, to check them off on some big list and make sure they were all severed.

But there could always be one that he hadn't foreseen, not even thought about. Something that the police could follow like a thread that would lead them to his door. Was there a stray hair? Would one bit of spit be enough to trace him? Had someone seen his face? The vision changed to a running, anxiety dream. If he just went far enough, fast enough, he'd leave the last link behind.

When he woke the next day, he still felt cold and empty. He checked the news – on the other side of the country, relatives had been informed, and the press had worked themselves up into a frenzy. One of his housemates had taken the rubbish bag to the communal bin. This would be collected tomorrow, removing the last forensic link between killer and victim.

There were many miles and no physical, traceable link between them. She did however, live on in his mind. He had seen her for about 120 seconds, but he would never forget her face. It would haunt his waking moments and torment his dreams. In the months and years to come, he would try to avoid the Crimewatch appeals and crying relatives on the news. But, no matter how much he drank, his brain stored information – Emma Walters, aged twenty-five, brutally slain on her way home from a night out with friends. There would be no escaping his memory.

He sat up in bed and reached for the half empty vodka bottle.

CHAPTER 2

February 23, 2015

DC Jonah Greene looked at DI Linwood across a desk cluttered with paper.

"So, um, are you feeling better after all the, ah, problems?" Linwood leaned back on his worn chair.

Okay, Jonah thought, it's going to be euphemisms. He wasn't surprised – Linwood had never faced a personnel matter head on.

DI Linwood filled the pause with, "I mean, are you, you know, well, better?"

"Yes, yes, time off and some help was all I needed," Jonah said cursing himself for his forced jollity. "I mean, that is to say, fighting fit and ready to get back to work."

"Back to work, yes, you see, that is the thing isn't it..." Linwood paused to tug at his ear, adding more dandruff to his shoulder. "That's why I wanted you to come in here to see me before the team. We, that is, management have decided that, well, team morale and everything."

Jonah's stomach tied itself in knots. He tuned out the DI talking in half-sentences. He tried to remember what his union rep had said about whether he could be made to leave his job. He knew that he either had to quit for good or go back. He couldn't face any more daytime TV and putting up with disapproving looks from his wife, Alex.

"...overall team dynamic. As a senior officer, it's my responsibility to have group oversight..."

It was his first day back after three months enforced sick leave. There had been a thick layer of frost on his car this morning. He hadn't expected it and had used a credit card to scrape it off, freezing his fingers and making him late. Then his hands had swelled up and gone red in the car, and now they were itching.

"...of course, moving forward as an effective organisation..."

Jonah discreetly rubbed his hands on his trousers. His jacket was by his side, in a puddle on the carpet. Halfway to work, it had started sleeting, and when he got to the station, he was escorted straight to his boss's office without a chance to visit his desk or hang up his coat.

"...we don't want to move you to another force. Relocation expenses, upheaval." Jonah wondered how Linwood kept his job. The DI's beer belly threatened to escape from his striped shirt while his tie had no hope of ever meeting his belt. He was probably about Jonah's age, but looked unhealthy. He had a ruddy face and wiry salt-and-pepper hair. His skin was dull, and he was shorter than Jonah.

"Should be right up your street, sympathy, and helping people with the paperwork. A bit less, ah, um, stressful than, well you know." He paused; the thread momentarily lost. "Anyway, Rob's been looking to retire for some time, seemed to be for the best, all been agreed." The DI slid a pile of papers towards Jonah.

He picked them up and hid behind them while he tried

to figure out what the conversation had been about. 'Coroner's Officer – Job Description' he read on the top sheet. Now he understood. Rob Underwood was the current coroner's officer and he was nearing, if not past, retirement age.

"So, you'd be in the same building, but on a different floor," Linwood said. Away from the CID, Jonah thought. When he'd considered returning to work, he had feared that he would be shut out by the rest of his team. Or put in impossible situations so he'd have to leave. Now he was being spared all that, but he would be hidden away – out of sight and out of mind.

"But I'd still be your boss, for personnel issues. Annual leave, er, sick leave, all that stuff." He brightened as he moved away from dangerous waters. "But day to day work assignment and the like, that'll be the coroner himself."

There was a pause and Jonah looked up from his paperwork. For all that this was a done deal, he still needed to agree to it. Before Jonah could find the right words, Linwood was talking again.

"Ah, yes, how could I forget? You passed your sergeant's exam," he rifled through the papers on his desk, "nearly three years ago." He appeared to have taken Jonah's silence as a negotiating stance. "Well, with this post, we've got the budget to put that through, as your pay grade for coroner's officer."

Jonah looked around the grim office. Replacing all the grey filing cabinets with light wood units hadn't made it any more cheerful. It was still untidy and unwelcoming although Linwood was making the atmosphere worse. He looked as if he would rather be anywhere but here. For a man who would willingly be the first through a door on a drugs raid, Linwood was useless at facing up to emotions.

Unable to stand looking at Linwood or his office any

longer, Jonah gazed out of the window at the massed desks of the CID open-plan area. They didn't want him there, and it would be a living nightmare being frozen out, even if he found a way back. He caught the eye of a woman in a hijab. He didn't recognise her – obviously she'd joined the team while he was on leave. She gave him a funny lopsided smile that said, 'You're being carpeted but chin up, it'll get better!' He turned back and Linwood was still looking at him, a hopeful expression on his face.

"Oh, yes," Jonah said, "I'll take it." Sergeant pay grade, he thought. "So, I'll still be a police officer, not a civilian?"

"Yes, that's right." Linwood stroked his moustache thoughtfully. "Warrant card, police federation, the whole nine yards. But answering to the coroner and working within his offices." He dug around on his desk before passing more paperwork to Jonah. "If you could, ah, just sign and date, here and here, we can get it all done."

Jonah glanced at the clock. It was only nine fifteen on Monday morning and he'd already lost his job. Or been given a promotion. He wasn't quite sure which. As he signed the papers, Linwood rose and opened the door behind him.

Jonah followed him out into the office which was unnaturally quiet. The only officers present were diligently looking at their monitors or talking on phones. The grapevine was working as well as it always had. He was no longer welcome and the message was clear.

"Hope you don't mind, we, ah, took the liberty, well that is to say, desk space, and uh, your replacement." Jonah followed him as he went to a waist-high filing cupboard and took down a cardboard box. It had once held 'A4 Paper, 5 Reams, Laser Printer Quality, White'.

Jonah took it from Linwood and looked at the motley

contents – a framed photo of Alex and their children, Gareth and Emily, some pens, a sandwich box, holiday postcards and a paperback. So, there really had been no choice at all. He dropped the coroner's paperwork on top of it all, covering it up.

Linwood was expertly steering him towards the door. On the way the woman in the hijab gave Jonah a thumbs up only he could see. When they reached the edge of CID territory, Linwood held out a hand, and there was awkwardness as Jonah shuffled the box from one arm to another without dropping his jacket before shaking his DI's damp hand.

"Well, good luck in your new job," he was saying, calmer and more relaxed. "Obviously any suspicious deaths, our paths will cross. And I'll approve all your leave and whatnot by email, no problem."

"Yes, sir," Jonah said, still slightly in a daze. Before he knew it, he was standing outside the office, holding the contents of his desk in his hands. He knew he had left his job in CID behind but had no idea what the future held.

DOWN TWO FLIGHTS of stairs and he was in a different world. Without warning he had been banished from the CID offices that had been his place of work for the past four years. He was in new territory.

Like all CID officers, Jonah had dealt with the coroner before. But his dealings were usually work related and short term – mostly reporting the date, time and circumstances of finding a body. His impression was that the coroner was ex medical and a bit formal. Jonah also had a measure of superstition about someone who chose to spend his career working with the dead. Still, whatever he thought, he was about to meet his new boss.

The coroner had a suite of offices that were next to the Coroner's Court. Perhaps suite was too grand a word – there were two small offices, one larger one, and a meeting room arranged around a reception area.

Denise, the coroner's secretary, welcomed Jonah and showed him that one of the smaller offices was his. This was the first good news of the morning – no more sharing an open-plan area.

Jonah wondered what the coroner thought of the politics that had obviously caused Rob's retirement, but his curiosity remained unsatisfied. "Timothy's out of the office today, but he says you're to make yourself at home," Denise informed him, before showing Jonah the coffee machine. A phone call interrupted her, leaving Jonah alone. Another deserted office, he thought. Maybe the remainder of his time with the police would be spent in empty offices as news of the reason for his time off spread? Was the coroner really busy or just putting off their first meeting?

He wondered if all those late-night discussions with Alex had resulted in the wrong decision. Maybe he should have transferred to another force? But then, he thought, it would take one, "Aren't you the policeman who...?" conversation and he'd be back to square one.

Attempting to banish self-doubt, Jonah got himself a coffee and arranged his photo and other objects just right on his desk. The office had been cleared of all his predecessor's personal belongings, leaving only official documentation.

Out of the window, Cathays Park was beautiful even in the murky, grey weather. At his desk he scanned the paperwork that Linwood had given him. He wondered what he could read into the empty office. Had Rob been keen to retire or was he pushed out? Jonah had expected to see him for at least a short handover period.

Now he had a new job to do and only the official paperwork to tell him what to do. He knew from bitter experience that the job description was often less than half of what was involved. Still, he had discussed returning to work with his counsellor. It would be like putting on a uniform, even if he was plain clothes now. Once he settled in, to the same environment, his reactions would return. He would adopt the persona of a professional policeman. He just hoped that he wouldn't have exactly the same responses as previously.

His introspection was broken by the phone ringing.

"Hello?"

"Is that the coroner's office?"

"Yes, sorry, DS Greene here." The new rank still felt unfamiliar to him. "What can I help you with?"

"PC Marston here. We've got an unidentified dead body." Jonah could hear the traffic in the background. "Male, forties, probably homeless, under a hedge near Roath Park. Wasn't there last night so it's fresh."

"Okay." Jonah scanned through the paperwork. "Do you need me out there?" He looked out of the window at the grey sky. Sleet had just started falling again.

"No, we've already cordoned off the scene and arranged for photographs to be taken, and documented the possessions, such as there are." There was a sigh from the other end of the line. "Mind you, those possessions included two vodka bottles and there was a frost last night, so I don't think we're looking at suspicious circumstances. Still, better follow procedure."

"Okay then," Jonah said, reading rapidly and half listening. "I'll arrange transport and liaise with the morgue. You said unidentified, no documentation on the body?"

"No, I've done a quick search, but no identifying documents found."

"No problem, I'll go down to the hospital to meet the body and get photographs so we can start on identification."

Jonah sat back in his chair and rubbed his chin. He knew what he expected a coroner's officer to do from his perspective as a policeman, so now he just had to do the job as best he could in the absence of any guidance. Rob had left the office well organised but had relied more on paper than the computer. There was a directory of phone numbers so Jonah phoned the hospital. Once he had introduced himself and explained that he'd taken over Rob's job, he arranged transport and informed the morgue. Jonah gave Rob a silent prayer of thanks when he found a stack of blank forms, all labelled and carefully arranged.

He looked at one of the forms and shook his head. He could hardly fill in any boxes – name, address, date of birth, place of birth – all had to be blank. His pen hovered over date of death, but there was no certainty that he died after midnight today, and likewise time of death was blank. He didn't even want to write NFA under address until he established that there really wasn't an address where the deceased might have lived. In the end, he ticked Male and laid the form to one side.

He introduced himself by email to the coroner and explained what had happened and how he could be reached. He checked the clock – he had a couple of minutes before he needed to leave for the hospital. He needed to phone Alex.

As he waited for her to answer, he looked at her photo on the desk. It had been taken in a restaurant on one of their rare family meals out. Crowded around the table were Alex, looking elfin and beautiful as always, her face framed by dark hair in a feathered cut, and their children, Gareth on her left and Emily on her right. Gareth was now at a technical college learning plumbing. His personality was solid and dependable, and he looked it. He had a square-set face and ginger hair, long on top, with sideburns. Emily was more of a concern to Jonah. When Jonah looked closely at the photo, he could see the marks under the eyes and disarranged hair. She had forgotten about the meal out and had been up all night at a party the night before.

She was living in a shared house, supposedly painting jam jars and selling them as candle holders at the local market. She also bought and sold cheap jewellery on the same stall. Jonah suspected that someone in the house was selling drugs, but there was nothing he could do. He knew Emily was a bit of a dreamer and would never be organised or stupid enough to get involved in drug dealing, but he hoped she wouldn't get caught up in the scene unwittingly.

Alex's voice broke his reverie. "Hey, honey," she answered. "How's your first day back at work going so far?"

Jonah told her how his meeting with Linwood had gone and what his role was now. He had expected that with his return to work there would be a thaw in their relationship but she sounded as distant as ever.

Jonah outlined the duties, which mainly involved cataloguing and investigating sudden deaths. It sounded more and more like a career dead end. He was even boring himself.

"Anyway! I'm back behind a desk and not just sitting around the house. And I got a promotion." He hoped that this was what Alex wanted to hear.

"Is it really a promotion though?" Alex asked. "I know you've got your sergeant's rank, but you passed your exam three years ago. I just can't see where you can go from here?"

"Well," Jonah faltered. He knew Alex was right, the next step should be inspector. Which would be difficult as he'd then have to move department again, maybe even back to CID. "Still, the money will be useful. And I need to get my feet under the table here before I see about moving on. Can't be seen to be too flighty." He winced silently. This was his third promotion in twenty years.

"Is this more a desk job then? Based in the office nine-to-five?"

Jonah considered the question and the unspoken message. Like Linwood, Alex clearly didn't believe that he could ever return to his old role. He wouldn't be the officer he'd been before taking sick leave. He decided to ignore the implication and answer the question she'd asked.

"Well, I do have to go and deal with relatives and help them through the process in sudden deaths. And of course, people die at all times of day and night so there'll be a rota. But yes, most of the office work should be more nine-to-five."

Jonah quietly flicked through a folder on his desk. He stopped at a flow chart that Rob had drawn by hand and tried to figure out where he was in the process with the frozen homeless man.

"Oh, I'm off out tonight, you remember Karen?"

"Uh-huh," Jonah moved his finger across the chart.

"We're meeting up for a drink and she knows someone who's selling a motorbike. We'll probably grab something to eat later."

"Okay, I'll get my own dinner."

"I'll walk the dog before I go," Alex promised.

"Fine. Love you and I'll see you when you get home tonight."

"Love you too."

Jonah sat back and wondered what Alex had said about

the motorbike. But then he slid the papers back into their folder and set out for the hospital.

It was a brief drive to University Hospital Wales. Like the police station, it was late sixties to early seventies concrete architecture. Instead of one building though, the hospital was a massive sprawling complex of large buildings and car parks. Once Jonah had found his way to the morgue, he chatted to the pathologist while the orderlies sorted out the body and loaded it into a freezer.

"Of course I'll run the post-mortem, as per procedure, but off the record he had a blood alcohol over two hundred and there was a heavy frost last night. Don't think he stood a chance."

"Do you think he was genuinely homeless?" Jonah asked. In his experience sometimes people would go out on a drinking binge and sleep rough over several days despite having a home to go back to.

"He certainly fits the bill – the hair hasn't been washed for weeks, the dirt is properly ingrained into the skin, all his clothes are totally worn out. I'd say he's spent weeks at least, if not months or years living rough. Of course, this'll have to wait for my official report, but just to give you a heads-up."

"Thank you. Have you got a decent photo of his face?"

"I should be able to get something good enough for an identification. I'll email it to you by the end of today."

"Thanks."

The rest of the day was spent at the hospital. First, he went to the canteen for lunch – a limp sandwich – and filled in some of the paperwork for the pathologist. Then he returned to the morgue to help with cataloguing the deceased's possessions as evidence. This was a depressing task as his clothes were threadbare, and the only other items of note were two bottles of vodka, one nearly empty. Even when it was stripped and waiting in the morgue, the body yielded up no form of identification. There was just enough time for Jonah to go back to the office and find the address of the main homeless shelter before his first day in his new job was over.

Back at his desk, Jonah read an email from his new boss, Timothy Carlton, Coroner for Cardiff and the Vale of Glamorgan. The message was sent from an iPhone, apparently while Carlton was at a conference on modernising the court system.

But his new boss sounded happy that Jonah was using his initiative. He was also praised for sending an email, which only reinforced his suspicions that Rob had been too old-fashioned and had been forced out. He made a mental note to make sure he was seen using technology. He had a lot of ground to make up.

Easing back from his desk, he breathed out. Going back to work he had been prepared for a fight. He'd had his arguments marshalled and was ready to go, only to be faced with one boss who didn't even want to be on the same floor as him and another who wasn't even in the building. On top of this his wife wasn't going to be home when he got there. He felt all wound up with no outlet.

Pulling himself towards the desk, he opened an email with a photo of the face of the dead man. He read the report from the PC who'd found the body. Jonah traced the path from initial phone call, through to the responding PC, the paramedics and finally the mortuary team who recovered the body. He was strangely grateful that he had a body to deal with. Spending the first day with nothing to do in the office would have been unbearable.

Jonah switched back to have another look at the face of the dead man. Then he reached down a battered Cardiff A-

Z. The street where he was found sounded familiar. He found it in the atlas – as he thought, it was in an area called Cyncoed. This bordered Roath Park and was one of the most affluent suburbs in the city.

Jonah lived right on the edge of Cyncoed, a fact that used to lead to light-hearted ribbing about his salary. However, he knew one thing – it was not somewhere the homeless often went. He had started his police career on the beat and knew this was not a good area to doss down. There were lots of concerned residents with twitching curtains and very few warm doorways or business premises.

That left one question in Jonah's mind – what was a homeless man doing out there on a dangerously cold night?

JONAH DROVE one handed and ate his Big Mac with the other. Over a speed bump, his fries slid down the passenger seat into the crack at the back. At the next junction, he put the burger down next to the remains of his fries. They were wilted like flowers two days past their best, making the whole car smell rank and greasy. He briefly imagined going home. Now that both children had left home and knowing that Alex would be out, he could picture the empty house, him on the sofa watching rubbish on TV. But, he thought, not drinking lager. He remembered now that the fridge was empty and he had meant to pick up some more.

Making up his mind, Jonah changed his route and pulled into the car park of a pub. What he really wanted was to grumble to Alex about his day, but she was out. He briefly imagined her somewhere having drinks with a friend. In his mind's eye it was all very quiet and refined, a wine bar or upmarket restaurant.

The pub he chose was a square modern building that served good food and hadn't yet succumbed to the tide of chain-pub franchises currently sweeping through the suburbs. It had two further points in its favour – it was one of the pubs favoured by the local police, and at a pinch, he could walk home in twenty minutes if he drank too much. The walk back the following day would add some time onto his morning routine, but he knew from experience it was perfectly achievable.

The bar was unusually busy, and Jonah saw people moving in and out of a private room. He sighed and looked for an empty table. He saw only one and it was in the corner, nicely out of the way. He swung past it, noted the number, then ordered a proper burger and chips and a pint.

As he threaded his way through the tables, he noticed someone doing the same thing and heading for the same table. He arrived at the same time as the woman in the hijab from CID that morning.

"This is my table," she said, indicating a dark cardigan over the back of a chair that he had missed.

Jonah took a breath. He gave the rest of the pub a quick scan but he knew that there was nothing free. He felt the weight of all the little battles he'd been unable to fight throughout the day. His counsellor had told him he must pick small battles and make a stand over them, to build his confidence.

"I didn't see that, and I've just given them this table number." He kept his voice level. He didn't want to make any more enemies. "There wasn't a drink on the table," Jonah explained.

She held up a drink for him to see, "I just got this one

from the bar, they must've cleared my empty." She looked at him levelly, "I know enough to time my toilet breaks so I don't leave a drink on the table. And there was my cardigan."

Jonah looked around again, but every table was still occupied. "Anyway, where else could I go?" he asked, almost to himself, looking for a way out.

"You could drink at the bar?"

"I told you, I've just paid and ordered my food." Polite but firm, just like he'd been taught. "They needed a table number and I gave them this one." They stood each side of the table, facing off.

"You were nicer this morning," he said experimentally.

"I felt sorry for you," she said, softening up a little. She sat down and indicated the chair opposite him. "Come on then, never let it be said I kept a man from his food."

As he sat opposite her, she said, "It's Joseph something isn't it?"

"Jonah Greene."

"Farida Phillips," she answered. "Did you keep your job? You looked like Linwood was leading you to your execution."

"Yeah, kind of. I even got a promotion."

"Wow! I've never seen anyone look so glum about being promoted. Was it that bad?"

"Well," Jonah hesitated, unaware how much of his personal history she knew. "I had some time off and I didn't know if my job would still be here when I came back."

"And you'd be worried that you'd be frozen out if you did have your job?" Obviously, there were no secrets within the station. "A promotion was probably a good thing, though. I know what it's like to be frozen out and it's not fun at all."

"Yes, but they promoted me out of CID; got me out of the office. I'm on a different floor now – I'm the new coroner's officer."

"And they put you up to DS for that?" Jonah nodded and took a sip of his pint. "But, that won't last, will it? Aren't those posts becoming civilianised?"

"Yes and no, there's a post over at the council called bereavement officer," Jonah explained. "All the paperwork if there's a death without any family to deal with it. Not to mention the fact that the council are talking about merging several of the coroner's offices into one."

"So, what is your job now?"

"Well, there's a long list of conditions under which a death is reported to the coroner for investigation. What it boils down to though is, if someone doesn't die in a hospital, or after a doctor has told them they're seriously ill, then I get to give it a look over. I then sort them into misadventure or murder or whatever. But ultimately most of my job is just seeing where to pass the cases on to."

"I think you're being unfair about your new role. Sounds like there's a lot more to it than that. I mean, the days of a single detective solving a murder are long gone anyway – it's more like a Major Incident Team grinding through the data to solve it. But there are plenty of outcomes between outright murder and natural causes. And that is proper detective work – finding out what exactly happened." She looked straight at him, to gauge his response. "After all, isn't that what police work should be? Providing answers?"

"What do you mean?"

"Well, imagine you have a teenage lad who goes out for a drink, disappears, and turns up dead in a river. Wouldn't you want to know if he'd been murdered, or had an accident? If you could build up a picture of his last hours, you'd be doing a real service to his family, even if no crime had been committed that you could detect."

"Service?"

"Yes, helping people. Isn't that what the job is now?" Farida frowned at Jonah. "Or are you an old-fashioned thief-taker? All about banging on the handcuffs and 'You're nicked!'"

"I see!" Jonah said in mock outrage, "just because I'm the wrong side of forty you think it's all The Sweeney, Life on Mars and that old-fashioned stuff!"

"No," she said, dipping her head slightly, "and I didn't think you were old enough for The Sweeney."

"Well, if anything, I was born too early," he said morosely. "If I was coming up through the ranks now, I could get a computer science degree and hop onto a fast-track. Get one of those central jobs on NCA or something. White collar crime, fraud, online scams, databases and all that."

"You could still do that, though?"

"No, not really. I'll be fifty in a minute. Whether I went Open University or took three years off and did it full time, I'd be too close to retirement. I've already got over twenty years served so that'd put me near to the thirty year limit. Anyway, it'd be so depressing to be sat there going through interviews with bright young things half my age!"

"But how long is coroner's officer going to be a police role? As I said, they might civilianise it," Farida countered.

Jonah took a longer swig of his pint. "Yes, it might take a few years. And it's not as bad as it could be. Even civilianised, I'd still have to have access to a lot of the police databases and do the investigative work. Anyway, I can take retirement from the police, and go straight to the same job as a civilian. I'd still have a salary and my pension."

"It's so depressing for you to be talking about your pension!"

"Oh, I'm sorry, it's just been a bit of a weird day. I was wondering how it'd be going back to work after the time off but now I'm not even in the office." The silence stretched out awkwardly. The conversation had become too personal too fast. Finally, Jonah couldn't stand it and blurted out "What's someone like you doing here anyway?"

"Muslim you mean?" Her laughter tinkled, far more girlishly than expected. "It's a leaving do for DCI Wetherington – he's been here forever so the pub's full. I don't drink so I agreed to drive my best friend home, but the private room was too oppressive. That happens if you get too many drunk people together in one place. I'd rather wait out here with my orange juice and lemonade."

"And you're allowed to be here with a man?"

"If I couldn't talk to a man on my own, then I'd be pretty useless at my job!"

"Point taken." Jonah's meal arrived then and saved him from digging himself any further into a hole. "So, what did you mean about being frozen out?" He picked up his first chip.

"Well, I know it's the twenty-first century and we're all multicultural, but a Muslim woman on the force is still more than a lot of folk know how to deal with. I get everything from the 'Make us a cup of tea, love' brigade down to those who just ignore me because they don't know how to talk to me." She softened and smiled. "Of course, that's not all of them, otherwise it'd be intolerable going to work in the morning."

"Why do you do it though?" Jonah asked, "I mean, the job."

She gave him a long look, weighing up if she could trust

him. Eventually she said, "Within my community, there was a lot of pressure to become a housewife. But I needed to actually do something, make a difference, have my own life outside the home. And I stand by what I said earlier, about service. I know the job can be boring and repetitive and some weeks you're just rounding up the same stupid criminals over and over again. But, there are bright moments where you feel like you've served your community and made a difference." She stopped and laughed. "Now I sound like the one who's old-fashioned, right back to Dixon of Dock Green!" There was a pause as she tried to gauge Jonah's reaction. "When I was choosing a career, I knew I wanted to serve in some way, and I was rubbish at biology so all the medical options were out. And I can't see myself charging into a burning building. The police are so desperate for diversity, this was the easy option." She stopped again, looked at Jonah. "Mind you, if I divorced the husband and married a disabled, black lesbian I'd make Chief Constable in five years!"

Jonah gave a short bark of laughter and the tension was broken.

They exchanged names of children, spouses, potted histories of their careers in the police force. As he drove home, he thought about Farida. She was attractive, but there was no spark there, no danger. Instead, they were both isolated within the force and had enough in common to be friends. Sometimes one friend was all you needed to make the isolation bearable.

When he got home, Alex was curled up on the sofa, drinking a hot chocolate. Jonah stopped in the doorway for a moment. His wife always looked tiny when she sat like that with her feet under her at the end of the sofa.

"You're back late," she said, more of an observation than

an accusation. Jonah strained to find any sign of a thaw in her attitude, but she sounded disinterested.

"Did you have a good night?"

"Yeah, it was lovely to catch up." Alex drained her mug and stood up. "I'm going up to bed, you coming?"

As they passed in the doorway, she stretched up to brush her lips against his. Jonah watched her leave. I'm scared that no one will talk to me, he wanted to say. He moved slightly toward her, wished he could bridge the gap, reach out and hug her. Whisper into her hair that he feared he wouldn't be able to do the job. But he didn't move.

"I'll be up in a bit, don't feel tired yet," Jonah said defeated.

He moved to the armchair, turning the day over in his head.

Once he could hear Alex moving about upstairs, Jonah switched on the TV and flicked through the channels. He switched it off and the whole house fell quiet enough for him to hear it creaking and sighing in the night.

Until he knew how Timothy Carlton would react to him, he couldn't properly settle into his new job. Still, some things never changed. Tomorrow he had paperwork to do and he would be going round the homeless shelters. Like his previous job, he would be trying to identify people and get information out of the reluctant. Hopefully he would get answers to his own doubts. He needed to prove to himself that he was capable.

CHAPTER 3

THE NEXT MORNING, Jonah headed for the largest homeless shelter in Cardiff, housed in a hall under a city centre church. He stopped at the office first to pick up all the paperwork about the body and the photograph.

Well wrapped up against the cold, he pushed open the heavy wooden door. Inside was a long, low room with benches and tables. A counter at one end was being cleared from breakfast. A few faces turned towards him, all etched with despair and boredom.

Before he could take in any more details, Jonah found his view blocked by the chest of a taller man. He kept walking, forcing Jonah to take a step back. He loomed over Jonah and scowled at him. The man was a full head taller, had a hard face, and cropped hair the colour of steel wool.

"Police?" He spat the single word out as a question.

Jonah nodded.

"Warrant?"

Jonah shook his head and found himself hustled awkwardly back up the steps and onto the pavement. Recovering his equilibrium slightly, Jonah took a step or two back, throwing the man off balance. While Jonah seethed inwardly, the man got his elbow in a vice-like grip and steered him down the street.

As soon as he could, Jonah threw off the other man's hold and whirled to face him. "I could have you for assaulting a police officer!"

The man simply took a step back and held his hands out inviting Jonah to put him in handcuffs.

For a moment the two men stared at each other. Jonah had slipped straight back into his role as a policeman. He had the same reaction to being manhandled as any other officer. He felt a brief burst of relief – he had not frozen when it came to the sharp end. Calming down, he now realised that he needed this man, needed the information he had.

"Okay. Not this time. But you can't go pushing the police around."

"What are you doing here, man?" He had a noticeable Scandinavian accent.

"I'm DS Greene and I need some information."

"Information? Listen, have you seen the weather?"

"Weather?" Jonah was taken aback by the change of direction but recovered quickly. "What's the weather got to do with anything?"

"Yes, weather." The man emphasised the word, as if Jonah was either deaf or a bit slow. "Last few nights there was a frost and this weather's going to keep up for a few days as well. Sleet, freezing rain, maybe wet snow. I need to get as many people into the shelter and fed with hot meals as I can." He turned to glare at Jonah. "You go in there with your tie and expensive walking jacket, folder under your arm, you might as well still be in uniform. If word gets around, my clients will desert the shelter, just when they need it most!" He indicated a small alley and with exaggerated care led Jonah down there without touching him. "We have a strict policy of no police unless you can get a warrant. It makes them feel safer."

Jonah attempted to look contrite and offended at the same time, "I'm not here to arrest your clients. I need information from them."

"So you said."

Jonah got out a notebook, a habit from his days in uniform. "So, your name is?"

"Per Smorgenson," he spelt out both parts.

"And you run the shelter?"

"Yes, I'm the director and have been for the last eight years. Before that I was a padre in the Swedish army." Jonah nodded and made notes.

"Okay, and have you seen this man anywhere?" He passed over the photo he had printed out.

"Paddy," Per said slowly. "He looks dead in this photo?"

"I'm sorry, yes he is," Jonah confirmed. "Found yesterday morning out near Roath Park under a hedge."

Per frowned and shook his head. "That's a long way out in the suburbs, away from where we could help him."

"I'm sorry," Jonah continued, "but we need a formal identification, find next of kin, arrange a funeral. You said he was called Paddy?"

"His name was Patrick or Paddy."

"Surname? Date of birth?" Jonah asked.

"No." Per shook his head with a rueful chuckle, handing back the photo. "No, that's not how the shelter works. If someone turns up sober and not causing trouble, they can have a meal and keep warm for a bit. But we don't keep records or fill out forms or anything like that. It's an open-door policy."

"Could you ask around?" Jonah asked, passing back the photo. "No one's in trouble, it was a cold night and he was drinking. Accidental death. I'm not looking to harass anyone, just need name and date of birth so we can find his relatives and give him a decent burial."

Per nodded slowly. "Okay. But you don't come back here." He checked his watch. "I have to organise things ready for lunch now. Two o'clock I'll meet you in Julie's Café on Bridge Street, tell you if I've found anything."

"Okay." Jonah handed his card over, then snatched it back. When Per frowned, he said, "Sorry, I've moved offices." He scribbled his mobile number on the back, together with his new office number.

Back at his office, Jonah spent the rest of his morning going through the case lists. Although every death briefly passed over his desk, most of them were simple natural causes, or more rarely suicides. But, as an investigator he had to give each one a quick look before turning them over to the coroner. A very few made it through to being investigated and even fewer were sent for inquest.

He ate lunch at his desk then made the short walk across town. He was glad of his 'expensive walking jacket' as the weather settled on an icy wind for the afternoon. As he expected, Per was waiting for him inside the greasy spoon café. He ordered himself a coffee and sat down opposite the padre, warming his hands on the mug.

"Well, I've just made your job easier," he said with a smile. "Patrick Kinsale, age mid to late thirties." He took a sip of his coffee. His entire demeanour was closed off and self-contained and Jonah had the feeling he treated everyone this way, from street sleepers upwards.

"Wait." Jonah held up a hand. "He wasn't even forty yet?"

"That's what people say." Per shook his head. "Been living on the streets on and off for years; it ages a person. When he was off the streets, word is he went back to his wife out in one of the suburbs. Anyway, he was a drinker and had been in trouble with you lot in the past." He slid the photo back across the table. "That should be enough for you, yes?"

Jonah slid the photo into a pocket and nodded. "Yes, thank you. I'll run him through the computer and see what we can find. Maybe he gave his wife's address one time."

"Can you let me know about the funeral, please?" Per asked. Jonah thought there was a slight vulnerability creeping into his demeanour.

"Sure, I'll check with the family about what the arrangements will be."

"You mean, if his friends would be welcome?" Per said, his cynicism wiping away the previous vulnerability. "Besides there might not be family. Some of these people are totally alone."

There was nothing to say, so Jonah nodded and drank in silence with Per, who finished his coffee and left first.

Once he was back in his office, Jonah had no trouble in finding all the details of Patrick's short life. Born on March 30, 1976, Patrick James Kinsale had bounced around the system for years. Mostly he was arrested and then released, cautioned, and occasionally fined or locked up for a few days.

Jonah flicked between the mortuary photo and the police record – it was the same man. Everything matched up, the stubbly face, the grey eyes, even the general look of being weathered by living out of doors. It was enough to convince him. In the morning he would arrange for fingerprints, just to make sure.

There was also an address on record for a Fiona Kinsale on an upmarket estate between Cardiff and Newport. Jonah was just about to set off to inform her of her husband's death when there was a knock at the door, almost too quiet to hear.

HE LOOKED up as a bearded face appeared around the door frame. "Come on in." The face was ingrained with dirt and the beard and hair were dirty and unkempt.

"Are you police? Investigating the death of Patrick Kinsale?" The figure loitered in the doorway. He was average height and build but his clothes were tatty, and carefully layered to keep the warmth in.

"Yes, I am police, but working for the coroner. I'm handling the paperwork following Patrick's death." The visitor was filthy, from his grubby, once-white trainers, to his greasy grey hair. Having already wrongly estimated Patrick's age, Jonah peered at the man, and guessed that even with the ageing effects of the street life, this man must be over fifty. He stepped into the office with a rucksack over one shoulder. He was at odds with the modern office, as if he belonged in an underpass, or on a park bench. Jonah pulled his notepad across the desk and clicked his pen. "Sorry, who are you?"

"I'm the Prof." The man came in and settled into the chair on the other side of the desk. "You lot gave me the bloody runaround. Word of Patrick's death was all over the shelter, so I went to the main reception at Cardiff Bay and they'd never heard of Patrick. They tried CID both there and over here with no luck. Then one of them suggested that I try the coroner. I can be an awkward bastard when I want to and I thought it might just be a way to make me walk across town and leave them alone. Anyway, here I am." He paused and looked around the anonymous office, seeming, despite his appearance, quite at home in these modern surroundings. "Could do with a coffee after all that walking around."

Jonah sighed. Tact and compassion, he remembered from what Linwood had said the previous morning. He levered himself up, and led the Prof to the coffee machine, trying not to breathe in through his nose. No, he thought, this man might have just lost his best friend. This is my job now, to help him understand the process and what's going to happen next. Doesn't matter if he lives in a mansion, or on the street, he's lost a friend and he needs my help.

When they were sitting down with coffee, Jonah picked up his pen again. "So, Mr...?" he said, with his pen hovering over the blank page.

"Oh, give it a rest! I could give you a name for your form but it doesn't matter. It's not like I've got an address or phone number. Just call me Prof." When Jonah frowned, he continued. "A lot of the people on the streets have problems you know, can't even read or write. I help them out if they need to deal with social services, or hostels, or the DHSS, anywhere they need forms filling in and such. So, they call me the Prof, on account of my advanced education." He grinned wickedly.

There was something about the way Prof had settled into the office and accepted his coffee that Jonah recognised. "You're not fooling me, though," he said. "You've had office jobs, a regular life before, haven't you?"

"You got me," Prof admitted. "I used to be a regular working Joe, what they'd call a white collar. Even worked in colleges for a bit, so it's fitting that they'd call me Prof, I suppose."

"What happened?"

"What always happens," he answered with a shrug. "Redundancy, wife left, money ran out." He moved his hand from side to side, floating down. "It's like those shells and stuff that settle down through the sea to make chalk. One minute you're on the surface, then you're not. One event after another, could happen to anyone. We're all a lot closer to the street than we think."

"You've never wanted to leave?"

"Leave? Of course I bloody want to leave! But once you're past fifty-five you're not employable, especially not without an address. And without a job you're just a number on a waiting list for a halfway house, place in a shelter." He gave a grim smile. "Oh, I know the system, fill in the forms, I'll find a place in a shelter for a bit sooner or later." He rubbed his hands together. "Anyway! I'm sure you don't want me sitting here in your lovely office telling my sob story! Although I could sit here all day and drink your coffee and keep warm. It's certainly nicer than anywhere else I could be!"

"Okay then, Prof, I take it you knew Patrick? I'm sorry for your loss."

Prof nodded, "He came to see me about a week ago, give or take." Prof stopped and looked down at his fingernails. "Thanks for your condolences, though I don't know if you mean it or not. I bet you didn't even know who he was yesterday." Prof took a deep breath. "Patrick was all right, you know. Sure, he had his demons and all, and liked his drink more than was good for him. There again, who doesn't? But he had a bit of learning, interest in the world around him. Could talk about what was in the news, read books when he could get them. When he was sober anyway. And he was a good sort. Always knew where houses were that were being done up, no one living there. Sometimes he'd take me with him and we'd either sneak in to kip or just use the shed or garden. Either way it was warmer and safer than being on the streets." He stopped again and stared out of the window. "Anyway, about a week, maybe ten days ago, he came to me. He was quite agitated, a bit upset, but excited too. He said that if he was killed, I was to go to the police and hand you this piece of paper. He asked me because he said he wanted it done properly, with receipts and everything. He didn't want to go to all that trouble just to have you chuck it in the bin." Prof's hand disappeared into one of the large pockets on his grimy overcoat. He brought out a mess of paper, mostly small handwritten notes.

As he sorted through the scraps of paper, Jonah's mind was whirling. Why had the Prof just implied that Patrick was killed? Surely a homeless death in winter wasn't that exceptional.

Meanwhile, the Prof selected one piece of paper, folded in four. He leant forward to smooth it out on the desk, before handing it ceremonially over to Jonah.

It was a page torn from a reporter's notebook, slightly grimy and with the top perforated. It had a list of seven names printed vertically down it, in block capitals in Biro. There were two columns, one of three names, the other of four.

EMMA WALTERS

MIKE KHAN PETER CALNE

ELIZABETH BARRYBILL WORMSLEA

JONAH TURNED IT OVER. There was no more writing on the back. He turned it back to the front. He looked up at Prof.

"What's it mean then?"

Prof simply shrugged. "I dunno. He seemed to think it would be obvious to you lot. It was his final request, if you like. Only it was all done in advance. Almost like he knew somehow." He stopped to consider the meaning of this profound statement for a couple of seconds. "Can you do the paperwork now?"

"Yeah, sure." Jonah left the note on the table and looked through some cupboards until he found an evidence bag. He carefully sealed the note inside, then filled in the panel, using the computer to look up the case reference. He winced as he noticed that he hadn't yet had a chance to fill in the correct name and date of birth. Finally, he found a receipt book and gave the Prof a proper receipt.

"Why did you come? Patrick said you were to come if he was killed – this looks like natural causes."

Prof frowned and said, "Less than two weeks ago he was worried someone would try to kill him, and now he's dead. Just 'cos it doesn't look like he was killed doesn't mean he wasn't."

Jonah nodded soberly, his mind working overtime. Patrick and the Prof were homeless, the lowest strata of society. It was understandable if they wanted to feel more important than they were. On the other hand, his gut instinct was to trust the Prof. He came across as more trustworthy and likeable than most of the people he dealt with.

Still undecided, he pointed to the receipt. "I've left your

name blank," he explained. "You can fill it in when you've left if you want."

"Much obliged, governor!" Prof was a lot happier now that he had discharged his duty. "And thanks for the coffee." He gave a mock salute as he left the office.

Jonah sat at his desk and looked at the note in its sterile plastic bag. He picked up his notebook and made some quick notes of the conversation while it was fresh in his mind. When he got to Prof's explanation of how he ended up on the street, he shivered.

Jonah wondered how close he had he come to the edge himself. When that raid had gone wrong, he had been lucky to find a federation rep who was on his side. A medical explanation was found, and mandatory sick leave agreed. If that hadn't happened, he would have left the force on a disciplinary. He would have struggled to find a new job. Alex would have stayed, but without the children to keep them together, for how long? He could see her become 'the wife in the suburbs' as he moved into temporary accommodation. Then he'd be one crisis away from living on the street.

He shook his head as if this could banish his dark thoughts and resolved to be kinder to any homeless people he met in the future.

As a distraction, he walked over to the photocopier and made a copy of the list. Walking back to his desk, he studied it.

Seven names, without any date of birth, or location. Jonah knew how useless this was. Many people shared their name with tens, hundreds or even thousands of people. What he needed was some extra information – middle names, rough ages or marital status would narrow the list down. Wormslea, he thought, that could be a way in, can't be many of them. And Calne, too, reading the list, that might be traceable. But even if he found two matches, he'd have no way of telling which name meant anything to Patrick Kinsale.

Hell, he thought darkly to himself, they might not even be real names, or they might not be anything to do with Patrick. They could be the result of the workings of a deluded mind. Or he might have plucked them from a newspaper. Patrick was wrong – it wasn't obvious to this policeman.

But one thing was certain, these seven names had been important enough to Patrick that he wanted the police to know about them after his death.

Jonah deliberately put the list over to one side and reached for the keyboard. He had work to do. He copied the details across onto his new record. Now he had a name and date of birth, the next step would be confirmation by next of kin. It was the end of the working day, a perfect time to call on the wife.

He looked from his mobile to the photo of his wife and children and back to his mobile. In his head he was preparing to deliver the bad news to Mrs Kinsale, while also wondering about the seven names. In the back of his thoughts was his near miss with homelessness. He couldn't face talking to Alex; if he picked up any sense of distance it would amplify his black mood. He felt that, somehow, he disappointed Alex, but he couldn't figure out why. Maybe, he thought in the voice of his therapist, he disappointed himself.

Whatever was going on in his head, he needed to tell Alex that he would be late back so he sent her a text. Then he sorted out where Fiona Kinsale lived and noted down the postcode for his sat-nav. He picked up the copy of the list as well.

Looking at it he could sense the desperation of Patrick to trust the Prof with it. He had no one else to turn to, a distance between himself and society.

He looked up from the piece of paper. The office was empty and the building quiet. Prof had come and gone like a shade. All he'd left behind was a used coffee cup, a faint musty smell and a list of names. He hadn't even left his name.

CHAPTER 4

Jonah checked the house number and parked up outside Fiona Kinsale's house. Out of long habit, he checked his surroundings. As he thought, St Mellons wasn't quite as affluent as Cyncoed, but it was a long way from being a problem suburb. The houses were smart 1930s semis with large gardens leading onto wide streets.

It was already dark, and winter showed no sign of releasing its grip on the weather. The light glowing around the curtain edges made Mrs Kinsale's house look welcoming. He wondered if this was how his house would look to an outsider. He knew from experience that every house on this street hid its own secrets.

He stepped from the car and felt the same cold night air that had killed Patrick. The wind gusted, looking for chinks in Jonah's coat.

The house was tidy and well looked after, as was the front garden.

A woman opened the door, drying her hands on a tea towel. She was tall and thin but not willowy with wide shoulders and an air of strength, healthy tanned skin, and dark ringlets falling past her shoulders.

She looked young and exotic – cast from the same mould as Catherine Zeta-Jones, dark and beautiful. Typical, Jonah thought, for the area around Swansea. He wondered where she came from before moving to Cardiff.

She was half-turned towards the house and not really paying attention to who was on her doorstep.

When she moved into the light, Jonah could see the crow's feet just starting around her eyes. If this was Patrick's wife, he would expect her to be around forty.

"Mrs Kinsale?" he asked.

"Yes." She turned and focused properly on Jonah. He felt a pang of sympathy for her. So far, her evening was progressing smoothly; she was unaware that she was about to move from ex-wife to widow. He was holding his warrant card, but she knew from his demeanour who he was. "Oh shit! Police. What's he done now? You'd better come in then."

She walked through to the kitchen, leaving the door open for Jonah to follow. On the way past, she shut the door to a lounge, but not before Jonah had seen two children eating dinner while engrossed in the television.

When they were both in the kitchen, she shut that door as well and leant one hip against the worktop. "Go on, then, what this time? If he needs bailing out again, you can leave him in the cell overnight. I'm not getting a babysitter and going out now."

"Mrs Kinsale, you'd better sit down, I think." She didn't argue, but collapsed into a chair, resting her elbows on the table. She propped her chin on her hands and all her confidence ebbed away.

"How bad is it?"

"I'm really sorry, but a man was found dead this morning. Preliminary identification suggests that, well actually we're fairly certain that it is your husband, Patrick." He slid the best of the photos towards her.

She nodded and big tears fell onto the table. "Ex-husband," she corrected when she had herself together. Jonah found the kettle and started filling it. She looked at him as if he were an alien. Then she snapped out of it and said calmly, "Strong tea, please, lots of sugar. And call me Fiona."

There was a pause while Jonah opened cupboards and made the tea. The kitchen, like the rest of the house, was tastefully decorated. Everything was clean, there were no DIY jobs waiting to be done. It was obviously a family home, but not untidy at all.

When Fiona had a steaming cup, she started speaking, looking down at the liquid. "Stupid bastard! I don't even know why I'm crying, I kicked him out years ago."

"It's just the shock, it's natural."

"I've seen the way you look round this place," she snapped, "I know what you're thinking! How can she live in a place like this and leave her husband to die on the streets? I must be some cold-hearted bitch." Before Jonah could respond, she continued. "He was a property developer; did you know that? Ha! That has to be the worst joke ever – a homeless property developer.

"Of course, he chucked the lot of it away, didn't he? He was bloody useless. Every now and again he'd get it on him and put everything he owned up for auction. Wouldn't care if it was recession or good times. Didn't matter if he was halfway through restoring it, or if he'd just bought it. It was like he just woke up one morning and gave up on it all.

"Of course, the drinking didn't help. He ended up being

blacklisted by all the subcontractors in the area. Either double-booking or forgetting he'd booked or being late making payment. Then I'd turn up when he was meant to be working and find him sleeping off the latest binge, just kipping down on a building site. I guess that's when he started living rough."

"I'm so sorry," Jonah said cautiously.

"Of course you are! Typical Patrick, being inconvenient, even when he's dead!" She shook her head; sipped her tea before rubbing her eyes with her knuckles. She reached in her handbag for a tissue to blow her nose, before picking up the photo again. She stared at it thoughtfully.

"I kind of hoped, you know, that I'd look at it and it wouldn't be him. But I knew. I knew this day would come, even if I didn't want it to. There was something in him that ate him up from the inside. I always felt that he was never going to grow old." She turned the photo over, face down on the table. "Don't want to remember him like that." Again, she looked in her handbag, finally sliding a photo in a small leather case across the table. Jonah picked it up. A much younger Fiona and Patrick were crammed into a photo booth, laughing. Patrick looked much younger, clean-shaven and smiling.

"When we met, he was all that, you know? Young, flash, always a drink in his hand, always ready with the money. Wasn't like the other Irish boys though – he was a bit calmer and quieter, not with all the charm and chat-up lines. At the time it made him more attractive because he had a bit of darkness in him. Of course, it's what ate him up in the end."

There was a silence. Jonah listened to the TV next door sounding tinny and muted through the solid walls. He wondered how long the children would take to finish their tea, and if they'd just continue watching TV after that.

"How did he die?" Fiona asked. "Can you tell me that?" She looked at him, hope and fear etched on her face.

"This is an initial assessment, but it appears he froze to death. Probably had too much to drink and couldn't get somewhere warm. It has been colder than usual these past few days."

Fiona nodded glumly, as if it was what she expected to hear. She frowned slightly. "He always seemed quite together, even when he was drinking, you know, he'd find somewhere safe to doss down."

Jonah shrugged. "The trouble is, it's a precarious life. It only takes one mistake. How long has he been like this?"

"Living on the street?" Jonah nodded. "Before Connor was born, he'd just go off on a bender sometimes and not come back for days, or even weeks. Turn up out of the blue when he ran out of cash. Then Connor was born, and while he was little, he'd sometimes stay over on site if he had a lot of work to do." Again, the wry smile crossed her lips. "As I said, more often than not he was hiding out and drinking. But children always grow up, don't they? One night, Connor had been asking about his daddy and if he was going to stay. Patrick was asleep upstairs, just waltzed in, had a shower and passed out on the bed. I sat here, right in this chair and sobbed because I knew I had to choose. How do you choose between your child and his father?

"The next morning, I got Connor off to school and sat down with Patrick. I told him he was either going at it full-on; rehab, giving up the booze, therapy, whatever it took, or he'd just spent his last night in the family home. We had a huge row. Apparently, there were things I didn't understand, he didn't want to be like he was, but it was impossible to change. Looking back, I genuinely think he was scared."

She stopped to think. "That was when Connor was in Year One so it must be nearly five years ago now."

Jonah looked up from his tea. This was the second person today who'd said that Patrick was afraid. And had been afraid for over five years. Now was obviously not the time to ask Fiona about it, but he filed it away in his memory before asking, "Are the children...?"

"Connor's his, Liam isn't. When I was pregnant with Connor, he signed this place over to me." She wiped some tears aside as she said this. "It was in a bit of a state, but it's a solid house and I've done some work on it. It meant it was the one place he could come back to as he couldn't sell it when he had one of his moods.

"That's what happens when you become a mother. You get ruthless. I suppose I knew, even way back then, I knew he wasn't good father material. It took me another seven years to finally put him on the spot, but I knew which way he'd go, and that I needed a house." She looked straight at Jonah, "I still feel bad when I think about it, getting him to sign it over when he was hungover. But," she shrugged, "what can you do?"

"I think you did the right thing," Jonah reassured her. "As a policeman I wish more mothers would do what you've done to look after your kids. If they'd grown up with an unreliable drunken dad floating in and out of their lives, there's more of a chance they'd have ended up coming to our attention sooner or later."

Jonah was unsure if he was just reassuring her or if he really meant it. In his career he had seen plenty of people graduate from good homes to a life of crime. Likewise, he'd seen people drag themselves up from awful families to make something good of themselves.

"You're too kind," she said. She looked around at the

house as if she was expecting it to all change now Patrick was dead. There was a burst of laughter from next door, and Fiona looked up, suddenly alert. For a second both of them waited, but the muted sound of the TV and chatter reassured them that everything was all right.

"We've got a bit of paperwork to do, but I don't think we'll need you to view the body, unless you want to." Fiona shook her head. "Patrick was arrested by us a few times, so we'll run fingerprints." Jonah did some quick mental calculations. "You're divorced, but Connor is your child with Patrick?"

"That's right," Fiona said suspiciously.

"I think, unless there's a will, that means that Connor gets all his possessions, and as you're his legal guardian, you'd better deal with all that. Probably some sort of trust thing or something, not that there'll be enough to cause a problem." Fiona nodded. "But all that can wait a day or two if you want. Also, can I put out a simple press release? Just name and such like. Might find some people who knew him for the funeral?"

Fiona nodded again, and then her eyes widened in surprise.

"Sorry! It's been such a shock, but I've just remembered something. Hold on there a moment," and she left the room.

Jonah heard her reassuring the children, then she returned with a dark red A4 envelope folder. "This is Patrick's. It's his bank account and other stuff. He told me he didn't want it to get stolen, but I think it was more that he didn't want to be buying booze with it. He used to ring me up and I'd meet him when the kids were at school. I'd give him a bit of money or help him buy stuff or even book him into a Travelodge if he needed it. It was like having another kid – I even took him to the doctor once."

She slid the folder to Jonah.

"He had a bank account? But he was on the streets?"

"I've thought about it lots," Fiona said, "since we split up. I think he hated himself. I think the drink, the drugs, living rough, I think they were all ways of punishing himself. But I never thought he'd want to end it all."

"I'm going to leave you to get on with your evening," Jonah said standing up. "I've just got a couple more questions." Fiona looked up at him, looking both tired and slightly wary. "When did you last see Patrick?"

"Errm, after Christmas, I think. January, he got some money out of the DSS, some grant or something. We met up and I took him to an army surplus place and got him a warm jacket and a decent sleeping bag. We had a hot meal and a chat too, he seemed all right then." She paused. "Well, as all right as he ever was."

"And where were you last night?"

Fiona laughed, "I was here, as always, putting the boys to bed!" She then looked serious. "Do you really think he was killed?"

"No," Jonah said automatically, even though doubts were creeping in. He sorted through his folder and pulled out the copy of the list and passed it to Fiona. "Do you recognise any of these names?"

Fiona burst into fresh tears, this time proper sobs that were shaking her whole body. After a moment, she got herself back under control. "Sorry, it's his handwriting. Took me right back. Right." She put on her glasses and carefully read the list, following it with her finger. "No," she shook her head, "nothing occurs to me. Not friends or anything. Might be suppliers or subcontractors who he felt screwed him over? Or people he knew on the street. He hardly ever talked about the time before I knew him though, could be from then."

"What do you know about that time?"

"We did swap details when we were first getting to know each other," Fiona explained. "After that he never said a thing. He's from London, Kentish Town, still got family there that he never sees. Went to University of Swindon, then moved out here about two years before I met him. Like I say, he never talked about the past, I never met any of his relatives or old friends." She thought a moment, her eyes rolling up and to the left. "I've got a phone number for an uncle somewhere. I'll let him know and he can organise the London family if any of them want to come up for the funeral."

There was a pause as Jonah gathered up the photo and list and put it all together. He put a hand on the folder of bank details. "Can I keep these? I'll just take a few copies and give it back tomorrow?"

"Yes, of course."

There was nothing more to be said. Jonah left. He sat in his car in the darkness and thought over Fiona's words. Patrick Kinsale had a mysterious past, a self-destructive streak, and a feeling he would be killed.

CHAPTER 5

JONAH SAT UP IN BED, making Alex roll over and snuffle slightly. He had been going back over the day, trying to make sense of everything. Two unconnected items had floated together in his consciousness.

Suspicious death, that was how Prof had said Patrick was worried about being killed. This linked with what Fiona had said to him as well. Something somewhere started to make sense. In his mind's eye, he saw the property report and read down the list. He swung his legs out of bed and went to look for a drink or something to eat. This feeling reminded him of a Sherlock Holmes story where he had to look for something that wasn't there.

As he padded downstairs in his bare feet he tried to think carefully and see what links he was missing. Abandoning water for something stronger, he reached for the Apple Schnapps and sat cradling a glass in the dark on the sofa.

Upstairs the toilet flushed and he heard footsteps above him. "You coming back to bed?"

"Can't sleep! Be up soon!"

Jonah couldn't pull the thoughts out of his head, so he went in another direction. He switched on his laptop and went to Google. Without access to all the police databases, he was limited in what he could do from home. But he was also restless; something didn't really make sense.

Adding Patrick's name to the other seven, he tried combinations in Google together with Kentish Town and University of Swindon. Nothing significant came up until he searched for Peter Calne and Swindon – he was the secretary for the University of Swindon Alumni Society. Jonah frowned in the darkness. He had found his link, Patrick had gone there too.

The names 'Mike Khan' and 'Bill Wormslea' showed up in the news results. Mike Khan had been 'helping police with their enquiries' connected to heroin and cocaine distribution. Reading further, Jonah learnt that he was always acquitted.

Bill Wormslea had been murdered about twenty years before. The other names were too common and generated hundreds of hits, covering all the events of life; births, marriages and deaths, along with a smattering of hairdressers, plumbers, car salesmen, party organisers and life coaches. They were too vague as names on their own – he'd need either a location or an age or some other information to pin them down to the relevant individual.

What Jonah really needed was a clear head and some better databases, not to mention talking to Peter Calne and seeing if he had any more information. One thing was clear, sitting on the sofa in the early hours wouldn't do him any good. He went up to bed and slept fitfully through to morning.

Despite his broken night, Jonah arrived at the office early to try to contact Peter Calne. The phone was answered on the second ring, but Peter turned out to be evasive. He kept mentioning the Data Protection Act as if it was a shield that couldn't be got round. He was also reluctant to look up eight names over the phone. Even a reassurance that he could use directory enquiries to call Cardiff Coroners and get through to Jonah didn't work.

Eventually they reached a compromise. If Jonah came out to see him in person, with his warrant card and documentation, then Peter Calne would put all the names through his database.

Sighing, Jonah pulled out a battered map and wondered how long it would take to get to Swindon and back.

He then emailed a quick note to the local paper, asking them to put in a message about the death, asking for information. He sat back and reached for the current death notices to start sorting through them, but was interrupted by his boss, Timothy Carlton.

He was older than Jonah, and better dressed. He had fine blond hair, parted on a ruler-straight line to the left. One look was enough to tell that Timothy's suit and immaculately pressed shirt were of far better quality than his and definitely put DI Linwood to shame. The tie was held down with what looked suspiciously like a gold tie pin.

Jonah wasn't sure how to react to the fact he was so well attired. His natural instinct was to distrust him, but he knew this was unfair. It also made him feel slightly shabby and down at heel. Even though Timothy was older than him, he wasn't going to seed. Jonah had developed a bit of a beer gut and since he'd given up rugby, he was losing his fitness. Timothy somehow managed to look trim and fit, while obviously older than Jonah.

He steered Jonah into his office and sat down behind the desk.

"So, Jonah, welcome to the team!" Timothy was all effusive charm. "I believe that we are here to provide a service to our clients. I also have the view that everything should be above board. After all, aren't we now an inclusive service? So, I've reviewed your personnel file, and it's all fine by me. If the psychiatrist says you're fit to work, then that's good." Jonah nodded, dumbstruck by the contrast to DI Linwood. "This job looks like it'll be a good fit. More desk work, less kicking in drug dealers' doors."

"Well, I hope so," Jonah mumbled.

"If I can be honest with you, I'll be glad of a fresh face." He held up his hands. "No, don't get me wrong, I had all the time in the world for Rob! Fine officer, hard worker! But he wasn't on the same page as me. I look at all the new technology out there – tablets and smartphones – and see how it could be used to drag the coroner's office into the twenty-first century." He rubbed his hands together, "Now, let me know about this new body you've been investigating."

Jonah outlined what he had learned about Patrick Kinsale.

"I spoke to his wife and one of the other street people, and it all seems to be a bit weird. He was only wearing a shirt and a fleece – no sleeping bag or coat. And he had two bottles of expensive vodka with him. Mrs Kinsale said that she bought him a coat and sleeping bag last time she saw him. Something doesn't add up."

"He was living on the street; anything could have happened. We can't go down the route of unlawful killing based on a hunch."

"What else could've happened?"

"What is the estimated time of death?" The coroner leaned forward on his elbows.

"Between midnight and two am."

"There you go!" Timothy exclaimed. "Someone could have come across the body and taken some warm clothes. If you're living on the street, you're not going to pass up the chance. Of course, they'd never own up and you won't be able to find them."

"But that wasn't an area usually frequented by the homeless," Jonah countered. "The odds of someone homeless stumbling across the body and stripping it of warm stuff..."

"Would be low, but not impossible. When you've been in this job a long time, you'll realise that all kinds of very unlikely things happen. You see people who walk home after a night out and slip and fall into a freezing river. And when you start, you think why did he slip there, and not just five minutes earlier or later? But when you put in a few years, you realise, God throws the dice and he's very capricious. Sometimes people get really lucky; others, it's really bad luck."

"It smells bad to me," Jonah said, cursing himself for sounding weak. "The combination of the missing clothes, the location and the vodka."

"Okay," Timothy was on a roll, "he could've found or stolen some money to buy the vodka." After a pause he snapped his fingers and added, "or, he went on a bender, and sold his clothes to afford the vodka."

Jonah started, and stopped again. He was about to point out that he had died of hypothermia, so it was more likely that he lost his clothes first and that led to his death. The timeline didn't add up – Patrick couldn't have died first, then been robbed.

Jonah took a deep breath and prepared his arguments in his head.

"I know what you're going to say," Timothy held up a

hand. "You're from CID and you're used to long complex cases where you spend weeks and months digging into the deep background. But this job isn't like this. We have a process to follow."

Jonah opened his mouth to speak again, but Timothy hadn't finished. "I know with your background you'll always feel you have something to prove. But that's not the case with me. Just do the job and we'll get on fine."

Jonah's worst fears had just been realised. Those words, 'with your background' would follow him around. He knew the case was rotten, something didn't add up. But he also realised with a sinking feeling that he'd never persuade his boss. He decided to play along while he thought of a new strategy to deal with the coroner.

"No, you're right, it's a dead end," Jonah conceded, "there's no way we could trace a street person who would then confess to messing with a body or stealing." Jonah nodded to persuade Timothy that he was agreeing with him.

They stared at each other. Jonah had no idea if Timothy had bought his act or not. "Listen, let's come back to basics. You've located a next of kin?"

Jonah nodded. "He had a son, Connor, under-sixteen, he's living with Fiona, the ex-wife."

"And how happy is she with the way that the investigation is progressing?"

"She's fine," Jonah said. "Well, obviously not fine, but she has no complaints with the coroner's office or the police."

"Well, there you go then. We are doing our job. When we start collecting metrics about customer satisfaction, she'll be within the required level."

"But..."

"No, there is no but. I won't have you chasing off after

some half-baked theories." He leaned in closer, as if sharing a confidence. "Most of the people who are living on the street have mental health problems. I'm not surprised you've come across stuff like this. It's all a bit paranoid. Their lives are a bit empty and so they make stuff up." He saw Jonah's shocked face. "Oh, I don't mean on purpose. They probably believe it, see two things and connect them. But this kind of random stuff is unsurprising."

Jonah sat back and thought for a moment. "I've got a list of people from Patrick Kinsale. Looks like people who he wanted at his funeral. He was university educated so they might be his old friends from back then."

"Right, go on."

"Well, I really need the up-to-date addresses and phone numbers for them. I thought if I went over the alumni office then it'd be the quickest way to get the information."

"Couldn't you just phone or email?"

"I could, but I thought the personal touch would achieve results faster. I could be there and back before the end of business today. Otherwise it could just drag on; some people take days just to answer one email." He paused before delivering his killer blow. "Just think how happy Mrs Kinsale and her son would be if we had a proper funeral with a decent attendance."

"You could speak to Denise. Forward your calls to your mobile and set up your email."

"Of course," Jonah gave a big smile which felt false to him but reassured Timothy. "That way I can respond immediately to anything that comes up."

"Okay, but that's it then. You've done really good work, to get a formal identification done in a tricky case within a couple of days." He looked at Jonah with a serious expression. "How badly do you need to go and see this guy?"

"I think it'd help move things forward."

"Well, I'll let you be the judge of that. But I have to be honest with you, I can't see that it needs to be done in person and I always have to bear the budget in mind. I can let you go in office hours, if you check your phone and emails. But we won't be able to pay any expenses or mileage."

"Okay then," Jonah said. He thought quickly – Swindon and back wouldn't be too bad on petrol and he was used to service station sandwiches for lunch.

"Finally, the important thing is to close the case and move on to the next one. I know you used to be a detective, but I'm sure there's no crime here to be solved."

"Fair enough," Jonah said out loud. But in his head, he was compiling a case. He had made a complete mess of his career as a detective – now he wasn't going to let go of his one chance of redemption.

"HELLO, DS Greene here, how may I help you?" Jonah cradled the phone under his ear and dragged a pen and pad across the desk. He had only just sat down at his desk to sort out his email and phone messages before heading out to Swindon.

"Yes, is this the right number for Patrick Kinsale? I mean, I know he's dead, I saw it in the paper. I just..." The voice was well spoken and female.

"Yes?" The pause had dragged out uncomfortably long for Jonah.

"I thought, maybe, how old was he?" Despite the vagueness of her words, there was an intensity about the caller.

"Thirty-seven," Jonah answered automatically. "Did you know him?"

"I don't know, I knew someone a long time ago, another lifetime really. Another world." Again the silence stretched out with no background sound on either end of the phone.

"What can I help you with?" Jonah asked. "Miss, or Mrs..."

"Oh no, I can't give my name, can't be connected. No, I just wanted to, you know make sure, I read it on the Internet but you never, you know, believe until you speak to someone."

"Well if you did know him, it must have come as a shock, and you have our condolences." Jonah felt that he needed to move carefully, reel her in like a fish on the line. He paused and was met with silence. He wondered briefly if she was even there. "There'll be a funeral, if you wanted to attend or send flowers?"

"Funeral? I'll get the details from the paper," she sounded distracted now. "What I need to know is, how was he killed?" There was desperation in her voice. "Do you know what happened yet?"

"Killed?" Jonah thought quickly. "Enquiries are still ongoing, madam, but if you have any information that could help us..."

"No, sorry, slip of the tongue. Just, he was young, wasn't he? And I mean, people that age don't just drop dead." A pause, and a deep breath. "Yes, probably natural causes, sorry to have bothered you."

The phone line went dead.

CHAPTER 6

On the drive up, Jonah reviewed his conversation with Timothy. The further he got from Cardiff, the more determined he was. His job was to investigate deaths, and he felt that this was one that ought to be investigated. He didn't know if the coroner had one eye on the politics and statistics or if he was prejudiced against Patrick because he was homeless.

But Jonah had already had a glimpse of his life and, from the Prof, an insight into how fragile everyone's existence was. He refused to see Patrick as anything other than a member of the public who needed his help.

By the time he arrived at the address, Jonah had resolved to go further than names and addresses, if at all possible. First though, he had to find the place. He had no idea what to expect from a university alumni society, but it wasn't a bungalow in a quiet residential estate on the outskirts of Swindon. He checked the number and looked up and down in case he had missed a name plaque or something.

He rang the bell. If nothing else, he could ask for directions. He was thrown when the door was opened by a man in a wheelchair. He wasn't old – younger than Jonah and had a full beard and collar-length black hair. "You must be Jonah Greene? Or should I call you DS Greene? I'm never sure!" He smiled to break the tension. "Don't worry, you're not the first to be struck dumb. Come on in and you can help with the coffee and we'll see what we can find on this list of yours."

With that he wheeled expertly around and disappeared into the house. Now that he knew what to look for, Jonah could see that the bungalow was equipped with ramps from street level and all the doorways were wide.

"You must be Peter Calne," Jonah said walking into the kitchen.

"Yes, typical police, check your facts first. Do you want my date of birth? Eighth December 1975."

Jonah nodded, wondering if that date was significant. Something tickled at the back of his brain. He also needed to know why Calne was so comfortable with police procedure as to be almost mocking of it.

Again, Jonah found himself making drinks in someone else's kitchen. This time however, Peter helped, leaving Jonah to carry the two cups through to the office.

Jonah nodded at the wheelchair. "That explains why you're not in an office on the campus."

"Yes," Peter answered, "I've got everything I need here and it's just not worth the aggravation of me commuting in and out to the campus every day. The site itself is properly done for wheelchairs, but it's the travelling. With modern technology, I'm as connected here as I would be on site."

Jonah looked around the room, low-level desk, at least

two computers, fan, modern phone, and racks of box files. The only anachronism was what looked like an old library card index system.

"Anyway," Peter said, "what about this list? It must be quite important for you to come out here in a hurry."

"Not so much important, just I don't know what it is." Jonah handed over the photocopy, and Peter scanned down the list.

"Where did this list come from again?"

"It came to us in connection with a fatality. Patrick Kinsale was sleeping rough and it appears that the cold killed him a few nights ago." Jonah decided to downplay his worries that Patrick was killed. "We found out that Patrick was ex Swindon, so I checked the other names with the University of Swindon and that led me to you. I wondered if these were all his classmates or something? Maybe he wanted them at his funeral?"

"Well, that should be easy enough to tell," Peter said with forced brightness. "Can I take a copy?" When Jonah nodded, he fed it into his printer.

There was silence as Peter tapped away at his computer and made notes on his copy. "Do you do the lottery?" he asked. "Because you have got some good matches here. If you add Patrick into this gap in the first column, then this column is all University of Swindon Alumni. Hold on, I'll write down when they were at uni." He scribbled for a minute, then sat back in his chair and rubbed his chin. "Oh, well, that changes things." He passed his copy over to Jonah.

Patrick had been added to the top, together with 'English 94–95'. Andrew had 'Economics 93–95' and Elizabeth, 'History 93–95'. Mike was marked down as 'Law 92–94', and Peter was 'Computer Studies 94–95'.

"Are these the years that they were all at university?" Jonah asked.

"Yes, that's what's odd. They, I mean, we would've all be there together." He paused. "Of course, it's a big campus; any one year there'd be around four thousand students there plus the MSc, PhD and other students. But even so, we were all there at the same time." He frowned at the list. "I wonder why I'm in the other column then?"

"And why was Patrick only down for two years?"

Peter consulted the computer. "No idea. He is registered as retiring from the course for non-attendance. Looks like he just didn't show up in October."

"But the other three names?"

"No match at all. Which is also weird."

"And do you remember any of them? Patrick for example? Would you go to his funeral?"

Peter shook his head. "No, but that's not surprising. Did you look me up on police computers before you got here?" Jonah shook his head. Things had been moving too fast for him to get around to that yet.

"Why?" Jonah asked. In his experience people didn't generally tell police officers that they were criminals but there was something off about Peter. He knew too much about police work and was trying to control the conversation.

"Oh. Right. This is why I wanted you to come here, I can't do this over the phone." Peter took a deep breath and blew it out. He drank several gulps of his coffee. Jonah could see him steadying his nerves and sorting his thoughts. "On the fifteenth of April 1995 I was thrown over a concrete walkway at university and fell over twenty feet to the ground below." Jonah had all the training and experience as a police officer, so he didn't visibly react. He did however wonder what it said about Peter that he could state something so traumatic so flatly, without emotion. "A nursing student called Susie Garrett happened to walk past at just the right time and she saved my life." He banged the wheel of the chair. "This is the result, plus various other problems, like a serious head injury. Most of my memories of university have come back but I don't trust them particularly. I don't remember Patrick or anyone else on this list. Of course, I may have sat in a class with them, or watched a film in the same cinema but there's no way to tell." He stopped again and studied Jonah. "That's all you could learn from the police report, which I'm sure you'll call up when you get back to the office."

Jonah nodded. "So you said 1995 – that would make you nineteen?" He wondered what a nineteen-year-old could do to provoke such a brutal attack.

"I need you to know that I'm not mad, the attack didn't affect me like that. I'm just," he searched for the word, "focused."

Jonah nodded. "An incident like that would change anyone. I'm not here to judge."

"No, you seem to be okay. Not like some other police I've dealt with. I sought out this job. No one else wanted it and I wanted access to a database of everyone who was on campus the night I was attacked." He held up a hand. "And, I do my job properly. Of course, I have a personal interest in students from the mid-nineties, but I treat all of them the same. I arrange the reunions and I send out magazines and all that." He turned to the card index. "There were 4,678 people at the university that day. I've discounted over 2,500 of them because the walkway had a four-foot-high concrete wall. No way that a frail woman, or a short man could do it. From there, I went through all the records I could and put them onto cards, one per person." He patted the wooden cabinet. "I got this from the library when they put in the computer system. It lets me record opinions and speculations without running up against the Data Protection Act. I eliminated people if they were in teams that were playing away that weekend, and others were definitely at home, or at one of several parties that were down in town. Also, the nightclubs were doing a good trade."

"That's so much work," said Jonah in awe. "How many people remembered where they were?"

"Most of it was done in the first four or five years. Like you say, after that it was harder to get new information. Now it's mostly keeping track of the suspects and hoping that someone will let something slip after so many years."

"So, the three names, four including Patrick, on this list," Jonah tapped the piece of paper, "they would have all been in your original list of people who were at university that night."

"And the question is, have they made the cut?" asked Peter, as he wheeled around and started pulling drawers out and flicking through cards. Jonah could see that they had small coloured stickers in the corners. The tiny circles flickered as the cards were sorted through. "Oh," he said, "all of them are possibles. Elizabeth is an outside chance, she's a woman, but possibly tall enough. I don't know exactly what happened that night, whether I was knocked out first and then tossed over or not. Either way, she might know something.

"I can't pin down where any of them were that night. Some people think they were drinking in the Hub." When Jonah looked confused, he explained. "There's a place called the Hub at Swindon Uni. It's got a bar, meeting rooms, canteen, common rooms, all that sort of stuff. As far as I can tell, I was drinking there on that night. The Hub is linked by walkways to the colleges, classrooms and lecture halls, like spokes but at different heights. But nothing was locked up at the time, so people tended to cut through and across the walkways to take a shortcut home.

"That's probably what I did, except I was ambushed and thrown over the walkway. So, my main focus is someone who was drinking in the bar. It happened between eleven and half past, so that figures. The walkway is not a common part of college so I'm assuming a student or someone who knows the campus."

There was an awkward pause as both men assimilated what had just been said. "Sorry for going at it full-on," Peter said, "it's just that I've been living with it for nearly twenty years and I get used to explaining it to people. Also, this is the first lead I've had in years."

"It's a lead?"

"There's a dead man with a list in his pocket that lists me and three of my possible suspects. Maybe the other three are also suspects, possibly from the town who wouldn't be on my database?"

"But why would Patrick be trying to solve your attack?" Jonah asked. If he was trying to solve this incident, he would have put Peter's name at the top of the list, or underlined it. There should be some mark if this was the purpose of the list. "Have you considered that maybe this isn't the best approach?"

Peter sighed heavily, "I know what you're thinking. Twenty years ago, they tried the other approach and got nowhere. They went back over my past with a fine-tooth comb and found nothing, no motive at all." Jonah nodded, but he thought that it was the best approach.

"No! I mean it! I'm so fed up with the restrictive police view! I was clean as a whistle! Sure, I had a few one-night stands, and smoked a bit of gear when it was around. But there were no pissed off boyfriends or husbands, no dodgy drug dealers I owed money to, nothing! This was random and done by one of the people in the bar that night!"

"Okay," Jonah tried to placate him. "You have to understand that we're all trained to ask the questions. We all think the same way, I'm just coming at this from a different angle, twenty years too late."

Peter took a deep breath and stared out of the window. Jonah could see his jaw muscles clenching and releasing. After an uncomfortably long pause he turned back to Jonah with a shaky smile. "Sorry, head injury stuff. Moods all over the place."

There was an awkward silence, so Jonah decided to steer into safer territory. "All this," he waved his hand around, "it's a nice setup. Does the Alumni society pay that well?"

"No," Peter shook his head. "And before you ask, compensation is kind of patchy, especially when they haven't caught the criminal. And being a single man when it happened, I was low on the list of council priorities."

"So..."

"So, the nuns came to my rescue."

"Nuns?"

"The Sisters from The Ministry of Capernaum and Bethesda." When Jonah looked blank, he continued, "I thought it was a scam too. But I checked them out on the Internet. They're genuine, a small nunnery who devote themselves to helping the paralysed. They started out before the NHS, supplying wheelchairs and crutches to the poor. Now they fill in the gaps in care around the NHS, still focusing on the crippled. They helped me set this place up, all the railings, ramps, low-level desk. They were happy to work with the university, sort out grants that kind of stuff. It's been invaluable."

"It is a very nice setup."

"And I'd give it all back in a second if I could stand up and walk away from this damn chair!" Peter wheeled back to the desk to hide the emotion on his face. He picked up the copy of the list and studied it. "Obviously I won't know what the significance is of this list straight away, but it is a good start," he said enthusiastically. Jonah nodded, trying and failing to imagine what he was going through. He had been perfectly normal on his nineteenth birthday and by his twentieth he had been in rehab, learning how to live with a wheelchair.

Peter started writing while explaining to Jonah what he was doing. "Right, Elizabeth Barry, you probably won't find, she married Jonathon Gardner in ninety-nine and took his name. Andrew McRae shouldn't be too hard to track down, he moved to Telford and opened a car dealership. Now he's got a chain, half a dozen of them, taking in Shrewsbury too. Mike, ah, yes," Jonah wheeled himself away from the computer. "I'll put down his date of birth, but that's it." Jonah frowned at him. "Your lot might have more luck. Word is that he went into selling drugs in a big way, moved up the supply chain. At the same time as he did that, he dropped off the radar altogether. I've had no contact for well over a decade. No idea where he lives apart from the fact that he's around Birmingham somewhere."

"Thanks for all of that," Jonah said looking down the list.

"Wow! Elizabeth did well for herself that's a Docklands address in London, isn't it?"

"Yes," Peter nodded. "The man she married, Jonathon, was another alumnus, a couple of years ahead of her. Graduated well and became a hedge fund manager. I should think Andrew isn't short of a bob or two either."

"What do the index cards say about them?"

"Patrick, Andrew and Michael are possibles, right place and time, physically capable of it. As I said, Elizabeth is far less likely, but she might know something. A few people reported that Andrew and Michael knew each other, were seen talking, but not often. Maybe in passing. I think Elizabeth moved in different circles, the May Ball type of crowd."

"All that's on your cards?" Jonah asked.

"Yes, I collect associations and rank them out of ten, as to how close they are. It's like a huge network on cardboard." There was a pause as Peter weighed what to say next. "You could solve the rest of the list with your databases though."

Jonah shook his head. "No, the names are still too vague."

"But what are the chances that they are totally unconnected? Either in time or space?" When Jonah looked confused, he continued, "I'd lay good odds that those other three either had something to do with the mid-nineties or were somewhere around the Swindon area. Otherwise they wouldn't fit in with the rest of the list."

Jonah wasn't totally convinced. He disliked Peter for telling him how to do his job. He knew he should make allowances for the physical damage that Peter's brain had sustained, never mind the amount of stress and emotional pressure. He had put a lot of himself into the massive task of trying to catch his attacker. But, Jonah conceded to himself, the information on the computer was likely to be straight from the university authorities and therefore good quality. He was less happy with the card index. He wasn't even sure it was exempt from data protection and it contained uncorroborated memories and opinions with no record of the original interviews.

Jonah admitted something else to himself – he had no other openings so there was nothing to be lost from trying Peter's approach of linking the other names to either Swindon or the mid-nineties.

"That has to be worth something though," Peter was still talking. "I mean, I know I can't access the police databases, but you could tell me what you learn?" He leaned forward, eager for more data.

"I could see what I could do," Jonah said non-committally. "There isn't even an active case for this one, it's just accidental death. I'm even going above and beyond a bit to try to round up some mourners for the funeral."

"Yes, but my case?"

"Your case will be with a cold case unit with Wiltshire." He weighed his words carefully. "I could offer to help if I find anything. But these things need gentle handling. If I went barging into their investigation, well, it could be taken as a criticism."

"But if you could help, surely they'd be grateful."

"Listen, I don't mean to be harsh, but you have to manage your expectations. There are all sorts of politics. An officer from Cardiff can't suddenly poke his nose into Wiltshire's cold cases. Can you let me know who dealt with you, is there anyone who I could talk to?"

"I deal with a DC called Kate Best. She wasn't on the original case. I think she's new and been given a whole basket of cold cases. I haven't spoken to her for a good while, but she always has time for me."

Poor sod, thought Jonah, including both DC Best and Peter in that thought. One with no hope of finding who tried to kill him, the other given the dregs of unsolvable cases. "Right then, I'll give her a courtesy call when I get back. Let her know I've been to see you, and what we've talked about."

JONAH DROVE HOME that night comparing two phone calls in his head. Firstly, his mysterious female caller who had assumed that Patrick Kinsale was murdered. The more he thought, the surer he was that she was unhinged in some way.

Then, he had called DC Kate Best who was struggling under a huge load of cold cases. It was clear that this was verging on hazing her before she could be accepted into CID properly. She was sympathetic towards Peter Calne, but quite dismissive of his research. She pointed out that it would be a miracle if he whittled more than four thousand suspects down to hundreds. And, if by some miracle he managed to get the suspects into double or single figures, it would still be useless as they couldn't follow up that many leads on a twenty-year-old case.

When he neared home, Jonah drove down wide, leafy avenues with nice big brick-built homes each side. Without thinking, he checked his mirrors and slowed down for his turning.

AS HE CLEARED the flanking houses, he got his first view of his home. Preparing to park, his headlights swept across the garage door and illuminated a motorbike that was parked there. It was one of these new weird looking machines – mostly black, the front mudguard was orange and the line of it was followed back to the tank. Then it came down and back up again towards the tail of the bike in a zigzag like a piece of modern art.

His heart sank. He really needed a quiet night in to decompress after a busy day, and was not in the mood to be polite to a visitor. As he got out of the car, he mentally ran through their friends, trying and failing to think of someone they knew who rode a motorbike. He walked into the house and looked curiously into the living room.

"Who's here?" he called out.

"Why?" Alex frowned up at him from her usual spot at the end of the sofa.

"Well there's a bike out front."

"Yes, I bought that today. I did tell you I was going out looking the other day." Alex spoke as is this was the most obvious thing in the world.

"Looking is one thing," Jonah said, his anger rising, "I didn't think you'd buy it!"

"Well, why not? There's no point in looking if you're not buying is there?"

"But, I mean, a motorbike?" Jonah was struggling for words as he stretched his mind around the fact that the machine on the drive belonged to his wife.

"I know what you're going to say," Alex said bitterly, "and I did everything you asked when I went for my license."

Jonah thought back to the rows three years ago when she had got her bike license. He'd just decided he was too old for rugby and had sat around the house at weekends with nothing to do while she threw herself into her new hobby. When she'd passed, he'd made her go on approved extra courses about hazard avoidance and defensive riding, and even made sure one of the motorcycle police had advised her on what kit to buy.

"But..." Jonah wanted to say that she couldn't ride a motorbike, but that was plainly not true. He knew he should stop her, keep her safe at home, away from trouble, but he couldn't find the words. A small voice at the back of his mind said that if he denied her this, then she might leave. He could see her literally riding off into the sunset.

"That's okay then, is it?" Alex asked. There was a challenge in her face, a quizzical expression. Jonah could not fathom what she was looking for. Did she want him to object and put his foot down or was that the last thing she wanted?

"I guess," said Jonah warily. "What are you going to do with it?"

"Ride it, obviously." The bitterness was back, easy for Jonah to read.

Jonah moved away from her, towards the office. The house was designed around a staircase and had several separate rooms on the ground floor. When they had restored it, Alex had insisted on keeping the layout instead of modernising it by knocking into one open-plan space with 'flow'.

Jonah was grateful for this now as he had a sanctuary in his office. Still standing, he gazed out of the window at the trees behind the house. He looked around at the mismatched furniture and thought of Peter in his low-level office, all new desks and printers.

He reached for the keyboard and fired up Google and methodically searched for each name, followed by a year starting from 1994 and working forwards. If that failed, he'd try Swindon, Wiltshire or West Midlands Police.

In practice, his task was easier than he expected. On a search for Emma Walters together with 1995, he found a whole host of hits. Mostly in the category of lurid, unsolved murder sites. He skimmed a couple and got the basic facts out.

On August 27, 1995, aged twenty-two, Emma Walters had been on her way home from a nightclub when she had been attacked and stabbed three times. The last blow had been fatal and left her pinned to the ground. It had been Saturday night on a bank holiday weekend, and she was last seen at 2 am, until her body was found at eight the next morning by a member of the public. There were all sorts of sites, establishing charities and calling for justice for Emma. Now he had the facts, he remembered the name and the fuss it had caused at the time. Everyone had been on alert for a serial killer starting his run. But there had been no follow-up killing, nothing else to link to it. Even stranger, there had been no sexual element, just a cold, brutal slaying. There was no shortage of evidence and there were photographs released by the police all over the web pages – the boiler suit, the bayonet used to stab her. Someone called Colin Bailey was initially arrested and put through the wringer. He had a previous conviction for exposing himself in parks and had also received a caution for threatening an ex with a bayonet, and he lived near Southend.

Jonah read more and as he did so he drew the conclusion that Colin wasn't Emma's killer. He was only a suspect because he'd been in the area and had a caution with a big knife. For a start there was nothing sexual about Emma's murder and most of Colin's crimes were opportunistic and almost chaotic in their execution. Jonah went back to the initial description of Emma's murder and saw how organised it was. The more he read, the more he formed a mental profile of the killer – clinical and efficient, well organised and pre-planned.

He had just opened a new tab to search for Bill Wormslea when he was interrupted.

"You can't just run away from this, Jonah!" Alex called out from the hallway. She was reluctant to enter his office. "I have my own money you know!"

Jonah remembered the old arguments when they had met. No one thought the relationship would last – the tiny elfin Alex, nearly a foot shorter than the burly, uncouth, rugby playing policeman. Also, no one else understood that her fiery personality meant she gave as good as she got in arguments. But they had ironed out their differences and both having jobs, had kept their own money.

She had progressed through the ranks of hospital administration. Friends who didn't know her well thought this a contradiction, but she had a steely determination when she needed it. This aspect of her personality had passed to her daughter.

He was still staring at the Google home page, grinding his teeth. He heard a small impatient movement behind him.

He tried to imagine what it'd be like to be walking home from the pub one night, and suddenly be paralysed. Or, he thought soberly, riding your motorbike. One moment everything is normal, the next it's all police and ambulance, the sterility of hospitals and solicitous doctors and nurses explaining how the rest of your life will pan out.

With his counsellor he had discussed his tendency to put himself in other people's shoes. It helped him to do his job, but it also threatened his stability.

He turned and looked at Alex who had just shrugged expressively at his lack of response. He watched her disappear towards the kitchen and wondered how life would be if he lost her. Suddenly he could see that he had an impossible choice – would he lose her to a motorbike crash, spend the rest of his life pushing her wheelchair?

Or would he insist now that she give up her motorbike? He could see if he did this that their slow drift apart would be accelerated, maybe even to divorce. With this new bleak thought, he wondered what his future would be like, family home sold, flats bought. The children had already left home so it wouldn't be too traumatic. Just another sad old policeman without a family.

Jonah tried to remember what his counsellor had told him – control his thoughts and manage the physical symptoms of panic. He took a deep steadying breath and tried to still his mind. But his thoughts wouldn't be tamed. For a civilian maybe it would work but he had spent twenty years on the force, listening to the canteen chat about motorcycle accidents they'd had to clear up. He smiled wryly as he realised that the police force was hardly the place to look for advice on stable relationships and long marriages either.

With another deep, calming breath, he decided that one problem could be addressed. With wooden legs, he slowly left his office and approached the kitchen. Alex was pointedly not turning around even though she'd heard him approach.

"So," he said in what he hoped was a conciliatory tone, "what is it?"

"What do you mean," she bristled.

"Your bike, what make is it?"

"You really want to know?" Alex turned to look at him, a wary expression on her face.

"Yes, I'm not going to change your mind, so I might as

well be a part of it." He grinned lopsidedly, a tactic that had won her over in the past.

"It's a BMW, F800. Come outside and look?"

They trooped outside together and Alex explained about the optional extras, lowered seat and ABS, while Jonah counted his breaths. Alex told him that the seller was moving up to a bigger machine, so the price was very good while Jonah tried to banish images of the bike on the back of a recovery truck, all bashed up. Alex was still talking; about how she could get both feet down and have enough torque to be able to pull out of difficult situations.

"The bloke who was selling it was one of those obsessive types, you'd have liked him," Alex said, checking his face for reproach. Seeing none, she carried on. "He checked everything every time he put it away and when he got it back out again." There was an awkward pause as Jonah knew she just wasn't the type. She was flighty and impulsive instead. Jonah didn't want to point it out though, break the mood.

"Maybe I could check it over, once in a while?" he offered.

"You?" Alex couldn't hide her surprise.

"Well," he said looking closer at the machine. "I could do the basics, it's still got a petrol engine, brakes, steering..." He started seeing how much could go wrong. He stepped back slightly, moving subconsciously.

Alex stayed the other side of the motorbike sensing that she'd gone as far as she could.

"I'm in the middle of something, work stuff," Jonah said awkwardly, half-turning back to the house.

"Thank you, Jonah," Alex said softly. Taking this as permission, he made good his escape, back to the house and the safety of his office. He entered a world far easier to deal with. All complicated emotions and unknowable motivations were reduced to data on a screen. Jonah understood data, could navigate his way through histories and make connections.

Bill Wormslea had an unusual name and was easy to trace. On the April 13, 1996 Bill Wormslea, aged fifty-seven, had taken his usual morning constitutional along the coast east of Bournemouth. He had been shot, once in the chest, probably by a rifle. Jonah looked out the window as he did some mental calculations. Bill, Emma and Peter had all been attacked within a year.

Looking back at the screen, he skimmed through the range of websites, from the ghoulish to the pleading, all asking the unanswerable questions. Bill had been shot walking on the surf line as the tide was coming in, the body had dropped into the surf and been tumbled with pebbles. There was no way to tell where the shot had been fired from. It could've come from anywhere on shore, or even from a boat, although that would have been a one in a million shot. There was also no trace of the bullet and all the forensics were compromised by the action of the sea. It was no surprise that this case was also marked as open. He read a bit more of the information, trying to see where, as a detective he would've made progress. The pathologist had carried out analysis of the wound and declared that the bullet was around the calibre of either 0.300 inches or 7.62mm.

As this was a common size of bullet, in both military and civilian use, it gave rise to speculation and wild conspiracy theories. These were based around anyone from Mossad through Spetsnaz to UK special forces or the CIA testing out new sniper rifles on innocent members of the public.

He rubbed his eyes as he tried to put the information

together. To his already disparate list of university students, he now had one stabbing and one shooting.

"I put shepherd's pie in the oven," Alex called out from the kitchen, "will you come through and eat dinner?"

"Give me five minutes," he called back. He was grateful to have patched things up with Alex, but he still needed to finish his searches.

Justin Day was a very common name, but Google was now skewing his results towards murders and was throwing up different pages on the same websites as the previous two queries. On December 22, 1995 Justin Day was involved in a car accident while driving through Worksop. It had been the final Friday before a four-day weekend over Christmas and Boxing Day. Traffic had been heavy and tempers short. When the immense amount of traffic chaos had been sorted out, and the paramedics and firemen had done their work, something was found to be wrong. His injuries weren't consistent with a fairly low-speed car accident. Further investigation revealed that he'd been shot while waiting at red lights, and this had caused the accident. Jonah winced when he read that a sawn-off shotgun had been used, both barrels straight in through the window. There was no other possible outcome, it would kill anyone stone dead. In this case, Justin had been sat on a hill, with his foot on the brake and clutch, so as soon as he died, his car leapt forward through the red light and into the oncoming traffic, causing chaos. Luckily no one else was killed, but it took the police several hours to determine that a murder had been committed, and by then the emergency services had compromised the evidence. A lone motorcyclist was picked up on CCTV leaning in and firing the shot but, by the time anyone checked, twelve hours had passed and the rider could've been anywhere in the country. The number plates proved to be false and the motorbike was never traced.

He shut down the computer and went to get some dinner. As they ate, a silence fell across the table. Jonah's mind was miles away as he pondered.

Bournemouth, Southend and Worksop. All within eighteen months and nowhere near Swindon. All the victims on Patrick's list had been featured on Crimewatch. But then he thought about Patrick, and he couldn't imagine him watching Crimewatch.

Finally, Alex broke into his thoughts, "Come on then, what's on your mind?"

"It's just this case I'm working on." He paused, weighing up what to say. "What do you remember about the nineties?"

"What do you mean? The whole ten-year period?"

"Well, no, just that some things from the nineties have come up. Trying to put myself back there."

"The music was Britpop, wasn't it?" Alex asked. "Blur versus Oasis and all that. When did Princess Di have that accident in Paris, and everyone went mad?"

"That was 1997 or 1998, I think. The end of a whole summer when the paparazzi were chasing them all over the world, photos from the yacht and all that."

"Oh God, yes!" Alex got excited. "The politics. John Major losing out to Tony Blair. The feeling of hope."

"And there was no Internet either, was there?" Jonah asked. "And I got my first mobile in the nineties. It was when I chucked in the IT career and joined the force as well. It all seemed to be so much simpler back then."

Alex reached out to hold his hand across the table. They chatted easily about the time they'd met, the jobs they'd had, and just what it had been like twenty years ago.

Even though he was talking to Alex, a part of Jonah's mind still turned over the problem. One thing was clear, something else had happened around then and Patrick had known what it was. The question was, had he been killed because of it?

CHAPTER 7

THE FOLLOWING MORNING, Jonah waited in the same café he'd met Per in two days earlier. It was cold damp weather and he couldn't see the street because of the condensation on the window. He cradled his weak coffee and wondered if the coffee rings on the plastic tablecloth were those from several days ago. He also tried to work out why he wanted to see Per again but didn't want to bring him to the station.

Timothy Carlton, the coroner, had made his feelings perfectly clear – he was to close the case. But Jonah needed to know more about the names on the list. And now he had three unsolved, cold case murders so it was a police matter. He just wished he didn't have to convince himself.

Per walked in, allowing a blast of cold air to sweep around the café before the door slammed shut behind him. He nodded at the waitress who started making his cup of coffee.

"Well?" Per asked, not disguising his annoyance. "I do have better things to do."

"I just wondered how well you knew Patrick, really?"

"What did you want to know?"

He briefly explained about the Prof delivering the note. "I just wanted to get a bit of a feel for what he was like. He was trying to tell me something with the note, but I don't know what."

Per leaned back, accepting that this wouldn't be a short meeting. "A lot of my clients fit into categories, most of them either have mental health problems or are ex-services or out of prison, sometimes all three. But it's a mistake to lump them all together, they all have their own personalities, they're all people, just a bit sad and lost sometimes."

"And Patrick?"

Per frowned, "I know this sounds weird, but I think he was kinder to other people than he was to himself. It's tough living on the streets, but I can think of several times when he helped someone out. Didn't have to, but he just wanted to."

"But not himself?"

"No," Per shook his head, "I don't think he thought he was worth it."

"Well, he was found with no coat or sleeping bag, but two expensive bottles of vodka. Could he have killed himself?"

"It's a very slow way to go. Takes a lot of organising and there's no guarantee. Also, it gives you too much time to change your mind. If it was suicide, I'd have expected something quick and final like under a train or off a multi-storey." Jonah looked up and caught his eyes. This wasn't theory for Per, but something he had considered, a demon he had faced.

Per rubbed the side of his face and looked out of the window. "Patrick wasn't too bad. He was an alcoholic and wouldn't have turned down a drink. But he did seem to know what he was doing if you see what I mean. I never saw him without his coat and he always had a sleeping bag in this weather."

"Yes, his wife bought him one in January." Jonah moved his coffee cup to and fro, unwilling to look up and meet the other man's eyes again. "Could he have sold it for vodka?"

Per chuckled softly. "He'd been living in it for over two months. No one would even want to carry it to the kerb, never mind pay for it!"

"So, there are two mysteries then, where did the vodka come from and where did the warm clothing go?"

Per shrugged and Jonah changed tack.

"Was Kinsale into true crime at all? Those tacky magazines, books, Crimewatch?"

"Not that I knew. There's a crowd that like to spend time in the libraries and museum to keep warm. They can get quite inventive with ways to avoid security guards. But I don't ever think Patrick was part of them. Why do you ask?"

"Three of the names on the list were murdered. The other four were at university with Patrick."

Per shrugged, "There you go then. He was always sad. Something ate him up from the inside. Maybe he is just unlucky and knew three people who were killed. It happens."

Jonah nodded, wondering if he could pull the case files from all over the country and find a link back to Patrick. Or maybe phone the officers with the cold cases and ask if Patrick was anywhere in their files. That was not a phone call he was looking forward to.

"What about the Prof then? Would you trust him?"

"Yes, for someone on the street, he's all right. When he's having a good day, anyway. If he seemed normal to you then he was probably okay."

"Why would Patrick have used him for the note?"

"He was probably the best person for the job."

There seemed to be nothing more to say. Per gulped down his coffee and, as before, left abruptly. As Jonah made his way back through the streets to the station, some blue sky began to show. It was still grey and there were puddles, but he felt that the season had at last started to turn a corner. But, he was struggling to grasp what Patrick had been like, what he was still trying to tell him.

On impulse he used his mobile to call Fiona, partly to check in and partly to confirm what Per had said. He didn't learn anything new – Patrick had been helpful to others, but not himself. He wasn't suicidal and tried to avoid any kind of trouble.

BACK AT THE office Jonah worked through some paperwork, sorting open cases into the right piles. He also took the opportunity to look up Mike Khan but got nowhere. The file was blocked. The only way to read it was to apply directly to a Detective Chief Superintendent Blackmore. There was no way that a detective sergeant could bother someone of that rank merely to uncover information on a speculative case. It was a code that carried a warning – you'd better have something cast iron or be of ACPO rank before you can see the file. He wondered about his coroner and decided that he would be no hope. Likewise, Linwood was only a DI. He had the feeling that neither man was the type who'd want to rock the boat. He'd have to leave that route blocked for now.

Jonah looked at the rest of the list and started making phone calls. He left a message for Elizabeth on her answerphone – her voice was bright and chirpy yet also managed to be businesslike. It sounded familiar, but the message was short, and she was being formal, so he couldn't place it. He left a standard message for her to call him back.

He then moved on to phone Andrew. As all he'd been doing all day was leaving messages for people, he found himself waiting for three rings before a machine went click to take his message.

"Hello, Andrew McRae speaking." The phone had been picked up.

"Ah, yes, this is DS Jonah Greene of Cardiff Crown Court."

"How can I help?"

"Have you heard of a Patrick Kinsale?"

"Patrick who?"

"Kinsale, K-I-N-S-A-L-E."

There was a pause, then, "Do you know what I do for a living?"

"Yes, I believe you're a used car salesman."

There was a burst of warm laughter down the phone. "Oh dear, you make me sound like a dodgy character with half a dozen cars, some bunting round a lot and a rundown caravan. No, I own six dealerships that between them shift over a thousand cars a year. I still do hands-on sales, so I might have run into this Patrick Whatshisname, even shaken his hand and not even know it."

"It's not that, he was at university with you." Jonah was trying to figure out why he didn't trust Andrew McRae. On the surface he was all warmth and charm.

"Along with thousands of other students."

"Well, yes, that's why we're calling."

"You're calling because we were both at the same university at the same time?"

"No," Jonah felt himself becoming frustrated. McRae

was unable or unwilling to answer a straight question. "I'm sorry to say that Patrick was found dead a couple of days ago. We're trying to trace anyone who may have known him for the funeral."

"You said he was in my year at university?"

"Yes."

"That's terribly sad if he was the same age as me. I feel like I'm in the prime of life." There was a pause. "Are you phoning all of the people in his year? There must have been hundreds, if not thousands."

"Well, no. It's a bit delicate. He was living on the streets and he had this list. We assumed it was people he'd want us to contact, maybe for his funeral, so we're phoning them."

"Right, and who else was on this list?"

"I'm afraid I can't really discuss that with you." Jonah made the decision to withhold the information in an instant. He definitely didn't trust McRae, even if he didn't know why yet.

"I just thought that I might know someone on the list who also knew Patrick and assumed we knew each other. It might trigger a memory from those days."

"I still don't think it's the kind of thing I should discuss over the phone," Jonah said firmly but politely.

"And yet, you think it's okay to phone me up, disturb me at work and ask if I had anything to do with a dead vagrant who just happens to have my name in his pocket?" A hard edge had crept into McRae's voice; he was angry but tightly in control. "He might have been at university with me, but that was nearly twenty years ago, and he died over a hundred miles away! I'll tell you again, as you're obviously not getting it straight. I advertise a lot and people travel from all over to buy my cars. The business is called Andrew McRae Cars – my name is my bond. I run adverts in so many local newspapers, my name and face are everywhere, that's what sells cars. Your vagrant probably picked up a newspaper, remembered I used to sit in his class or we had a friend in common, and fixated on it." There was a pause. "Is that all you wanted to know?" he snapped.

"There's no need to get upset about it."

"If I'm upset, it's because you are phoning me up and making improper allegations about who I might be associated with. My time is valuable and I could do without being bothered by half-baked theories. Who did you say you were again? DS Greene from Cardiff Courts?"

"Yes, sir," Jonah confirmed glumly. He could picture Andrew as someone who'd make notes as he spoke on the phone.

"Right then!" And with that Andrew hung up the phone. As he made a record of the phone call, he tried to pinpoint the moment when McRae had lost his temper. Jonah shook his head when he realised that it was when he refused to name the other people on the list. He mentally marked Andrew McRae down as someone who was used to getting what he wanted and who couldn't handle being defied.

CHAPTER 8

THE NEXT MORNING, Jonah sat in his office and stared at his computer. DI Linwood had sent him a meeting request, in his office, in less than an hour's time. He was 'required to attend'. Maybe Timothy Carlton wanted to transfer Patrick Kinsale's file over to CID. That was something Jonah would welcome. If nothing else, it would provide a way back and allow him to demonstrate that he could now be trusted.

As he climbed the stairs to CID, he planned out the best approach. He could lead with the fact that Patrick's death could be suspicious. The missing coat and expensive vodka on their own made it worth exploring. Add in the list with three cold case murders on it then it started to look like a workable case. Maybe not a full-on major investigation yet, but something that a couple of officers ought to be checking over.

When he walked into Linwood's office his carefully organised thoughts collapsed like a house of cards. His DI was not alone; this wasn't going to be a cosy one-to-one where he could ask for help. Two other people sat awkwardly on chairs to either side of him, all facing a single chair. They were just off the corners of the desk and had chosen not to lean in awkwardly and were instead folding their hands in their laps, making them look a little lost and uncomfortable.

"Ah, yes, Greene, come on in," Linwood said. "Nothing to worry about." On his right was Timothy Carlton the coroner – he hadn't mentioned to Jonah about this meeting. The woman on his left Jonah didn't recognise. She was neat and tidy, with a sleek black bob. She had a clipboard on her lap. He studied her subtly for a second. Smart and fashionable, but not in a flamboyant way. In her thirties, attractive but a bit severe looking. Some instinct told him that she wasn't uniform but a civilian who was comfortable here, someone in one of the support roles.

"Okay then," Jonah said warily. He struggled to regain his inner equilibrium as he abandoned his initial plan of asking for help – first he needed to understand what was going on.

"I've called this meeting because I've been reviewing your progress on your current case." Linwood paused but Jonah refused to fill in the gap, so he carried on. "Ah, yes, well, it seems to be taking up quite a lot of your time." He looked through some papers on his desk. "It seems that you've already met two people here in Cardiff, and driven to Swindon and back on business, as well as making phone calls around the country."

"Is there a problem?" Jonah asked. "I haven't exactly been trained or given a formal handover but I thought this was my job."

"Well, umm, yes. Now I can see how you might get confused. It must be a change of pace from being a detective. As you said, the circumstances of your transfer to the coroner's office were not ideal. You didn't get the briefing and support that might have been necessary. You see, this job is more of a liaison role, to act as a human face between the grieving relatives and the official process that must, perforce, accompany a death that falls within our purview."

"So, what exactly have I done wrong?"

"Not wrong per se, I just feel that you might need a steer on the correct emphasis and balance that you give to each case. Am I right in thinking that you've informed the wife of the deceased?"

"Ex-wife, but yes," Jonah confirmed.

"And you've also made contact with the manager of a homeless shelter, who knew him?" Linwood asked and was answered with a nod. "So, really there's nothing more to be said." He frowned at the paperwork again. "There's something here about a list of names?"

"Yes, one of the other street people handed in a list of seven names that Kinsale had written prior to his death. I've been trying to find out if they are people who knew him and might want to attend the funeral."

"You see, that's your old detective training coming in. If you've shown this list to the ex-wife, then it's up to her to do the guest list for the funeral. You're only here to help when she interfaces with officialdom – post-mortem, inquest, things like that. It's time to put this case to bed and move on."

There was an awkward silence as Jonah digested this instruction. It was remarkably heavy handed to bring the four of them together to deliver a message which could've been just as easily sent in an email. It also didn't ring completely true. Jonah looked straight at Linwood, a man he'd known for over ten years. He screened out the other two and spoke directly to him. "George, what's this really about? I've just started in the job and I have nothing else to do. There are strange circumstances and I was just looking into it. Am I being warned off?"

Linwood nervously looked left and right, gaining imperceptible nods from the other two people in the room.

"Jonah, I do take offence that you think I'm warning you off, I'm just trying to help." There was another awkward pause which Jonah again refused to fill. "But yes, there might be more to it than we at first said. I'm given to believe that you contacted a Mr Andrew McRae of Shropshire by telephone yesterday afternoon. Is that correct?"

Jonah nodded and thought, 'given to believe' meant he was deep in trouble now. That phrase meant that Linwood was worried that this might come down to some sort of official enquiry. He obviously knew that the phone call had taken place, but as he hadn't witnessed it directly, he was hiding behind language..

"And did you take any notes during the conversation, or even a recording?"

"No," Jonah shook his head. A recording? This was worse than he had feared.

"Oh, well, all we're trying to do is establish the facts. Why didn't you take notes?"

"Well, it was just an informal enquiry. I was following up and his name was on the list. As I said, he might have wanted to attend the funeral."

"But you didn't just leave the list with the ex-wife?"

"No, she doesn't have the resources that we have for finding people."

"But, as I've said you have to be careful how you allocate those resources." Another pause followed. "Anyway, so you found his name on the list and decided to phone him up. Why did you think he'd want to know about it?"

"Well, as I said, a fellow rough sleeper brought me the

list and," Jonah thought for a moment. Now was not the time to tell an outright lie to his superior. He glanced at the woman who was now writing on a clipboard perched on her lap. "And he said that Patrick Kinsale was concerned about dying and asked that the list be handed in if he should die. It was a logical inference."

"Right, right, yes, I see." Linwood said before lapsing back into silence.

"Am I under suspicion here?" Jonah countered. "Do I need a police fed rep here?"

"No, no, perish the thought," Linwood spread his hands out to show how open he was being. "It's just that we've had a complaint. Mr McRae is very concerned that you phoned him up and accused him of being involved in the death of a vagrant here in Cardiff. The public know what it means if you start asking questions like when did he last see the victim and what was he doing at the time of death."

"But I didn't..." Jonah started and then saw the trap that he'd been led into.

"What you didn't do was keep records of the conversation," Linwood finished for him. "We have no choice but to assume that Mr McRae's complaint is valid. Which is why we tried to steer you towards closing this case. But now you know. This must be closed or his complaint might move from being an informal discussion to something more formal."

"Doesn't any of this strike you as odd?" Jonah asked. When he got blank looks, he continued. "All I did was phone up Mr McRae, and he starts threatening a formal complaint!"

"Mr McRae is well within his rights to make whatever representations he feels appropriate."

"But," Jonah started, "Kinsale was in the wrong place –

Cyncoed is not where they usually," he searched for a word, "congregate. And there's the vodka and the coat too," he said weakly. He wished he had been eloquent, but the three stony faces staring at him sucked all the passion out of him.

"Jonah," Linwood leaned back with sigh, "if a commuter suddenly decides not to catch his usual train, and instead spends the day at Swansea, eating ice cream, then something's wrong. That's a break in his pattern of behaviour. But these are homeless people. They don't have usual. They are not normal. Chaos and unusual behaviour are their stock in trade!"

Jonah wanted to say that he'd known homeless people with routines. Begging and busking pitches were keenly fought over and regularly used. These people had places they felt comfortable, favourite sleeping spots; behaviour as entrenched as any commuter.

Linwood gave a sideways glance at the woman to his right, then leant forward. More quietly he said, "Jonah, there is more going on here than you know. This could seriously affect your career. So, I'm advising you again, as a friend, to close the case."

A wave of oppression swept over Jonah. He felt the room closing in, the three faces looming over him. He recognised what was happening because his counsellor had explained it – he was being bullied and pressured. He knew he should push back but at that moment he felt he could hardly breathe.

The cold of the door handle in his grip brought him back to himself. He had automatically got out of his chair and tried to flee the room without realising what he was doing. He could storm out but that would leave too much unanswered.

The sense of injustice that had swept him out of his

chair was now replaced by anger. Not for himself – this kind of office politics was always the same in any job, any station around the country. But he found himself angry for Patrick. He had been inside the house that he had bought for his wife and child. He had been such a desperate person, and it was no way for anyone to die. Alone and literally freezing to death. And here he was, reduced by this group of suits to an item on an agenda. Now Patrick was just an unfortunate detail, something that had cropped up to disrupt their lives. His life was too complicated and was taking up too much time – like trying to find the right item in the supermarket and then giving up and just taking the first thing that comes to hand before moving.

He took a deep breath and couldn't just storm out. That would be failing Patrick. That would mean that all the idiots he put up with, the drunks and the criminals, the evil and the plain stupid, would be for nothing. All the dross of humanity that he waded through to help the occasional Patrick here and there would be for nothing. No, he would master his anger, say nothing, turn around and sit down. Give as little as possible while learning as much as he could.

"Excuse me," he said turning to the woman with perfect politeness, dripping with venom, "I don't believe we've been introduced."

"I'm Ms Cross," she answered icily. "I'm here from HR to ensure there's an independent record of this conversation. I know you're DS Jonah Greene, and I read your file before coming over here." The look that she gave him made it clear that she knew his full history.

"Listen, Greene, your previous, ah, problem was deemed to be medical in nature. So, we can't do anything about that," Linwood shot a glance at Ms Cross and got a nod back. "But now we've got someone prepared to make an official complaint, and that can go on your record and affect your performance review." He looked straight at Jonah to make sure he got the message. "So, why don't we rewind a moment. How about you give us your account and we'll see what we can do to save your career."

Jonah took a big sigh and dropped back into his chair. "We found an unidentified body out by Roath Park. We identified him as Patrick Kinsale, a homeless man who was living rough in the city. One of his friends brought in a list of seven names that had been given to him by Patrick before he died. Andrew McRae was on that list. So, I contacted him to see if he knew Patrick from before he was homeless and further, if he wanted to attend the funeral."

There was a silence, broken by the scratching of Ms Cross's pen. Linwood furrowed his brow and Carlton looked like he'd rather be anywhere else at all. Sod it, thought Jonah, this had gone far enough.

He stared down at the carpet. He had been properly done up. He'd expected, even after the last six months, that he would have some loyalty from his old boss, but now that was a distant dream. He was on his own. Something hardened inside him – he knew that he had never been the most popular officer, but he'd assumed that he would have some support.

"Listen," Linwood spoke again, "there's a bereavement officer over at the council whose job is to organise funerals – they can take over a lot of the support with the ex-wife. Your primary focus is to work on establishing the cause of death and making your report to the coroner." Linwood indicated Carlton on his left as if Greene would've been unaware of who the coroner was.

"Yes," Jonah said, aware of the lifeline he was being

offered. "I'll investigate the circumstances leading to the death."

"But you'll stay away from Andrew McRae. One whisper from him and it's on your record." This time it was Ms Cross who was favoured with a nod from Linwood.

"So, you said, there were seven names. What happened with the other six?" The conversation was picked up by Carlton.

"Three of them are dead," Jonah said, editing his thoughts as he spoke, "I've met one and he didn't know Patrick Kinsale and I've left one message and the last one can't be traced." He paused and prepared himself to watch the tiny reactions on their faces, before he said. "The one who can't be traced is Mike Khan." Carlton and Ms Cross looked blank, but Linwood's eyebrows twitched upwards – surprise or fear? The expression was there and gone in a second, but Jonah knew what he had seen.

Unaware of what had happened, the coroner continued. "So the matter has been concluded then. We can choose misadventure with alcohol abuse as a contributing factor when the post-mortem comes in. No need for an inquest unless the post-mortem throws up something unusual. I think we can all agree that you made best efforts, no, efforts above and beyond, to trace friends of this poor lost soul. But ultimately it was a dead end, and no further action need be taken."

Linwood was nodding along and Cross looked more relaxed. This was obviously the ending they had all planned.

"Fine," Jonah said when he realised a response was needed. "I'll close the case." He looked at Timothy Carlton, "It'll need a couple of days; it's complicated. We've got an ex-wife and a child who'll inherit, but he's a minor. Obviously no will, but she can act as guardian." He stopped talking because no one really cared about the details. Timothy Carlton nodded and that served to end the meeting, apart from the usual pleasantries and farewells.

Jonah was the first to leave and he made straight for his office. He shut the door and sat behind his desk attempting to bring his thoughts into order. He needed more information about Andrew McRae. He pulled his keyboard across the desk and called up the Google homepage. And he saw the beady eyed Ms Cross reading a report from IT and making notes in his file.

He slipped out of his office and strode into town. The local library was refreshingly anonymous, and now he knew what to search for. "Andrew McRae car dealer Shropshire". The page filled with adverts, reviews and his official site. Jonah clicked the link for news results and started reading.

As he read each entry, just a headline and a few lines of text, his blood chilled a bit more. Here was Andrew being accepted by the selection committee for a safe Conservative seat. There he was in the background of photo of a local mayor planting a tree. Here he was handing over a giant cheque to a road safety initiative. Jonah clicked on that link and saw even in the grainy black and white photograph how warmly Andrew and the Chief Constable looked at each other.

He sat back after half a dozen results. Somehow, he had rattled the cage of some rising star of the Conservative party – someone about to enter parliament. Why was his name on a list with several murder victims?

Jonah scrubbed at his eyes with the heel of his hand. This was the case he'd been waiting for. Something with logic and databases that would respond to his particular skills. And now he was blocked. He looked at the screen and every result confirmed that the sensible decision was to walk away from this case.

He pulled the keyboard closer, cleared the search box and typed in:

'Mike Khan drug dealer Birmingham'.

ELIZABETH

CHAPTER 9

April 13, 1996

The woman who would be a killer waited inside the car, lying flat. She saw a lone figure approaching from the other end of the beach. She was well prepared and grimly determined. She was ready to start her own journey.

She looked both ways and saw that he was alone. She was properly prepared and raised a spotting scope to her eye. This was a cross between a telescope and a rifle sight and showed her target walking across the surf. She identified him from her previous visits. Her prey had been tracked, his movements noted, common areas staked out. She knew from many previous visits that he came out here early every morning for a walk.

His name was Bill Wormslea and he had been chosen very carefully. She knew from looking at him that he was in his fifties, so nearing the end of his useful life. He had initially been selected because of his routine of walking alone on the beach first thing in the morning. After that she had followed him at different times in the day. Once he had been seen leaving the Job Centre, he became a very interesting prospect. Another factor in his choosing was that he smoked, using his daily stroll to get through several roll-up cigarettes. Soon, the killer reasoned, he would be a burden on society.

He lived in a one-bedroom flat with no sign of a family, no children or grandchildren to visit. He shuttled between the Job Centre, the newsagent and the post office. There wasn't even any sign of a cat or dog to mourn his passing. This wouldn't be murder, it would be more like a cull, thinning the herd in order to make it stronger.

She had agreed to carry out one murder, announced in advance and confirmed by newspaper cuttings. But there was no reason for her to take someone young, or someone on whom a family depended. She had fulfilled her side of the agreement and kept her conscience clear.

Like a hunter with a hide, she had arrived twenty minutes early, partly to allow for traffic and partly so she didn't spook her target. She had eaten a fast-food breakfast while waiting and keeping a close eye on the promenade. Once she was finished, she lay in the back of the car, gun to her side, all loaded and ready.

While she waited, the killer thought of her family, especially her father. He had pretensions of being a proper country gent. He had never understood that you could hang around the shoots, attend the fringes of the hunts and never be accepted. If you were born to be a beater, a follower, to go lamping for rabbits, then that is where you would stay for the rest of your life. But, lying in that car, the killer was grateful. She now had a familiarity with death, an aptitude for guns, and a calm demeanour when the moment came.

This was always going to be a difficult shot to take. There would be no sighting shot, no practice. There was no wind, a cautious glance at the flags on the shore confirmed this. Distance had been estimated as well as possible. The only option was to use book values to set the sight on the rifle and trust that eye and hand would remain steady. The car was a Volvo estate, plenty of room to lie in the back if you lifted your feet slightly. The back was deliberately messy – a ladder, some drop cloths and a few paint cans suggested that she was a painter or decorator. But that was all part of the cover, elaborate stage props in case of a random stop and search. A piece of blue rope had been tied to the tailgate to stop it opening all the way. Now it offered a slit through which the rifle could be aimed.

Her target, Bill Wormslea was now level with a groyne that had been chosen as the mark. Much to his misfortune, and the killer's good luck, he chose this moment to stop. While he patted his pocket to find his tobacco tin, the killer carefully laid down the spotting scope. A quick check assured her that he was still alone on the beach.

She was in the proper position, resting on a couple of folded dust sheets. She very deliberately went through a quick relaxation exercise. When all tension had left her body, she rested her cheek against the stock of the rifle, feeling its coolness. Everything on the gun had been designed around the human body. Her hands fitted perfectly onto the grips, and if she shut one eye she could look straight down the scope. She felt as if the rifle was part of her, an extension of her arm. She flowed into the weapon, one complete unit, her awareness moving down her arms, through her eye and down the scope.

Tiny movements of the rifle were exaggerated by the magnification. Bill suddenly filled the sights. He was average height, grey and balding. He was slightly overweight. The expression on his face was one of calm contemplation. His doughy face was showing stubble. For a second, he looked straight down the scope and the killer wondered if she'd been seen.

But it was a trick – she could have been stood next to him, but she was off the beach and he was at the tideline. Bill raised the cigarette to his lips and took a long drag, his florid cheeks caving in. He had a long look around the beach. It was the motion of someone preparing to start walking again and spurred the killer into action.

Gently she lowered the rifle 'til the cross hairs were centred on his body. White shirt with thin blue check showed through his dirty raincoat. She centred just to the left of his shirt pocket. Her brain took in all the details on a surface level only – she was in the zone.

She held her next in breath. Gave the trigger a gentle squeeze. She took the shot.

She was punched in the shoulder and her ears were assaulted with the report. This was deafening even through ear defenders. Being in the car with the doors nearly all closed meant that the sound had been magnified and reflected within.

She felt a quick flush of satisfaction. She hadn't flinched, hadn't pulled on the shot. It was as smooth and easy as if she were on the range.

Birds wheeled into the air, shrieking angrily at the disturbance. The sound echoed and rolled off the cliffs. The killer knew she had hit the mark; through the sights Bill had disappeared in a cloud of red. He had in fact dropped to his knees, tottered, then fallen face first into the surf. But that was not her immediate interest now. Without the scope, the killer scanned through the side windows of the estate car. Were any of the doors opening in the houses that overlooked the sea from high on the cliff? Was anyone running towards the beach? Were any cars stopped on the road?

There were no signs that the gunshot had attracted any attention, so the scope was picked up again. Now there was a body on the beach. Blood was pooling into the water; the action of the surf gave the body gave a simulacrum of life. The hands bobbed up and down in the waves, the coat billowed out and back in again. But the body seemed lifeless, lying in the sea as clouds of blood billowed around it.

Abandoning the scope a second time, she scanned up and down the beach. The café further down was still closed and the beach and promenade were deserted. She considered taking a second or third shot but discarded that idea. Even if a car stopped now, or someone walked over the dunes, it would take them five or ten minutes to reach her victim. From there, it would be more time before they found a phone and summoned help. By her calculation he was a good twenty minutes away from help, and therefore if not dead already, he soon would be.

For one final check, she focused the scope on the body again. The tide was coming in and she watched a wave break over the back of his head. There was no movement, no spluttering, so he was already dead. She knew that she had been fortunate because a single shot to the body could be survivable, if medical assistance was given immediately.

The killer was, not happy, but grimly satisfied. It had been a good clean shot, maybe a touch lucky, but luck favours the prepared. She pulled in the gun, tugged on the rope, heard the catch as the boot closed properly. There was an awkward moment as she squirmed around. The first job was to drop the gun behind the front seats, where it would rest under the folded up rear seats, all but invisible. The dust sheets and the debris from a McDonald's breakfast completed the scene. Then, with more contortions, she got back into the front seat and started the engine. She removed her ear defenders and stuffed them in the glove box.

Driving cautiously, with the windows open to dissipate the scent of cordite and stale food, she left the car park. Bill was now nothing more than a hump on the beach, a dark bundle that looked like it had been washed up. Seagulls, bolder now the sound had gone, strutted over to have a look, see if there was any food.

By the time the body was discovered, the Volvo had merged into the tens of thousands of cars making up that morning's rush hour. The ringing noise had left the killer's ears. All the clever props in the boot had not been needed.

It was only in the weeks that followed that the killer found the fault in her logic. The research had been sketchy, not enough time committed to build up a true picture of the target. Bill was given something like a military funeral as he had been a lynchpin of the Sea Cadets for nearly thirty years. The church was filled with colleagues of all ages who were heartbroken and dumbstruck that their mentor had been taken from them so callously. Further, some senior figures from the Catholic church graced the funeral, in their mysterious black robes, with their rings and sashes indicating their status and rank. Bill had been a theologian, a regular correspondent with the Catholic Herald. Described as someone with a lot to offer, the mourners spoke of how he had been snatched from them when he still had so much to live for.

In the months, then years that followed, the killer wondered what solace theology brought Bill? Was he now sat at the hand of his God in heaven? Perversely, this led her closer to the church as the only way to atone for her sins.

CHAPTER 10

March 13, 2015

Jonah's phone rang and interrupted him from work. He was painstakingly researching the family tree of a man who was found dead in his flat, aged ninety-three. His body had been there for over a week before he was found, making Jonah very glad he was out of uniform. His job was to find any relatives.

"Hello DS Greene, coroner's officer."

"Hello, I'm Elizabeth Gardner, you left a message for me to contact you? I really must apologise; I've been away for a bit and I only just got the message. It was left just over two weeks ago?" The voice was female and perfectly modulated and now he'd heard a couple of sentences, Jonah recognised it. She was the caller who'd rung up, refused to give their name and then hung up.

"Yes, thank you for calling back," Jonah made a quick decision to hold his information back for the moment. He didn't want to risk another hang up. "I'm investigating a homeless man who was found dead a couple of weeks ago. Did you know someone called Patrick Kinsale?"

There was a deep breath on the other end of the line. "Patrick Kinsale did you say?"

"Yes, you were at university together? Swindon?" Jonah looked suspiciously at the open door. He held the phone to his ear and moved round the desk to try to shut the door.

"I may have heard the name, why are you interested?" She was now sounding wary.

In the two weeks since he was warned off, Jonah had called round a few of his friends and colleagues. Over twenty years he had accumulated contacts going back to his days at Hendon. Very quietly, often in the evenings, he called them up and asked for off the record help getting some information on Mike Khan. He never used email or left a message and always pointed out that this was unofficial.

This was the first progress, so he decided to play Elizabeth like a fish, let out a bit of line, then reel her back in. Stretching the phone wire, he caught the door with his heel and it swung a bit more closed, but didn't latch. It was now out of reach and the phone was dangerously close to the edge of the desk.

"It's part of, errm, an ongoing investigation. That is to say, I am very interested."

"So, you are investigating his death?"

There was a pause. "Yes, I am. So, did you know Patrick Kinsale, he studied English at university? He'd have been a year above you and I think you overlapped each other by only one year. But you were both in humanities."

"So you really have been looking into this? Done your research?" There was a pause. "Are you going to see this through?"

Jonah considered this question. Two weeks ago, he

would've said 'yes' without a doubt. But his initial fire had dimmed.

For all his enquiries he had got nothing back. His friends had listened carefully and promised to keep to in touch. They'd always 'get right back' to him, or 'see what they can dig up'. But the result was always the same – no further contact. After a week he had run out of avenues. But in the quiet minutes before the day started, or on his lunch break, he found himself staring at the list, wondering what he'd missed, what else Patrick had meant to impart.

"What do you mean?" Jonah asked carefully, regaining his seat.

"Well, I can't just go about talking to anyone. This has been buried for a long time and it needs to be sorted out once and for all. I'm not starting something and then not finishing it."

"I said that I'm investigating," Jonah argued.

"Yes, but you lied, no hold on, you didn't lie. It was an obfuscation, a diversion, a half-truth." Her words were speeding up now, tumbling out of her mouth and down the phone line. "You repeated my words back to me and you hesitated before you admitted whether you were investigating, and you sounded too definite when I challenged you, like you were trying to convince yourself as well as me. So, something's up. How am I doing so far? Have I caught you out yet? What is really going on?"

"Okay, Elizabeth, take a breath for a minute. Calm down." Jonah questioned himself – was he right to get so personal with someone he'd hardly spoken to before? The line went silent for a couple of moments, amplifying his doubt.

"And now you're avoiding the question, aren't you?" She sounded calmer now.

Jonah thought fast. "Okay, but I need something from you. Did you definitely know Patrick Kinsale at the University of Swindon?"

"Yes, but you need to answer my question, are you really investigating?"

Damn, Jonah thought, time to reel in some line and see if the fish swims away or stays hooked. "Listen, this isn't precisely an investigation per se. Officially our remit is to investigate the circumstances of a sudden death. And in this case we have established that there is a definite cause of death. But, on the other hand, there is one further matter which does merit further enquiry." He hated himself as he said this, but he needed to keep her talking. "But I do intend to keep on with this. I feel we need to do justice to Patrick. He trusted me with the list and I'm not going to let..." Jonah realised he hadn't yet told Elizabeth about the list.

"What list?"

"People who he wanted at his funeral; your name was on it." Jonah crossed his fingers and hoped that she would let the matter drop.

"And who else was?"

"I can't say that right now."

"Will you come down and see me?"

"I'm the policeman here. You don't get to tell me what to do and where to go!"

"But I need to know, to see if you are the one who can bring redemption, or retribution, maybe even resolution. One of those words like that. What is it you police do now? Rehabilitation?"

"Elizabeth!" Jonah said sharply, "you're getting manic again! What are you on about?" Jonah looked nervously at the door. Had his raised voice been heard or not? There was no reaction from the office.

"Are you all right?" he asked in a much softer tone, now expressing concern.

"All right?" there was a soft, throaty laugh, "I haven't been all right for a very long time. But I do have good days and bad days. Sometimes I let it all get to me and get carried away. But I have a strange feeling that you'll be able to cope. You seem to keep me in line."

"Thank you, Elizabeth." Time to start pulling her back in. "But I'm not here to be your counsellor, I need to understand your relationship with Patrick while at university. Is there anything you can tell me to shed light on that period?"

"I would like to see this list," Elizabeth mused, almost to herself, "How about we meet up? In person? I'm in the Cotswolds over the weekend, so that's better for you if you're in Cardiff?"

"No!Your duty is to help the police, not set conditions."

"No need to get all bossy with me!" There was a dangerous pause where Jonah prayed she'd stay on the line. "If this is an unofficial investigation, I'm not really helping the police, am I? It's you that I'm helping. And in return for that, I'd like to meet you. I want to see this list of yours. On the other hand, you want some information out of me. We can both win. How about I sweeten the deal, I'll buy you lunch as well? Tomorrow? I know a lovely little pub, does exquisite food, right off the beaten track, no tourists."

Jonah couldn't work out how to get out of this. She was right, he did need information, and it sounded like she could provide it. Reluctantly he agreed to meet up and noted down the name and address of a pub deep in the countryside up past Gloucester. At least I won't end up paying for the bridge, he thought glumly, although he was unsure how he'd sell the idea to Alex.

He put his head down on the desk and wondered how

he'd managed to get the interview so badly wrong. Everything he'd learned, hell, everything a cadet knew, had gone out of the window. And now he had agreed to an interview with no recording, no corroboration. Any information would be useless. But, he argued with himself, PACE didn't apply. He had no crime, no victim, no witness. He was heading into dangerous territory – his only motivation was to do right by Patrick Kinsale. He had tried to communicate something to Jonah from beyond the grave. Elizabeth was the only one on the list he could talk to, so he felt he must. He was working for a dead man and there were no rules.

JONAH HAD GOT into the habit of eating his lunch in the gardens around the Central Police Station. It helped him avoid his former colleagues in the canteen and he loved the area – Cathays Park. After his phone call with Elizabeth, he'd texted Farida to see if she was in the office and wanted lunch. She texted back immediately 'YES!'.

He walked out of the station and through Cathays Park. It was a place built on optimism – late Victorian philanthropists had designed and paid for it to be built to propel Cardiff from large town to city status and then on to the capital of Wales.

Finished in the Edwardian era, it was a triumph of classical architecture. All around there were white stone frontages, classical columns, manicured lawns edged with granite. The avenues were wide and expansive, dotted with monuments to Wales' fallen soldiers. Any spaces that were left between buildings were filled in with formal gardens. The whole area was segregated from the main shopping centre of Cardiff by the main road and the castle. In the middle of this area, the Central Police Station had a different sort of optimism. It was built in the late 1960s and was unashamedly modern. It had stark, brutal vertical lines, now the depressing grey that you only get from forty-year-old concrete. Someone in the sixties had thought that this design was equal to and fit to sit alongside the grand Victorian and Edwardian buildings around it.

Jonah found Farida sat on a bench in Gorsedd Park. It had a modern stone circle to celebrate some eisteddfod or other. The walk had calmed him down – his head had been swimming after the phone call with Elizabeth. Soon they were eating their sandwiches with the spring sunshine filtering through the trees.

"What a morning!" she said, "three of the lads in the department went off on a counter-terrorism course and came back today." She rolled her eyes expressively. "They don't know whether to ask me stupid questions about Islam or to treat me like a potential suicide bomber."

"Couldn't you lodge a complaint about harassment?"

"No, there's no point. I like to, what's the phrase, keep my powder dry. If I kick off about this, then if anything really nasty happens, I won't be believed. This is just office high jinks and them larking around. I've got a contact within the Police Fed and I know how bad it can get."

"Are you sure? It could escalate."

"No, as long as I can sneak out and decompress and complain about them, I'll be fine." Farida then turned to Jonah. "Distraction, that's what I need. Why were you so keen to escape from your office?"

Jonah gave her a brief overview of his conversation with Elizabeth. He squirmed internally; when he recounted it, he heard how bad it sounded. "At one point I even started to sound like DI Linwood."

"So, this Elizabeth Barry is on the list?"

"Yes, except she's married now and called Gardner. I called her and left a message about ten days ago. I forgot about her to be honest." He gave her a quick recap of what he had learnt so far, including the fact that he had been warned off by his boss.

"So, you're convinced that this Patrick Kinsale was killed, by someone stealing his coat and sleeping bag and buying him vodka?"

"Pretty much," Jonah said. "I mean, he lost his warm clothes and he got thirty quid's worth of vodka from somewhere. If I'm right, then the real question is why was he killed, and I think the list is something to do with it."

"Okay, but have you thought about the ex-wife and child?"

"No?"

"Well the ex-wife is getting her funeral and all the paperwork sorted out for her," Farida explained, "that's all she wants. Do you really think she is going to thank you for digging up some murky past that her ex may have? All you're doing is storing up more grief for that moment when her teenage son asks, 'what was my dad like?'"

"It's what you said when we met though," Jonah countered, "it's service. If someone did kill him, then don't they have a right to know? Don't you think when that son grows up, he'd want to know?"

"I'm just worried that you're doing this for your career and not for better reasons."

"It's not just Patrick," Jonah said defensively, and Farida raised her eyebrows. "It's Elizabeth too. She's vulnerable and her mental state seems unstable. She needs me, needs some answers as well."

"At last we agree about something; she does need you.

That's because she's using you. She's playing some game or other and you're one of her pieces. Remind me again, where she lives and what she does for a living?"

"You know! She doesn't work and she lives either in the Cotswolds or Docklands."

"Precisely. I know the type. She's loaded and manipulative. Much harder to deal with than the 'my taxes pay your wages' crowd, because she'd never say it, just use it as an attitude to beat you with." She looked directly at Jonah. "You said yourself that she was unstable. She might not even be aware herself of what game she's playing but you're fooling yourself if you think you can help her."

"So, what am I doing then?"

"I think you're digging yourself into a hole. I take it you remember Colin Stagg and Rachel Nickell?"

"This is different, it's not a high-profile murder," Jonah protested.

"You are right, this is different. When the whole Nickell case went wrong, they had the support of an MIT, and a professional psychiatrist. That still went so badly wrong that the policewoman involved left and sued the Met for psychological damage. Now you're treading the same path without any support."

"But Elizabeth isn't a murderer and isn't deranged."

"Just because she's rich and middle-class, doesn't mean she's safe," Farida argued. "I'm just showing you where and how it can go wrong."

"Okay, I'll take it easy. And I'll look up Rachel Nickell on the Internet, try not to make the same mistakes. But I know there's something, whether it is the murder of Patrick Kinsale or something further back in the past. It's kind of like an itch, you know, I need to know."

"That's more honest, you're doing it for yourself," Farida

agreed, "because it doesn't feel right. Underneath all the paperwork and reviews and intelligence reports, you're still a detective playing a hunch!" She paused, then asked, "What does your boss think of all this?"

"Which boss?"

"Either? Both?"

"Well, the case has been formally closed, verdict recorded of death by misadventure with alcohol as a factor. Death certificate issued, probate all nicely sorted, the whole lot."

"So, what exactly is your remit here, what crime are you investigating?"

"There isn't one. Well, I don't know. I've got three cold-case murders."

"That no one's managed to solve for nearly twenty years!" Farida interrupted.

"And Mike Khan's obviously dodgy – ask anyone and he's described as a drug dealer."

"But," Farida countered, "he's obviously under the eye of the West Midlands lot – and at a senior level. There are some fairly big toes you'll be treading on."

"Yes, but what if they're linked?" Jonah persisted. "Peter, he's another crime victim, he was attacked too."

"But the only link is one piece of paper scribbled on by a down-and-out! And what's on it? A victim of an attack, a known criminal, a car dealer, some rich woman who's a bit mad and three murder victims, all unsolved cold cases. Isn't it possible that Patrick had no idea at all?"

"Okay, that's just what Timothy said. But, how did he die? And how come he knew he was going to die? This wasn't some list that the Prof had been holding on to for years, he was given it less than two weeks before Patrick died."

Farida held her hands up in surrender. "Okay, but you're still going against your boss who's already warned you that he's got a formal complaint in the wings. Add that to a pissed off DCI from another force and the other cold cases around the country and your career is on the line."

"But, look at it the other way round – if I sort out this tangle, bring Mike Khan to justice, then my career will be resurrected. I'll be doing the proper job I thought I would be twenty years ago when I started."

"That's a big 'if'!"

Jonah nodded to himself. He knew he had broken most of the rules. He hadn't controlled the conversation and had been backed into a corner by a witness. He smiled to himself, he didn't even have a crime for her to be witness to. He had gone wrong because before he started, he was already off the map. When Elizabeth called back, he should have told her the funeral date, and that a formal verdict had been made by the coroner and then hung up.

He knew what his problem was – he had discussed it in therapy. He identified too closely with the people he worked with. Of course, properly under control it was a great strength in a policeman. An ability to empathise and see all sides of an argument was an asset indeed. But he took it too far, he imagined what it would be like to be the victim. If he wasn't careful, he took it home with him.

No, he thought, I haven't done that. It's about service – he should be serving Patrick Kinsale. But, talking to Farida, he had clarified something else in his head. He would have to tread a narrow path. One standard interview strategy was to gain the trust of the interviewee, pretend to be on their side, get them to confide. The challenge would be to do this while still avoiding any charges of entrapment or getting sucked in and damaged himself.

So, ultimately, he had no case, no legal justification to investigate. As his coroner was keen to point out, he should close the file and move on to the next one. Except that the list wouldn't let him alone. Patrick had been certain that his life was in danger and it was conceivable that someone had acted to do him harm – either to kill him or warn him off.

Elizabeth had known Patrick. Both of them knew something, so there must have been something to know. And it was a something that was, in theory, worth killing Patrick over. Which in turn made it something that Jonah wanted to know.

"You're not going to stop, are you?"

"Probably not," Jonah answered. He considered a moment. "Mind you, I might be at a dead end. I've got as much as I can out of Calne, McCrae is close to putting in a complaint, and Khan is totally off limits. If Elizabeth Gardner doesn't tell me anything useful, it's hard to see where to go next."

"Well, whatever you do, be careful."

BACK AT HIS DESK, Jonah replayed his conversation with Farida in his head. Even though she was sceptical, he felt that the case now had legs again. He had seven names, three of whom were murdered, one had been interviewed and one was not contactable. Now he was about to meet with Elizabeth, he felt he needed more background on the final name on his list.

Aware that he could be bringing his career to a halt, he phoned through to the Shrewsbury Local Information Unit, and got through to a DS called Terry Mannings. With some trepidation, he asked about Andrew McRae.

"Please tell me you want to know about some poor kid who happens to have the same name as a major car dealership in the town?" The accent was local. Figures, thought Jonah, he'd know the place inside out.

"Unfortunately not," he admitted.

"Christ!" There was a pause, "how are you playing this? Is this an official enquiry, with a case number that I have to put into the system? Or am I just on the phone with a friend?"

"There isn't a case number for you to log it against."

"Jesus wept! Are you mad? You want to go poking that tiger with a very short stick?"

"No, I'm not poking any tigers," Jonah sounded offended. "I just want to get a feel for him, what he's like."

"You want to get a feel for him?" There was a sneer in the words. "Why don't you buy a place at one of those five-hundred-pound-a-plate charity dinners, and you might get to sit next to him. Or, you could always stump up the green fees and take up golf, I'm sure you'd run into each other at the clubhouse. If all that fails, just give our chief constable a bell, and see if he'll put in a good word for you!"

"There's no need to be sarcastic! His name just came up, tangential to a case, and I wondered what the score was." He paused for effect, "I guess now I know." I know that he's bought the local force, he added to himself.

There was such a long pause that he thought the LIO man had hung up. "You calling from the office phone?"

"Yes," Jonah admitted.

Terry muttered something under his breath that sounded a lot like 'stupid!'. Aloud he said, "You could, as you're a friend, phone me at home this evening."

"But..." Jonah started to say.

"You said you were a detective!" Terry snapped, and this time he did hang up.

Jonah had access to many databases and his main job was tracking down people. He thought of his conversation with Terry, and decided he was Shropshire born and bred, and probably in his fifties. Wouldn't be living that far from Shrewsbury, so should be easy to track down.

When he got home that night, he had a phone number written on a Post-it folded up in his pocket. He was wondering how quickly he'd be able to lock himself in the study to call Terry back and find out what he couldn't say at work.

The house was empty, with a note from Alex saying that she'd gone out to 'a party with a live band' and would be 'back late'. What didn't suit his plans so well was Pickford, their dog, sat on the mat, whining and looking up at the hook where his lead hung.

Cursing under his breath, Jonah didn't bother taking off his jacket. He chose one the shorter routes even though the night was calm and clear. As he walked, his mind roamed, both over his day and to Alex. Where was she and what was happening?

Then he returned to his other problem. So far, he was certain that DS Mannings wouldn't report him. At the moment he was safe from the official complaint that was hanging over him. But, if he made the phone call when he got home, then he would be set on a course that could end his career.

He glanced at the large houses set way back from the road. He passed a communal area of grass, ringed by ordered flowerbeds and low hedges. This was near the area where Patrick Kinsale had died. He wondered how it had happened. Would it be easy to lure a homeless man into a car? Once he was there, removing his coat, stealing his sleeping bag and giving him vodka would be easy. Or would you give him the vodka first? Then it would be equally easy to push him out of the car somewhere inhospitable.

It was about an hour to walk back from here to the centre of town. But, drunk and disoriented, Patrick would have been totally isolated. Jonah shivered even though it was a mild spring night. He knew from working night shifts that the temperature dropped alarmingly overnight. He couldn't imagine what Patrick's final hours would have been like.

He was now resolved – he would risk his career to get justice for Patrick Kinsale.

Finally, he was home. He had a cold beer, a sleeping dog, and a ready meal in the oven. Time to phone Terry.

"Hello! I wondered if I'd hear from you this evening!"

"So, what's the score on McRae?"

"Well, the first thing is that there is a general feeling that he buys information," Terry explained. "It's a very grey area, I don't think he's ever put pressure on anyone to change their investigation, to do things differently, but he's known to be generous if you put things his way. Maybe not with money, but he can help a career with a word in the right ear. Or the other way round if you get on the wrong side of him."

"Right, that figures. So you didn't want to talk in the office."

"No, and if you're going after him, it'd better be bulletproof."

"So, what else is there?"

"Well, he's clean as far as police records are concerned." Terry paused for effect.

"So, that doesn't tell me much," Jonah complained.

"It tells you a lot. He's an old-fashioned car dealer. He

turned up in Shrewsbury nearly twenty years ago and started from the bottom, trawling the auctions for cheap cars, polishing them up and then putting them on his lot. Eventually he got enough money together to have his own mechanic, a lad to clean cars for him, that kind of stuff. Then he bought shares in a body shop so he could do his own bodywork on the cheap. From there it was a steady progression to the person he is now, owner of a chain of six modern dealerships; he must be worth millions.

"The weird thing is that there is no hint that he ever broke the law, going back nearly twenty years. Not a caution, not even a note in an intelligence report, nothing."

"There can't be many successful car dealers who can say that. Really nothing?"

"Not a thing. I had a quite chat over a cigarette with our esteemed desk sergeant. He's been around forever and won't go running back to someone like Andrew who he sees as a newcomer. But he said that, around two thousand four or five when he was getting big, CID were working a scrote who was flogging bent car parts. We leaned on him, because he'd been working for McRae. Apparently, he'd stored some of the bent stuff at the back of the garage and Andrew found out. He went ballistic, made him load the lot into his own car, and then fired him on the spot!"

"That is weird," Jonah agreed, "most garage owners would be after their own cut, or maybe give the guy time to sell it all and tell him not to do it again. The garage trade is shorthand for petty criminals."

"There's one other thing I can tell you. Just after that incident, he had a fire at his yard."

"That's more interesting, insurance scam?"

"No," Terry sounded disappointed, "we had an off the record chat with the adjuster. Apparently, he wasn't padding at all. Mostly it was invoices, receipts, paperwork, computers that he lost. Even the cars with fire damage weren't written off, he just ran them through his own body shop and charged costs only to the claim."

"So," Jonah summarised, "this guy is a saint. He won't trade in stolen parts, he won't cheat his insurance, he donates to charity and he's friends with high-ups in the police and society."

"Exactly," Terry confirmed. "The message he always puts out is that he works hard and got lucky."

There was a pregnant pause before Jonah said what they were both thinking. "So, what's he hiding?"

"Since you phoned up, I've been asking myself the same thing. Do me a favour though – if you find out, please let me know."

When the call was over, Jonah sat in his dark house wondering if he now knew more or less having spoken to the LIO.

CHAPTER 11

JONAH SLEPT BADLY and woke up still feeling tired. The first thing he did was roll over and feel the empty side of the bed where Alex should be. It was cold. He sat up in bed and listened to the house. There was no sound, he could tell that he was alone. He grabbed his mobile from the bedside table. There was a stream of texts assuring him that she was fine, just a little drunk and not keen on riding. They petered out around three in the morning so he wasn't expecting her home soon.

He got up and made himself some coffee. Now the children had left home, the house was unnaturally quiet. For the sake of something to do he got the lead and took Pickford for a walk. It wasn't as relaxing as it could have been as he checked his mobile every few minutes to see if Alex had woken up yet wherever she was.

He hadn't had a chance yet to tell Alex that he'd arranged a meeting with Elizabeth for lunchtime. He had breakfast, checked Google Maps and worked out when he should leave. He nervously watched as the clock ticked around to and then past his departure time. He really didn't want to leave without at least seeing Alex. Finally, he heard the rumble of the engine, then a moment later Alex turned into the drive and coasted to a halt.

"There you are!" He was already in the porch as she took her helmet off. "I'm really sorry, but I've got to go – I have an appointment."

Alex blinked as she pulled the helmet off. "Appointments? On a Saturday?"

"Well, not exactly an appointment, but I agreed to meet someone at a pub. It's over in England, towards Gloucester." He looked nervously at his watch. "Listen, you're okay?" he asked. She nodded and Jonah said, "Sorry, I've got to go." Without looking back, he slid into his car and left.

As he expected, Jonah was late to the pub. His sat-nav had struggled and the expected arrival time kept creeping upwards. He had to resist the urge to speed as he was on unfamiliar roads.

When he was parked up in the car park, he got out of his car and looked around. It was an ingrained habit to check out his surroundings. He was deep in the countryside, and all was quiet around him. He'd last seen a house about five minutes before arriving at the pub. It was a long, low building, with thatched roof hanging low over the whitewashed walls. The car park was shaded by mature trees and full of expensive cars on personal plates. Range Rovers and other 4x4s loomed over low-slung sports cars.

Squaring his shoulders and wondering if he should have dressed smarter, Jonah prepared to enter the lion's den. He had reached the door and wondered how to identify Elizabeth. From the outside, he imagined that the pub would be full of rich, middle-aged women.

However, when he got to the authentic porch under a bump in the thatch, he was grabbed by a well-manicured hand and dragged into the dim interior. He was in a lobby that was trying too hard to be a mixture between an old pub and country house. Hunting trophies loomed over leather sofas, and tables with leaflet racks.

"Are you DS Greene?" When he nodded, she continued, "Elizabeth Gardner." In the dim light, he could tell she was beautiful. She had platinum blonde hair in a very flattering short bob. She was quite thin and frail looking, about average height. "Sorry to grab you like that but I was followed here."

"Followed?"

"From Waitrose." Elizabeth nodded. "At first I wasn't sure. I mean, the middle of Cheltenham is busy. But the closer I got to the pub, further out into the countryside, the more I was sure. There's a dark green Mercedes out there." She waved at the window.

Jonah laughed. "Half that car park is full of Mercedes! What's so suspicious?"

"No! Not a shiny, last year's model. One of those boxy ones from years ago with a proper grille. Looks a bit tatty. Still got two guys sat in it." Jonah turned to the window. Now this got his interest. Two men, driving out to a remote pub, then waiting in the car park? Something wasn't right. "They're not out there, they went to the overflow car park round the back."

Jonah frowned, partly because his fourteen-year-old Mondeo stuck out like a sore thumb. He looked through a window of the pub-restaurant. It was busy and he couldn't see through to the back. But on the other hand, there were enough empty tables and seats at the bar. There was no reason for two people to wait in their car.

"What do you drive?"

"The white Lexus sports car, up the end there," Elizabeth said.

"Stay here, get us a table. Preferably one with a view of the back," Jonah instructed her. He doubted there was anything in her story, but if he checked now, he could reassure her and she would be more likely to talk.

He walked out, phone in hand. The car park ran up to the end, then a road led around to the rear car park. If they were following her, they'd have parked where they could see her Lexus parked.

Relying on this, he walked straight to it, while looking at his phone. He was loading up the camera. When he reached the car, he lifted up the phone and frowned at it, as if reading something. He surreptitiously snapped a few photos of the tatty old Mercedes sat in the car park, with its nose facing the Lexus. There were two people in it, one behind a paper, the other with his head down, reading something.

When they were both seated at a table, Elizabeth still looked quiet and withdrawn. He quickly reported what he'd seen.

"You mean they really were following me?"

Jonah thought of the car, sticking out like a sore thumb, pointing at her Lexus. "Maybe. They could be here for any number of reasons." He called the picture up on his phone and zoomed in to read the plate. "I'll just have to pop out a minute to check this number plate," he said. A waiter was approaching their table, so he said to Elizabeth, "I'll have the field mushrooms with garlic butter to start, followed by steak and chips." They were the only two items he'd recognised from the menu.

He made his way between the tables back out the way he'd come in. Outside the restaurant he stopped in the lobby, sandwiched between the diners inside and the smokers outside. Jonah perched on a low leather sofa while he phoned in a PNC check and scribbled down the information. KDM Cars, from Birmingham. Private hire company that had its own cars. So, was the second man a fare paying passenger or was the driver off on his own with a friend?

The starters were waiting when Jonah got back to the table. Over mouthfuls of mushroom, he mentioned that the two men in the Mercedes were acting strangely and happened to be from Birmingham. A chilly silence fell over the table, so obvious that Jonah was sure he wasn't imagining it. So, he thought, there is a link between Mike Khan in Birmingham and Elizabeth Gardner. And she admitted to knowing Patrick Kinsale.

He ate in silence, watching Elizabeth closely. Although still pale, she'd recovered some of her composure after Jonah had seen the men who followed her. Now that he'd mentioned Birmingham, the pinched, haunted look had reappeared on her face.

To break the tension, he slid his photocopy of the list across the table. It was the clean one that didn't have Peter's notes on it. She glanced down at it, then moved her empty plate aside to study it more closely.

"That proves it – I haven't had any contact with Patrick for years!" she said stabbing a finger at her own name. "I've been married fifteen years and he wrote down my maiden name. Whatever this list is about, it's nothing recent," she said, then stopped suddenly. Jonah was about to ask how she knew Patrick, what their time at university had been like when she started speaking again. "This one, Mike Khan, he's the one you need to watch out for. Have you done your research yet?"

Jonah nodded, then added, "He's a drug dealer." He didn't want to scare her any further, so he didn't mention that he was suspected to be in Birmingham.

Elizabeth chuckled softly. "That's less than half of it. He's a proper nasty piece of work." She shook her head. "Seems to like hurting people, wielding power over them." Jonah looked up with an unspoken question. "I'm a wealthy woman, I'm sure you know that. And I get bored, so sometimes I look up my old friends – and not just on the Internet – if you have the money, you'd be amazed what you can learn."

Jonah's head was swimming with questions when the food arrived. He was pleased to see that at least the main part – the steak and chips – were fairly normal and substantial. He eyed the onion marmalade on the salad suspiciously, along with the roasted fennel. Elizabeth for her part made a great show of eating and avoiding eye contact. As he ate, Jonah felt himself getting frustrated with the lack of progress.

Over coffees, he finally asked, "Elizabeth, what are we doing here?" She looked up quizzically. "I mean, you invite me out here, treat me to lunch and then what? You clam up and don't tell me anything! You obviously knew Patrick and Mike at university, what about the other names?" He jabbed the list with his finger.

"I'm scared," she looked at him with big eyes, "I'm being followed. I don't know who I've upset or what they might do if they find out I'm talking to the police." Jonah had a feeling that she knew exactly who she was afraid of and she wasn't telling.

"Okay, but you were all at university at the same time, and you've already said you know Patrick and Mike, what about Andrew?"

"I know the name, but I'm not sure I'd recognise him now," she reluctantly admitted, brushing her hair back behind her ear.

"And Peter?" Jonah tapped the list with his finger.

"Peter? Peter Calne? That does ring a bell," Elizabeth said, her brow furrowing. Jonah felt hopeful that at last he might get something out of this meeting. But then Elizabeth continued. "Everyone knew the name; it was all over the papers. When was that, ninety-four, no, ninety-five or ninety-six? I can't really remember. But I do remember all those lovely rugby types who were suddenly only too keen to walk me home at night. Everyone thought there was some maniac stalking the campus, throwing people off the walkways, waiting to jump out at any moment." She stopped and sipped her coffee. "Of course, you know what university life is like. It went on for a couple of months, then he woke up and no one on else was attacked. By the time we left for summer holidays I think the whole fuss was over." Jonah looked hopefully at her, so she continued, "But I never actually knew him personally or ever met him." She looked straight at him. "Can we go now. Those men out there are spooking me."

As they walked out to the car park, Elizabeth stopped him in the porch again. "Can you do anything about them?" She looked up at him with big eyes turning on her full woman-in-distress act.

"Don't worry. You leave the car park first, and if they do try to follow, I'll get between your car and theirs. Go nice and fast, and I'll slow them up. Once you get past two or three junctions, they won't have a clue where you've gone. And I'll give you my mobile number, so you can get in touch if you ever feel scared again." Jonah thought that if they'd come all the way out here from Birmingham then they had probably started following her from her home. This wasn't, however, something worth sharing with Elizabeth.

AT FIRST JONAH thought that Elizabeth was jumping at shadows. He started his engine first and expertly peeled out of his space right behind her Lexus. He turned onto the main road and automatically checked his rear-view mirror. He was wrong – there was the Mercedes right behind him. He kept an eye on it, noting when it swung out to get a better view past him at the Lexus.

Soon, Elizabeth turned off the main road into a much smaller lane. It was now narrower and impossible to overtake so he eased off the accelerator. He didn't want to show brake lights, but he did want to increase the distance. Predictably, the Mercedes behind him closed up to threaten him.

Experimentally he jabbed the brake lights and was rewarded with a flash from the car behind. By now he had lost sight of Elizabeth in front. At the next junction, he had no idea which way to turn, so he stopped his car and got a map out, holding it high so the car behind could see. He had positioned his car to stop the Mercedes getting past. He could hear, faintly through the window, shouting from the car behind and a revving engine. Just to be careful, Jonah leant on the door lock and heard a reassuring click of central locking.

The driver behind was now leaning on his horn.

Jonah looked around – he was totally alone in the countryside with two adversaries. He had no idea where he was and had only given Alex the briefest outline. He could picture Elizabeth heading safely home, with no idea where he was.

He looked at his phone and saw it had no signal. Disgusted, he threw it onto the passenger seat next to him.

The drone of the horn became a background noise. He could see the lurid tabloid headlines about the brutal slaying of an off-duty policeman in a rural idyll. His stomach turned over slowly.

Jonah felt a slight, but definite jolt. The Mercedes had got fed up waiting and nudged his car. He didn't think it'd be hard enough to leave a mark, but it was unsettling, a sign of an impending confrontation. They had got inside his personal space. Elizabeth had a very good head start now, so he'd better get moving.

He glanced in his rear-view mirror and saw a door open behind him. Jonah tried to ease the clutch up to roll forward, but his leg spasmed and the car lurched forward half a length and stalled.

Jonah could feel the car closing in, no air in it for him to breathe. The sky had turned a leaden grey making the light outside the car flat and oppressive.

He was paralysed the same as he had been four months earlier, at the top of those stairs. Unable to move, that time he had failed his colleagues. Now, in the car, he had put himself was in danger.

Breathe, he told himself, breathe and move. The car was locked, he was safe, he just needed to start the engine and get moving. His right arm felt heavy and he struggled to release his grip on the steering wheel. Key, he thought through the fog in his brain. He felt cool plastic under his fingers and the brush of the other keys on his palm.

Do I turn it towards me or away? I can't remember how

to start a car, never mind drive it, his panicked mind screamed at him.

The rear window shattered in a spray of safety glass, thousands of fake diamonds all over the rear seat. The sound, the impact, the sudden rush of fresh air overcame Jonah's paralysis. He even felt a few fragments of glass on the back of his neck. He didn't wait for the next blow. In one fluid movement, he depressed the clutch, snicked the gear lever into first, fired up the engine and tore away from the junction with a squeal of tyres. It was obviously not what they were expecting – Jonah saw his assailant stood by the side of the road, wheel brace dangling from one hand. The Mercedes started moving as Jonah disappeared around a bend.

Mercifully, he was only ten minutes from the A436. Soon he had blended into the traffic and was doing a safe fifty-five mph as he headed for Gloucester. He had not seen the green Mercedes since the attack and was starting to calm down. The car was noisy and blowy with one window broken.

He heart was still thumping and his hands were slick on the steering wheel. With a start he stamped too hard on the brakes as he'd drifted up behind a slow lorry. The car behind him hooted and swerved. Nervously he checked but it was just a driver annoyed by his driving.

His stomach churned and his heart hammered away. As the adrenalin left his system, he clamped his hands onto the wheel to stop them shaking.

The next time he saw a garage, he stopped for some coffee, tape and a couple of plastic bags. While the coffee cooled, he made temporary repairs to the car. The weather was colder now, and a fitful breeze kept trying to grab the plastic from his hands.

When he got back on the road, he made an effort to drive calmly, blending into the traffic around him. He berated himself as he drove. What had he been thinking? All that play acting with the map. As soon as Elizabeth's car had cleared the junction, he should have turned in a different direction, set the sat-nav and headed for home.

He'd worried that he wasn't ready to return to the police. He'd done untold courses in defensive driving and risk assessment. Yet, the minute Elizabeth used her puppy dog eyes it all went out of the window. How had he allowed himself to be dragged into her drama? Maybe Farida was right – he was being played by Elizabeth.

More concerning was the fact that he'd frozen. Now the moment was in the past he was hard on himself. It had been explained to him over and over that a panic attack was a physical thing, but he still felt it was weakness. He was just thankful that it didn't happen on duty. He should never have been there, so the police service need never know. Whether he could live with himself knowing was another matter.

Alex was dozing on the sofa when he got back. They looked at each other and then said, at the same time, "where have you been?" Jonah raised his eyebrows and Alex spoke first.

"Got too drunk to ride home and crashed out at the clubhouse," she said groggily.

"Clubhouse? What kind of party was it?" Jonah had visions of hard-core bike gangs, his wife there with tattooed bikers dealing in drugs and guns.

"It was just a live band in a pub. But this group of 'em, well the landlord's one of them and he has a spare function room on the side. I just kipped on one of the benches in there."

Jonah felt everything closing in – he was finding it hard to breathe again. It all came rushing at him in a jumble, Elizabeth's paranoia, the thugs in the Mercedes, Alex partying with bikers – he turned away and went to sit down heavily in the kitchen. He stared out at the garden – there was plenty to do but a light rain had just started falling.

"Are you alright, love?" Alex had glided into the kitchen, silent as a ghost. "Don't worry about the bikers, they're good people. They don't even have a club name, patch or anything like that. Listen, it's the Crown, down towards Ogmore, you can ask around at your work, it's not a bad place."

"Yeah, thanks, I'll do that." Jonah suddenly felt exhausted and fed up with it all. "Listen, I haven't sorted out the garden recently, I ought to." He went to get changed but when he came back Alex waylaid him. She was more awake now, cradling a coffee.

"I know I shouldn't have stayed out late, but where did you go? Did you get overtime or time off in lieu?"

"No," Jonah shook his head, "it was a bit off the record. Just some background stuff."

"You're not going to ruin it again, are you? You've built a good career; I'd hate to see you throw it all away now."

Jonah shrugged – he hadn't thrown it away; it had been taken from him. He wished Alex could understand, would support him, especially when he was unable to do so himself. Also, he balked at the idea that his career was good. He saw each step as taking him closer to retirement without having achieved anything.

"It's okay," he said to Alex, "like I said, someone got in touch who had some background information. It's nothing that could come back and bite me."

"What happened today?" Alex asked, "I saw the car outside? The window?"

"Oh, that," Jonah replied, "something and nothing. I stopped in services, and when I went back to the car someone was standing there. I called out, a bit stupid of me, I know, and he took off like a hare. I guess he must've just done the window and was about to open it up and see what he could steal. He had too much head start so I just drove it round to the petrol station and taped it up."

"Are you going to report it? There'd be CCTV."

"I don't think it's worth it." He looked at her, trying to appear honest. "I know, I could get my own crime number, talk straight to the right person in Gloucestershire, and all that. But it's just criminal damage and I've already left the scene." He shook his head as if making his mind up. "No. There's a glass place near work, I'll pop in at lunchtime and get it fixed. It's no bother."

Alex studied him carefully with her head on one side. "Okay then," she said before drifting off to the lounge.

The rain was easing, so he decided to wait another couple of minutes before heading out to the garden. He slipped into his office. With the door shut, he phoned the LIU for central Birmingham and asked them about KDM Cars.

"Well, if you want minor crimes, they're the people to go to," the sergeant told him. "Of course, that's all intelligence, we can't actually pin anything on the company."

"Hmm," Jonah said, "I'm not too bothered about proving anything. What does the intelligence say?"

"If someone's got a grudge, or needs a debt repaying, or any other message conveying with violence, then they tend, more times than not, to use one of their cars to get to and from the crime scene. Of course, as a private hire firm, they can claim to be blissfully unaware of what their customers get up to. But their name can only come up so many times, before you start to see a pattern. Can I ask what they were up to?"

Jonah briefly described what had happened over the afternoon, carefully describing Elizabeth as a friend.

"Did you want to report it? Or were this afternoon's activities strictly off the record?"

"Off the record," said Jonah, happy to let the other man think that he was having an affair and was doing his mistress a favour. "Can I ask one more question? Does this company have anything to do with Mike Khan?"

"Oh, I wish you hadn't asked me that." The line went quiet for a few seconds. "I'm really glad you want this off the record. This is way over my head, that's all I'm going to say. There's an ongoing investigation and it's kept very tightly locked down. You put that name on a report, and all the paperwork will vanish."

"Sorry," Jonah said, while thinking that the sergeant on the other end of the phone sounded more scared than anything else. "Forget I said anything about that name. And thank you for the information."

"Thank you too, it all helps." There was another slight pause. "It's a bit odd though, they were way out of their area, they usually hang around the city. I wonder what they were up to?"

Jonah said his goodbyes and left the sergeant to ponder the connections with his local criminals. Back in the kitchen, Alex was waiting for the kettle to boil. "Come here you," Jonah beckoned, "give me a kiss!" She walked over, reached up slightly and kissed him before resting her head against his chest.

Jonah breathed in deeply through his nose, not really

sure what he was looking for. She didn't feel different; she hadn't been either more passionate or more distant than usual. Unless he was a useless detective, his wife was no more having an affair than he was with Elizabeth. Something was going on, but what Alex had said about last night had been the truth.

"Off to the garden!" he said, gently detaching her. His counsellor had suggested he rekindle his passion for gardening. He'd been taught by his dad and he found the repetitive physical work helped quiet his restless mind.

After losing himself in hard work, followed by takeaway food and beer, Jonah awoke the next morning feeling much restored.

"What's up with your phone?" Alex rolled over onto one elbow, "I tried getting in touch yesterday afternoon and you didn't answer."

"Shit! I was out of signal and chucked the phone on the seat. Must've fallen under it. I'd better find it." Jonah pulled on a few clothes and went to retrieve his phone. When he did there were missed calls from Alex, interspersed with some from work.

CHAPTER 12

"I've got to go into the office," Jonah announced as he returned indoors. A steady rain had started falling so he'd sat in the car to pick up his messages. "While I was out yesterday some old guy tripped over and died. They've been trying to reach me ever since."

"But it's Sunday, surely they'll just keep him in the morgue 'til tomorrow?"

"Nope, he's Jewish and the family are creating because they want the funeral within twenty-four hours. They've grudgingly accepted forty-eight but there's still a ton of work to do between now and then."

"I hoped we could have a quiet Sunday." Alex looked disappointed.

"Me too, but my name will be mud because I wasn't available yesterday, so I'd better show my face now."

The rain reminded Jonah of the last time he'd been in CID for his back-to-work meeting. Then he'd been hustled out of there by Linwood before he had to face his colleagues. Now his stomach knotted up as he climbed the familiar stairs to the open plan office. He had to work hard not to look for his old desk and see what the new occupant had done with it. He looked around the familiar mix of desks, cabinets, water coolers and printers, looking for the on-duty officer who had handled the case so far. The fact that, once again, he had let them down didn't help matters.

He was expecting anything from a curt explanation of the situation to being completely ignored. Instead he saw the familiar figure of Farida weaving her way through the desks towards him. As it was the weekend, she was dressed casually in jeans and a long-sleeved pea green top together with a dark brown hijab.

"You're in trouble now," she said playfully as a greeting.

"I know." He rolled his eyes.

"What happened? Where were you yesterday..." she trailed off, shocked when she saw the guilty look on Jonah's face. "Elizabeth? After everything I said you still went off to meet her?"

Jonah nodded sadly, then recounted the events of yesterday. "So, with the patchy reception, my phone under the seat and the wind howling through the broken window, I just didn't get any messages until this morning." He decided not to tell her about Alex's vanishing act yet. Their relationship might be purely platonic, but he felt really uncomfortable about criticising his wife to another woman.

"So, tell me about this new body." Jonah was desperate to get the conversation back on course.

Farida led him back to her desk. He pulled over a neighbouring chair while she flicked open a notepad. "David Rose, aged fifty-seven. Left synagogue at 1 pm after the Saturday morning service. Went to a daughter-in-law's house for lunch. Left there to go back to his place to fetch a book, it was only a couple of minutes up the road. On the way there he tripped and fell against a wall. Banged his head and dropped dead."

"So, he tripped over," Jonah asked, "and that killed him?"

"Yes, we've avoided a post-mortem so far. The pathologist examined him thoroughly and there were no signs of a struggle. Apparently, he hit the edge of a wall – it was one of those one in a million things, just the right knock on just the right part of the head. The attending constable said nothing was stolen. Everyone else in the party was in the house at the time. All the timelines add up, not even five minutes missing anywhere. All the locations, the two houses and the synagogue are within easy walking distance of each other."

"What about all the Jewish complications?"

"Well, it's been an education, I can tell you. It's similar to strict Islamic law but also quite different. We've got the burial society attached to the synagogue involved, they're handling all the appropriate ritual and prayers. I've been in long conversations with the rabbi. He's the one who approved the extension for the funeral. Also, they won't allow an autopsy unless it's strictly medically necessary. The pathologist has been brilliant, doing his job while also respecting their religion."

Jonah nodded thoughtfully. "Looks like you've been doing all the hard work. Unless there's something else going on, looks like simple accidental death. I think we can let them have their funeral. As long as everyone else is happy?"

Farida nodded. "There is just a stack of paperwork," she said hopefully.

"I'd better start making up for yesterday. I'll still be in the shit with Linwood but the more I can do today the better it'll go."

"And I'd better get back to manning the phones and doing my proper job."

"Thanks for all this!" Jonah said as he scooped up a big pile of files. He didn't need to go back to his office, so he found a meeting room and got started. From the moment Mr Rose had fallen over, phone calls had started, and increasingly more people had been called in. There were official reports from the emergency centre who logged the 999 call, the attending constable, duty CID and medical personnel that all needed reading and collating. On the other side there were statements from the family, and advice from the burial society and the rabbi.

After about two hours, Jonah had all the paperwork in really good shape and was happy to advise accidental death and allow the burial to take place as planned on Monday morning. He had all the forms lined up and ready for Timothy Carlton to approve first thing. It all looked a bit tight, so he decided to call him at home to make sure he would be in early and would definitely approve what he'd done.

The conversation was a bit stilted. The coroner was clearly displeased, both that his officer had been out of contact and that he was being disturbed on a Sunday. However, as Jonah laid out what was being done, how he'd got all the opinions and reports in order, he mellowed a bit. Finally, he conceded that Jonah had done a good job, and authorised him to call the rabbi and let the funeral go ahead in the morning.

While the funeral was taking place, he would still have a mountain of work to do, but at least it would be fairly routine now he had spent the time arranging the paperwork.

Jonah went home to find Alex in conciliatory mood. There was roast lamb in the oven, and she was flitting around chopping vegetables and tidying the kitchen. "I'm glad you're back – I made a big roast, your favourite."

"Thanks," said Jonah, wondering what he should acknowledge. "Work's all tidied up for the day. I'll have to be in early tomorrow, but I think I've repaired the damage."

The rest of the evening was like time had rewound. It was as if the past four years hadn't happened – there was no tension, no bitterness. Also, they very carefully didn't talk about the day before and both their mysterious disappearances.

As expected, Jonah was called in to see Linwood as soon as he got into work. He explained that he'd gone to have lunch with an old friend and about his mobile and the window.

"Did you report it?" Linwood asked.

"No," Jonah said, and repeated the lie that he'd told Alex, about the service station. "Anyway, it's easier sometimes to just go to one of those quick glass places than hassle about all the insurance and everything."

Linwood frowned at him. They both knew that he could get a crime number easily and have it all official. Jonah didn't want to lie in an official police document and he certainly didn't want his weekend on the record either. After an awkward silence, Linwood spoke again.

"Anyway, there's a place come up at the last minute on a training course. If you can be in Manchester on Wednesday morning there's a three-day course running on," he pulled a piece of paper towards him, "Using Disparate Data Sources in Complex Investigations. I know you were thrown into the role abruptly, so it'll be good to get you up to speed."

"What's the situation on the budget?" Jonah asked. He privately thought that he couldn't pay for three nights in Manchester.

"That's all covered, expenses, hotel, meal allowance. It's an eight thirty registration for a nine o'clock start, so if you want a room on Tuesday night, that'll be covered too."

"But," Jonah frowned, trying to find the words, "I thought you said the budget was stretched."

"That's a different department." Linwood waved his hand expansively. "This is money that's been ring-fenced for training. We have to spend it, or we lose it next year. Anyway, your name's been put down and cover has been arranged."

Jonah thought quickly. It was eleven in the morning, and all this had been done. Something about Linwood's dismissive manner put him on guard. While he was trying to find a way to say what was on his mind, Linwood carried on talking.

"It might do you good to get away for a few days. Take a break and think about things. That complaint from the car dealer is still hanging around. You might want to think about what's best for your career."

"How can that still be around?" Jonah asked. "The case is closed, everything filed, the funeral's next week and I haven't contacted Andrew McRae since our meeting."

"Good, good!" Linwood nodded to himself. "Just keep it that way. No extra-curricular activities, strictly what you've been told to do. As I said, a few days away, chance to reflect. We all need that from time to time."

"Sir, has there been a further complaint?" Jonah wondered if any of his contacts had asked around about him.

"No, no, nothing of the sort. Just talking generalities, best case scenario, that kind of thing. Now, you've got to sort out that Rose case, put that to bed, then I want everything shipshape before you go to Manchester."

When he was back at his desk Jonah realised two things. Firstly, he had never agreed to go on the course, yet it was all signed off and booked in his absence. Secondly, he had been warned off again, much more subtly this time, but still warned off. In fact, he was being sent out of the area for a bit, to put a stop to his investigations.

When Denise delivered his hotel booking and course information in the afternoon, he'd already made his mind up. He was sitting on three cold case murders, a serious assault and one major crime figure, together with a dead homeless man. Somewhere in there had to be some benefit for him. If he could either solve a cold case or bring down Mike Khan, he'd redeem some of his career. It was too big a prize to ignore, and every attempt to deflect him not only failed but further convinced him of the value of his investigation.

JONAH WOKE up and for a second was unaware of where he was. He sat up and looked around the dull hotel room and remembered that he'd been sent on a course. He was now in a Novotel attached to a combined leisure, business and retail park. The bland uniformity of the room was matched by the rest of the complex. It was a series of car parks linked by roads with speed bumps. Around the car parks were grouped motels, shops, cinemas and chain restaurants.

As Jonah walked, first to a Costa Coffee for breakfast and then on to the office block, he didn't see one business that was genuinely local. Everything was part of a national chain, and the entire place could have been anywhere from Aberdeen to Penzance.

The course was as dull as Jonah expected. Inside the office building, everything was tastefully arranged to offend no one. Grey carpets led to beige walls. All the furniture was pale ash and brushed aluminium. The course itself was taught in a room with all the computers facing a large screen. The instructor droned through PowerPoint presentations demonstrating the linking of databases and how to compare data sources. The delegates then used their computers to complete exercises. There was a coffee machine, a lounge and a canteen. The trouble was, no one knew each other, and they had all been thrown together. They all had roughly similar jobs, although some of them were from various council or government enforcement departments, and one from the British Transport Police.

On the final night a group of them had gathered in an overpriced bar, determined to spend their expenses. During a lull in conversation, Jonah seized a chance and asked the group. "What do you think our instructor has missed?" When they frowned at him, he continued, "Well, this is all up to date, with the PNC and everything. But what if, in theory, you were looking for people from twenty years ago, before it was all put on computers? Where would you go then?"

"Paper," Derek said. He was a portly investigator for the DSS fraud office. "People always overlook it now that it's all on computer but there's so much stuff still on paper, tucked away in archives. What exactly are you trying to do? Find these people now?"

"Not exactly, they were all at university together and denying that they knew each other. I think they're lying about that, and probably something else. But if I can prove they were lying about the first thing, it'll be a crack that I can use to find out more."

Derek took a sip of his pint and looked thoughtful. He was younger than Jonah, with dark wavy hair and glasses. He looked like an archetypal computer nerd, so he was surprised that he was so keen on paper.

"That is a good problem. Well, you're police, aren't you? So there's pocketbooks for a start. And there are so many things that have to be licensed, stuff that people don't realise. Like, if they're renting out houses, there should be a license for multiple occupation."

"It's too late for dog licenses to still be a thing, isn't it?" The exchange had caught the imagination of the rest of the group.

"Or did they get a caution for something. If one of them was stopped while driving, were any of the others in the car with them?"

"What about firearms licenses, fishing licenses, that kind of thing."

"That's a good point – sports clubs. You might struggle to find records going back that far, but it'll prove they socialised together."

"And just because you're police, don't forget the other agencies." Derek returned to the fray. "The councils have mountains of paperwork, old housing benefit forms or, not Job-seekers back then, but unemployment benefit. A lot of those forms have to list who was sharing a house with who, even if there was no relationship. I don't know how far back electoral rolls go, but they might be useful. Likewise, you might find some tax stuff, but a lot of it is destroyed after ten years."

"Yeah, but you can forget about police notebooks – they are useless," one of the older policemen present spoke up. "They're generally only kept for six or seven years. And to be honest, unless you knew exactly the right PC and the right date, you'd have way too much information. You'd spend half your life reading about them sorting out traffic problems and rounding up drunks, and still be no further forward."

Derek nodded, "I think licensing is probably the best bet, a lot of that is paperwork and some forces just don't clear out old records. Especially if the license is still valid or only expired a few years ago."

"Thanks, guys," said Jonah absent mindedly. University of Swindon, he thought to himself, that'd have a local police station. Chances are, in that part of town, that it's been there for more than twenty years. It might have paper records in the basement. He remembered too, Linwood's warning and Alex's growing dissatisfaction with his continued absences.

The next morning played right into his hands. The tutor had been cutting short their lunch breaks and keeping them an extra half hour at the end of the day. No one minded because they had nothing else to do, being stuck in a hotel miles from home. On Friday morning, he announced that he'd end the course at 12:30 and they would all be able to go home and enjoy the weekend.

Jonah got his phone out and made notes on a scrap of paper. Three hours to Swindon, arrive there before four. Leave Swindon at seven, still make it home by eight thirty, as if he'd left Manchester at five and got caught in traffic.

JONAH WAS IN LUCK – when the university was built, they hadn't rebuilt the police station. Instead, it had expanded by buying buildings each side, then adding on ugly, 1970s extensions out the back. The whole place was a confusing maze of different styles and floor levels.

However, he was soon entrusted with the archive, such as it was. His excuse, "Just passing, deep background on cold cases", was accepted without enthusiasm. The desk staff were looking forward to the weekend off, while the uniforms were gearing up for another Friday night.

Without a central index, or anything stored on computer, there was no way to plug in the names and see what came out. The main system of organisation was by year, so he went back to October 1992 – the first date any of his suspects arrived at Swindon to start university.

Dogs, fishing, cautions and electoral rolls all drew a blank. He was scanning down lists and flicking through forms in binders. Everything was handwritten and some boxes were out of order.

By seven that evening, Jonah was tired, dusty and frustrated. His three hours in the files had felt like three days. He decided to give up and with faint misgivings he signed himself back out. On the drive back home, he thought over how best to continue. He decided to take one day as annual leave to tackle the biggest set of files – firearms licensing. Each license issued had interviews, home visits and referees to guarantee good character. Even if he couldn't find a direct link between the names on his list, he still hoped that he might find something useful.

When he was back in the office, he applied for annual leave for the following Friday. Queried by Linwood, he simply stated he had a family event and had taken his advice to not obsess about work but take things slowly. He lied similarly to Alex and left for work as normal on Friday. Instead, he went straight back to the archive room in Swindon and carried on trawling through Firearms Certificates. There were far fewer of them and they were better organised.

Finally, just before lunch, he struck gold. Patrick Kinsale, Mike Khan, Elizabeth Barry and Andrew McRae all had applied for, and been granted licenses in mid-1995. Even more significantly, the same name, Gerald Dunton was listed as one of the referees on each form. Taking photocopies, Jonah's mind turned over. When he had the copies, he went outside to use his mobile.

"Hi, Peter, it's DS Greene, I came to see you a few weeks back..."

"Jonah, yes! Have you found anything?" The hope in his voice was painful to hear.

"Not directly about your case, but I am making a bit of progress. I could do with some help though, another name for you to check."

"Could it be another suspect?" Peter sounded a bit more disappointed this time. Jonah tried to picture him, alone in his bungalow, trapped in his chair.

"I doubt it, it's more, err, tangential than that. It might be someone who knew all four of my suspects while they were at university."

"Okay then." Peter wasn't trying to hide his feelings. "Give me a minute while I get the databases up."

"The name I'm looking for is Gerald Dunton." Jonah waited while Peter worked his magic.

"Ah, yes, a shade earlier than you might like. Started in 1990, but never moved away from Swindon, still here now in fact. What else did you want to know?"

"You don't keep societies or clubs on there do you?"

"Of course I do. That's how I can cross people off my master list – if they were in a sports team that had an away fixture that weekend. Let's see, our man Gerald Dunton was President of the Rifle Club for years, even after he officially left." Peter then told Jonah the most up to date address and phone numbers he had for him.

Once again Jonah found himself in an anonymous coffee shop, this time on Swindon High Street. Gerald arrived while he was still in the queue. Jonah bought him a coffee, but he indicated a plastic bag with his packed lunch so didn't want anything else. The weather was fine, so they took an outside table with the smokers, where Dunton felt comfortable eating his lunch.

Jonah self-consciously ate his bought sandwich while he sized up Mr Gerald Dunton. He had thinning sandy hair and a solidity about him. Jonah suspected that he looked middle-aged even when he was at university. He had a careful way of talking too. Eventually they got through the small talk and down to business.

"I certainly remember those days. Very tricky they were. I was shooting before I went to university, but it was a bit of an awkward thing after Hungerford. As it was, the society was small when I started in 1990. We had lots of discussion with the Ents Officer, and eventually opened it up to people from the town as well, as long as it still had a majority of students. I was about to step down after nearly six years when Dunblane happened. Then of course, we had to deal with the backlash from that as well. It was around then that we changed to incorporate two other local organisations, the clay pigeon lot and the local shooting range. As I say there weren't enough of us to maintain three organisations. Especially once the restrictions came in and people either gave up or moved abroad."

"What about these applications? You guaranteed them all? I know it was a long time ago, but you might remember something?"

He studied each of the photocopied sheets. "I hope I

didn't do anything wrong? It was standard practice to have the president of the club authorise these. The fact they were in a target shooting society helps with the license."

"No, it's fine, I just wondered if you knew them, what they were like, whether they were friends, anything like that?"

"Well, Elizabeth I do remember. A bit of a shame really, excellent shot. Didn't need to settle down and sight in, she could just turn up and start hitting the centre from the word go. And she had a sensitivity. She had this old Steyr rifle," he tapped the entry on the firearms license. "I remember when she bought it, it was in a right state. But she borrowed some tools and really patiently took it all apart, cleaned and oiled it. Once she'd finished it was a nice thing, a bit out of date, but coming up on match quality. If she'd kept up with the shooting, she could have shot for her country." He turned an accusatory gaze on Jonah. "Well, if she'd moved out to Switzerland that is. The new laws after 1996 made it very hard to be competitive in this country. The other three don't ring a bell, I'm afraid. You must understand, students can be a bit insensitive, and I'm sure some only joined because of the fuss about Hungerford. A bit of rebellion.

"Also, firing a gun is a very odd thing. Everyone's seen TV and films, guns are part of our culture, but hardly anyone who's not police or army have ever fired one. There's a lot of mystique there. Add in your average student's thirst for rebellion and they join up. But you find they drift off after a year or so, which is probably what happened here. The licenses are good for five years, were they renewed?"

Jonah flicked through his paperwork and shook his head. "No, all lapsed."

"There you go then, a passing interest at best."

"So, the club wasn't big? They might have known each other?"

"Almost certainly. I wouldn't sign off on their forms unless they were committed to the club, turning up to shoot most weeks for at least six months. Some days, only a handful of people turned up so they must have known each other. Especially as we sometimes went to competitions around the country, sharing cars and arranging lifts so, yes."

When Jonah went back to the archive to take a few more copies and sign out formally, he found he was thinking more about Andrew McRae than the other three people on his list. Patrick and Mike were unreachable for different reasons and Elizabeth had pretty much admitted that they knew each other at university. But Andrew was denying it and making formal complaints. Now Jonah had documented evidence that he was lying, he had a bit of leverage. An up and coming MP couldn't afford a scandal involving lies and guns.

All this went out of his head when he got home that evening.

"How was work?" Alex asked casually.

"Usual sort of stuff," Jonah said, feeling wary.

"Were you in the office?"

Jonah paused just a fraction too long, "in and out really, why, what's up?"

"All your emails came back with the 'from my iPhone' stamp on the bottom, so I called the office and got your voicemail, apparently you were off today but I could either call CID or wait til Monday."

"It's not what you think..."

"You don't know what I think," Alex snapped back at him. "I don't think you're having an affair, but there's something you're not telling me."

"It's just work, filling in the blanks a bit, that's all."

"If it's work, why take annual leave?"

"My boss thinks the case is closed."

Alex shut her eyes and took a deep breath. "If your boss thinks the case is closed, then the case is closed. I think you sometimes forget that I'm a manager too." She held up her hand to silence him. "I know the police isn't the same as the NHS, but management skills are the same. If I found out one of my workers was sneaking around behind my back, trying to prove me wrong, I'd be livid. I'd probably have them fired!"

"But," said Jonah, wounded, "what if I was right? There's something here and I can prove that I was right."

"You really don't get it," Alex shook her head sadly. "For your bosses it's not about right and wrong, it's about how they look and whether you're embarrassing them or not."

"That is where the police is different. I might make them look like fools, but catching the bad guys is still our job that we're meant to do."

"That's not really it, is it? From what you've said there isn't a case so there can't really be a bad guy. Or a crime. I just wondered why you were pushing so hard."

"You know." Jonah took a breath and tried to arrange his thoughts into words. "It's like if I wake up and grab two black socks, one from Marks and Spencer, and one from Asda. I know they'll look the same if I wear them, but I just can't do it." He looked up to a blank look from Alex. "Or like, having the knife, fork and spoon all matching and lined up the right way round? Or the loo roll hanging the right way round!" Another blank look. "Oh, you do know! It's like that, like an itch in my brain. But this time I can't just say, oh, it's because I'm tired, or stressed, but my rational brain knows it doesn't really matter. This is, quite literally, life or death. I've got three cold case murders, one homeless man who may or may not have been murdered, a nasty assault. And it's all like a sore tooth, something I just can't, and won't, stop fidgeting at until it's all unravelled. And I'm making slow progress."

Without a word, Alex moved in and gave him a hug.

"Well if I were you, I'd be very careful, get better at sneaking around." She looked him full in the face. "I do know managers and if this ever pans out to something, you'd better think about how to do it." He frowned and she continued. "Your career will go a lot better if you can let your boss think that it was all his idea!"

CHAPTER 13

Jonah's mobile vibrated across his bedside table. In the dark, he saw two glowing displays. It was twenty past one and his phone displayed a number instead of the name of a saved contact.

"Hello, DS Greene speaking, how can I help?" After twenty years in the police, he could answer the phone in this official way even before he'd properly woken up. He sat up and checked Alex. She was stirring.

"Jonah? Is that you? It's Elizabeth!" She sounded slightly manic.

"Elizabeth?" Jonah glanced sideways as Alex's eyes opened slightly beneath her frowning brows. He slid quietly from the bed, making calming motions at Alex. "What's up? Are you all right?"

"Yes, fine, I just had a couple of drinks, and I know I shouldn't what with the meds I'm on and what the doctor said but I started thinking that it's Patrick's funeral tomorrow and I ought to raise at least one glass, and then I got to thinking..."

"Elizabeth!" Jonah was sharp now that he was on the

landing and out of earshot of Alex. "Just take a moment. What's up, why have you phoned? Are you hurt?"

"Hurt?" There was genuine bafflement at the end of the phone. "No, not physically anyway. I just wanted to chat, and you gave me your number."

"It's..." Jonah was going to say the middle of the night but decided there was no point. She was so far divorced from reality that it wouldn't matter. "It's nice to hear from you. What did you want to talk about?"

"Well," Elizabeth said as Jonah sat on the sofa and winced at the cold leather against his bare back. "I was thinking about the last time we met at the pub and I couldn't remember if I told you about Mike, Mike Khan?"

"You did mention that you knew him, that you'd looked him up on the Internet."

"No! It's more than that. He's evil. We made him that way, and now he's evil. Of course, we had no idea at the time, that's the point isn't it? You're young and you do things and have no idea how far off course they'll career and where they'll end up. I need you to stop him."

"Stop him?" Jonah's tired brain was slow to wake up and none of this was making much sense.

"Yes, stop him. You're the police and he's a bad man, a very bad man, so you need to stop him."

"It's not quite that easy. We need to find evidence that he's committed a crime and arrest him and charge him. We can't just stop him like that."

"But I've told you about him, that should be enough!"

"I'm afraid it isn't – I'll need more. Ultimately my job is to gather evidence to pass over to the CPS. It has to be good enough that they'll then decide to prosecute him."

There was a pause. The entire house was quiet and

there was not even a crackle down the phone line. In the moment of stillness, Jonah found his head swimming.

"He's going to be an MP, you know. We haven't got long." Now Elizabeth sounded admonishing, like a school-teacher getting frustrated with a slow pupil.

"MP? Mike?"

"No, not Mike, Andrew. I mean, I know I let it all slide for a bit, but that's a bit strong isn't it. No, we really need to do something now. Before it gets too far."

"Okay, Elizabeth, it's okay. I'll make an effort to get both of them." He paused, then realised he had little left to lose. "What do you think I should investigate them for? What can I arrest them for?"

"What for? Honestly! Weren't you listening, they're bad, we all are, we've all done things, such bad things. My therapist said I wasn't to think about the things that we've all done. But that's fine in the daylight, when you're sober. At this time of night though, the thoughts creep up on you. It's like they're hiding during the day and ambush you at night. The bad thoughts, I mean, not anything else. I haven't been bothered by those two people in their car since you sorted them out for me."

"Elizabeth! You're babbling again!"

"Am I? Did you know you're really rude? I'm not sure I like you always shouting at me! Goodnight!"

Jonah stared stupidly at his phone for a while, 'til it went dark. He reached over for a notepad and tried to make some notes about the conversation. But Elizabeth really hadn't made enough sense. He wasn't even sure that she knew who she was talking about.

Jonah returned to bed, to sleep fitfully. Elizabeth's words and madness infected his dreams. In the morning, he had Patrick's funeral to attend. He had cleared it with both his bosses. He insisted that it was a duty, when someone died with hardly any family, to make up numbers at the funeral. He could tell that he wasn't completely believed, but he was going.

As he expected, it was a sparse, drab affair at Thornhill Cemetery and Crematorium. Everything was beautifully laid out, manicured lawns, rows of graves and perfect flowerbeds. The weather was a mockery – it was a perfect spring day. A clear blue sky was dotted with fluffy clouds and a light breeze kept the temperature down. Jonah parked and made his way to the low, off-white municipal building.

Once inside, it was painfully obvious how poorly attended the funeral was. The chapel had row after row of empty seats. Jonah sat to one end of the front row after exchanging condolences with Fiona and being introduced to one uncle who was the only representative from his London family. He nodded briefly to the Prof, who was sat one row back. Aside from that the only other mourners were two women. They were middle-aged and had set, stern faces. Jonah idly studied them as they sat, heads bowed in prayer. There was something about the similarity of their clothes, that he couldn't place. They both wore long, charcoal grey dresses over white blouses. They also both had dark blue cardigans and headscarves. In a weird way, he was reminded of school uniform, especially when he noted their sensible black shoes.

The minister gave a perfunctory service. He kept referring to a sheet that Fiona had pressed into his hand before he started. He didn't ask for any eulogies and the whole affair was even more depressing than usual. Jonah thought back to his father's funeral. At the time he'd felt overwhelmed with the large service – distant relatives and half-known friends had filled the tiny chapel where it was held.

Now he understood, a full church diluted the grief somehow, made it less obvious.

Here, it was raw and intense, hard to comprehend. When the coffin had slid between the curtains, he went outside.

He shook hands with Fiona. He gripped her elbow and apologised before moving to intercept the two women he'd seen earlier.

"Hi," Jonah said, slightly breathless. "Did you know Patrick?"

"No," the taller of the two women said. "We were asked to pray for him."

"Okay," Jonah replied, unsure of how to continue.

"Sister Imelda." She extended her hand and indicated her companion, "and Sister Patricia."

"DS Jonah Greene," he said. "I dealt with all the paperwork, the police side of it." He paused, then a thought struck him. "Have you heard of the Ministry of Bethesda?"

"The Ministry of Capernaum and Bethesda?" Sister Imelda asked. When Jonah nodded, she continued, "Yes, that's our order. We don't often meet people who've ever heard of us." This last statement had the inflection of a question.

"I read something somewhere," Jonah said, "a leaflet about how you started supplying crutches and wheelchairs to the poor, before the NHS."

"Alas, even with the NHS, there are still many out there who require our help."

"Anyway, I just came to remember Patrick, it didn't seem right that he should, you know, be forgotten."

"No," Sister Imelda replied, "we're here to pray for his soul as well, to intercede that he might find more peace after this life than he did during it."

"Right, so, you were asked, or..."

"Please don't fish, DS Greene!" Although Sister Imelda had a stern face there was a sense of fun in her eyes. "One of our most generous donors asked if we could intercede for Patrick's soul, make sure that the right prayers were said, and we agreed." She shot a warning look at Jonah. "And no, we will not tell you who. They want their privacy and we respect that."

Jonah was about to reply when a movement behind the nuns caught his eye. A car had just left the car park, a battered old green Mercedes. "Thank you for your frankness," he said, while studying the car park. He could not remember if the car had been there throughout the funeral, but he thought so. "And thank you for praying for Patrick. It doesn't seem as if life was very kind to him."

"God cares for us all, it's just that some of us are unable to reach out and accept that love," Sister Imelda said. "Anyway, Fiona's about to leave and we want a word."

With that, Jonah was left alone. The Prof was already walking out through the gate and the minister was unlocking his car. Seven people didn't seem enough to remember a life, he thought, watching them all go their separate ways.

WHEN JONAH GOT BACK to the office, the phone was ringing. It was Elizabeth in contrite mood.

"I'm sorry about last night, I should know better than to drink when I'm taking my medication."

"That's all right," Jonah said. He felt far from all right, with the combination of the funeral and not enough sleep. "Thanks for the apology, you didn't need to call."

"But I also had to call to give you something. I don't remember much about last night, but I do remember that you need to have some proof." Jonah felt a brief smattering of hope. "It's Jonathon's accountant, Darren Farrell. I found out that he's been helping to finance Andrew's parliamentary campaign. Doesn't that strike you as dodgy? What do you think he's up to?"

"That I could look into," Jonah said, already wondering how he could arrange it. "Where is he based?"

"Well, that's what's weird. He's not in London, he's out of the way in Newbury, down the M4. Of all the accountants to choose, why do you think he went there?"

"Okay then," Jonah wrote down the details, "I'll see what I can do." There was an awkward pause as they both recalled her behaviour the night before.

"Thanks, bye," Elizabeth said finally.

Needing to find some clarity, Jonah sought out Farida to meet him for lunch and thrash out the latest theories. Soon they were sat side by side on a bench in Cathays Park. Shielded from the wind, the sun was warm.

"Have you thought about a military connection?" Farida asked.

"Not really, why?"

"Well, give me the list of murders," she said. When she had the list, she ran her finger down them. "There's one long range shot, that could be sniper training."

"Now you sound as bad as the people on the Internet. Last time I checked the army didn't use the general public for target practice."

Farida ignored his sarcasm. "But then this one in Worksop. There was a case in Iran where Mossad had two operatives on a motorcycle. They would ride up to a target, usually a nuclear scientist, and the pillion would stick an explosive on the driver's window, before disappearing into the traffic. Doesn't that sound familiar?"

"Except there's one person with a shotgun, instead of a bomb," Jonah argued. "And it was in Worksop, not the Middle-East!"

"It could still be connected. Shotguns are easier to come by."

"What about the third one? What part of army training involves stabbing innocent young women?"

"They did use a bayonet," Farida countered.

"That's weak. You're stretching the evidence to make it fit your theory now." Farida nodded morosely. "Have you pulled the files then?"

"Yes, we're allowed to do research and background on old cases when there's nothing major going on. I'm second tier so I'm only allocated onto MIT when something big is happening."

"What did you learn from the files?" Jonah asked hopefully.

"Very little. The investigations were done well but with little flair. I can't see anywhere they slipped up or were corrupt. And I can't see how they could be solved. The only thing linking them is the lack of concrete evidence."

"But the stabbing, Emma Walters, there were lots of things left at the scene."

"Yes, but they didn't have any of the killer's DNA on them, or any fingerprints. Not that it would have helped, they didn't really have any suspects to start with. And what it does tell us really doesn't help. Probably a man, but not necessarily. Around the five foot ten mark and medium build although they may have deliberately worn an ill-fitting boiler suit. And probably right-handed." She shook her head.

"It's hardly anything to go on at all," Jonah admitted. "Listen, can you think of any way I can get over to Newbury to shake down a dodgy accountant?"

"You could report it to me and I'll ask for you to help me. I'll make up some story about how you have local knowledge and I need you to come along?"

"That would be brilliant." He explained the whole sequence of phone calls with Elizabeth. "I think this has more legs than your theory about the military."

"Why?"

"Well, if these four knew each other at university, then they could've met up again later. And hatched a plan to get Andrew elected to parliament. Mike's some sort of drug dealer, quite high-level judging by the police interest. Jonathon is brought in by Elizabeth as the one who can do the money laundering and get accountants involved, and Andrew has the charisma and publicity to actually get elected."

Farida nodded. "That does make more sense than anything else. Except," she held up fingers and counted off them, "why put four other names on the list? Also, if Andrew owns a chain of dealerships, why would he need the money from somewhere dodgy like drugs? Finally, how did Patrick find out and did it lead to him being killed?" Farida thought for a moment. "Unless... Andrew's going to be something in the Ministry of Defence and cover up something in the past?"

"Still doesn't cover Peter. He doesn't fit in anywhere at all."

Farida stood up suddenly. She balled up her sandwich wrapper and launched it into a nearby bin. "Well I give up then! Let's head off to Newbury and see what we can shake out of that tree."

CHAPTER 14

Two days later Jonah was late home from work. It was already getting dark and once again Pickford was whining on the doormat, looking up at his lead. With a shrug, Jonah got him sorted and went straight back out into the gathering dusk. A light drizzle started falling and he didn't fancy the local park so he decided to walk about a mile route around a network of quiet streets that would bring him back to the house.

As he left the long drive and turned onto the main road, a car started up some way behind him. Something niggled, so Jonah turned to look, but it was a plain silver car that slipped out of its parking spot and drove away from him.

He carried on walking, unaware of Pickford pulling on the lead as he surged forward to sniff trees. He turned it over in his mind and then realised that he hadn't heard anything during his walk down the drive. His house had been built on a plot of land behind an already established row of houses. It had a good sized plot, but had to be approached down a narrow drive from the main road. If someone had left a house, he should have heard a door slam, or maybe voices saying goodbye, the end of a conversation.

When he'd driven home about five minutes earlier, the street had been quiet as well. Had the driver been sat in the car, waiting for him to go past? He turned around sharply. Pickford gave a yelp, and tugged Jonah forward. He knew the route and couldn't understand why it was changing.

Jonah doubled back past the end of his drive. Pickford adapted to this change and eagerly investigated some new trees and lampposts. The road was quiet now, wide, with the houses set well back. The pavements were generous, separated from the road by grass verges that were broken into small rectangles by the driveways.

Jonah stopped at the space the car had left. He looked up and down the road. He could see the end of his drive clearly, but anyone parked here would be inconspicuous to him. Pickford seized the opportunity to cock his leg and mark his own lamppost. Then he started casting around in circles, unsure of which direction he was going next. Jonah crouched down to scratch between his ears, equally unsure of his next direction.

Jonah was spared from any more thought when his phone chirped with an incoming text from his daughter. Emily asked if he was free to meet in a launderette tonight. Jonah looked down at Pickford who was now sat, his liquid brown eyes focused on Jonah, alert for any clue as to what was happening next. Swiftly, Jonah arranged to meet Emily in about ninety minutes – enough time to finish his walk, grab some change and get into central Cardiff.

All his tasks completed, Jonah arrived first at the launderette. Sitting in a hard plastic chair he wondered how long he'd give it before he texted her again. Emily was independent but in strange ways. She wouldn't accept any money or allowance from her parents, but Jonah had emptied his change drawer before coming over, as he knew he would be paying for the powder, the wash and dry. On other occasions, he had taken her shopping for groceries and picked up the tab. But she wouldn't directly take money from her parents.

He saw his daughter before she saw him. A light rain had started and the drops sparkled in her hair. As always, he was struck by how vulnerable she looked. She was thin and elfin with fine blonde hair. He could always see the little girl still in her features. Some days he couldn't believe she'd grown up at all. She was lugging a large Sports Direct bag full of washing, illuminated by the light spilling out of the window. They exchanged greetings before she loaded the machine while he inserted money and bought a small box of powder. Emily came over to sit beside him while they watched the washing go round.

"Why do you live around here, Em?" Jonah was watching the people walking past on the street outside. With the dark, the streetlights, and the rain, the whole scene twinkled slightly. People moved in and out of the light. Asian and white, old and young, in a procession. It was definitely a colourful neighbourhood.

"You know, it's cheap." She glanced sideways at her father who suspected her of living in a squat. "There are great people around, lots of," she searched for the right word, "vibrancy?"

"But, those people, you know, they might be dangerous."

"Dad!" She thumped his arm playfully. "You know as well as I do, you could arrest as many people in Cyncoed as you could around here. Just 'cos someone wears a suit doesn't mean they're not a criminal. In fact, they're more likely to be."

Jonah grunted non-committally. This argument was habitual and went round amicably every time.

"Anyway, Dad," she said pointedly. "I've found this warehouse and I can get a lift out there every two weeks. It's wholesale jewellery and I can sell it on the stall at a mark-up."

Jonah gave Emily a long hard look. "I always thought you were the creative dreamer in the family. Head in the clouds. Took after your mother."

"She's not as soft as you think," Emily said, "and neither am I." After a pause, she continued, "Look, the rent's really cheap and they're all friends from art school so they're all broke." Jonah frowned in confusion, so she continued. "Well, they're not all going out to posh restaurants or night-clubs spending their money. It's more a case of a few bottles of supermarket wine and Netflix. So, I can sell stuff on the stall and put the money by instead."

"What are you saving up for?"

"I don't know," she said. "And don't give me that look! You changed career when you were nearly thirty! How can you expect me to know what I'm going to do when I'm not yet twenty-one?"

They sat in silence for a bit, Jonah wondering when his daughter had got so wise. He looked up and frowned at the window. "Who is that? Older than you, long dirty blond hair, thin face, army jacket. That's the third time he's walked past and each time he stares at us."

Jonah was wondering if he could be the driver of the silver car. Somehow, he didn't seem like it, he looked too scruffy and poor. But that could be an act.

Emily went quiet, staring at the bright red numbers counting down on the washing machine. "Well, shall I go out there and have a chat?" Jonah asked.

"No! Thank you!" She held his arm and laid her head on his shoulder. "Really, just sit there, that's fine."

"Seriously, is he any problem? Not dangerous?" He wanted to go out there and find him. Take him out for a drive and make sure he understood. Or just put his name in to the beat police and let them make his life hell. Or the good old-fashioned, slam him against a wall and whisper into his ear the ways he would hurt him if he ever went near his daughter again.

"No, he's just, a bit, you know, besotted. Do him good to know who my Dad is." Emily looked up at Jonah who grunted again. He knew he was being used by her, but he also didn't really mind.

"Besotted? Where did that come from?"

"Eh? Oh, I'm reading Jane Austen at the moment. We were meant to do them in school, but I never really got into them then." Emily looked at her father. "What are you doing?"

Jonah had his phone out and was holding it out towards the window at arm's length, tapping on the screen. Then he got out a notepad and very obviously made notes. "Just enjoying myself," he explained, nodding at the window. Emily's admirer, with his lank hair had been staring at him, like a rabbit in the headlights. Suddenly, he twitched himself back into action. He half-stumbled then scrambled down the street, a look of terror on his face.

Emily collapsed in giggles and Jonah said innocently, "That's what you wanted, isn't it?" Emily nodded, still unable to speak. "What's his name? I've got his description here."

"Sean Barnes," Emily said when she recovered. "But leave him alone. He really is harmless, and I doubt I'll see him again for weeks now!"

CHAPTER 15

Farida and Jonah were approaching the Severn Bridge when he finally asked the question. "What exactly did you tell Linwood?"

"I dug around and found a long running operation to do with targeting criminals who steal loads from HGVs at service stations up and down the M4. There's a hint that Cardiff Gate might be the base for one of the gangs. I offered to make some routine enquiries and suggested that you had knowledge of the investigation before your medical leave." She glanced sideways at him before looking at the road again. "Anyway, no one checked, and your workload is quite light, so here we are."

"And are we actually going to do it?"

"Of course. We'll stop at all the services along the way, chat with the managers, ask some drivers if they've seen anything suspicious. As you owe me a favour now, you can write up all the reports, prove that we've been working."

"We'll go as far as Reading, quick stop for lunch in Newbury, and then come back?"

"Pretty much, yeah."

After a mind-numbing morning driving up the M4 and interviewing site managers and lorry drivers, they turned off towards Newbury. As they followed the sat-nav it became clear that they were heading more towards Bracknell. Jonah found himself getting more depressed the further they went. It was a maze of dual carriageways linking dull chains of pubs, cinemas and shopping centres. Even the housing estates they glimpsed were full of cookie-cutter modern houses. Finally, they arrived in the car park of a bland, modern office block. It was all very nice, well kept, but utterly lacking in character. Jonah looked around for what he was missing. Wherever he went, even in the built-up areas of Cardiff and Newport, he knew he was near the mountains, wild areas or sea. Here, there was nothing but more of the same in one direction and London in the other. No nature, no wilderness, just city as far as you could see. Even the hills seemed to have been rubbed smooth by suburbia.

They were met inside the chrome and glass foyer by a receptionist who was immaculately made-up. Soon Darren Farell, accountant to Andrew McRae, had been summoned. He was wearing a rumpled grey suit over a blue shirt with red tie. He was running to seed, slightly overweight, with receding, short curly blond hair.

He waved them over to some low leather sofas, "I won't invite you up to the office, I'm meeting a client in a few minutes, so this'll have to be quick. How can I help you?"

They introduced themselves and explained that they were making preliminary enquiries about the funding of political campaigns.

"Well, there's not a lot I can say without a warrant. And, frankly, I'm surprised you came all the way from Wales just for a preliminary enquiry. Surely our local force could've helped in some way?"

"Well, we came across some information that was relevant, and we happened to be in the area," Jonah explained. Farida chose to remain silent. "Do you know an Andrew McRae?"

"Of course," Darren's face opened in a smile. "You won't get very far there though. I'm his accountant for his campaign to become an MP. Obviously, there are many things that I'm not allowed to tell you, but I can tell you this, he is dedicated to changing the way that politics is run. Openness will be a big feature of his campaign; he'll be publishing records of where his donations come from, the businesses he owns. He's going beyond what is required of him in terms of disclosure. After the expenses scandal, he wants to be part of a new breed of MPs that will be fighting to regain the public trust." He took out his business card and started writing on the back. "Here's his campaign website, you can download lots of data from there. And my details are on the front, should you want to return with a warrant to get more information."

"Thanks," Jonah started to say, accepting the card from Darren. But before he could say more, Darren leapt to his feet.

"Ah, here's the man himself, maybe you could ask him any further questions?"

The man who was walking towards them across the marble floor should have been unimpressive. He was of average height, with dark hair neatly side-parted. He had wire rim glasses and his face was pleasant without being outstandingly good looking. But he had two factors in his favour – firstly he carried himself with poise, as if he were entering a stage and expected every eye to turn in his direction. Secondly, his clothes were so well chosen and cut that even Jonah could tell that they were expensive. In short, he exuded power and wealth.

"DS Greene," Andrew McRae said without thinking. They stopped and stared at each other.

"I recognise you from your website," Jonah said slowly, "but how do you know who I am?" The other man stayed quiet, regarding Jonah with a stony gaze. "You must have paid some private investigator to follow me. You've seen photos of me."

Farida and Darren were watching silently, their gazes flicking between the two men.

"DS Greene," McRae repeated. "I believe you've already been warned to stop harassing me."

"Andrew, I didn't know," Darren started explaining, before being silenced by a wave of Andrew's hand.

Jonah immediately flashed back to the feelings he'd had when faced with his bosses and the woman from HR. He felt trapped and short of breath. Had he blown his entire career by coming here, challenging Andrew? "But," he started and trailed off. Andrew's gaze bored into him. "But," he said forcing himself to speak, "you've been carrying out surveillance on a serving police officer. Those aren't the actions of an innocent man."

"Surely," McRae said smoothly, "I am innocent until proven guilty?"

"I know you lied to me," Jonah said, regaining some confidence, "I have paperwork to prove you knew Patrick, Elizabeth and Mike at university."

McRae took a step back, his eyes widening. Then he regained his poise. "Who are Elizabeth and Mike? You only asked about Patrick Kinsale last time we spoke?" He was condescending now. "I suggest that next time you consider hounding someone, you get all your facts straight."

"I have plenty of facts and I might share some of them with your selection committee."

McRae fixed Jonah with an icy stare. Then, without a word, he beckoned Darren, turned on his heel and stalked out of the lobby towards the lifts.

Darren looked around uncomfortably. "Well, as you can see, my next appointment. Really, this is most irregular, you should have been much more up front. I feel taken advantage of."

And then Jonah and Farida were left alone. Without a word, they nodded to the receptionist and left.

Back in the car, Jonah and Farida both wrote up accounts of their conversations. Not in their notebooks, but still done properly, as if they were formal records. That way they could be used later but wouldn't have to be reported in.

When they were back under way, this time heading for the M4 westbound, Farida broke the silence. "It seems you were right after all. McRae definitely didn't like it when you asked about his university chums."

"I've been thinking about what he said, this time and when I phoned him a couple of weeks ago. He's very slick, I don't think he's ever actually denied knowing them. I think he just spouts a lot of words that don't mean much and lets his listener make assumptions."

"I hate people like that," Farida said.

"Like what?"

"Oh, you know, all full of hot air. Say a lot, make a lot of fuss and when you analyse it there's nothing behind it. Sound and fury signifying nothing." There was a pause as Farida tried to find a way to change the subject.

Finally, as they negotiated the slip road down onto the

M4, she said, "You shouldn't let people bully you, you know."

"Do you think that's what happens?" Jonah frowned.

"Yes, it's a feeling you give off. All your confidence disappears and people notice, even subliminally. Like just now, with McRae. Your shoulders drooped and you looked away. Of course, McRae is such a manipulator that he'd pick up on it immediately."

"I didn't totally roll over though," Jonah countered.

"No, I think once you'd upset him with those names you got some of your confidence back."

"How do you do it?" Farida glanced over at him, momentarily taking her eyes off the road. "I've seen you talk to lorry drivers and people who are a foot taller than you without batting an eyelid."

"Well, what's there to be frightened of?" Farida said. "Once you've prepared properly you can face anything. I do keep up with self-defence classes when I can work them around my shifts. And I'm a police officer – I have training, experience, and a huge network behind me. Once you know that then you have confidence, and people can sense it."

"All I can think is what can go wrong," Jonah said. "Like today, we were totally out of our depth, miles away from our area, no backup, and we got caught out by someone who's already done his level best to finish off my career."

"Yeah, but he doesn't know that, does he? And you know what the police are like, even on a different force. Any sign of trouble they'd barrel in and help us out. It's only afterwards, behind closed doors that we'd get caned."

"Maybe."

"Definitely."

A silence fell between them.

"Is that why you," Farida stopped, "well, you know, you had that three months off. Special leave?"

"Not exactly," Jonah sighed. "I, well, kind of froze in the middle of an operation. Wasn't there to back my colleagues up."

An easy silence fell between them. After a while Farida said, "Here's the next services."

"Mind if I stay in the car," Jonah asked, "I've got my laptop and I can check out that campaign website."

"Yeah, fine."

When Farida came back, Jonah was downcast. "I don't know if he's trying to hide something or if the whole thing is above board. But I do know one thing; he's released enough information here to keep the forensic accountants busy for ages."

"That would be if this was official enough to involve that kind of support."

"Exactly," Jonah said in a depressed voice. "He's certainly being open about the information it's just a question of whether any of it is useful."

"Well, given how far off the record this investigation is, that's the end of it there."

"I could try downloading stuff, but I'd have no idea what I'm looking for."

"So, what's the next move then?" Farida asked.

"Next move?"

"Well, you're right, something incredibly odd happened twenty years ago when they were all at university together. And you haven't found anyone yet who wants to talk about it."

"Well, I suppose the next move would be to speak to Mike Khan. I mean, I can't really get anywhere with

McRae, I've spoken to Peter, Elizabeth's not stable enough to be reliable, and Patrick's dead."

"What's stopping you?"

"There's a block on the file," Jonah explained. "A Chief Superintendent Blackmore from West Midlands. There's absolutely no access to the file; you've got to ask him for permission. I don't really have a strong enough case to even make contact."

"West Midlands," Farida said thoughtfully, "I may have contacts. Not at that kind of level, but he'll be running a department, have people under him. I might be able to get in touch with someone else in the team. I'll have a poke around and see who I can find."

"That would be brilliant," Jonah said, "I'm so glad I've persuaded you."

"It wasn't really you; it was McRae. I know a guilty person when I see one."

THE FOLLOWING EVENING, Jonah was on his way out of Tesco. Since his latest run-in with McRae he had been even more worried than usual. Thankfully, his official work was going smoothly. He had spent an edgy day at work, waiting for Linwood to call him in for another carpeting, or worse. But so far McRae had not filed an official complaint. Jonah hated having the thought of it hanging over him.

He had taken his laptop home with him, so he could do some work in the evening. But, his increasing sense of unease meant that he took the laptop shopping with him. He felt slightly foolish with the case wedged in the trolley seat, in place of a small child.

When he came out of the shop and into the car park, his

feelings were justified. He did a double-take as he approached his car. Someone was trying to force the door open on his Mondeo. They were hunched over, facing him, working on the driver's door. He didn't need to be a policeman to know what was going on.

"Oi! That's my car!" Jonah cried out. Secretly he was hoping the man would flee. He looked up, straight at Jonah. He had a shaven head but aside from that looked quite ordinary. The man moved around, away from Jonah. Then his eyes lit on the trolley and he changed direction, edging up between the Mondeo and the car next to it.

Jonah remembered what Farida had told him the day before. He was a police officer, he was trained, experienced and had backup. And this time he was on his own turf.

"What were you doing to my car?" Jonah demanded.

"Nothing mate, just dropped my keys," the man said with a shrug. But he did keep moving, as if he was going to squeeze past Jonah to escape.

"What's your name?" Jonah fell back to routine police work and also kept his trolley blocking the other man's way.

"Nothing to you," he said, with a slight trace of an Eastern European accent. "Excuse me!"

"Hold on! You were trying to break into my car. Give me your name and address or I'll have you down the station to answer questions!"

Without a word or any warning, the man dived between Jonah and his trolley, breaking his grip and sending the trolley crashing into his car. With horror, Jonah saw that the man had grabbed the handle of his laptop case as he went past. That simple black case was his entire career. The moment he lost it, he was finished.

Jonah spun round and immediately assessed the situation. The man was younger than him and running easily, glancing back to check. With a lifetime's experience on the rugby pitch, Jonah saw the move.

A car was moving slowly down the row towards them, driver's head swivelling left and right as they searched for a space. His adversary would have to move left to avoid running into the car. Jonah started running, grabbing the trolley as went. When he had a good head of speed, he released the trolley full of shopping straight into the gap to the left of the car.

At just the right moment, his quarry saw he was about to run into the bonnet of a moving car and jinked left to avoid it. Unfortunately for him, he did this just as the full trolley drew level with him. It hit him square on the hip and he cartwheeled over it, taking the trolley down to the ground with him. His momentum meant he rolled forward into the gap next to the car. This had now braked to a halt, and Jonah was still running. He now had to improvise a hurdle jump to clear the tipped over trolley. As he landed his left foot hit a can of peaches, rolled sideways and his whole weight twisted through his knee as he landed heavily on the ground.

Pain flared in his knee. The initial agony of the injury was followed quickly by the sick realisation that something had gone wrong inside his leg. Jonah pushed all these thoughts out of his head as he looked around him. The man was further on, lying between the car and the parked cars, and the laptop case was lying on the ground between them.

With a superhuman effort, Jonah half rose and hopped on his right leg, he wobbled as soon as he tried to put any weight on his left leg, and collapsed on top of his laptop case. The other man slowly got to his feet, checking himself for any permanent injury. He looked at Jonah, clearly calculating his chances of being able to grab the laptop case.

The woman driver opened her door a crack, "Are you all right?" It wasn't clear who she was most concerned for, Jonah or his victim. "What did you do that for?"

Jonah wasn't sure he could open his mouth without being sick, so he nodded stupidly. The other man glanced over his shoulder, then turned on his heel and ran away. Twisting round, Jonah could see a couple of shopworkers and some bystanders slowly coming to investigate the noise of the trolley going over plus the squeal of tyres on tarmac.

"No, no, she didn't run me over," he managed to say as someone helped him to his feet. The Tesco assistant righted his trolley and reloaded his shopping for him. Jonah managed to wedge himself upright by leaning heavily on the trolley.

"No, someone tried to grab my laptop case," he found himself saying, "It's okay, I'm police, I'll put the report through myself. I'm sure someone will be round for the CCTV at some point." He waved his warrant card vaguely around. Now the car was gone, the shopping saved and the drama over, the crowd was starting to disperse.

Jonah hobbled back to the store, bought a pack of frozen peas, and sat in the café with a strong coffee while he waited for Alex to arrive by taxi to take him home in his own car. His leg didn't feel in good enough shape to drive. He was experienced enough with rugby injuries to know that he might have to hire an automatic car for a few days.

He could've taken a taxi home but one thing he had learnt from his years on the job was to take care of the details. At some point his car would have to be recovered, but this way, he'd have everything in the right place at the right time.

Alex arrived, seemingly more annoyed than concerned, "You really want me to drive you home?"

"Well, yes, I wouldn't like to try the clutch."

When he limped to his feet, she looked at him and said, "Come on, A&E for you."

He groaned. "That's four hours of my life I won't get back!"

"Yes, but look at you. Your face has gone grey and you can't put any weight on it."

"I've done worse on the rugby pitch and been fine," Jonah complained, still following Alex out to his car.

"Yes, but you were younger then," Alex pointed out. "Come on, let's get you checked out properly."

Jonah had little choice but to sit in the passenger seat and let his wife take him to A&E. Despite his protestations, Jonah was glad that Alex had been there at the hospital. It had been very useful, not because she could use her position to gain an unfair advantage, but because she knew how the system worked. The fact that he was a policeman also helped to get the best care available.

The time in the waiting room had been spent in sullen silence interspersed with Jonah's attempts to persuade Alex that if he'd lost his laptop he'd be out of a job.

"I'm one warning away from being in proper trouble anyway," Jonah explained, "and it doesn't matter how well encrypted a laptop is, it's the publicity; it looks bad if the police have something stolen. The press usually makes a story out of it."

"Yes, well, if you'd paid more attention to what your manager was thinking, then you wouldn't be in this position in the first place," Alex argued.

"My job isn't to please my senior officers and play politics, it's to serve the public," Jonah said, hating how pompous he sounded.

"Well, I still think you need to be more careful, chasing people around and brawling at your age!"

"Oi," said Jonah, "I'm still less than ten years older than you, just like when we met!" He attempted to sound light-hearted about it but there was still an edge of bitterness in his voice.

Alex rubbed his arm tenderly and lapsed into silence. Jonah simmered – he hated these arguments that just fizzled out with nothing resolved. But there was nothing that he could do. He closed his hand over hers, and before he could think of anything to say, he was called for another stage of the process.

Finally, he was allowed home and watched as Alex efficiently put all the shopping away. He felt frustrated and impotent, although he still had his laptop with him.

Late that night, propped up in bed with his leg out straight, Jonah reviewed the situation with Alex.

"I said I didn't need A&E. I've seen far worse on the rugby pitch!"

"Yes, but what did you do? Leap over a trolley and land on a can? At your, well, with your..."

"I think you mean, at my age and weight I shouldn't be doing stuff like that," he said with a grin. "Maybe I'll find a quiet job, potter in the garden and wear slippers and cardigans!"

"I'm still glad you went; it could've been anything." She turned to look at him. "Are you going to keep going to work?"

"Yes," Jonah said, "they recommended that I keep moving it. Between painkillers and a stick, I should be fine."

Alex turned to look closely at her husband. "It's not connected is it? With all this 'off the record' and 'just doing background checks' stuff that you're doing, is it?"

Jonah squeezed his eyes tightly shut as his knee throbbed despite the drugs. He felt the pressure of both his injury and Alex's disapproval. "I don't know!" he snapped, "could be or it might not be. Next time someone attacks me and runs away, I'll remember to ask them if they've got an ulterior motive!"

Once again, the argument wasn't resolved as Alex picked up her book. After ten minutes of pointedly silent reading, she clicked her light off, still without a word spoken.

CHAPTER 16

Jonah pulled his car to a stop on the estate and checked the address Farida had given him. It was more of a rumour than a definite, but this should be the wife of an undercover officer who was working on the Mike Khan case. It was three days since his trip to A&E and he was feeling slightly sick from the painkillers and broken sleep.

He looked around at the rather disappointing houses – all red brick and built in the last fifteen years. They were close to being identical with small added features to make them all look subtly different. One thing was the same though, they all had tiny gardens at the front, mostly given over to driveways.

When the door opened, a tired, drawn looking woman answered. She was short and frail, with blonde hair in a short ponytail. Her roots were showing, and she was wearing tracksuit bottoms and a scruffy polo shirt. Behind her, Jonah could see stacks of cardboard boxes.

"Yes?" There was aggression in her voice.

"I've come to ask you about your husband," Jonah started.

"Press? You can fuck off! I've got nothing to say."

"No," he said hastily, "police." She glared at him even more aggressively than before. He handed over his warrant card.

"Oh," she said, examining his card carefully. "South Wales? Not his lot? I suppose you'd better come in." She led the way into the house. "Sorry about the mess," she said, not sounding at all sorry.

"And you are Cathy Porton? Wife of Ron Porton?"

"Yep, that's me," she said as she made coffee. "There's no space in here, boxes everywhere, let's take these out to the garden."

Jonah manoeuvred through the house, his progress made awkward by his knee that had stiffened up on the drive over and his stick. The back garden was as small as the front. There was a strip of patio close to the house, and the rest of the garden was split between a tiny patch of lawn and a huge rockery with a water feature.

"So, you'd better tell me why you've come all the way from South Wales to talk to me?"

"Well, I was investigating a suspicious death and came across Mike Khan's name and that led me to your husband. I've been getting nowhere at all through official channels."

"So, they don't know you're here?" The was something in her voice, almost excitement.

"You mean anyone from West Midlands, no." There was a long pause, during which Jonah wondered if he'd blown it already.

"They're no friends of mine," Cathy said finally. "This whole thing has been a complete fuck-up from the beginning. Ron was left out there with no support whatsoever. Hold on a minute," and she went back into the house. In a moment she returned with a framed photo.

"Here he is," she handed it over. It showed a man with sandy hair and an infectious grin, covered in mud, leaning against a football goal. "He was the keeper for the force team."

"Where is he now?" Jonah asked gently.

Cathy gave a low chuckle. "As far as anyone knows, New Zealand. We're husband and wife but we communicate like spies, setting up new email accounts and phoning from cheap mobiles." There was no hiding the bitterness in her voice.

"Do you have any children?"

"No." Tears rolled slowly down her face. "I'm sorry, it was four years ago, but it still catches me out." She took a deep breath. "I had a miscarriage. That was when it all went wrong. I don't think Ron knew how to cope. He refused to go to counselling, then he volunteered for undercover work. We'd only just moved to the area, so he was accepted straight away." Cathy dried her tears with hard swipes, annoyed at her own weakness.

"So," Jonah said, keen to keep the conversation moving, "will you be going out to New Zealand with him?"

"I don't know." Cathy shrugged. "He's trying to sort things out that end, but it's difficult. He just cut and run. Now West Midlands HR are dragging their feet, trying to decide if he's resigned or retired or been sacked. They keep talking about a disciplinary board, and the police fed rep keeps saying it was a failure of management. Everyone keeps talking, having meetings and sending memos and nothing's getting done!"

"Listen, I've got some information on Mike Khan and I'm going to try to bring him to justice. But I need more, I need to know what he's done."

"This has to be off the record. If you turn up waving

your pocketbook in court claiming I said this and I said that, I'll tell them that I sent you off with a flea in your ear. If anyone asks, we spent ten minutes in the garden sharing pruning tips." She got up and went to a switch on the wall. Behind Jonah the fountain sprang into life. It should've been impressive, a cherub perched on a rock disgorging water eternally from an urn under one arm. But it was obviously a cheap item bought from some DIY chain and the water trickled rather than gushed. Finally, it overflowed and started to trickle down the rockery.

Cathy went to stand by it and beckoned Jonah over. "I'm sorry about all the cloak and dagger stuff, but Ron has worked undercover, seen some of the things they do to gather evidence. If we stand here, even a long-range microphone would struggle over the background noise."

Jonah levered himself to his feet and leant on his stick as he walked over to join her.

"Are you all right to stand for a minute?" Cathy asked.

"It's best to keep it mobile," Jonah explained. "Do you really think that they're spying on you?"

"Do you really think they're not? Have you read the papers recently? They spied on Stephen Lawrence's family for God's sake! They sent officers so far undercover they had kids with the people they were supposed to be following and investigating. I could cost them a lot of money, and worse. If what I'm about to tell you got out, a lot of embarrassment."

"It's okay," Jonah reassured her. "I'll only use it for my investigation, to build background. It won't turn up anywhere official."

"I suppose I've been waiting to tell the story; it's awfully lonely you know. We're new to the area and I'm not welcome among the other police wives. I've pieced together bits and pieces from what Ron's told me over the phone. He never puts this stuff in an email and it's always the first phone call on a new phone. You know that he was undercover in Mike's gang. No, not gang, organisation. That's what they are, very organised. And ruthless. It didn't take him long to realise that everyone was afraid of Mike. The lower levels, the street dealers, protection guys, phone thieves, people like that, viewed him as some sort of mythical figure, like the bogey man.

"Anyway, Ron did his job really well." There was pride in her voice and for the first time, she looked animated, almost happy. Jonah studied her on the other side of the fountain. Etched on her face was how much she'd been through and how she still loved her husband. "He mixed it with the criminals but showed enough flair and brains to get marked out fairly early. The strange thing is, the way he tells it, it was just like a business. A bit of luck, taking risks, knowing the right people and you get marked out for promotion. And that's what happened to Ron. He was getting there. Took him years, mind you, Mike's so slippery. Ron was told to remain undercover until he had absolutely solid evidence of Mike himself committing crime. None of this issuing orders or conspiracy or something he could weasel out of.

"Of course, I knew none of this at the time, I just knew he'd vanish for weeks on end. Anyway, one day, about three months ago, Ron gets scooped up by Mike's closest bodyguards. He's absolutely panicking because one minute he's in a meeting, next minute he's in the back of a car being driven away. You can see already how smart Mike is, no chance to tip off his handlers, no idea where he's going. He's already fearing the worst, wondering if he'll see me again." Cathy stopped for a minute to dab at her eyes. "Anyway, he gets to this godforsaken place. It was a warehouse on a small estate out in the countryside. No way anyone could approach without being spotted, no way he was followed by his handlers. Inside this warehouse is Mike himself. Very few people actually get to meet him you see. He's about six foot six, and big built as well. He just stands up and intimidates people.

"But he wasn't there alone. There were another ten or so people there, all looking scared like Ron. He knew they were all at about his level in the organisation – rising stars. People who were about to make it into Mike's inner circle. Calm as anything, Mike drags another person out, duct taped to a chair. You must remember, as well as Mike and the ten of them there were armed men at the doors. This is just outside Birmingham you know, not Detroit. You see that many guns and you know that it just got serious." Cathy stopped to take a deep, shuddering breath. "Anyway, Ron won't be drawn on details, but Mike tortured this guy. He can't have been over twenty-five. Apparently, he'd signed up as a Confidential Informant and Mike had seen the paperwork. That's an indication of how powerful he is, how much he's bought his way into the police. So, Ron is thinking that this is the money, this is what he's there for, watching Mike torture this poor kid with a samurai sword. He wasn't gagged so everyone could hear him screaming and begging for mercy. Then, someone brings out a wheelbarrow full of rocks. They're these big, fist size smooth stones, you know, like you'd get from a DIY store. And Mike tells everyone to stone the guy to death. They're all trapped, nowhere to go, so they all pitch in and chuck rocks until the guy is dead." Tears ran down Cathy's face now, totally unheeded, but she didn't stop with the story. "Mike walked among them, making sure that no one wore gloves, that everyone was picking up a stone and throwing it. Swinging his fucking samurai sword like it was a knife making sure that there was nothing half-hearted going on.

"You can bet there were hidden cameras in that room. That those rocks, covered in blood, hair, and fingerprints will be stored up somewhere in a safe, together with the footage." She turned to ask Jonah, "What do you think he should've done then? Joined in? Taken a stand, and if he was lucky a bullet to the head? Although the choice was almost certainly, take part, or find yourself taped to another chair."

Jonah shook his head. What do you do? Having a nervous breakdown and running away to New Zealand looked like a reasonable choice.

"Ron wasn't the only one who couldn't cope with Mike's little show. There was at least one suicide in the week after, and another disappearance. I guess that was the point, sort out the wheat from the chaff."

Jonah was saved from saying anything when a man burst into the back garden, apparently out of breath. He was thin and cadaverous with hollow cheeks and pale skin. His dark hair was receding and cropped close to disguise the fact.

"Who..." Jonah started saying before being interrupted by Cathy.

"What are you doing in my garden?" she shouted at the man, "How many times do I have to tell you I'm not talking to you? If you want Ron, you'll have to bloody well find him yourself!"

He glared at her and Jonah, jealousy and anger writ large across his face.

"Who is this?" He asked sharply, obviously expecting to be obeyed.

"Sorry, how rude of me not to introduce everyone," Cathy said, dripping with sarcasm. "DS Greene, meet DI Bridges of West Midlands CID."

"Which force are you from?" DI Bridges said with all the pleasantness of a tom cat finding another cat on his territory.

"South Wales," Jonah admitted.

"Right, and your boss knows you're here, does he?" While he was speaking his phone chirruped. Without any hint of embarrassment, he pulled it out and read a message.

"Cathy," DI Bridges said, trying to sound more charming now. "This man has been poking around our investigation for ages, trying to find out what's going on. Your husband was undercover, so you know the risks he was taking, and the dangers that officers like this man Greene can pose. He's putting lives at risk, the lives of decent officers."

"Strange isn't it then," Cathy replied evenly, not breaking eye contact with him, "that I trust him far more than I trust you and the rest of your team."

"I think we're going to have to deal with that through official channels," DI Bridges said to Cathy before turning to Jonah. "You, on the other hand, are our problem." He gripped Jonah by the upper arm and started to lead him from the garden.

Emboldened by what Farida had said, he pulled his arm away. "I'm here visiting a friend; you don't get to order me out of the way."

"You are on our turf, sticking your nose into our business and it's time you left before we make this official and I call your boss."

"I said, I wasn't conducting an investigation, just visiting a friend." He glanced at Cathy who nodded slightly. He wondered about the speed with which DI Bridges had appeared and realised that he'd been listening in to their conversation, right up to the point where they moved near the water feature. He also guessed that he wouldn't want to put it on record that he'd been spying on the wife of a fellow officer.

"Cathy," DI Bridges said, changing tack. "Your attempt to get any money, whether it's pension or redundancy or anything like that is dependent on co-operating with CID. We could believe that Ron hasn't confided in you. But do you really want to be known as associating with officers from other forces, possibly jeopardising any future enquiry?"

Cathy sighed. "Play their stupid games, Jonah. It was lovely to see you, but I'd better get on with packing and sorting things out. With a bit of luck, I'll be moving soon."

"Bye then," Jonah said resignedly. He turned and left, uncomfortably aware of DI Bridges right at his back. He wasn't surprised when he saw a flashy car parked right behind his own hire car. He limped over to his vehicle, watching Bridges go off to his.

Something snapped inside Jonah – all the setbacks, Farida's jibes about his being bullied, and now this self-important DI was shutting down his one best lead. Without thinking he walked over behind Bridges. As the DI opened his car door, Jonah reached past him and pushed it shut with the end of his stick.

"WHAT? I THOUGHT YOU'D GONE?"

"What, thought you'd dismissed me? Sent me back home with my tail between my legs?"

Bridges slapped the cane out of the way and rounded on

him. Although he was thin, he was wiry, strong and younger than Jonah. "What are you going to do then? Fall over on your bad knee or simply freeze up?"

"Neither," said Jonah pretending to be braver than he felt. "I want to know what makes you so bloody certain you're right and you can just walk in here and order everyone around."

"It's my case," Bridges took a step forward, "it's on my turf," another step, shoving Jonah backwards, "and I outrank you." He gave final shove and Jonah stumbled slightly, putting his cane behind him to steady himself.

Jonah's brain was still turning over what DI Bridges had said – was he was hinting that he'd read his personnel file?

He levered himself upright, practically nose to nose with Bridges. "Has it ever occurred to you that I might know something you don't? That I could offer you information about Khan that you haven't yet discovered, or thought was important?"

The two men surveyed each other icily. Inside, Jonah was quaking, but knew he had to portray confidence. If you went onto the rugby pitch fearing a big tackle, you'd be finished before the first whistle.

Close up he could see that the other man was uncertain. His eyes widened slightly and there was a tightening around his mouth. He broke eye contact for a second, as if he was looking around for help. He didn't want to be here and didn't agree with his orders.

"Just tell me what it is about Mike Khan?" Jonah persisted. "I can see he's got under your skin; everyone I've spoken to seems to be afraid of him."

"We are not afraid of that man!" DI Bridges snapped. "But neither do we underestimate him. He is intelligent and dangerous."

"Right, so don't give him a chance. I just want exchange of information, nothing more. Let me help you."

DI Bridges spun on his heel and opened his door again. He gave a slight nod of his head to indicate that Jonah should get into the passenger seat. He limped around the car, noting it was a nearly new Vauxhall Omega with a high trim level. Inside, he settled into the leather seat and saw how neat and clean it was. Bridges put the key in and started the radio. Still without speaking, he switched to Radio 4 and turned it up. The warm sounds of Gardener's Question Time filled the car.

"I shouldn't be speaking to you," DI Bridges said. "This operation has gone tits up so many times, you'd think it was cursed. Everyone on the team is vetted and once you began poking around, you got checked out too." He paused for effect. "You failed to make the grade."

"What? You had no right!" Jonah said, outraged.

"We have every right!" DI Bridges countered. "Do you have any idea who we're dealing with? How far have you got with your own research into Mike Khan?"

The radio was talking about the best way to care for rose bushes and if teabags really did help them grow.

"Well, he went to university, studied law..."

"...and graduated with a first," DI Bridges interrupted.

"After that he seems to have become a rather nasty, sadistic, drug dealing criminal."

DI Bridges nodded. "I don't think you really have any idea of his reach. He's not just a drug dealer, he's got fingers in criminal pies all over the Black Country. And you're right, he appears to be very nasty." He paused, appearing to weigh up how much he could divulge to Jonah. "This operation was started personally by the deputy chief constable. He has handpicked the chief super to put together a team to work on him. A lot of the information on it is kept on paper files in his offices. No one gets on unless they pass vetting, not a hint of scandal or that they could be corrupted. Everything else is locked down, beyond tight."

"And you're the enforcer for the operation?"

"Among other things," DI Bridges said darkly. "What have you got so far?"

Jonah considered offering a trade, but that wasn't how it was going to work. He'd offer up what he had and see what came back. He had come close to assaulting a senior officer from a different force and could still be in all sorts of trouble.

He outlined what he'd learnt, starting with Patrick's death, and the list. Bridges was interested that four of them knew each other at university and all denied it.

"Could we have their contact details? Get in touch and see what they remember about Mike Khan? Could be good deep background."

"No," Jonah shook his head, "Elizabeth Gardner is seriously unstable. She takes medication that alters her mood and disappears for weeks on end, probably a retreat or maybe even a hospital or some such. McRae is running for MP and has already threatened to ruin my career. You can have a pop at him but go very high up. He's friendly with his local chief constable, conservative party, and local council. Peter Calne's odd, he claims not to have known any of them at university but that might not be true. He's had a serious head injury so we can't trust his memory. He's quite obsessed too – if you speak to him, he'll want help with figuring out what happened to him."

Bridges nodded slowly, obviously deciding what approach would be best. "So, Elizabeth Gardner would be unreliable due to her mental state, Peter Calne likewise due to his head injury, and we could expect McRae to lie and refuse to co-operate." Jonah nodded. "Well, I'll pass that further up the chain and see what they decide."

Jonah looked around hopefully at DI Bridges. He sighed and said, "I can't give you anything operational, but I can fill in some background for you. As you're interested in his university years, I'll give you the next chapter. We've pieced together his early movements from intelligence reports. A year or two after he left university, Mike showed up in Birmingham. At first he was just buying drugs, but soon he started pressuring his dealers, asking them to move up the chain, meet the person they were buying from. Sometimes he'd offer money, other times, he'd just threaten them.

"Anyway, that kind of behaviour doesn't go unnoticed so once he got to quite a high level, people buying in tens of kilos and splitting it, they sent an enforcer out to see who he was and what his game was. Basically, trying to see if he was one of us undercover. That guy vanished off the face of the earth. Now he had the attention of some seriously nasty guys, the proper top-of-the-tree dealers. And with those guys, killing one of their thugs is a declaration of war.

"They responded by sending out one of their worst enforcers – the kind where you just have to mention his name and people are scared. We knew his name because he was tied into various murders and beatings. He was top of our list for quite a while. Anyway, this bloke, the one they're all afraid of comes back to them in a wheelchair, properly messed up. Within a week he's dead – apparently he'd been force fed some radioactive crap that there's no antidote to and just eats you up from the inside."

Jonah turned to look at DI Bridges with a look of horror on his face. "I told you he was nasty, that you didn't have any idea who you were dealing with. It gets worse. Of course, they did the only thing they could, they arranged to have a sit down, a meeting of all the heads in Birmingham to discuss whether to work with Mike or bring him down together. They met above a nightclub in early 1998, after hours." Bridges turned to look at Jonah to see if anything registered. Jonah nodded slowly. "Yep, DS Greene, that nightclub fire. Thirteen dead and more horribly injured. We found one in the alley with his head stoved in, could have been a baseball bat, could've fallen out of the building."

"So," Jonah filled in the pieces, "he wiped them out? In one night?"

"Pretty much. You have to understand; this is all conjecture. The people who told us parts of this story are mostly dead or in prison. Certainly, none of them will repeat it under oath. Not while Mike Khan's still alive, for sure. But this is what we learnt after years of combing intelligence reports, putting together snippets from CIs and asking around."

"And once he had a power vacuum..." Jonah said.

"...he just moved in to fill it," DI Bridges completed the sentence. "We're not sure how exactly, but he was able to pick up most of the import and distribution deals."

"Mike Khan's most likely to have made a mistake early on in his criminal career. There might be something in the mid-nineties that you can use to nail him now," Jonah said.

DI Bridges stroked his chin. "Maybe. It'd have to be big to carry enough weight now. And there would have to be evidence too. Concrete evidence. Tell you what, I'll plug these names into the system and see what pops out. And I'll bear in mind what you said about Elizabeth Gardner, Peter Calne and Andrew McRae."

"Any chance you can keep me in the loop?"

"Not much." DI Bridges shook his head. "You'll never be accepted with your record." He handed over a business card, "but that doesn't mean you can't tell us what you know." He paused, then added, "but if it's not current, I can let you know what we discover about his movements in the nineties, on the quiet."

"I'd appreciate that."

"You know, you've got a lot of balls for an old guy with a stick!"

"And there aren't that many youngsters who know when to back down."

With that, Jonah got out of the car and limped back to his own, with more questions than answers running around his head.

MIKE

CHAPTER 17

April 15, 1995

The man who would be Peter Calne's murderer had been waiting for him, even though the two men had never met until this night. Hunkered down into his donkey jacket he had spent twenty minutes checking his watch. He wanted to look like he was waiting for someone even though he was alone on the concrete walkway.

He used the time to contemplate his life so far. Because after tonight he was going to be a different person. He would not only transform his own life but drag others up with him. He was taking a big step, out of the humdrum, into an extraordinary life.

When he first saw his victim, he knew it was all going to work. Peter was alone and weaving slightly. Not obviously falling down drunk, just a little tipsy. God was making it easy for him. The attacker stood up from the pillar and stepped into the centre of the path. This caused Peter to stop.

The walkway was part of an early sixties' concrete monstrosity. It linked together the various buildings of the

University of Swindon. It was bounded by thick, four-foot-high walls, and a roof about seven feet up, all made out of concrete. The effect was to leave long thin slits, reminiscent of World War II German sea defences. However, constructed in the sixties, it was all irregular, jutting off at strange angles and built at different heights.

Peter's attacker moved forward rapidly and swung a huge roundhouse punch straight at his ear. It connected solidly, knocking his victim to his knees. As if he was suddenly being helpful, the attacker rushed forward and gripped Peter by the upper arms.

However, he didn't raise him up to his feet, he kept on lifting until he had hoisted him clear off the deck.

"Hey!" was all Peter managed to say before he was being pushed through the slot at the edge of the walkway like a letter through a post box. For a moment the attacker locked eyes with Peter. This was a moment to remember – the dawning of realisation. The look of surprise slid from Peter's face to be replaced by terror. He now knew what was happening.

This was not proving to be as easy as he had imagined. The attacker cursed himself. He hadn't hit Peter hard enough in the initial assault. He should have knocked him out.

The struggle assumed almost comical aspects. Every time the attacker pried up a finger or released a hand, Peter found another way to anchor himself to the concrete.

The attacker had many advantages – he was stronger, sober, and on the walkway. Peter was rapidly running out of room. Small patches of blood spotted the concrete as he grazed his knuckles, elbows and ankles. His attacker meanwhile had adopted a methodical approach. His feet were dug into the walkway and every time he released a hand or foot, he shoved it brutally nearer the edge.

Finally, there was only one foot hooked over the edge. With glee, his assailant picked up the ankle and thrust it deep into the gap. With nothing holding him there, Peter thrashed and twisted to try to find another handhold. But his attacker seized his chance, set his feet on the floor and threw his weight behind one huge shove.

Peter's feet slid through and out over open space, followed by his hips. For a second, he hung in the balance, right over the edge. His attacker leaned in, keen to capture the moment. With one punch to the shoulder, the job was done. The last he saw of his victim was two white hands, fluttering like wounded birds before they lost purchase and he was gone.

Up above, as he left the scene, his assailant drank in the experience. He was disappointed with himself; it hadn't gone as smoothly as planned. He should have hit him several times, he thought, until he was unconscious and then pushed his body through head first. That would have made sure.

He reached the end of the walkway unwittingly retracing Peter's route, threading down corridors and stairs. Once he entered the bar, he felt safer. There were still a few students around, finishing up their drinks even though the bar was shuttered. From here there were at least half a dozen exits.

As he stood in the foyer, he replayed events in his mind. He savoured the look in his victim's eyes. The sheer terror washing away the alcohol. His victim must have suddenly felt totally alive, aware of every sensation, just seconds before eternal blackness.

The power coursed through him all over again. He had

seized his destiny, changed his life, altered the world around him.

He'd always known he was destined for greatness but now he had taken a major step on the path. He had crossed boundaries, done the unthinkable, set himself aside. He looked around; through the doors rain was falling in the night.

He needed a drink, and as the bar was closed, he would have to walk into town to one of the nightclubs. He didn't need a taxi, or to worry about the rain. He felt superhuman and invincible. After a drink what he needed was a girl. He knew that tonight, he couldn't fail at whatever he tried. If he ever felt an opportunity slipping away, he could just conjure up that face, the way it disappeared into the black void and know that he was capable of anything.

Yes, he thought to himself, go to a nightclub, find someone pretty and take them home for a night of debauchery. Tomorrow was the first day of the rest of his life, and everything was possible.

News of the unprovoked attack spread round the campus like wildfire. When the attacker came back to lectures on Monday morning, his ebullient mood was punctured. The word sweeping around campus was that his victim had survived. He was critically ill in hospital but stable.

For several weeks, in parallel with Peter Calne, his assailant lived a half-existence. At any moment, his victim could wake up and accuse him. His attacker knew his limitations. If he had been studying medicine, he might have attempted to trick his way into the hospital. Then he could have found some clever way to finish the job – something that would look like a normal death for a comatose trauma casualty. But he didn't have enough knowledge, and couldn't be sure that he'd kill his victim without leaving clues. And, having made one mistake, he wasn't prepared to take any more chances.

Instead, he took to his area of speciality – the law. He researched previous cases and precedents and developed a strategy to carry out if the worst should happen. He would co-operate fully with the police. He would point out how unreliable memory was, even in a healthy brain, never mind a damaged one. He would highlight that his excessive size made him stand out. It was entirely reasonable that he had encountered Peter in the bar that night and stuck in his memory for some reason. He would fabricate a spilled pint or some other casual contact. This was safest as he had been in the bar that night and any number of witnesses had seen him. He was big enough to carry out the attack. So, the police would already have him on means and opportunity. His trump card was that they would never find a motive. And without that, and without evidence, he was convinced he would walk free.

Finally, sixteen days later, he found his reprieve in a local newspaper. His victim had awoken but had significant memory loss. In particular, the police were not hopeful that he'd ever be able to reliably identify his attacker. He breathed a sigh of relief that all his painstaking research had been for nothing.

While this caused him to relax, it did not do much to lift his mood. He still remembered those forty-eight hours when he'd felt superhuman. He had been cheated – and he needed to reclaim his prize. He was cursed to be forever chasing that feeling of ultimate power over another person.

CHAPTER 18

For all his bravado facing up to DI Bridges, Jonah's mood gradually deflated over the next few days. Bridges hadn't phoned up and told Jonah how much his information had helped. Neither had McRae made any more threatening moves to Jonah's career. Nothing at all happened apart from the routine of sorting through the dead and their associated paperwork.

But the truth was he still had plenty of mundane work to do and hadn't really made any forward progress with the list. Rather, he had shifted his focus. He now clearly identified Mike Khan as the bad guy, someone who needed to be stopped. He stood by what he'd said earlier – it was most likely that Mike had made mistakes early on his career, and that was where he'd be caught out.

His current case was a murder, but was frustratingly mundane, if murder ever could be described as such. A young woman had been killed by a jealous ex-boyfriend. It was a clear case of unlawful death and the ex had already been arrested by uniform, with the blood still on his clothes. His fingerprints also matched those found at the scene.

Depressed by how futile and stupid the crime was, Jonah went to lunch early. The weather was perfect late spring day – clear blue sky and bright green bursting from the trees. The improving weather was indicated by the increase in the number of coaches. He dodged past a line of foreign students in matching backpacks, snaking their way from the castle to the museum.

Rather than heading straight to his favourite spot for lunch, Jonah made a point of walking for at least ten minutes. Sitting still all morning made his knee seize up, and although walking was slow and painful, it did ease the stiffness. He finished his walk in Gorsedd Park, scanning the people, and looking for a quiet bench to eat his lunch. He did a double-take – middle-aged, blonde hair, fine bone structure, well dressed. Away from the Cotswold countryside this was Elizabeth Gardner.

"Jonah! Hi!" She appeared to be genuinely surprised.

"Spare me," Jonah barked, "were you here looking for me?"

"Can't I just do some shopping, get a spot of lunch?" Elizabeth tried her hardest to look innocent.

"Not when you're hours from either of your homes and just happen to be walking towards the police station where I'm based."

Elizabeth tried her most winning smile. "I was going to apologise, but I didn't think you'd take a phone call from me."

"Okay," Jonah said, thinking that she was probably right. He took a deep steadying breath and remembered his planned interview strategy. He attempted to view all his interactions with Elizabeth over the past few months as an extended interview – and his job now was to build a rapport, get Elizabeth believing he was on her side.

"I'm sorry. I was angry with Jonathon and I knew one of his accountants had dealt with Andrew, so I thought..." She looked around. "Shall we sit," she indicated his stick. Jonah nodded and lowered himself onto the bench. His knee was feeling sore and throbbing slightly, so he welcomed her suggestion. He got himself comfortable and Elizabeth perched on the edge of the seat, turned slightly towards him.

"Thank you for taking the time to come over and apologise," Jonah said. "I think I managed to get away with it at work, but it was a bit touch and go."

"I didn't realise you could get in trouble over it." Elizabeth acted contrite but Jonah wasn't buying any of it.

"Well, my job should be dealing with sudden deaths, not running over all the country interviewing accountants at the drop of a hat."

"Of course, of course, I didn't realise really."

"But, don't let that stop you. If it wasn't for you and your information, I would have stopped the investigation into Patrick's death ages ago."

"Thank you, as well, I thought I'd messed everything up." She stood and paced nervously.

"No, I realised that you were right about Mike, he is the monster here, the one we need to stop. But I'm trying to find some concrete evidence to actually do some good, bring him down."

"Is he though?" Elizabeth said thoughtfully, as if to herself. "I mean, look at me and Andrew, out here in your society, wearing the right clothes, paying into the right charities, as we appear to fit in."

"I'm not sure I'm following you."

"Well, who's the real monster? Someone like Mike who lives and operates in a criminal world; the only people he'll really hurt are other criminals." Jonah bit his tongue – now was not the time to point out the real damage people like Mike did to society. "And then you've got other people who are criminal, but they just keep their heads down, wear suits, run for parliament or waste time as a rich man's wife. I mean, even Patrick, God rest his soul, he was as guilty as the rest of us! Who's to say Mike's any worse? Maybe we made him the way he is? Maybe we're all monsters?"

"That's a bit of a philosophical argument," Jonah said. "Here in the police, we arrest criminals wherever we find them when we have evidence."

"There's another reason why I came out here. The clock is ticking on Andrew as well."

"What do you mean?"

"Well, the deadline for registering candidates is only next week. If we can get some solid evidence to the selection committee before then, they can withdraw him and go with another candidate. If we don't, then it all becomes complicated – getting him disbarred and triggering a by-election and all that."

Jonah looked up at her in stunned silence. He wanted to ask her if he should be prioritising Mike or Andrew. But he had a strategy to stick to. "Right," he asked, "how long exactly have we got?"

Elizabeth thought for a moment, then said, "until end of business a week on Tuesday. If you get some arrests, then we can put all of it together." Jonah frowned at her, so she continued. "I have the paperwork to put all of this to an end now. But if I did that, then I'd take myself out of the equation. And if I'm honest, I don't trust the police to properly get to grips with both Mike and Andrew. They're both too clever and too slippery. I think they'd slide out of it." She nodded to herself, working out her strategy as she spoke.

"So, if you get Mike or Andrew out of the way, properly banged up, I'll hand over what I've got, and it'll all be wrapped up. Okay?"

"That sounds fair to me," Jonah said, even though he had very little idea what she was talking about. "You'll hand over the paperwork when I've arrested either Mike or Andrew."

"Yes."

"And this paperwork..." He stopped, unsure of how far he could push her. Was she on the verge of confessing? He wasn't sure how aware she was of what she was saying. In the end, he backed down. "Listen, we both want the same thing, to find a way to do the right thing. But it has to be done the right way as well. Is there anything further you feel you ought to be telling me?"

"Hmmm." Elizabeth turned to study Jonah. He felt uncomfortable sitting while she stood over him but didn't want to stand and tower over her. "So, concrete evidence," she said, disregarding her previous philosophical musings. "How about we see if you can get Mike first, and then we'll see if there's anything further I want to tell you. If I can bring you something, you'll use it? You're not afraid of your boss?"

"Afraid? No?" Jonah thought fast. "But if I lose my job, I can't help you." He grew firmer. "So I can't go off tilting at windmills any more. If you really want to help me, I need definite information."

"Definite," Elizabeth repeated, "definite." While she was talking, she slowly backed away. Without any word of departure, she turned on her heel and left.

Jonah thoughtfully opened his sandwiches and watched her retreat. He had the feeling that he'd unleashed something. He wondered what Elizabeth heard, what she had understood from his words. He had released a loose cannon and only time would tell what she would do next.

WHEN HE RETURNED to his office, he found that the front desk had called, asking if he was free to see a Fiona Kinsale. He called back and checked if she was still there. The fact that she had come piqued Jonah's curiosity. He was soon in a meeting room with her. It wasn't a formal interview room with cameras and tape decks, but a less intimidating setting.

She asked, "Is it okay to talk to you about Patrick?"

"Of course," Jonah said, his mood lifting.

"I was just wondering, because you know, we've had the funeral and the verdict, certificates, probate, probably the whole thing's done and dusted for you."

"Well, all the official stuff has been done, but I'm always happy to listen and see if there's anything else I could help with."

"I know it sounds a bit odd, but I've only just got round to sorting out his paperwork. He didn't have much, but he did have a few bits that he didn't want to lose on the streets. Anyway, I found this notebook, and it's a bit disturbing. I don't know why he wrote it. Or what to do with it."

"Have you got it with you?" Jonah asked.

Fiona nodded and handed it across the desk. At first Jonah's heart sank as it was like a school exercise book. The list had been torn from a reporter's notebook, so he wasn't going to find anything else that explained the list. But as he flicked through the notebook, he saw that it had a value of its own.

It contained drafts of letters, to a Mr and Mrs Walters. The first page had their address in Southend.

I don't know how to write this letter, but it is very difficult for me to explain. You might want to know that your daughter didn't suffer, she seemed happy and then she was dead. I didn't want to hurt her, but it was necessary.

Underneath this entry was scrawled the words. 'No good, too brutal.'

I can't imagine the pain and damage I have wrought upon your family. That was never my intention, I acted with the haste and stupidity of youth, seeing Emma as a means to an end, instead of a living human being. I am truly sorry and filled with remorse. I have spent the rest of my life trying to atone, to be a better person.

Again, this was annotated underneath with the words 'Nope. Too much about me, not enough about them.'

Jonah flicked through more pages, catching phrases as he went – it wasn't her fault, she seemed really happy right until the end, it wasn't anything personal, I was young and didn't realise, still won't help, won't give them anything.

"Does it help?" Fiona asked. "It is his handwriting."

"I'm not sure," Jonah hedged. "I think so. I'm going to need a quick statement from you. Nothing special, just saying where and when you found it and that you believe he wrote it. Do you have any idea when it was written?"

Fiona thought for a moment. "I've had that box of stuff for ages, I don't know, say, five years at least. But I don't know when he wrote it or put it in the box."

Jonah nodded. He was already preparing the statement for Fiona to sign. Once he had it all entered into evidence and the system, he started making the phone calls that he'd been looking forward to since he'd first seen the notebook.

"I'm DS Greene and I'm calling from Cardiff Police

Station. I'd like to speak to someone who's dealing with the Emma Walters cold case from 1995." Jonah repeated this phrase several times as he got passed around the departments. Finally he got through to a harassed sounding DC Dave Jenkins. Carefully, Jonah outlined what he'd found. It was a relief to actually talk about it in the open.

"Okay, so we've got something of a description, it might be our suspect," Dave said. "That type of bayonet was quite rare and we found a shop in London that might have sold it. Interestingly, we got a similar description from passengers on the first train out of Southend that morning." There was a rustling of paper. "Trouble is, it doesn't really help. Male, young, maybe twenties, average height, let's say, five nine to six foot. Brown or dark hair clipped short. No distinguishing features." There was a big sigh that reached down the line to Jonah. "What have you got your end."

Jonah did some mental arithmetic. "Patrick would've been nineteen and a half. I guess he'd look like he was in his early twenties. And he was five foot ten, with dark brown hair and eyes."

"Hmmm, like about half the population. Got any connection with Southend?"

"Nope, born in London, university in Swindon, moved out this way before he died. Is there any evidence from what was left behind? DNA or prints or anything you could check?"

"No," Dave sounded despondent. "At first we were excited because he left the knife and the boiler suit. But it turns out the only trace on those was from the victim. It was quite clever really, because if we'd found something at a suspect's house with Emma's blood on it, we'd have had him. By leaving it behind, he managed to avoid that."

"No hairs or anything?" Jonah asked.

"No, if the sighting we had is our killer, he had very short hair. Shows a level of planning." There was a pause. "Thanks anyway. Without a connection to Southend, and without anyone remembering where he was twenty years ago, we don't have much. I'd say with the list and notebook the most we're looking at is a nutter who obsessed on the murder. I don't suppose he actually admits killing Emma, does he?"

Jonah flicked through the book, even though he'd already read it cover to cover. There were many pages with a few words and more that were entirely blank. "No, he admits to being young and stupid and regrets what he did, apologises to the parents. But nowhere does he say, 'I killed Emma Walters'."

"What's your gut feeling?" Dave asked.

"My gut feeling is that he's your killer, but you might never prove it," Jonah answered. "Everyone I've spoken to said that he was eaten up from the inside, something happened to him, made him feel guilty and drove him to drink. Ultimately I think it killed him."

"Thanks for that," Dave answered, still sounding morose. Jonah knew it was the last thing any detective wanted to hear – the crime would never result in a conviction.

Jonah said his goodbyes, then spent the rest of the afternoon sorting out the paperwork to transfer the notebook over to Southend to see if they could do anything with it. It felt good to be actively involved in a case again in an official capacity.

WHEN HE GOT HOME that night, Jonah saw Alex working on her motorbike. Feigning interest, he wandered over and watched her attaching a wing mirror to the handlebar.

"Nearly done it," Alex said without looking up. "Then I'll clean up and come in to figure out what's for dinner."

"What's up with it?"

"This? Oh, nothing, needed doing when I bought it," Alex said.

Jonah nudged the discarded wing mirror with his foot, turning it over to reveal a cracked surface. His glance then fell to the side of the bike. The edges of the fairing were more scuffed than last time and on closer inspection some of the stickers were scratched now.

"Alex," Jonah said carefully. "What really happened to the bike?" And you, he wanted to add.

Alex followed Jonah's glance along the side of the bike. "What, oh, it was nothing, just a few scratches."

Jonah ran his finger along the side of the bike, lifting one of the shredded stickers slightly and looked at Alex. As always, he was reminded of the gulf between them and his inability to find the right words to bridge that gap. "Why don't just tell me what happened?"

"Now you sound like a policeman investigating."

"Well, I am a policeman!" Jonah snapped, marvelling how Alex could irritate him with just a few words. "And your husband," he softened his tone slightly, "and I worry about you."

She glared up at him sulkily, still unsure of what she wanted. What the point was of being independent if she wanted to run into Jonah's arms the minute things went wrong?

"Okay," he said with exaggerated formality. "Madam,

could you tell me where you were when the incident occurred."

"Just coming off the main road into Thornhill," she admitted. "I was waiting to turn right, and some idiot couldn't get past so he leant on his horn. I had nowhere to go so he tried to push past and nudged me over."

"So he actually hit you? Are you okay?"

"Well, it was more like he kind of nudged past me, just caught the rear wheel and I couldn't really hold it upright, that's all." She paused trying to judge his mood. "I must've looked quite silly really. I leant over to get out of the way, then just kept going over further and further. I ended up hopping on one leg before I kind of toppled over and put the bike down."

"But you're not hurt?"

"No," Alex admitted, but what she really wanted him to do was to demand the description of the driver so he could call down the full weight of the traffic police on their head.

"Well, as long as you're fine," Jonah said. "I mean, bikes and bodywork and stuff can all be fixed, can't they?" He was beaten down from his previous encounters – he wished he could find the other driver, but he didn't know what good it would do. A year ago, he would've had a quiet chat with someone from traffic and it would've all been sorted. Now he didn't know where he stood, either with the rest of the force, or with Alex. There was no one to help him.

There was an uneasy silence between them, so Jonah took the easy way out and went into the house. On the hall table was a plain white envelope, printed label, addressed to him. Frowning he took it into the kitchen and slit it open. Inside was a cutting from a local paper. He checked both sides but there was only one complete story – a spate of cars being stolen and burnt out around Shrewsbury the previous week. No suspects, usual opinion piece about the youth of today and the worry that it was the beginning of a new crime wave. He reread the story carefully and learnt that there were three cars burnt out on one night. Jonah checked the envelope, but it was plain white, sold in millions, no return address, blurred postmark, just his address printed on a sticker and stuck on the front. He shook it out but there was nothing else in there. Without access to police computers, there wasn't anything he could do, so he replaced the cutting and slid it into his inside pocket, his first job when he got in tomorrow morning.

Alex came back in about half an hour later and they had a sullen dinner together, after which she announced she was having a bath before bed. By the time he came up, she was already in bed, wearing pyjamas so he had no chance of seeing the large bruise flowering over her hip, nor of seeing how stiffly she had got into the bath.

When he reached the office in the morning, he was disciplined. He cleared his emails and paperwork so it would look like he was doing his job. Then he took out the cutting and started his searching. Luckily for him, it was a far more restrictive list than the one from the Prof. He knew the place and the date and soon pulled up three crime reports from West Mercia Police. He immediately saw that it was going to be complicated. He didn't fancy using anything traceable so he went to grab some paper from the printer. Every report was short on detail. Each car was set alight outside a dealership, one in Shrewsbury, one near Westbury and one near Ketley. On a hunch, he went to Google and checked – each one was owned by Andrew McRae. While he was at the computer, he pulled up a map and saw that everything was centred around Shrewsbury. Scratching his head, he went back and read through the reports. Once the fire brigade had finished with the cars, there wasn't much left. The police who dealt with the incidents simply left the comment on the forms that they'd checked the addresses through DVLA and they were faked. Likewise, the driving license details on the new owner section of the logbooks were found to be false. That was where the details stopped. Luckily, the officers on the case had recorded the number plates recovered from the VINs on the burnt-out hulks.

Jonah divided his sheet of paper up into three and started with the first case. He called up the DVLA computer to get some more details. As soon as the record came up, a chill went down his spine. The car was registered to Patrick Kinsale. Jonah's first thought was that he had owned it at some point in the past, and it had for some reason been stolen and burnt outside one of McRae's businesses. But when he went back to check the date of transfer, he found it was just over a week ago. Scrolling through the record, he looked past the name at the current address – a posh address outside Shrewsbury that also rang a bell. Jonah pulled out a well-worn photocopy and smoothed it out on his desk. Finally, he scrolled back through the previous owner details and jotted down the previous address on his piece of paper.

Now he had the whole picture he was more confused than ever. Someone had gone into one of Andrew's dealerships and bought a car using Patrick's name and Andrew's address on a fake driving license. Then, they laid it up somewhere for about a week, and then drove it to another of his dealerships and set fire to it. It made no sense whatsoever to Jonah, so he looked at the other two cases to see if there was a pattern.

The second one had exactly the same history, bought on

the same day from one of Andrew's lots, then torched on the same day. This one was registered to Elizabeth Gardner. Jonah was totally unsurprised to find the final car was bought on the same day and registered to Mike Khan at the same address.

He looked at all the details on his piece of paper. He tried to imagine the minimum amount of effort required to carry it out. Two people, one to pretend to be Patrick and Mike, and a woman to impersonate Elizabeth. Then they could be driving each other around to arrange collecting the cars and parking them up somewhere. The three cars were cheap part-exchanges so the whole thing could have been done on two different days with under ten thousand pounds to finance it all. So, it wasn't a hard thing to arrange, he thought, but why? What purpose did it all serve?

He looked at his notes, and one thing leapt out at him. He put the list that he had carried around for the last few weeks next to his notes on the car arsons. They were the same, the first three names, plus Patrick.

Whoever had sent the newspaper cutting had been very clever, Jonah thought. He had only been given information that was already public knowledge, nothing from the police computers. Of course, whoever had sent it knew that he was interested in Andrew McRae and had given him information that no one could trace. Jonah thought of the LIO from Shrewsbury and sent him a silent prayer of thanks.

Jonah selected a fresh sheet of paper and tore it into eight slips. He wrote one name from the list on each piece with Patrick on the eighth. Now he could slide the pieces around and try to make sense of it. He put Patrick top left and listed Andrew, Mike and Elizabeth underneath. This was his original list. Now, McRae had unwittingly presented him with a new list, this time with the same other three people on. For that matter, he thought Elizabeth had told him that she knew Andrew, Patrick and Mike.

So, now he had the other four in a similar list opposite the four from university. So, Patrick felt guilty in some way about Emma's death. Was he responsible? With his training, Jonah thought about joint enterprise.

This legal concept had been at the heart of the Derek Bentley case back in 1952. Derek Bentley famously said, "Let him have it!" and therefore was considered to be guilty of murder even though his accomplice Christopher Craig actually pulled the trigger.

In effect, if everyone was involved in the same enterprise and it resulted in death then all of them could be guilty of murder, regardless of who actually committed the crime.

Jonah looked down at his list. The gang of four must have had some knowledge of the murders. By not acting to stop them, they were on the way to being accessories, and if they were involved in some common enterprise then they would have all been equally guilty of murder.

Was this the reason why the list was divided into two columns? Murderers one side, victims on the other?

He remembered a famous film – Strangers on a Train, where two strangers agree to swap murders so there'll be no link between attacker and victim. Is this what he'd found, he wondered?

More to have something to do than for any other reason, Jonah Googled Andrew McRae. He had the most extensive online presence of all four of them. Through his dealership, and political ambitions, there were a few potted biographies of him online. Jonah thought that if he could find a link between McRae and one victim, he could start to prove something.

Skim reading, Jonah failed to find any references to Worksop, Southend or Bournemouth in Andrew's life. He had grown up in a Bedfordshire commuter town, attended University of Swindon then moved to Shropshire. He then did a search of the known information on the three victims, but none of them were university educated, and had never been near either Swindon or Bedfordshire.

So, there probably wasn't some great murder swap, Strangers on a Train conspiracy. He couldn't see any way that four university students would all have someone they'd want to kill never mind how they would meet and exchange names.

University reminded Jonah of something, so he now moved Peter Calne over to the left, as he was at university with the other four. Maybe he was the first accident or victim or whatever. He hadn't been in the gun club, so maybe he hadn't been a part of their gang. Whatever they were up to, maybe it started with Peter and spread outward from there.

Over the next twenty years, there would have to have been a conspiracy to keep silence, maybe one that was slowly unravelling. Which one was panicking, Jonah wondered? McRae on the verge of parliament, or Mike beset by the police at every turn? But, if that was the case, then why had Patrick felt so guilty?

Jonah went back to his original plan, the four members of the gun club in a list on the left. Then, as if he was a magician doing a card trick, he held the remaining four names in his hand. He dealt Emma Walters to lie next to Patrick. He looked at the remaining three victims and considered what he knew about the other three members. Mike was supposed to be big and strong, so he put Peter Calne down next to Mike Khan. That left two victims, Bill

Wormslea and Justin Day. He remembered what the gun club president had said about Elizabeth being an expert shot and placed Bill down next to her. So, then, he thought, Andrew McRae was paired up with Justin Day. He liked that arrangement, as this was the one murder involving vehicles and McRae was now selling cars.

He looked down at the desk, four victims and four suspects? He swept everything into one big messy pile and screwed it into a ball. As an experienced policeman he knew it was never that simple. Elizabeth could have surprised Peter with a baseball bat. Patrick might have had a lucky shot. Anyone could have stabbed Emma or shot Justin. Just because they lined up, didn't make it so. Until he had a motive, and maybe some evidence, he couldn't move anything forward.

CHAPTER 19

THE ENTIRE DRIVE NORTH, Jonah told himself he was making a mistake. He was putting his career on the line. He was betting everything on a half-baked theory he had cooked up with Farida. But then he thought of those names on bits of paper, moving on his desk, lining up so neatly.

He had tossed and turned all night, trying to see if there was any other option. He could however think of only one way to tell if his theory was correct – confront Andrew.

The M50 unwound in front of the car. This early in the morning it was totally deserted, two lanes up and two down carving their way through the woods and countryside of the Welsh Marches. Jonah knew that the best way to catch someone like Andrew was to turn up at his house early in the morning. Somewhere around half past eight would do the trick. Catch him over breakfast before he left for work – if he was going in.

Finally, he was moving through the Shropshire countryside, looking for one very isolated house. Thankfully the driveway gate was open, so Jonah could drive straight up to the front door.

It was one of those strange houses that sat alone at the edge of a village, on a slight rise so it could be seen from miles around. It was square and Georgian, all yellow brick and sash frames. It looked like a four-bedroom house and Jonah briefly wondered if there was a family anywhere that he hadn't yet found out about. There was one car on the drive, a low-slung Mercedes.

Andrew McRae himself opened the door and his face registered genuine surprise. "You?" he said finally. Jonah was once again amazed by the obvious charisma of Andrew. Even this early in the morning, he was well turned out in an ironed shirt and pressed chinos. Not a hair was out of place and he was at ease.

"Me," Jonah said. "Can I come in?"

"All right then," he said warily. "You've got a nerve coming here. I could phone my solicitor right now, get him here to witness you harassing a businessman."

"You could..." Jonah nodded in agreement, following him down a corridor to a kitchen at the back of the house. Everything Jonah had seen indicated the house was beautiful but soulless. "...but I don't think you will." Andrew inclined his head to indicate that he should continue. "You've had plenty of chance to go official before now, and you've not taken it. If you went to an official complaint, you know how much mud I can throw. I don't know a lot about politics but I'm guessing that a selection committee wouldn't take kindly to a new candidate being mixed up with the police. I can always bandy around phrases like helping the police with their enquiries or even being deliberately obstructive."

Andrew pursed his lips and stared out at his perfectly landscaped garden. Jonah leant his stick against a cupboard and used the action as an excuse to glance around the kitchen. It looked like something out of a magazine – beautifully designed and equipped, modern and up to date, but betraying no hint of personality. The only disturbance was one chair pulled away from the table, where Andrew had obviously been sitting, eating toast, drinking coffee and reading the paper.

"So, you're prepared to gamble on mutually assured destruction? That if I try to take you down, you'll drag me with you?" Andrew asked, and Jonah nodded, "I'll concede I hadn't thought you would be that desperate. Okay then, it must be important." He stopped and went to the filter machine. "How rude of me. You've obviously driven a long way to see me, would you like a coffee? I can assure you it's the best, I don't tolerate anything less."

Jonah waited for him to make the coffee. He had come here to see McRae's reaction to the list, so he wanted his undivided attention. He thought that McRae would try to mask his true feelings, so he needed to be careful.

Finally, they were sitting with their coffees. "So, what brings you here," McRae asked as genially as a politician about to be interviewed for a Sunday colour supplement feature.

"You know Patrick left a list behind, with your name on it, among others." Andrew leaned forward. "So, I thought I'd tell you who was on it. You, of course, and your friends from university, Elizabeth Barry and Mike Khan."

Andrew held up a hand, "I wouldn't say friends. I'll accept that our paths may have crossed, but given your dire warnings about the selection committee, I won't have it said that I was a friend to a drug dealer."

"Your paths did cross, together with Patrick's, at the shooting club," Jonah corrected him and Andrew nodded. "But I'll accept that it was a long time ago. I'm more interested in the other names on the list. Peter Calne, Emma Walters, Bill Wormslea and Justin Day." There was a slight twitch at the last name, but to Jonah it looked more like a half-smile, a fleeting expression of self-satisfaction.

"There was something about a student who fell off a walkway and ended up in a coma, happened while I was at university," Andrew said frowning. "Was that Peter Calne?" Jonah nodded. "The other three, no idea," he said shrugging.

"Oh well," Jonah said, "it was a long shot."

"Was that it? You drove all this way for that? You could have phoned or emailed."

"I must admit, I wanted to see how you lived. You learn a lot about someone from their home."

"Nothing to hide," Andrew said, "but I hope you'll excuse me if I don't give you a guided tour."

"Not at all, just wondered how you did it all, without breaking any laws?"

"That's the trouble with policemen," Andrew said, rising from his seat. "You see everything in terms of a crime being committed. Has it ever occurred to you that I worked hard, made sacrifices and had a bit of luck? Look at my year at university. As you pointed out, I was in a club with both Mike Khan and Patrick Kinsale. Whereas I have made a success of my life, Patrick ended up living on the streets and Mike as a hardened criminal. It's just statistics. Probably ten or twenty of my alumni made it to be millionaires, along with me. Out of a thousand or so students, it's only a few per cent. Likewise, ultimately, Patrick was just a statistic. Some of our year were bound to end up homeless." Jonah could sense that Andrew was getting into his stride with a lecture so he only half-listened while considering what he'd learnt so far. "I came up in the whole time when Thatcher was a dirty word, until Blair came along to make us all feel good about ourselves again. But this," he waved his arm around the kitchen, "is the result of old-fashioned values. Did you know I still go into the dealership? I read the papers, not just the Financial Times, but the red tops too. That way I can see how the people are thinking, whether they're scared and want cheap cars, or if they feel good and want something flashy. My degree was economics, and this is the sharp end. It is theory put into practice, and if it isn't done right, then the business collapses.

"I know what you're thinking, why did I succeed where others failed? I don't know, and if you did know you wouldn't be a detective, scrabbling around with pieces of paper. You'd be writing books with titles like 'The Secret of Success' and 'Reprogram Your Life'."

Jonah wondered what he was hiding. While the speech had been excellently delivered, he did seem to be protesting a bit much. He was hiding something, Jonah decided, and he'd find out what. This whole kitchen, and indeed the house, were a stage set. It had been dressed to show off to the world how successful Andrew McRae had become. Even the coffee, which he had to reluctantly admit was the best he'd had, was part of the show.

"So, you just happen to have been lucky?" Jonah asked.

"Lucky and hardworking, and intelligent," Andrew corrected. He glanced theatrically up at the clock. "Was there anything else? I have to get on with the day."

"No, no," Jonah said, "you have been helpful. Really, thank you."

Before he knew it, Jonah was driving back south. Happy, he thought. Justin Day's name had made Andrew McRae happy. He was sure now that's what he'd seen in Andrew's face for a fraction of a second. Satisfaction at a job well done, he wondered?

CHAPTER 20

When nearly a week had gone by, Jonah assumed that the trail, like all the others had gone cold. He had initially been excited by the link between Patrick and Emma and then with the news from Shropshire. Something was finally starting to shake free. But now he was not so sure. In the quiet moments at work, he still tended to stare at the list, trying to see the links. But now it was more like a meditation, something familiar when his brain was in neutral. At night, he shut his eyes and saw those seven names, moving past each other in endless different combinations.

The office was quiet, and Jonah had the frayed photocopy in his hands again. He was jolted out of his reverie by a phone call. Refolding the paper, he picked up the phone.

"Hello, is that DS Greene? This is Jonathon Gardner."

He racked his brains for a moment, before saying "Oh, Elizabeth's husband?"

"For my sins, yes," he answered. Over the phone he sounded calm and confident, instantly assuming familiarity with Jonah. "I know it's a bit irregular, but she asked me to pass on a message to you."

"That's fine," Jonah reassured him. "I contacted her on a police matter, but then we became friends."

"She wanted me to tell you that we've been burgled. It rather looks as though someone was targeting us."

"Burgled? What was taken? Was anyone hurt?"

"Yep. Only expensive stuff that we can replace. Nothing that was personal. It'll be a pain going through insurance but that's what it's there for. And no, we were out at the time."

"Is that why you think you were targeted?"

"Well, when we went down to the Cotswolds for the weekend, we found that the house had been ransacked. We had to stay in a hotel and sort out all the police, insurance and everything else over the weekend. But, when we got back to London, the exact same thing had happened to our flat."

Jonah nodded, even though Jonathon couldn't see him. "That is odd. Why isn't Elizabeth telling me about this?"

"Ah, erm," Jonathon's confidence had a momentary falter. "Well, as I'm sure you realise, being her friend, she can be a bit, er, delicate and at times erratic. As I'm sure you can understand, these events have been most upsetting for her."

"Yes," Jonah searched for tactful words to describe his experience of Elizabeth. In the end he failed and asked a question. "Where is she at the moment?"

"Ah, she's gone to a convent," he chuckled softly. "Oh, that sounds so Dickensian, doesn't it? I don't know if you're aware of this, but Elizabeth gets great solace from her problems in the church. As far as I'm aware, they don't usually take guests or offer retreats, but she's grown very close to some of the nuns over the years. As I said, she does find the modern world so overwhelming and when things get a bit much, she can go up there to find her balance again."

"Would that be the Mission of Bethesda and something or other?" Jonah asked.

"The Ministry of Capernaum and Bethesda," Jonathon confirmed, surprise in his voice. "Did she mention it to you?"

"Yes," Jonah lied.

"Oh, well, she must trust you. But I take it then that you know not to bother her. She never stays more than a couple of weeks, but it must be absolute seclusion."

"No, no, that's fine. Understood. I know you said that the burglary upset her this time, but I can't help wondering if anything initially caused her, er, problems?"

"Not that I know of," Jonathon said. "When I met her, she was already struggling a bit. I went into the marriage with my eyes open, I knew she needed shielding from the world, protecting a bit. But I'm painting a very bleak picture here. Most of the time, she's witty and charming, such a quick mind and a warm heart. I know it's old fashioned and sexist, but I wouldn't have got to where I am without her. She can attend a cocktail party or whip up a dinner for guests perfectly. And without that in your armoury, your career as a hedge fund manager won't go far.

"You have to remember there might be no ghosts in her past, no skeletons in her closet. Sometimes, it's just the way we're built, you know. Like being born with a gammy leg or something." He paused to think, then continued. "But, something in these last few weeks has upset her. I wish I knew what it was so I could help. I haven't seen her this distracted since we first got together."

"You met just out of university, didn't you?"

"Well, I was over five years out, but she's younger than me, so yes I suppose so."

"Hmm, and no idea if something at university made her delicate? Upset her?"

"No, she never really talked about that, and we had very few friends in common. I know a few years doesn't sound like much now, but she was twenty-two and I was twenty-eight when we met. In university terms, that's different worlds."

"Thanks for that though," Jonah said, "and thanks for passing on the message."

"Oh God, yes! The message! Can I give you the crime numbers, could you have a chat with the local police? Make sure they're doing everything they can?"

"Of course," said Jonah, "I'll do what I can. But don't get your hopes up, they'll probably be Gloucestershire and the Met, so I don't hold much sway there. But I can certainly give the files a once-over and make sure nothing's been missed."

"I would appreciate that, and I know that Elizabeth would too," Jonathon said, before handing over the reference numbers.

With nothing better to do, he pulled the keyboard closer and started looking for details of the contacts in Gloucestershire and the Met. He decided the quickest way through the morass of bureaucracy was to talk on the phone. As he expected, the officers assigned to the case were only too glad to hand over the details. Any help in getting another case closed would be welcome. For good measure he fired off an email to the insurance loss adjuster as well.

With all the requests sent in and nothing else to do but wait, he went for lunch. He found Farida on a bench in the corner of Gorsedd Park. She looked guilty when he sat next to her, and he knew that, as he suspected, she really had been avoiding him.

"I've been warned," was how Farida greeted Jonah. "My boss had a closer look at our little trip down the M4 and he wasn't too happy. Nothing official but he's dropping snide hints about keeping a closer eye on me and making jokes about accountants."

"Do you think McRae had a hand in it?"

"Could have, but I was thinking about that."

"Go on."

"Well," Farida said, "if McRae does lodge a formal complaint against either of us, then our only real way to retaliate is to pass our information to the selection committee and expose him."

"Yes, and that's why we're holding him at bay."

"But are we?" Farida was getting more passionate. "What do we have? A couple of unrecorded conversations where he may or may not have denied knowing people twenty years ago."

"But I've got the lists," Jonah said with outrage. "I can prove they were all in the same shooting club at the same time."

"And," said Farida, just as passionately, "so what! He'll just claim that he got confused and couldn't remember what had happened. He hadn't met any of these people for years and couldn't bring their names to mind. Your real problem then is the same as it always has been – you're not investigating a crime. You can't point the finger and accuse him of anything."

Jonah sat back, deep in thought. "So why are we still in our jobs? He's treading very lightly here. If what you're saying is right, then he could launch a formal complaint. We've been acting out of area without authority, harassing him, asking him questions. We've broken half a dozen guidelines. You're right, even my evidence of the firearms licenses is from another force, I really shouldn't have that either. And it doesn't prove anything."

"You still think he's guilty of something, don't you?" Farida asked and Jonah nodded. "Well, if you can't get to McRae, what about Khan? How did that contact I gave you play out?"

Jonah recounted what he'd learned, both about the informant and the nightclub fire.

"I mean, it is useful," Jonah said, "and I'm grateful. But it's the same as the stuff on McRae. There's nothing we can use. If I go back there, the wife will clam up and I'm already known to West Midlands. They'd shut me down so fast if I even hinted at what they told me."

Farida shook her head, then said, "Anyway, it's all immaterial. I don't know what kind of game you're playing, or even who the other players are but I'm out. I've come close to getting something on my record already and I certainly don't want to get involved with undercover work from another force." There was another awkward pause, "Jonah, I need to ask you something." Jonah looked at her, hearing the nervousness in her voice. "I need to know what happened. You know, before you had your time off. People in the office are saying that I shouldn't be seen with you, that you can't be relied on."

Jonah sighed. "Is that what they're saying? That I let people down?"

"Well, yes," Farida looked slightly embarrassed, "but it's not easy to tell if they're just trying to put me off or if there's something behind it."

"Why does it matter?" Jonah snapped.

"It matters," Farida said icily, "because I don't want to believe bad things of my friends. I don't want to just feed the rumour mill all around the office."

"Really? You've already made your choice, just walk away from me."

"I'm not walking away because of what people are saying," Farida said angrily. "I'm not even believing what they're saying. I'm trying to protect my career. Losing our jobs won't make anything any easier."

Jonah deflated. "Well, what you heard is true. I can't be trusted. There was a drug raid, routine stuff. But there were a series of fuckups all the way along. A kid that I knew vaguely ran straight past me when I was well placed to stop him." Jonah stood up, sick of the whole conversation. "So, in truth, they're probably right. I am a cancer to people's careers. I've been the reason a colleague got stabbed, and now I'm dragging you down with me too. Well I like you too much to ruin your career as well." He stalked off without waiting for a reply.

For the next couple of days Jonah kept his head down and worked with a sense of grim determination. He was already avoiding his colleagues in the canteen and now didn't want to go to Cathays Park either. So he was reduced to eating his sandwiches at his desk, which just made his mood blacker. On the third day of his self-imposed exile, the morning brought all three responses to his queries about the burglaries at Elizabeth's properties. In the police internal mail, he had one CD and a memory stick. The loss adjuster had emailed a preliminary report across as well.

Jonah opened the files and read them all through trying to put them together into one narrative.

At first it looked simple; the Gardners were rich and their TV and stereo were definitely high-end. The cottage was a weekend retreat, so it was an easy target. Scanning down the insurance list, Jonah raised his eyebrows. Even the phone was Bang and Olufsen! Then on the next page he found the repair bills. An eye watering amount to an upholsterer to repair the three-piece suite. Flicking forward to the photos he found that every piece had been flipped over and the lining slashed from corner to corner.

He pushed back from his desk and frowned. The burglar hadn't deliberately destroyed the furniture – he'd simply opened it up as efficiently as possible. Was he looking for something? Jonah pulled himself back to the desk and flipped between the photos and repair bills. The frozen food was all dumped in the sink, the plinths taken off the kitchen units. Upstairs, the bath panels had been removed and the airing cupboard emptied. Similarly, the bedrooms had been searched.

He almost wondered if he was dealing with an off-duty police officer. Except that most of the searches he'd seen carried out had left more mess than this. Whoever did it knew what they were looking for. He flicked back to the photo of the frozen food in the sink. None of the packets were emptied out, so the burglar wasn't looking for something small and easily hidden like drugs, jewellery or any memory stick or card. Yet, they were looking inside furniture, under drawers. He rubbed his eyes and tried to figure out what the intruder was looking for.

Looking through the floor plan and the list of damage, Jonah could see that the entire house had been searched. He frowned, trying to get into the intruder's mind. Taking the TV and other equipment was window dressing. Somehow, he'd bypassed both the lock and alarm without damage. The first room he came to contained everything he stole. Yet, he took the time to methodically search the entire house, as quietly and efficiently as possible.

Jonah got up from his desk and paced around his room. He returned to his desk and skimmed over the Met Police report of the break-in at the Docklands flat. It was so similar he believed the same person carried out both, waiting until the first crime was discovered before committing the second. No room in either property was ignored. This implied that whoever was searching, they hadn't found what they were looking for.

Was this the elusive proof, that Elizabeth had constantly teased him with? And if so, who was looking for it? Andrew McRae or Mike Khan or someone else? Mike Khan had already targeted Elizabeth Gardner and was a criminal. He would have access to a professional burglar and the money to pay them.

But it could also be Andrew McRae, as he too certainly had the money. But then he remembered the newspaper clipping. Whoever arranged that series of car purchases and burnings was sending a message. Not to DS Jonah Greene, but to Andrew McRae. Taken together with the fact that Elizabeth was followed and burgled, and that he himself had been attacked twice and probably followed, there was only one conclusion. Something had seriously upset Mike Khan. So seriously that he was exerting whatever influence he had to shut it down.

Or, he thought, was there another actor in the drama? Maybe the four or five of them at university had uncovered a serial killer? One who was smart enough to spread his crimes around the country, using different methods. Except that they all felt guilty. Jonah rubbed his eyes in frustration. He was missing a part of puzzle. He got out his private folder, that held the list and his informal record of his conversations with Elizabeth.

He picked out phrases 'we're all guilty' and 'we made him'. Something definitely happened twenty years ago, but until Elizabeth gave him any more information, he would just go around in circles in his head.

His musings were interrupted by his phone. He frowned at the text – his children had summoned him to a meeting that evening.

JONAH SAT in the pub and looked at his two children. It was still a bit weird to see them in a pub having drinks. He'd spent so much of his life protecting them and now it was hard to accept them as adults even though they were old enough.

Gareth appeared too big for any table he sat at – long and rangy, he had to fold himself into the chair. He put his pint in front of himself and handed a strange coloured drink to Emily. His daughter took more after her mother – she was small and fey with short blonde hair framing her attractive face. Jonah could sometimes look at her and see who she was – not just his daughter – but also a pretty woman. She had high cheekbones, blue eyes and a tiny upturned nose. When he could see her beauty, it scared him, because she was often away in the clouds and wouldn't see the danger until it was too late. Jonah tried to push the thoughts out of his mind – the dangers of being both a policeman and a father.

"So," Jonah said, breaking the awkward silence, "this is new." Having left home, his children would usually pop into the family home when they needed something. Failing that, they would communicate by a combination of phone, text, email and Facebook. Being summoned to the pub by both of them was indeed new, and in his mind, serious.

Emily shot a mutinous look under her brows at her

brother. Clearly this wasn't a joint plan. Gareth caught the look. "Don't give me the evils, Em, you know we need to do this."

"Okay, okay, it's just, you know, awkward, isn't it?"

"Still needs to be done though," Gareth said. Jonah was now seeing what he'd always known would happen. The younger brother was proving more mature than his sister.

"Look you two." Jonah took charge. "It's lovely to see you in the pub and share a drink. And don't think I'm not enjoying the double act. All the sideways glances and winks – very funny. But seriously, what's bothering you?"

"Well, it's Mum," Gareth said. Jonah had suspected this was the answer as Alex was usually part of any family discussions. Her absence was more noticeable than her presence would have been. Gareth looked at Emily who was still keeping quiet. "Emily said, that she'd seen Mum, you know in the sort of pubs and places that she goes in."

"I don't always drink in biker pubs," Emily protested. "But you know when there's a good band on, or we get invited by someone..." She sipped her cocktail.

"But, well," Gareth picked up her thread, "it's a bit weird isn't it? I mean we have our places, and you know, you, er, older people, are another generation."

"We should keep to our old fogey's pubs?" Jonah asked mischievously.

"No! It's not that. It's just that, well, we're a bit worried about her."

"You're worried about Mum because she's drinking in the wrong pubs?"

"No! Yes! You don't think that it's a bit weird?"

"I don't know if you realise this," Jonah said, already weary of the conversation, "but we did have a life before children. And your mother has always been quite a bit younger than me. Maybe you might even say that she was younger than me in spirit as well as in years. But she is an adult and she can go where she wants and drink in whatever pubs she likes."

"Yes, but," Emily pleaded, "having your Mum turn up at the pub in leather, with a motorbike. Isn't that just a bit, creepy? And don't give me all that free spirit stuff. She wasn't like this a few years ago. If we go home, we like to know that Mum will be there for us, not roaring around the countryside on her motorbike."

"So, you think she should just stay home waiting to put your washing through, with a big casserole in the oven in case you're hungry?"

"No!" Gareth stepped in this time. "No, it's just that we're worried. Her behaviour seems to have changed and we don't think it's good." He paused to look at Emily, to see if he should change tack. She gave a small nod. "Well, it's just that, you know, we have heard, sometimes, at these pubs, they sell stuff. And you're a policeman, so..."

"I'm not on drug squad or vice," Jonah explained quietly. "Also, your mother is a professional, she works for the hospital and I think she's aware of what my job is. So, I don't think there's anything to worry about."

"So, you're really not worried," Emily asked. "You don't think she's behaving oddly?"

Jonah considered the question. He was worried about Alex, of course he was. But he wasn't about to be lectured on his relationship by his own children. He wasn't even willing to admit to them how much he was concerned. He took a deep breath. "All right, all right! I think that there is something going on. But it's not news to me. I am keeping an eye on things, I do know which pubs she drinks in, where she goes on that bike of hers."

"And you're okay with that?" Emily asked.

"I am, and if I am, you should be too! I don't like you dragging me here and quizzing me about the state of my marriage!"

"But she's our mother as well," Gareth said. "And we've been watching both of you and talking to each other for a while now. It doesn't seem to getting better."

"It doesn't have to get better!" Jonah said sharply. "Because there's nothing wrong. When you two are older, have grown up a bit, you'll realise that relationships don't stay static. People grow and change and as long as they grow and change together, then there isn't a problem. And that's how it is with your mum and me. We're fine!"

The three of them sat around their table without saying anything. Behind Gareth, the door opened, and a swirl of cold air swept into the pub. Jonah sipped his pint. He didn't want to make the situation worse by storming out. The last thing he needed now was to start a family feud. If he was honest with himself there was something awry in his relationship with Alex. But he was stymied as to how to fix it and was damned if he'd start taking advice from his own children.

"How's your new job?" Gareth asked in a conciliatory tone.

"Not too bad." Jonah shrugged. "It sounded good at first, more investigating, but it all becomes routine."

"But you spend all day with dead bodies!" Emily sounded outraged.

"I'm not a pathologist," Jonah said gently. "Mostly it's paperwork. Even when you die, there are lots of rules and regulations. Believe me, there's a proper way to do it – preferably in hospital with lots of doctors. But if you do die in another way then it's my job to find out who, where, why and how. Lots of forms to fill out."

"You make it sound all like boring or something." Emily sounded disappointed.

"I know you think I'm like some kind of hero," Jonah admitted, "but it is a lot of paperwork."

"Yes, but what about your knee? That seems better, I noticed you've left the stick at home."

"I was mugged for my laptop," Jonah explained. "That could have happened to anyone."

"Well, you did hang on to it though," Gareth said. After that, conversation died for a moment. Jonah thought he ought to reciprocate and he wanted to change the subject, so he asked after Gareth's class.

"Yeah," Gareth nodded thoughtfully, "yeah, it's good." He paused to think. "You know how I've been doing some DIY and odd jobs? Gets a bit of extra money in. Well, all the plumbing out there, most of it is just bodged. A lot of what I'm doing is just fixing other people's mistakes. I know what I'd like to do eventually. New builds and designing systems from scratch. You know, get it right from the start."

Jonah nodded, realising once again that his children were growing away from him. In a way it was the end of his job, to send them out into the world, part him, part Alex and part themselves. Secretly he was glad that Gareth was finding his place in the world, even though it gave him a moment of sadness. Jonah set his empty glass down.

"Are we okay?" he asked, indicating his empty glass. "Cos you know, this isn't really my kind of pub." Emily and Gareth gave embarrassed smiles and nodded. That was all Jonah needed so he excused himself and left. For the next few hours, he felt good about the state of his family.

CHAPTER 21

"JONAH IS THAT YOU?" Elizabeth sounded frantic.

"Of course it's me, who else would it be?" Jonah was irritated. Alex hadn't come home yet, and he was waiting for her to phone. That evening's conference with his children had put him on edge. If they'd ganged up on him, it must be serious.

"Are you okay?"

"Me, I'm fine," Jonah said, "why wouldn't I be?"

"I," Elizabeth hesitated, "I need to know where you live. Your address."

"My address? Why on earth would you want to know that?" Jonah said, still thinking about Alex.

"I've got, a contact, a friend, no not really a friend, someone I employ. He does a very dangerous job for me; he looks at Mike's computer."

"What do you mean? Looks at? Mike Khan?"

"Yes!" Now Elizabeth was exasperated, "Mike Khan! I've got someone spying on his computer. They sent a virus or something and now they can see what he does, without even having to break in. I told him to tell me anything out of the ordinary. He phoned me this evening and told me that Mike's looking at Google Maps, for directions to a place in South Wales somewhere. It's near Cardiff somewhere, so it reminded me of you. But if Mike's heading your way, well it can't be good can it?"

"So, Elizabeth," Jonah said slowly, "why don't you just tell me the address? If it's mine, I'll lock my doors and make sure my family is safe."

"And if it's not, you can phone up someone at work and they can check it out. They'll listen to you, won't they?"

Jonah went silent. He couldn't tell Elizabeth that his currency was very low with CID at the moment. That Elizabeth didn't appear anywhere on record and would have to go down as 'information received'. He might be able to phone the local station and ask them to swing by. But if he made it official, it'd get back to his boss and if he didn't then they might not do anything. He supposed he could swing by and have a look, once he was sure Alex was safe. Suddenly he realised that he hadn't answered. He said, more kindly than before, "Give me the address and I'll see what I can do."

"Twenty-four Mountain View, Aberdare," she said, and he wrote it down automatically.

He gave a short burst of laughter, relief that there wasn't one more problem for him. "No, that's a good hour or so north of Cardiff. But it is in our force's area, I'll see who I know up there."

"Thank you for trusting me," Elizabeth said, the closest she could come to an apology.

"Right." Jonah didn't know how to deal with contrite Elizabeth. "I'd better make some calls, see what Mike is up to."

When the call was over, he sat at his desk in his office for a moment. Northern Division, he thought, all the way up in Aberdare, properly into the Valleys. It felt like a world away from the inner-city policing of Cardiff. Aberdare had lost its station a few years ago, so it'd either be Pontypridd or Merthyr – both open until midnight. He pulled an old road map down from a shelf above the computer, flicked it open and decided that Merthyr was much closer, and bigger. He looked up their number on the computer and scribbled it down underneath the address. It was already past half ten so they'd be busy with the pubs chucking out and rounding up teenagers. He needed to consider his approach carefully. He was a DS so they would go out to an address if he asked, but an official report would be made. It all came down to how much he trusted Elizabeth. She had alternately helped and hindered him in the past and in no way could she be described as stable.

His reverie was broken by the phone ringing again. Worried about this new problem, he had temporarily forgotten all about waiting for Alex. It was nearing eleven and she still hadn't got in touch.

"Hello?" Jonah wondered what else the night would bring.

"Hi, is that Jonah Greene? Detective Sergeant Greene?" The voice was quiet even though there was quite a lot of noise in the background.

"Yes, who's calling?" Jonah asked this even though he could recognise the police manner easily.

"It's Sergeant Jones, on the desk at Barry Police Station," the voice continued, still quiet. "Nothing to worry about, no one hurt, nothing like that. Just thought you might like to know that we scooped up your wife, Alexandra Greene in a routine operation."

"What happened?"

"Some locals thought they'd be hard nuts and started

taunting some bikers down on the front. When they threw some chips at them, there was a bit of pushing and shoving. For what it's worth, it looks like your missus was trying to make peace. But you know what it's like – you get a van and round all of them up, sort it out later. Anyway, we're processing them all here, before they get transported over to Cardiff Bay." There was a short pause, and Jonah imagined the man checking he wasn't being overheard. "Thing is, if you were to get here, say within the hour, well, we might not have got around to processing her by then. And if you wanted to give her a lift home, make sure she's okay, you get my drift?"

"Loud and clear," confirmed Jonah, "and I don't forget favours like this either." Elizabeth and her problems were nearly pushed from his mind – at the last minute he tore off the page with the Aberdare address and folded it into his pocket.

On the drive out to Barry, Jonah's mind was whirling. He needed to do something, take a risk, make a change somewhere. In the end he reached his decision, as he pulled in as close to the station as he could get.

When he approached the front desk, the sergeant half turned and called out to someone in the back, "Cover the front desk for a moment, I'm taking a smoke break."

He nodded briefly to Jonah who fell into step beside him. They walked around the back as he lit a cigarette. Taking a deep drag, he said, "Where are you parked?"

Jonah nodded to his car, and the sergeant continued, "Okay, wait there, she'll come out in a minute, she hasn't been processed yet."

Within minutes, Jonah and Alex were driving away from the city. After a while, Alex spoke, "This isn't the way home."

"No," Jonah said simply and they lapsed back into silence. After more driving through the dark, he swung off the road and into a small car park, stopping with the car facing a sheer drop.

"Do you remember," he said, "when we first met? You were up from London, visiting a friend from university and we were drinking in the rugby club." Next to him, Alex nodded in the darkness. "We got into this huge argument because you were from London and always took your holidays in Dorset and Devon. You thought that the Valleys were all pithead winding engines and slag heaps and ugly buildings."

"And you were so passionate," she said, "trying to persuade me that it was all lovely up here."

"This is where I drove you when the bar closed. This exact spot. We sat here in the darkness, waiting for the sunrise to come up. I was so nervous; in case it was one of those crap sunrises where it's all just cloudy and overcast and slowly gets light."

"It would still have been beautiful," Alex said quietly. "It was just the thought, that you were bothered to take me, you know. Most blokes just show off and are all macho and stupid and hope that's enough to get you into bed."

"Then, the sun came up and there were these clouds that lit up all gold underneath. It was so good you got out of the car and danced, even though it was drizzling out there."

"You must've thought I was mad!" Alex laughed. This wasn't any part of Jonah's strategy. He just knew that he had to take action to save his marriage and he'd wanted to come back to the beginning, to where it had been good before. He thought that if they could remember when it had been good, when the spark was there, then there was a chance for them.

Somehow, a blockage was lifted and they chatted more naturally than they had in ages. They ranged back and forth across the years, remembering the births and marriages, the events that bound them together. For once there was no recrimination and they both seemed to know what to say. Jonah felt that he'd met an old friend he hadn't spoken to in years and was catching up.

Finally, as the sky started lightening, about an hour before sunrise, they lapsed into silence and half-dozed in the grey light.

"Look!" Alex said bringing Jonah out of his light sleep. "Look at the sunrise, the clouds!" She sounded like a small child at Christmas. The sun was still below the horizon, but rays of light were coming up, striking the horizontal bands of cloud that lay in front of them. Against the deep blue of the pre-dawn sky bands of pure gold were lighting up.

"Just like the first time we met," Jonah said sleepily.

"Do you think it's a sign?"

"I don't think there are signs in the universe," Jonah said. "I think you work hard and get what you're owed." After another moment, he asked, "Are you going to get out and dance?"

Alex shook her head. "No, not this time. How did you remember where it was?"

"I come up here sometimes when I need to think."

"And now?"

"Well, we need to figure out what's gone wrong with us," Jonah said, staring out through the windscreen.

"I hope you don't mind," Alex said, "but I've been talking to someone."

"What do you mean talking?"

"Well at work I know a psychiatrist, as a friend. I've seen

her a few times over lunch and after work. You know, just to talk things through."

"You never really liked me having counselling though, did you?" Jonah countered. "Once I had some time off work."

"No, I've been trying to figure out why I do things and why some things annoy me. Why I don't like the idea. I think it all goes back to my father, you know."

Jonah gave a snort, either of disgust or humour. Alex's father had taken off when she was young, and her mother had had no end of trouble. Even though she'd tried to insulate her daughter it was obviously a hard life. On the rare occasions she talked about it, Jonah learned that on more than one occasion they had moved suddenly to avoid either debt collectors or unsuitable stepfathers.

"I know, I know, it's very cliched. But I think that's why I fell in love with you in the first place. You were the opposite of my father – a rugby playing policeman, you couldn't have been more stable if you tried."

"It does sound all a bit Freudian," Jonah observed.

"But it matters, because that's who I fell in love with. Of course," she said, seeing Jonah's stricken face, "there's more to it than that. It's you I love, but some part of my psyche needs someone to protect me, to always be there, to be fiercely loyal."

"And I haven't?"

"Well you stopped playing rugby," Alex said, "and I know how shallow that sounds. And then there was all that fuss at work, and you had some time off and I don't know. It was like my foundation was all ripped away and I had no idea what was going on. I mean, if you're the stable one and you need a therapist and can't work, where does that leave me? I behaved badly, I just reacted without thinking it through. So, you know, I think it's time I thought about it a bit, you know, found out the facts, what was really going on with you. Not just what I thought I saw. Would you mind telling me what happened on that raid?"

"Do you want me to tell you?" Jonah asked. "I thought you knew already."

Alex hung her head. "Totally honestly, I don't think I was properly listening, and you didn't want to talk about it. I was just angry at you for being weak. So, no, I don't really know what happened. Could you tell me about that day? When you, well I don't really know what happened. You came home and went off sick. I know there was a big fuss, but I never really understood."

"I didn't think you wanted to understand."

"I didn't at the time. My rock was being chipped away and I was selfish." Her big, expressive eyes were downcast, almost hidden behind her lashes. "But we're a team, we need to know what's going on to work together."

"I suppose it all started some months before. I was waiting in the car park at college to give Gareth a lift home when this lad came over to talk to me. That's quite odd because they all know he's the policeman's son and they're afraid. Anyway, this lad comes over, Jules he was called, and he actually asks me for help. His family are well known to us – petty thieves and drug dealers. So, this lad wants my help to get out of it. He's doing a motor mechanics course and is finding it hard with the money and everything. I kept putting him forward to agencies and charities, try to make him one that we don't have to arrest.

"The morning of that drug raid, we'd had an overnight tip-off. A lot of our top targets tend to drift around without a fixed address. We got a call that some of these people were at a party. So, they arrange this dawn raid to catch them all in bed.

"The whole thing was a mess from the start. I was stationed at the top of the stairs. This guy Jules is in one of the bedrooms, but the bloke who's arresting him takes his eye off the ball and gets pushed over. He comes straight towards me, doing up the belt on his jeans as he runs.

"I really can't explain it. I just stared at him and he stared at me. And so many thoughts went through my head; I could tackle him, just slam him into a wall, even push him down the stairs. He knew me so I could've tried to talk him down. Made a connection. Anything. But it was like my brain went onto overload with too many options. I just froze.

"For each of those actions, I could see what could go wrong. If I tackled him, I might end up down the stairs, or he might have a hidden weapon or a syringe. Or I might mess up and end up in front of CIB if I hurt or even killed him.

"So, there I am, at the top of the stairs like a statue and he went past me. After that it got worse, he wasn't doing up his jeans, he was releasing a belt buckle knife. Rob Ford another DC came up the hall and tackled him. He was really lucky; the knife went off the stab vest and into his shoulder. He went down, obviously, and the whole cock-up was saved by the uniform on the door. He'd seen everything and already had his baton out. Smashed Jules straight on the wrist, twisted him round and had him in cuffs before he could do any more damage." Jonah rested his head on the steering wheel, utterly defeated by the memories. "If I hadn't had such a good fed rep that would've been the end of it. The truth is, that for all the talk about stress and how the body reacts, I broke the cardinal rule. I cracked and exposed another officer to harm. I was there to stop him, and I didn't." He smiled grimly. "In a way, this started when I gave up the rugby. Some days your thoughts just run away, and you wonder if this is going to be the match that I break my leg or my neck or something goes wrong. It's when you realise that everything depends on decisions. What if I decide to go for that tackle and it's the one that hurts me? The same with the job, you start second guessing yourself, becoming incapable of making a decision." Jonah paused before pressing on. "Apparently it's a common symptom of stress. Kind of like a slow motion post-traumatic stress disorder."

"So," said Alex, as a way to marshal her thoughts, "it was kind of a breakdown?"

"Kind of. But if I'd gone to that raid and fallen down the stairs and twisted my knee, then how would that have been different? My work would necessarily have changed because I can't go out to do my job, chasing people if I've got a gammy knee."

"And my therapist said that I've got a fragile image of you. That if you had sustained physical damage then I would still have reacted the same way – withdrawing and being angry."

There was a pause between them as they both watched the sunrise over the valleys. It was one of those misty mornings where it looked as if the landscape was painted onto stage backdrops, stacked one behind the other, fading away into the distance.

"So," Jonah said, facing his darkest fears, "you fell in love with me because I was a big bear who could keep you safe? And now I'm not, now I'm the one who needs help..." He was unable to finish the question.

"No!" Alex said, "No! It's a change and we ought to..."

Jonah never found out what they ought to do. His phone rang. He fished it out and glanced at the screen with an apologetic look at Alex. "I've got to get this – it's work."

"At five in the morning?"

"It must be important," he said, pressing the button. "Hello?"

"Is that DS Jonah Greene?"

"Yes."

"Sorry to wake you, sir, but there's been a major incident in Aberdare. There's been a murder and it's nasty. My next job is to wake up the detective super and see what he wants to do. Just thought I'd give you the heads-up as the coroner's officer. You'd better get up and get yourself into work."

JONAH FELT tired and his eyes were gritty. The next meeting was scheduled to start at eleven o'clock in the morning. Apart from dozing in his car, that made nearly thirty hours without sleep for him. The Major Incident Team had been convened and officers had been assigned to Family Liaison, Scene and Exhibits.

Jonah had been summoned to the meeting in Cardiff Bay station. It was modern, deep blue carpet, lots of glass and chrome. If it was ever quiet, Jonah imagined you'd hear the walls murmuring 'policing in the twenty-first century' and 'providing a modern police service'. He shut his eyes for a minute and the whole world tilted and spun. Bad idea, he thought, and decided to abandon his search for the right meeting room and instead find some coffee.

He smiled grimly as the machine made strange noises and struggled to produce evil tasting coffee. They might have a swish new headquarters, he thought, hell they've even got a new city in the bay, but the coffee machines haven't changed at all.

He finally found the right room. It was a suitable size for seven or eight to meet, or maybe ten at a push. Now nearly twenty people were already there. The lucky ones sat at the central table, the others either sat on lone chairs or leaned against walls. Jonah checked faces and saw Farida stonily ignoring him, plus a few of his previous colleagues. No one met his eye or spoke when he entered the room.

Although it was his job to be present, Jonah felt left out so he chose a chair and placed it at the back on the other side from the door, hoping he wouldn't be noticed. He clutched his machine coffee, burnt the tip of his tongue on it, and prayed for the moment it was cool enough to drink.

In the past the room would've been thick with cigarette smoke. But now the smells were of too many people in a small room and greasy breakfast rolls. There was a hum of chatter as everyone waited for the meeting to start.

Finally, Detective Superintendent Jack Castle strode into the room looking harassed. A few more senior officers who Jonah didn't recognise followed him in and waited near the front.

"So, welcome, guys." The detective superintendent's voice rolled over the assembled officers, quieting them down almost immediately. He was a tall man, rangy, with sandy hair and sideburns. He came across as laconic, almost lazy in the way he spoke and moved, but it was a mistake to underestimate him. He was around Jonah's age and already superintendent. He clutched his hands behind his back and launched into what was clearly a prepared speech.

"The first thing I have to say is that this will be big. This is a nasty murder. It's lurid and horrible so we can expect it to get a big slice of news time, lots of space in the tabloids.

Five, ten years down the line, there'll be documentaries on Channel 5. So, this is by the book. We will not cut corners, at all!" He glared around the room, meeting as many eyes as he could. "When you look at porn, you will not do it in the same room as your work computer, you do not use your work phone. Someone sends you a funny text or silly photo or joke email, you delete it immediately and, if necessary, report the sender up the line. Soon enough the press will get bored with the victim, and they'll move on to us. I won't have any of my team tarnish our reputation.

"Similarly, we want this to get through CPS and get this bastard locked up for good. So there'll be no hunches, no lone rangers running off, no uncorroborated intelligence from unnamed sources. Everything will, as I said before, be by the book. Evidence logged, informants logged, everything logged. If it's not in the computer, it's not happening. Are we clear?" There was silence from the room. He had their full attention and there were nods of agreement.

"Now, on to what we know already. For those who haven't had the pleasure, this is DCI Dave Whitlock, based here in Cardiff Bay." He indicated a short, thickset man to his left. He had dark, thick hair and his chin was showing stubble already. "Dave has had an initial look over the crime scene, so, I'll hand over to him." He stepped to one side, nearly tripping over the two portable whiteboards that had been wheeled into the room.

"Okay, we're establishing a preliminary timeline." Dave spoke in a Welsh accent, Swansea unless Jonah was very much mistaken. "I've visited the scene and been given a walk through by forensics and these are our thoughts.

"The emergency call came through at oh five oh seven from a neighbour who was leaving for work. He saw lights on and the door open, thought it was a bit odd at that time of the morning, so he did a quick check. He saw blood everywhere and called us. Now, he didn't want to hang around, but he's okay. His boss is a slave driver and he can't afford to be late. I think between that and all the blood, he just panicked. He's a lorry driver, expected back tomorrow, we can formally interview him then."

He turned to the whiteboard, pen in hand, and spoke as he wrote "So, we have ourselves a victim, Christopher John Harris, born April 10, 1950, died last night." As these facts appeared on the board, Jonah copied them onto a form he held on a clipboard on his lap. If someone died in his area, whether it was quietly at home, in a violent murder, or anywhere in between, then it was his job to file the forms. While everyone else was sorting out motives and forensics, he'd be making sure the death certificate was in order and the relatives could bury their dead.

"Everything indicates that he was killed in his home, where we found the body." DCI Whitlock wrote the address on the board as he spoke, "Twenty-four Mountain View, Aberdare."

In a trance, Jonah reached into his pocket and smoothed out the crumpled piece of paper he found in there. He gave a nervous glance at the other people in the room, but no one was paying him any attention. He looked from the paper to the board, but since the phone call calling him into work, he had known. It was inconceivable that he'd been warned about a maniac coming to a small town like Aberdare, and then, hours later, he would get a second call about an unconnected murder. Numbly he copied the address onto the form.

"We think Chris opened his front door sometime last night. It was dark, and he's not expecting anyone, so he puts the chain on the door. But, our suspect is powerful, so they just smash the door open, rip out the screws on the chain. It was a fairly shoddy one, and the force was enough to twist the door and damage the hinges. We found some blood drops in the hallway and the victim had his nose broken. We're assuming that either he got smacked in the face by the door or once it was open our killer punched him. I've put forensics onto it to check the door, but it doesn't really matter." He turned to the other board and labelled that one 'Suspect'. Under that heading he wrote 'physically strong'.

"Up to this point, what we're looking at is something very like the way we or the army would force entry to a property – quick and hard. Smash the door open, overwhelm whoever's inside. Although, hopefully, none of us would deliberately break someone's nose!" There was a murmur around the room, they had found the joke funny, but this wasn't the place for open laughter.

"Now Chris is ex-army but he's also sixty-five, so he's probably on his knees at this point. This is where we get into the psychology of our attacker. He could've pulled out the sword or a knife right there and finished it. In and out inside a minute, much safer. Instead, he drags his victim into the kitchen and duct tapes him to a chair." At the mention of duct tape, Jonah's head snapped up. He still hadn't been able to rid himself of the images planted in his head. Some poor Confidential Informant taped to a chair and then tortured and killed. When he'd got the call from Elizabeth, he'd imagined Mike bringing his brand of chaos to his own area. But he'd never thought it would happen. "Then he goes to work on him for, well who knows how long, all the cuts were painful, certainly, but not enough to kill him. Then he beheads him with two or three massive blows from a very sharp sword." There were more murmurs around the room at this point. Rumours about the crime had been swirling around the station, but this was the first official confirmation.

"Now we're going to have to work with experts here but swords like that aren't ten a penny. We're probably looking Japanese or Chinese, properly sharpened. The initial analysis from the smaller cuts is that it was extremely sharp. And obviously to remove the head it had to be quite sizeable as well. A preliminary theory is that all the injuries could have been inflicted by the same weapon. Once the post-mortem comes in, we'll be sure." Samurai sword, Jonah thought, it was a bloody samurai sword. Have I just ended my career? The DCI's opening remarks came back to him – by the book, no unregistered informants. The DI carried on talking over Jonah's turbulent thoughts.

"Somehow our suspect then leaves the scene. We'll wait for house to house to complete before we know if he was seen. In his favour, it could have been after midnight. Counting against him, he'd have been dripping with blood and carrying a big sword. All the way through I've been saying 'he' because it's probably a male suspect. The force to not only open, but damage the door, the strength needed to behead someone, all suggest a male. But I'm not ruling out a strong female, someone tall who plays rugby for example."

A hand came up on the left side. "I know no one else is going to say it, so can I just raise the issue. What about Muslim extremists? Ex army, beheaded?" There was a rustle around the room as they turned to stare at the DC who'd asked the question. Farida didn't know where to look. "The press are going to get there soon enough," he said defensively.

"No, no, valid point," said the DCI, flicking through his notebook before transferring details to the board, speaking as he did so. "Enlisted in 1968, served sixteen years, left in

1984. So," he paused, obviously thinking out loud, "way too early for any action in Iraq or Afghanistan. We're waiting for the army archives to send over details of where he was posted but I'd imagine we will be looking at Northern Ireland, followed up by the Falklands, maybe West Germany. But what's clear is that there is no indication whatsoever that there is a radical, terrorist aspect to this at all. He was out of the army over thirty years ago, towards the end of the cold war. It was a different time, the enemy then was the Russians, not the Arabs." He picked out a dour looking man with thinning hair, halfway down on the right. "Rob, could you look into that? We'll need to get his army career, as much detail as possible. It's not likely that someone would bear a grudge over thirty years, but let's cover it, okay?"

He turned back to talk to the room as a whole. "Initial forensics is quite disappointing; our suspect probably wore gloves. Obviously, there is a lot of blood and if our killer has cut himself in the attack it'll be a while before we find out if any of this blood belongs to him. Likewise, there could be hair or skin or fibres but the scene will need a lot of processing.

"While we're waiting for forensics to give us information on our attacker, we can take this opportunity to look the other way, at our victim. This has to be a very personal attack, so we're going right back to the beginning. Our victim is sixty-five so we have a lot of background to comb through and see who bears enough of a grudge to do this. I've put DI Helen Covey on this." He gestured a woman forward. She was dressed in a formal business suit with her blonde hair up in a bun.

"Starting at the beginning, Chris went to school in the sixties." She wrote the dates on the whiteboard labelled 'Victim'. "He left school and went into the army. John, can you go back to his school records and see if anything survives. Dig up anything you can – I know it's a long time ago but we need to build a picture of who he was. Likewise go back to his hometown, chat to people try to see if you can tell what he was like.

"We're still filling in the gaps, but we're lucky that he had a police record, so we already have a few definite details. He joined Securicor in 1987. He came to our attention in the mid-nineties when he was on the crew of a van that was attacked in an armed robbery. Several million stolen and no one in the frame for it, so we went through the guards, including our victim, with a fine-tooth comb to see if it was an inside job. Yes?"

"Did you say mid-nineties?" Jonah asked. He hadn't really been listening, but the mention of the date had broken his reverie.

"Sold to the man sitting at the back! It is indeed mid-nineties, sixteenth of July 1996 to be precise. Pull the files, there'll be plenty of paperwork on it, go over it, look for links, people out of prison, grudges. We need to revisit the checks that were done at the time to build up a history of Chris Harris – especially people he might have known who have criminal records. DC Kate Jones is in charge of computer records, she'll make sure you can see everything you need to. Anything seems out of place, or relates back to this crime, feed it back into the computer."

Jonah sat there in a daze as the rest of the meeting swirled around him. He was also cursing himself as he was only there as an official observer from the coroner's office. On a case this big, there would be a Family Liaison Officer to deal with the relatives. All he would have to do is to occasionally chat to them about the paperwork that was attached to any death.

At the end of the meeting he approached Superintendent Castle. "I'm sorry, sir," Jonah said with his eyes downcast, "I shouldn't have spoken up in the meeting. I'm the coroner's officer and I'm only meant to be here as an observer and to do the paperwork."

Castle frowned at him, then finally asked, "So why did you speak up?"

"I'm working on a case that goes back to the mid-nineties." Jonah paused, wondering what he should say. "Well I think it started in the nineties."

"Hmmm, so you've done some research?" Jonah nodded, and Castle continued, "Well, we need as many bodies as possible, there's a lot of ground to cover. I'll speak to your boss; the coroner isn't it?"

"Yes," Jonah said, "Timothy Carlton, but you'd better check in with DI Linwood as well."

Castle nodded soberly, made a note of the names, and with that Jonah had joined the Major Incident Team.

ANDREW

CHAPTER 22

December 22, 1995

The man who would be a killer was waiting for his victim. But he wasn't passively hiding, instead he was stalking the town, looking for his prey. He had been circling Worksop on a small motorbike for nearly two hours now. It was a bitterly cold, bleak day and he was well wrapped up. For totally different reasons than the cold he had two pairs of gloves on, thin ones under his winter motorbike gloves. He was perfecting his timing trying to arrive at this point at the right time – he had chosen this junction on a hill on purpose.

After all this time, in the cold, he was experiencing a moment of self-doubt. Was his plan overly complicated? He had his motorbike and a loaded shotgun, so it should be easy to find a lone person and end their life. But that was not in his make up. He didn't want to extemporise. He wanted a plan that he had worked out, that he had checked, seen every pitfall.

With these thoughts, he coasted gently down a hill until he got to the lights. He was at a four-way crossroads, and each of the routes was busy. The killer had watched this junction and knew its phasing. The phase he wanted was when the cars coming down the hill would be stopped to allow traffic from the right to move, either straight across, left or right. This junction was surrounded by a fish and chip shop, houses, small industrial units and a park. In this bleak weather, there would be no one hanging around to watch what was happening.

All he needed now was the perfect car at the front of the queue. He had decided to give in after this run, find a café to warm up in for half an hour, then return to have another go. He knew it was a risk as it increased his chances of being remembered, but he was getting so cold that soon he'd be unable to carry out his mission.

As he coasted down the hill however, the killer saw that his chance had finally come up. Brake lights glowed on the back of the dark blue car, showing that the car was held on the footbrake. He glanced left and right and saw no pedestrians waiting to cross. Perfect. He pulled alongside the left of the car, splitting the lanes. He pulled off his right glove with his teeth, reached into the bag strapped to the tank, pulled out a sawn-off shotgun and swung it clumsily at the window of the car next to him. The barrel clattered uselessly against the window. The driver, a slightly overweight young man turned to stare at him. He had slicked back dark hair and looked Greek. He was saying something that couldn't be heard over the wind and through his helmet. It looked like "What the fuck are you doing?"

Frustrated, the killer took a proper grip and jabbed the butt of the shotgun straight at the window. He was rewarded when the window shattered.

The killer leant on the car roof and twisted to try and see into the car. He was shielding what he was doing with his body. He hoped that from behind he looked like he was asking the driver something. It was far more awkward than he had imagined. He was half off his bike and could feel the heat and vibration of the engine against his right leg while his left was off the floor, halfway across the saddle. He swung the shotgun round to point into the car. The occupant now went white and raised his hands in a futile attempt to protect himself.

Taking as careful aim as he could with one hand, the killer fired both barrels at once. The combined load of shot and wadding spread instantly from the shortened barrels. His victim's outstretched hands were shredded. The main blast caught him in the left armpit, leaving a glistening dark red hole in his side. Further up his face and neck were peppered with tiny red dots.

With a convulsive spasm, he arched back, taking both feet off the pedals. The killer was nearly swept off his bike as the car leapt forward, kangaroo hopping straight into the traffic ahead. He fumbled and managed to catch the gun by the barrel in his left hand, which was thankfully gloved and immune to the heat.

In an ungainly fashion he pushed with his right leg and settled back down onto the saddle. Trying not to fumble, he stuffed the gun back into the bag and tugged the zips into place. Then he shoved the glove back onto his right hand, registering for the first time the pain in his wrist. He took a deep breath and his ribs hurt. The stock of the gun had raked across his body on the recoil. He was protected by his leather jacket and bulky jumper, but he could still feel some bruising starting to spread across his abdomen.

The killer swore under his breath. He had experience with guns, but he would have been banned from the range if he'd practised firing one handed. So, he had to make one assumption in his plan - that he could fire one handed. In practice it had been far more awkward and painful than he'd expected. It was only in action movies that you could get away with firing a shotgun like a pistol. He experimentally flexed his fingers and winced. Nothing broken, he thought, but it was definitely sore.

Everything sorted, he became aware of his surroundings. As he'd predicted, the dark blue car had shot forward into a stream of traffic that was crossing the junction. The resulting accident had not only blocked the left-right road, but also spilled over into the road ahead. The entire junction was now stationary and people were leaning on their horns. Soon, they'd brave the weather and get out of their cars to investigate.

He let out the clutch, gingerly revved the engine, aware of his damaged wrist, and edged forwards. Keeping both feet down, he managed to skirt around the accident, using gaps that were too small for cars. Once he was clear of the accident, the road was empty, and he picked up both feet and accelerated away. Within a minute from when he fired the shot, he was riding away from the scene, leaving outraged witnesses behind, incapable of following him.

He took a deep breath and tried to steady himself. He had done the hard thing, now he just needed to keep it together to ensure it was the perfect crime. Taking a route he had practised and memorised, soon he was out of town on a small road. At the top of a rise, he stopped, left the engine running, and put the bike onto its side stand. Taking a craft knife from his bag, he awkwardly slit the tape holding on his fake number plate. He hadn't dared remove his glove as he could feel the wrist swelling and throbbing. He removed the plate, revealing the real one underneath. Then he walked a bit further on, until he was on a bridge over a busy A-road. Unseen by the hundreds of commuters below, he let the plate slip from his fingers. It hit the hard shoulder, cracked and bounced into the weeds. The carriageway he had chosen was heading in the opposite direction to the one he needed to take to get home.

The rest of the day was cold and boring. He rode fifty miles to a lock-up garage where he swapped the bike for his car. He examined his ribs and found a long blunt graze with a bruise. His wrist was swollen and would need bandaging and protecting for a few days. The first thing he did when he got in the car was to turn up the heater, then he switched on the radio. It was the last shopping weekend before Christmas and the news was reporting that, as he'd predicted, the entire town centre was gridlocked. So far, there was no indication that anything other than a simple traffic accident had caused the chaos.

He smiled to himself as he pulled away from the lock-up. He had already fled the scene and changed vehicles, and the police didn't even know that they were dealing with a murder. He was untouchable now. As he drove back home for Christmas, he examined his feelings.

He didn't feel horror or revulsion or elation or anything much about what he had just done. It had taken a long time to come to this point – he had made plans and reconciled himself to what needed to be done. He had mapped out his future, and now he had taken a step on the path. That was just how he viewed it, one step on the road to a better place.

He also thought about the person he had just killed. He didn't feel remorse because he had learned at school that he was better than most of the people around him. He had dreams and life and vibrancy. The rest of them just trudged along with their lives, never dreaming to look up and reach for the stars. So, if one of those mundane lives was snuffed out as he took the chance to seize his future, what of it? He was moving forward, along his charted course.

When he got home, his mother, predictably, worried over his wrist.

"I went out for a drink last night, slipped on the way home," he said dismissively. "I landed a bit heavily and banged my ribs too."

"That's not like you," his sister chimed in, "you're usually so in control, I've never seen you drunk!"

"And that's why," he said easily. "It was silly of me, last night drinks with a few friends. I won't make that mistake again."

"Well, at least let me strap it up," his mother said, reaching for the first aid kit.

"Of course," he said, "a few days rest and it'll be fine."

And it was fine. By the time the physical injuries had healed, the killer had moved on with his life. A piece had been moved on the board, and he was one step closer to winning.

CHAPTER 23

JONAH THOUGHT he had escaped when Farida grabbed his elbow in a tight grip and steered him into an empty meeting room. She let go when he was in the room and she was blocking the door.

"What is up with you?" Her eyes were wide, nostrils flaring.

"What do you mean?" asked Jonah innocently.

"Don't take me for an idiot! You told me that Mike is known for taping people to chairs and going nuts with a big sword. Then we have that briefing and you look like a schoolboy who knows he's in trouble and about to go to the headmaster's office." Jonah instinctively checked his pocket for the scrap of paper and glanced at the door. "You knew," Farida said flatly. "You knew this was going to happen! What are you playing at?"

Jonah leant on the edge of a table and blew out slowly. "It's complicated..." He stopped. "I thought you didn't want to be involved?"

"I don't, but don't think I stopped caring about you. You look like shit, by the way."

"Thanks." Jonah's thoughts moved with all the speed of treacle. With no other option, he decided to tell some of the truth. "Elizabeth did phone last night and she gave me that address in Aberdare. But before I could sort it, I had a, er, family emergency. I never really got to bed; I was dozing in the car when the phone rang. Being coroner's officer, I was one of the first in."

Farida shook her head slowly. "You've got to tell the boss, the Super, Jack Castle."

"I can't," Jonah said simply.

"I don't mean in the middle of a meeting, just go to his office have a one-to-one. He'll chew you out a bit for breaking protocol but once you give him the killer, you'll be all right." Her look left him in no doubt that he would deserve whatever he got.

Jonah sat down at the table and rested his face in his hands. He tried to marshal his thoughts. He knew it was a bad idea, he just couldn't work out why. "I have two facts that imply Mike is guilty," he said slowly. "Firstly, what Cathy told me about his preferred method of killing people. Not only does that not directly implicate him, but it is also hearsay from the wife of an undercover officer. He shouldn't have told her, and she definitely shouldn't have told me. I know she won't repeat it on record. Not only are they in the middle of a legal dispute with West Midlands, they might well already have moved to New Zealand!"

"Fine!" Farida snapped. "But what did Elizabeth tell you last night? That must have been useful as you got the address before the crime had been committed."

"Elizabeth?" Jonah sneered. "The mentally unstable woman who was tangential to an enquiry that finished two months ago? She told me that she'd paid someone to place an illegal virus in Mike's computer and that's how she got the information!" Farida looked crestfallen and Jonah couldn't resist twisting the knife. "Mike Khan has a first-class honours in Law and money to spend. He's been dodging the police for the last fifteen years. With this level of evidence, he could go on legal aid and still walk free!"

"You still have to tell someone, pass it up the chain!"

"Why?"

"Because this is above your pay-grade, and mine. That's what the higher ranks are for. To make the hard decisions."

"No," Jonah said finally. "No, I'd lose my chance to save someone else and my career to boot."

"Maybe what you don't want to lose is your contact with Elizabeth?"

"Maybe," Jonah said quietly. He laid his head on the table, aching for sleep. He had no more fight left in him. He searched for a solution, but his brain wasn't co-operating. He raised his head. "If they find definite forensics, DNA or prints, something that Mike can't wriggle out of, then I'll call my contact in West Midlands. He can act on information received and get DNA or whatever to check against our crime scene."

"That means you'd lose out on all the glory," Farida observed.

"Do I look like I'm in it for the glory?" Jonah asked wearily. "Last night I made the wrong decision and now someone's dead because of it. I'll just be glad if he's stopped, that's all." The two stared at each other, the gulf between them wider than ever. "So, if there's definite forensics that we can't find a match for, I'll have a word with DI Bridges, and he'll do the link up with West Midlands. Is that okay with you?"

Farida opened her mouth and closed it again. She desperately wanted to argue, to push her point that it wasn't her decision to make – that it shouldn't be made at this pay-grade. In the end she said, "I'll stand by you," but she left the room.

TIMOTHY CARLTON PUT his head around Jonah's door and asked, "How's it going?"

"Listen, to be honest I wasn't expecting to come in today, so I was up late last night and in at five this morning. So, I've hardly had any sleep. If there's nothing else urgent, I was going to turn in, and have another go tomorrow."

"No, that's fine. No one expects you to be here on a Sunday. Did you show your face at the MIT meeting?"

"Yes. Have you spoken to Detective Superintendent Castle yet?" Jonah asked.

"No, why?"

"It turned out to be more than an observer's role. He's going to assign me over to the MIT temporarily."

"Oh." Timothy thought for a moment. "Hope he's not going to take up too much of your time."

"No, it's just some background research – the kind of stuff we usually do here anyway. The victim was sixty-five so there's a lot to get through. Should be able to fit it in around my regular duties."

"Well do your work, report in, offer whatever help you can. It'll do us all good to be seen to have interdepartmental co-operation. I've no objections, just let me know how you're allocating your time.

"When a death is as obviously violent as this one, then there's very little to be done from the perspective of the coroner. It's going to be unlawful killing, there's no doubt about that. On Monday, I'll open the inquest, establish identity, time, place and cause of death, neither of which should give us a problem. Then I'll adjourn and we'll just have to wait for the criminal case to finish before restarting. Usually that'll just be taking selected parts of whatever case MIT puts together for the CPS and reusing them in the coroner's report. We will need to inform the registrar though, so an intermediate certificate can be issued, and probate carried out. But a lot of the liaison work becomes an MIT issue, so can you touch base with the FLO tomorrow? Again, make sure you're visible and there to offer any support with our side of the process."

Jonah nodded. "That won't be a problem." He yawned. "Anyway, I'm about beat so I'll go home now, and get started on that work tomorrow."

"Okay."

He went home and loafed on the sofa. He knew from experience that the best way to cope was to stay out of bed until the night, then get a long night's sleep. So he half-dozed and half-watched the golf on television.

After a couple of hours, Alex came down from bed and curled up into him.

"What were we talking about this morning?" Jonah asked.

"Hmmm? I was saying how I needed to get a complete picture of you. I don't just love you because of what you represent, it's all of you, and our shared history." Jonah had his arm around her shoulders and her words were muffled as she spoke into his chest.

"So, we're okay then?" Jonah asked.

"Yes." Alex lifted her head to look at him. "Or no. But we will be. I'll stop charging around looking for what I want when in fact it's been here all along."

"Hmmm!" Another wave of tiredness washed over Jonah and he let his eyes slide closed.

"You sure you don't want to sleep in bed?" Alex asked.

"No, I'll hold out until evening," Jonah said, eyes still closed.

For the rest of the afternoon they ate snack food, cuddled, and dozed on the sofa. As soon as it was dark, Jonah gave in and went to bed, falling instantly into a deep sleep.

Jolted out of a nightmare, Jonah sat up in bed with his heart pounding. In his dream he had been in his car, waiting at a busy junction. He was trying to turn right, and the traffic kept sweeping past without a gap. Every time he felt he could go, a car or lorry emerged out of nowhere, going too fast. He edged forward, then let the car roll back a little. Behind him traffic was backing up and he could hear horns in the distance. He felt a sense of urgency, he was late, he must make this turn.

He looked to his left and saw Alex in the passenger seat, waiting serenely, totally not bothered. A big gap opened up in the traffic from the left. He edged forward, but then saw Gareth and Emily were in the back seat. He couldn't take the risk with his entire family in the car.

He looked the other way and caught something in the back seat. It was Christopher Harris, the murder victim, and he was headless. In that weird way that dreams have, this fact wasn't scary, instead he was at peace with it. Likewise, something weird was happening to the space inside the car, as he was now joined by Elizabeth and Andrew.

Unable to take any more, he shut his eyes and jammed his foot on the accelerator and shot out finally into the traffic. He heard the screech of tyres and tensed up for the inevitable impact.

Slowly he reasoned that it had been a dream and he was awake and safe.

He swung his legs out of bed and decided not to use his stick. He just needed to go downstairs, get a drink, make sure he didn't slip back into the nightmare.

The next morning, he awoke slowly and feeling groggy. At one point he'd been standing with a tie in each hand, unable to choose, for far too long. Once he'd had some toast and coffee, he went back upstairs to say goodbye to Alex, who was still in bed.

"I've got to pop into work," he said, sitting on his side of the bed.

"What?" Alex woke up and rumpled her hair, "you were in on a Sunday." She looked up at him through her eyelashes. "Couldn't you go in a bit later?"

"I'm sorry," he said, "really I am, but there's been a really big case, it'll make the national news in no time. A beheading out in the valleys, night before last. That's why I was phoned at five in the morning. We need to get ahead of it before the press go mad."

"In the valleys?" Concern creased her forehead. "You mean we were up there while some axe-wielding maniac was?"

"No, it was miles away," he said, while thinking about what she said. "Anyway, you know what these jobs are like, it's all hands to the pump."

"Off you go then, keep the good people of Cardiff safe from crime!"

As he drove into work, he realised that his worst fears had come true. He had been faced with the choice between saving his wife and doing his job. He'd had two phone calls and had made the choice between family and work. In fact, he mused, he hadn't even chosen. He hadn't given it a minute's thought. Once the police station in Barry had called, all thought of Elizabeth had flown from his head. He could've taken the moment to call Farida and ask her to swing by the address in Aberdare and check it out.

He was eaten up with guilt that he hadn't stopped a murder. He tried to imagine the timeline. While he was driving away from Aberdare, towards Barry, was Mike already on his way down the M4? Or was he already torturing Chris Harris while he was picking up Alex? The pathologist couldn't be exact about time of death, so Jonah didn't know what difference he could've made. Maybe he would have been in time to find the body? Maybe if he'd left Alex there his marriage would now be over?

He almost stopped the car when that thought occurred to him. Every decision was laced with danger. He'd just considered that he should've sent Farida in his place. From what he'd read, Mike had to be about a foot taller than her, and about twice her weight. And armed with a sword. He knew that the police trained you in unarmed combat, but there were limits.

Once he was in the office, he called up all files that had been allocated to him. As he expected, there was a wealth of detail on the Securicor van robbery in 1996. He started with the summary. It was a famous case and he remembered reading about it in the papers at the time. But he made himself re-read the police reports as he trusted neither the press nor his memory.

A van with fourteen million pounds on board had left the Cardiff depot and been stopped within ten miles. Four robbers had unloaded most of the cash into two cars before one of the guards tried to rush one of the robbers. One of the other robbers had opened fire and shot the guard and accidentally injured their co-conspiritor in the process. The whole thing sounded like a mess, even though they did get away with just over twelve million pounds.

The police investigation had stalled early on. Firstly, the informants in South Wales came up blank, and later on, a UK-wide trawl turned up no information. Even talking to all the Regional Crime Squads resulted in nothing. They had the DNA of the robber who'd been shot but that failed to turn up a match anywhere either.

Faced with this complete brick wall across their investigation, they turned to the only other option – an inside job. Some officers had registered on the files that they thought this was a dead end, because one guard had been shot. Others expressed the opinion that it could be a double-bluff or even a settling of scores. In any case, the wound had been serious, but not disabling, with the guard making a full recovery in time.

This was the part of the file that Jonah was interested in – the deep background work that had been done on the three guards. They were treated as suspects and every aspect of their life was gone over. As Chris Harris was ex-army, they thought that he had recruited some former soldiers to rob the van. Ultimately, this train of investigation petered out when it was found that none of the three received any kind of financial help or suspicious gifts either in the year before, or at any point after the robbery.

Obviously, Chris Harris had some dodgy friends who'd served alongside him during his sixteen years in the army. But, with a career that long, there were literally hundreds of soldiers who'd served alongside him. Simple maths said that a certain percentage of them would turn to crime or become homeless or turn to drink and drugs.

Nonetheless, those closest to Chris Harris had been diligently tracked down and their alibis checked. Jonah shuddered when he saw the work that had been put in. The army were notoriously difficult to get information out of, especially if you were trying to find ex-soldiers with criminal tendencies. There must have been months of painstaking work to track down all these people, unfortunately with no tangible result. As with every other line of enquiry, this finally went dead.

But it did provide Jonah with a potential list to start working with. All he had to do, was to get the list and work out who, for a start, was still alive. The robbery had been about nine years after Chris Harris left the army, but now that was nearly thirty years ago. A lot of people had passed on.

He went through the work mechanically, with no real enthusiasm. He knew the answer, and unless Mike Khan's name came up somewhere in this list, there was nothing he could do about it. He still wondered if there was a link to Patrick Kinsale, so he got his tatty copy of the list of names out. More out of hope than anything else, he checked every entry against his list. There might be a cousin or wife or husband of someone that would provide a link between this case and his original list.

He knew it was a really long shot, but there was something relaxing about doing mindless, pointless work. After his realisation that all decisions carried consequences, he needed to do something without any outcome. He didn't believe that anything he found in Chris Harris' past would explain why he was attacked.

As he worked though, he turned the problem over in his mind, still wondering why Mike Khan had attacked Chris Harris. He then paid a bit more attention to the list of Chris Harris' previous contacts, looking for anyone who might have been to Swindon or Birmingham or in any way intersected with Mike's world.

But he still came up with nothing. Elizabeth had given him Mike's name and told him that he was heading for Chris Harris' address in Aberdare. There was no way it was a lucky guess, so he had to assume she knew something, some connecting fact that made sense of the link between the two men. Other than knowing that Elizabeth didn't want to tell Jonah, he had no idea what she was hiding.

Eventually, he reached a point where he was just going over the same ground again and again, and gaining nothing. He'd battered his brain against a mountain of work for long enough.

Standing up to stretch his back and rub his eyes, he wondered yet again about Elizabeth. Something had prompted her to pay a private investigator to target Mike Khan. And then, out of all the data that it must have generated, she'd picked out this one Google map search. And that had made such an impression on her, that she'd phoned him out of the blue. She'd said at the time she was concerned for him, but something somewhere must have given Elizabeth the idea that Mike was coming here set on mayhem.

He needed an answer so, with serious misgivings, he phoned Elizabeth.

"Hi, it's Jonah," he said.

"Oh, hello," she sounded frosty. "I saw the news."

"I'm sorry, we did what we could."

"Not enough though! I gave you the address. I told you he was coming, and he still got away with it! How much more help do you need? I thought we were trying to save people here."

"It's not like that. You gave us a big help. We were able to get there much quicker," he lied, "and that means that we are much further ahead. Getting there right after the crime means the scene is fresh and there's more evidence. And," he improvised, "we're going over the crime scene right now and checking all the forensics. It helps a great deal that we now have a suspect to check them against."

"But there's been nothing in the news about Mike Khan being a suspect or anything." Elizabeth sounded exasperated now.

"You have to understand that this a complex, ongoing enquiry. You can't always release all the information to the press. And you have to remember that Mike does have both a good degree in law and access to a lot of money. We'll only get one chance to nail him and we must make sure it sticks. We can't afford to mess this up and we certainly don't want him knowing how close we are."

"Okay." Now she sounded more mollified. "But there's also the date to worry about. If we can get Mike before the end of April, then we could bring down Andrew as well. Once the nominations close for the election, then he'll have to stand for election, and we'll have to get him disbarred or sacked or something."

"What is the connection between Andrew and Mike? Why will bringing Mike down mean we can get Andrew?"

"It is all connected, but you just have to trust me." Elizabeth went quiet.

Jonah was the first to break the silence. "Listen, I need to ask you something. What is it about South Wales? Why did you think it was significant that Mike was coming here?"

"Well, it's because you're there and I was worried about you," Elizabeth said. Jonah wished he was talking to her face to face because he wasn't sure if she was lying or not.

"But there's no reason why, if you saw Mike looking up an address here, that you might think he was going to come here, intent on violence." He wanted to ask her what she was holding back, but as always, he didn't want to push her too hard.

There was silence from her end of the phone. "No," she said eventually. "No, it was just a lucky guess. I told the investigator to look for something unusual and he sent me the information." Now Jonah was sure she was lying, he just didn't know what about.

CHAPTER 24

The next day, Jonah didn't have any chance to go through the Chris Harris case. He'd updated the system with his list of surviving associates before going home the day before, so he knew he'd be seen to be helping.

Jonah was called mid-morning with a new case. It should have been straightforward. A woman in her early twenties had called the police, concerned that she couldn't reach her father who had failed to turn up at work. At first a PCSO had attended to assess the scene. When no one was able to raise a response, they radioed it in and made entry.

Mr Brian Royston was found, rather inelegantly, on the floor, halfway out of the bedroom, feet tangled in the bedclothes, stone dead. The PCSO had immediately comforted the daughter, Chloe, and a constable had arrived. Pretty soon, in the way of things, the duty inspector had joined the group and decided to play things safe. While talking to Jonah, he had said that he didn't want to disturb the scene until CID had cleared it but there was no one available at the moment as the MIT was taking up all their resources.

So, before lunch, Jonah had found himself in a bedroom, trying to remember his basic CID training. To be fair there was very little to do. There was one broken window in the back door where the PCSO had gained entry. The daughter, while distressed, could confirm that nothing had been disturbed. Everything was in order, all the usual electronics, money and a little jewellery were present and correct.

Mr Royston himself had that white, fixed, marble-like quality of a corpse. Without touching anything, Jonah could see a reddening of the exposed flesh towards the floor, indicating that the body hadn't been moved. There was no sign of injury or struggle.

Jonah had no problem signing off the forms to allow the mortuary assistants to remove the body. He had a feeling, unless the doctor revealed anything that the daughter didn't know, that an autopsy would be on the cards.

The whole incident had upset his balance a little, as the dead man was in his late forties, with a beer belly and greying hair. It wasn't quite a vision of his own mortality, but it was too close to home for Jonah to be comfortable. It made him wonder how he would look and when he'd meet his end. Of course, he always hoped, as most did, that the final moment would come when he was an old man. But his job was dealing with sudden death, and in his depressed mood, these thoughts were proving harder than ever to banish.

Finally, the body of Brian Royston was in the morgue freezer, the forms were filled in and the computer was up to date. Jonah had a quick check of the MIT system, but nothing had been allocated back to him yet. With a weariness that was more than just tiredness, he went home.

"It's the rugby club's quiz tonight, you said you wanted

to go." Alex's words interrupted his quiet reflection as he sat on the sofa.

"No, not tonight. I'm not much company, why don't you go?"

"Me? On my own? That'd be too weird. We haven't been there for over a year. I can't just waltz in and face everyone asking where you are." She paused to look at Jonah, pin him down with her gaze. "I don't know where you're at. I thought we'd really made progress after that night up in the valleys. But now, now it seems like we're not even in the same house."

"Hmph," Jonah said, wishing his wife wasn't quite so insightful. "I just don't feel like going out, socialising."

"You haven't since we got back that morning. I thought we'd made a breakthrough, sorted something out, but now you've taken six steps back." She stopped to gather her courage, before plunging on. "Did you want to carry on with the marriage or were you hoping that we'd drift apart?"

"No!" Jonah's voice betrayed his panic. "No! I don't want to lose you. That's why I took you up there, why I came out to get you from the police station, to try to put things back together." To himself, he added, that's why I chose you over a stranger. That's why he died, to save our marriage.

"So why don't you try then? You've just switched off."

"I don't know. It just seems that there are so many decisions and each one has consequences and well, sometimes it's just easier not to do anything."

"But it's no different to being an artist. You'll always be faced with a blank canvas. Sometimes you just have to put it all aside, pick up the brush and make your mark. It doesn't matter if it's good or bad, it'll just be better than a blank canvas."

"Hmmm," Jonah said non committally. "But it's the job

isn't it? I affect lives, I deal with life and death issues. It's not just a painting or some minor decision."

"But you've always done the job haven't you?" Alex tried, but Jonah didn't respond. "Come to that, it's the same every time you leave the house. Once you get in your car then you might make a decision that changes or ends someone's life. At the end of the day, you've just got to not think about it too much, just get your head down and get on with the day." Jonah still didn't respond. "What about the garden? You haven't touched it for days and it's spring and everything's growing."

"Since when have you been interested in the garden?" Jonah snapped.

"I'm not really," Alex explained, "but I know what it means to you and you haven't been out there."

Jonah didn't say anything, unwilling to admit that he was retreating from life. Alex tutted and stalked from the room.

Jonah knew when he was beaten. He needed to do something, anything. He didn't like the choice between going out and staying in but that's what was there. He imagined the guilt if he spent this evening sat on the sofa with cans of beer and rubbish on the telly. Waking up in the morning with a bad head and sour feeling between Alex and him.

He levered himself off the sofa and into the kitchen where Alex was washing up with excessive noise. "If you give me half an hour to have a shower and put some fresh clothes on, we still have time to get a table for the pub quiz if you want."

"I need to get all dressed up too," Alex said. "I'll do my make-up while you're in the shower." She stopped on the way past him in the doorway to give him a quick squeeze. "Thank you!"

Less than an hour later they were in the noisy function room of the rugby club. It was about as bad as Jonah had imagined. As soon as he had agreed to go, he'd regretted it. He knew that Alex was right – he was hiding away and trying to avoid making decisions. But she had cornered him, forced him to face his fears. The only reaction to that was to take a bold move – so now he was in the pub quiz.

The evening was a slow-motion hell on earth for Jonah. He went to get drinks while Alex secured a table. He saw a couple of his rugby acquaintances who were keen for a chat and to see where Jonah had been recently. They made small talk, and someone mentioned a rugby league for older players that was in the planning stage. Jonah had always shied away from admitting that he was getting older but now he could see the advantage in not trying to catch a twenty-five-year-old haring up the pitch, never mind not being tackled by the younger generation.

Jonah noticed that he wasn't being engaged at all by the few off duty police officers in the room.

"Hello, stranger, is Alex with you?" Jonah turned round to find Robin, a woman who worked with Alex at the hospital. She was in the ladies' team and met all the stereotypes, being well built with short hair. Just as Jonah was thinking this, he had to change his opinion as her husband joined her. Together they went back to the table. There was then some to and fro as Jonah made sure he sat with his back to the room. This usually made him feel uncomfortable, but at the moment he didn't want to risk accidental eye contact with anyone from work. He felt that he was being ignored and didn't have the mental or emotional strength to deal with it now.

In a quiet moment as papers were swapped, Jonah wondered if this was his lot in life. How would he be remembered when his time came? As a partly enthusiastic member of the rugby club and a policeman with a patchy career? The thought did nothing to lift his mood as he grabbed the paper to start marking.

JONAH STILL DIDN'T FEEL strong enough to face the bear pit of the main room over in Cardiff Bay, so he did everything by email. Now that he had dealt with Chris' army career, he turned his attention to the other checks that had been carried out nearly twenty years ago.

Also listed were the two other guards in the van – the driver Dave Black and Tony Evans who was in the back. Remembering the initial briefing, Jonah wondered if the guards were part of a secret that Chris may have been protecting. He knew that a shared traumatic experience tended to bind people together. Or, he thought darkly, in his case drive them apart.

He checked through his various databases to see where the remaining two guards had ended up. For at least ten years following the robbery, the case had undergone periodic case reviews. As time went on, they became simpler and more sporadic. But, as the main theory was an inside job, the guards' details had been kept up to date. Dave Black was listed as last address in Splott, less than a ten-minute drive from Cardiff Bay police station.

But that wasn't what Jonah wanted. He needed to stay in his office, insulated from the world and reach out by the safe mediums of phone and email. He checked Tony Evans and found that he was listed as 'moved abroad' in 2003.

Jonah dug deeper and found that he was now in Cork, Southern Ireland. It took him another half hour and several phone calls before he had a number for Tony Evans. He dialled, waited for the connection and finally got through.

"Hello is that Tony Evans?"

"Yes, who's calling?" The voice was guarded.

"It's DS Greene from South Wales Police..."

"I've got nothing to say to you! You've ruined my life and now you're coming back for another swing!"

"No," Jonah said calmly. "I am sorry for mistakes that were made in the past, but you might be in danger."

"Oh, come round at last have you," Evans said bitterly. "Twenty years too bloody late!"

"Listen, that was another generation," Jonah said. "When the robbery happened, I was getting blisters pounding the beat in Cardiff. Don't go having a go at me for someone else's mistakes."

"You're all the bloody same though, aren't you? Trying to pin the blame on someone, never mind the damage that gets done. Do you have any idea how hard it is to find work in security if you've spent a year under investigation by the police for an inside job? That is once I'd recovered from being shot in the leg! Let me tell you, if it was an inside job, we all did bloody poorly out of it. A stay in hospital, seven years on the dole and now I've had to leave the country to find any work at all. Proceeds of crime, my arse!"

"Okay," Jonah took a deep breath and mustered all his tact. "As I said, I am sorry, but I wanted to know if anything odd has happened to you recently."

"Why do you want to know that?" Tony sounded suspicious.

"Well, do you remember Chris Harris?"

"Of course I bloody remember! You don't forget something like that."

"He was killed last week, murdered."

"Oh, I see, and you're working a falling out between thieves angle, are you? Maybe seeing if we really did do it?"

"No," Jonah was getting frustrated and wondering why he was bothering trying to save this person. He tried to remember the briefing and how much he was allowed to say about the circumstances of the attack. He supposed he ought to try to be tactful as well, but that was a bit of a stretch. "The thing is that the attack on Chris was quite extreme. It's possible he was tortured, forced to reveal some secret. Or he might have known his killer. It wasn't a straightforward murder, there was a more personal edge to it."

Jonah heard a match being struck followed by a noisy drag on a cigarette. "That's harsh that is," Tony said finally. "He were a good sort, Chris, always kept his cool. No one deserves that. But I'm afraid I can't help you. I didn't really want to keep in touch with the other two after the event. I mean, I had my sympathies and all, but I was fighting my own battles. It was something I wanted to put behind me, not have yearly reunions and form a support group. Besides which, you lot might've made something out of it if we'd been fraternising."

"And have you seen anything odd, been followed, someone watching you?" Jonah asked, ignoring the other man's tirade.

"No," Tony said after another brief pause. There was another noisy drag on his cigarette. "Can't say that I have." He was reaching his limit for talking to the police.

"How did you end up in Cork?"

"Well, the security business is a bit of a closed shop.

Everyone talks to everyone else. And you know, once you lot start poking around, well it's a risk isn't it? Nothing's ever written on paper, but it didn't take a genius to figure out why I kept getting rejected from job applications. No, I was right down about it all and the nuns suggested I move out to Ireland. They've a place in Cork, so they could vouch for me, give me a fresh start. You know what Ireland's like – the church control everything. I'm now a painter, decorator and general handyman. I'm caretaker at the convent and get odd jobs on the side in the town." For the first time in the call there was a hint of pride in his voice.

Jonah however focused in on one part of his narrative. "Nuns?" he asked.

"Yeah, there was some charity available and I took advantage of it. That's not a crime now is it? It started off as some help with going private for the rehab. They offered to pay for it, well why not? And before you ask, check your paperwork, they all looked into it at the time and it was legit. Genuine charity, and all that – not the proceeds of crime. Anyway, they had this support service so when I'd had enough of South Wales, they were there to help."

"Was it the Mission of Bethesda and Capernaum by any chance? I've heard they do good work with leg injuries."

"You mean it's not in your files? You lot couldn't organise a piss up in a brewery! Yeah, that was them. What of it?"

"Nothing really, just getting some deep background, trying to build up a picture, see if we can understand the circumstances behind the killing of Chris Harris."

"Yeah well, that was them."

Jonah said thank you and hung up quickly. It wasn't hard as Tony didn't want to stay on the phone either.

He closed the files and walked over to the window. He stared out without seeing the trees and gardens beyond. He was on a useless quest. All the names had been checked twenty years ago, with a much bigger team. They had found nothing. Now, with the passage of time, he had found even less. Predictably a lot of them were impossible to trace, presumably dead. Certainly none of them shed any light on Chris Harris' killing.

With this in mind, he returned to his desk to take a moment to check through the forensic evidence from the house in Aberdare. He remembered his promise to Farida and was looking for something that would lead back to Mike Khan. One item caught his attention – due to the amount of blood around the body, they would have expected the killer to leave footprints extending from the scene. There were prints, but they were deliberately scrubbed out. With each step, the killer had put his foot down, then swivelled or slid to obscure the print. There was some technical detail about ultraviolet light and taking layers off, but the bottom line was that the foot that left the print was big. Not just big, but unnaturally big, probably in the size fourteen to fifteen region. Jonah's heart leapt, but when he scanned to the bottom of the report, he saw that they estimated that even if they found the shoe, there wasn't enough detail left in the print to make a positive match.

Jonah put his forehead down on the desk. He was so close; he could feel that there was a crack somewhere in this case. But, every avenue he tried, he was blocked.

CHAPTER 25

"Abdominal aortic aneurysm," the pathologist said to Jonah over the phone. "That's your cause of death. Most likely thing really. He was a bit young, but not unusually so."

The pathologist was phoning over the summary of the autopsy on Brian Royston. Jonah allowed himself a momentary feeling of relief – he had called it correctly. It had been a weird, random medical event and not foul play.

"You got round to him quickly," Jonah said. It was Thursday lunchtime and the body had been found on Tuesday.

"It's been quiet, and aneurysm was always the prime suspect."

"What is it anyway?" Jonah asked, pulling the paper forms over. He had already part-completed them, copying the details from the witness statement. Full name, date and place of birth, date and time of death. The whole human experience reduced to a simple set of numbers and figures.

"It's where a blood vessel stretches out in a big bubble as the walls get thinner. In this case it was the aorta that moves blood away from the heart around the body. They can happen without the patient having any idea, but if they burst, as in this case, they're nearly always fatal. Certainly at home in the early hours of the morning."

"That's cheerful," said Jonah sarcastically. "What's the cause?"

"Cause? Hm, could be lifestyle, usual culprits, weight, smoking and cholesterol, but a lot of people now think it has a genetic component. You get screened if you're over sixty-five, but your man Brian was quite some way south of that."

"Cheers for that, I'll fill in the paperwork while I'm waiting for your official report."

Jonah said goodbye and hung up the phone. He looked again at the form and saw a mistake. He'd put his own date of birth down instead of Brian's. He double-checked the form. They were both born in the same month in 1967. He shook his head, if they'd grown up near each other, they would've been classmates. All the time he was growing up, getting married and having a career, Brian was dogging his footsteps, living his own life. And now that life was snuffed out.

Somehow Jonah had always assumed that he had decades of time left. At least twenty years before normal retirement age, although he'd have to leave before that. Plenty of life. But now he had the thought of an aneurysm hovering over him. A time bomb ticking away inside the body that might be explode at any moment. A death sentence that wouldn't be his fault, but could be lurking in his genes, programmed in since birth.

The thought that he might be dead at any moment served to puncture his depression. Rather than wallowing, he realised he had a job to do. And it wasn't one he could do part-time with only half his brain.

Jonah knew he had merely skimmed the report on the armed robbery. Burdened by his bad decisions, he had done the bare minimum on the Chris Harris murder. Instead of reading the report, he'd focused on the list of known associates.

Filled with a new resolve, he started again, reading the report from the beginning.

At first, he grudgingly read the main report, darting off sideways into the witness reports and the forensic evidence. Soon he was building up a picture of the events.

On Tuesday July 16, 1996, a Securicor van had been making a routine journey from the depot with stacks of counted and sorted notes, ready to start making rounds of smaller depots. From those depots other vans would go round cash machines to refill them. The report listed four suspects, who all wore hooded sweatshirts, either black, dark grey or navy blue. They were disguised with sunglasses and dust masks like a builder or painter would wear. Their hoods were pulled up tight and they all wore blue jeans and trainers. Suspect 1 was slight and short and was probably female. Suspects 2 and 3 were both probably male and about the same height – between five foot nine and six foot, with an average build. Suspect 4 however was much taller, around six foot six inches and he was heavily built as well.

The first three suspects were believed to be IC1 – White North European. Suspect 4 was darker, he was recorded as IC2 Dark European although there was a note on the record that he might be IC6 Arabic or North African.

The other players in the drama were Dave Black, the driver, and next to him was Chris Harris, who was thirty-eight at the time. Tony Evans was an experienced guard at this point, and he was in the back of the van.

They had been less than ten miles from the depot, driving down a narrow lane, approaching the M4 motorway. A dark green Volvo estate had pulled out sharply across the lane, blocking the van in. When the driver had tried to reverse, a following gold coloured Volvo estate had swung across behind them. Before anyone had a chance to think, the passenger of the front Volvo, Suspect 4, had leapt out and slapped a piece of paper on the windscreen. With his other hand, he waved a revolver.

The piece of paper was a photo of the driver's wife dropping their two children off at school. The driver took one look at the picture and his face went white and he killed the engine. When he looked away from the photograph, he saw the driver had already got out of the lead Volvo, and was aiming a rifle straight at him, elbows resting on the roof of the car. He checked the wing mirrors and saw that robbers were rushing down each side of the van with guns already drawn.

So, the battle was over before it was even joined. The driver leapt down and was hassled to the centre of the road, where he was forced to sit down between Dave Black and Tony Evans. They were all made to place their hands on their heads as they rested against the van.

Suspect 1 was still leaning on the roof of the lead Volvo with a rifle aimed at all three crewmen. Suspect 3 was half sitting, half leaning on bonnet of the rear Volvo cradling a sawn-off shotgun.

There then followed a strangely quiet period. The three guards sat in the sun, wondering what the eyes behind the sunglasses looked like. The sun beat down on the tarmac from a blue, cloudless sky. Suspect 1 rested like a statue, finger alongside the trigger, rifle on the roof of the Volvo, perfectly covering the group of three people. At the other end of the scene, Suspect 3 was more mobile. He was restless, rubbing the back of his head, looking around occasionally, shifting the gun from one hand to the other. Sometimes he wiped sweat away from his eyes.

While these two looked on, Suspect 2 and Suspect 4 worked tirelessly to shift sacks of cash from the back of the Transit van to the rear Volvo. The guards sitting on the tarmac started sweating, but the two suspects loading the cash were dripping. When they were out of sight, they lifted their sunglasses and wiped their foreheads. Stains were starting to seep through their sweatshirts. But it didn't stop them; like robots they just went through the motions of grabbing bags and slinging them into the boot of the car.

Once the rear car was full and the bodywork was low over the rear wheels, they started the longer job. They moved the cash down the length of the van, between it and the verge, to load up the front car. They worked without talking, pointing occasionally and moving past each other with ease. They had weapons laid easily within reach, revolvers in pockets or belts, a machete and a baseball bat were in the rear of the cars.

A moment came when both Suspect 2 and Suspect 4 were down the side of the van. Suspect 2 was returning for a fresh sack and passed the heavily laden Suspect 4. The front Volvo was nearly loaded and they were having to reach deeper into the van for the last sacks. Suspect 3 took his moment of being unobserved to lay his gun down for a second and take a small bottle of vodka from his pocket.

Tony Evans took his chance. He had the other two guards between himself and Suspect 1's rifle, so he launched his way up and straight at Suspect 3. He never got there, as Suspect 2 emerged from the back of the van, dropping his sack of money. He tried to shove the guard back down and for a second they wrestled. Then they broke apart, Suspect 2 moving behind the car, and the guard stumbled clear of the other guards, over to the far side of the road. Suspect 1 saw her chance and fired a well-controlled shot, straight through his thigh. He collapsed and was dragged back by his two colleagues.

The silence following the shot was broken by Suspect 2.

"What the fuck have you done?" he shouted.

The bullet had travelled straight through Tony Evan's thigh and had hit Suspect 2 just below the knee. He was going white as blood ran down his leg, starting to leave big droplets on the road.

"Shit! Shit! Shit!" Suspect 3 was saying repetitively. Suspect 1 was slowly moving out and around the front of her car, still covering the three guards with the rifle. The guards were leaning over their fallen comrade, shouting obscenities at the robbers.

It could have dissolved into chaos right there. But Suspect 4 came around the rear of the van and cuffed Suspect 3 on the back of the head. He leapt to his feet, shotgun tucked into his shoulder, suddenly alert. Suspect 4 fired his revolver once into the air, and everyone went quiet. A large man, he loomed over the three guards, his stricken friend and the other two suspects who were stood in the open.

Everyone froze for a second. The smell of the cordite merged with the coppery smell of blood and sweaty bodies. Heat came off the road in waves. The pools and spots of blood glistened black and red in the sun, contrasting with the grey tarmac and the bright green of the leaves and grass. The sun was merciless, bleaching the colour out of everything and leaching the energy out of everyone.

In the calm that followed, Suspect 4 knelt down and slit

the leg of Suspect 2's jeans with a knife. He grabbed some empty cloth money sacks from the rear of the van and mopped up the blood. Suspect 1 reached into the cab of the van and threw a first aid kit to Suspect 4. He cut the leg of the jeans into thin strips and bound a large gauze pad over the injury. Finally, he pronounced, "Flesh wound," and half carried Suspect 2 into the passenger seat of the rear car.

"Cover them," Suspect 1 said to Suspect 4 when he returned. When they were covered, she ran to the front car, retrieved some yellow washing line, and proceeded to tie up the three guards. She tied them up simply, only one wrist on each of them, then looped it through the door frame of the van and tied it off securely before shutting the door on the knot. She locked the van and took the keys. Finally, she nudged the first aid kit towards the guards. With one hand free and the other tied, the two uninjured guards were able to start basic first aid on their colleague.

Suspect 4 got into the rear car with the injured Suspect 2, while the disgraced Suspect 3 got into the car with Suspect 1. Once the cars were gone, the guards searched the first aid kit and found some unnoticed scissors. Once they'd cut through the line, the youngest, Dave Black was sent to the nearest phone box to raise the alarm while Chris Harris tended his injured colleague.

Jonah sat back and rubbed his eyes. They just vanished after that, the four people in two cars. No gunshot wounds reported to local hospitals. Nothing from any confidential informant. They not only vanished, but also took £12.8 million with them. They would have had the whole fourteen million if it hadn't all gone wrong.

The rest of the police report made depressing reading to Jonah. They did have evidence, but it was useless. The washing line came from any branch of Woolworths. There were cash bags left at the scene stained with blood that didn't match Tony Evans. But without anyone to compare it to, the DNA it contained led nowhere. It had stayed in the database ever since, still waiting for a match. The only slight hope was that it was blood type A negative which was rare, less than ten per cent of the population.

Jonah could now see how the complete lack of evidence had led the enquiry to focus on the guards.

He went back over what he remembered of the witness reports of the event. Slowly, pieces started to fit together. Without conscious thought, he leafed through the typed sheets. With every phrase, every line he saw more connections. Cautiously, not daring to hope, he checked his working theory against the facts.

He pushed back from the desk and walked to the window. He was surprised to see that it was dark outside. There were no gaps, nothing that couldn't be explained. He still didn't have all the answers, but what he did have slotted together perfectly. More than that, this time he knew he wasn't reaching. There was none of that feeling where you're forcing your facts to fit your theory.

He was right. He knew it. Now, he just needed a way to prove it within the confines of the police service and the CPS. He packed up and prepared to head home, turning this new problem over in his head.

CHAPTER 26

"JONAH?" It was Elizabeth, sounding breathless. Instinctively Jonah looked at the clock – 10:47 pm. He had been watching the TV and finishing his beer when his mobile rang. Alex was already upstairs in bed.

"Elizabeth?" He couldn't help but think of the last time she'd called late at night. He moved silently through the house to his office. He switched on his computer as he sat at the cluttered desk.

"Mike's on the move again. Same as before, Google Maps and heading your way." She gave him an address in Splott. This was a suburb that was the other side of the docks from Cardiff Bay, where the main police station was.

"Okay." Jonah took a deep breath and wrote down the address, instinctively calling up his own Google Maps window. "When did he do the search?"

"Um, hold on," Jonah heard her tapping keys on the other end of the line. "I got the email, and it's got the details. Eight twenty-three tonight."

"How did it take so long to get to you?"

"After he did the search, then I think the program

sweeps his computer every hour or so and sends them to my source who forwards them on to me."

"Right." Jonah was thinking fast. "Right. I don't want to be too slow this time, so I'll get on over there and be in touch soon."

"Okay." She hung up. Jonah thought furiously. From what he'd read today, he knew who would be at the address in Splott. He also remembered his last argument with Farida.

He called up the stairs to tell Alex that he had to go in to work.

"At this time on a Thursday night?"

Jonah chose not to answer.

His mind made up, he grabbed his car keys and left the house. But he didn't go straight to the address that he had been given, instead he went into Cardiff Bay station. There he spent some time at the computer, first learning that Mike Khan was on his way, as he thought, to visit another one of the guards from the security van robbery. This gave Jonah his chance to make everything official. He linked together the two cases, Patrick's unexplained death and the robbery. On the screen he typed up his theory. Finally, he entered an action that he was heading out to interview the guard in Splott to see if he recognised any of the suspects.

All the paperwork covered, he went back to his car, ready now to find out what was waiting for him.

JONAH DROVE from the centre of Cardiff out to the east. Splott was only five minutes by car and his journey began by driving past pubs and night clubs. Even though it was a Thursday night the streets were still busy. He saw the uniformed officers standing around, chatting to people, just keeping an eye out. Trying to prevent trouble before it started. As his car came out onto the wide main roads, he wondered about the wisdom of always seeking promotion. Was he really better off out of uniform and into CID? At least those officers on the street knew what their job was, what was expected of them.

Soon, he pulled into Splott. This area was a grid of streets, mostly terraced houses. In the past it had also housed the vast steelworks that kept South Wales employed, but the work had long since gone overseas and the big industrial plants had shut. As the world changed, the pattern of the streets had been broken up by blocking off key roads to prevent commuter rat-runs forming. Jonah's target, Robb Street was one these that had been turned into a cul-de-sac. There would be only one chance to look at number thirty-five without arousing suspicion.

He drove down the street slowly, looking left and right, as if searching for an address. When he got to the right house, he noted that the wood was splintered on the door frame and the door was slightly ajar, just as it had been in Aberdare.

He drove a further five houses up and found a parking space. He weighed his police radio in his hands. He knew it could be set to silent, but it still made him nervous. He locked it in the glove box and got out of the car.

As if he knew what he was doing, he walked back to the house and, pulling a small torch from his pocket, ducked down a narrow passageway that led to the back where he turned left and dropped to his hands and knees.

Jonah couldn't help but feel stupid. He was crawling through some stranger's back garden like a kid on a dare. Luckily the back door was only half-glazed, and he was able to get past it without being seen. Beyond that there was a dangerous rectangle of light half on the lawn and half on the patio, thrown by the kitchen window. Hugging close to the wall, he managed to stay in the shadows.

He sat with his back against the wall. He was safe here, in the dark, unseen by anyone. He knew he had to make the decision, but for a moment he rested.

Ultimately, he had to take the chance. He gathered all his previous resolve and slowly moved to crouching, at the far corner of the window. All he needed was one glance in, confirm that a crime is occurring and then he could legitimately call in all the forces of the police to investigate.

With painstaking slowness, he inched higher until he could see the whole scene. He was looking through a milk bottle on the windowsill. He moved his head slowly to the left and got a clear view. He breathed out as he saw the back of a huge man, large enough to block half the window.

There was a flash of steel as he raised a sword and Jonah briefly saw another figure in the room. This was a man who looked much smaller and was taped to a chair. Dave Black. Blood ran into his eyes from a gash on his forehead, but he was awake and alert. He was securely bound with silver duct tape. He was pale and terrified.

Before he could be seen, Jonah slowly moved back until he was crouching beneath the window again. This was it; this was what had been set in motion the moment that Patrick entrusted his list of names to the Prof. He now had it all – and properly sewn up. He had a reason to be here, valid concerns because the door was broken, and he was a witness to a crime. All he needed to do was to crawl out of here and radio it in. He would do that sat in his car, where he couldn't be overheard. He quickly scanned the garden – there were no gates. The only way that Mike could leave would be out the front. On his own, he could easily keep watch.

This was the centre of Cardiff, not Aberdare. He could have specialist teams here with tasers and guns within minutes. He would be sure to emphasise the size and dangerous nature of the suspect. In his mind's eye he saw a team in riot gear charging into the tiny terrace house, subduing Mike Khan once and for all. Even his money and law degree wouldn't get him out of this one.

Ever so slowly and carefully, he crawled, keeping close to the wall, right under the window. Suddenly his bad knee went straight from aching slightly to full blown, stabbing pain. Somehow, he had knelt on a sharp stone that dug straight into the soft part below the knee.

Jonah managed to control the urge to cry out, but he did flinch and lift his knee, rising to a half crouch, up on one foot and one knee. He felt his shoulder brush something and turned to look. With a sinking feeling he saw a cheap garden incinerator. It was little more than a metal dustbin, with holes in the side and a chimney in the lid. In slow motion he watched the lid slide inexorably towards the patio. There was a small step in the patio, and he had nudged one foot of the incinerator over that.

Jonah reached out a hand, but his fingers futilely brushed the lid before it crashed to the paved surface. As it was ringing out like a cymbal, the main body of the incinerator followed suit, crashing and clanging as it rolled away from him.

The door banged opened and Mike Khan stood there silhouetted against the light. He ducked through the doorway, then stood up straight, blocking both the way into the house and Jonah's route back to the street. The descriptions were true, he was at least six foot six and heavily built, not gangly. His skin was either pale Asian or dark European, and his black hair was cropped close to his skin. His eyes glinted dangerously in his face and he was just starting to develop jowls.

"What the fuck?" he asked. "Who the fuck are you?" He had a sword dangling from his hand, blood staining the blade. There were dark spots across the navy-blue boiler suit he was wearing.

Jonah merely stood up and shrugged. He hadn't yet figured out how to play this.

"Mmm," Mike said, "get in there." He stepped aside to block the passage to the front and lazily indicated the kitchen with his sword. "For fuck's sake," he said when Jonah didn't move. "There's no other way out of this garden apart from through me. Now, do you want me to get all out of breath and sweaty chasing you around the garden before I drag you back into the kitchen? You don't want to see me when I'm upset."

Jonah's mind was spinning, trying to work out an angle. He looked around but Mike was right, there was no other way out. With that sword and his height, his reach was impossible to get past. In the end he shrugged again and went to the door. He passed by Mike, close enough to smell his aftershave mixed with blood and sweat. He could feel the presence of him. He couldn't believe how tall and wide he was as he passed him and entered the kitchen. His shoulder blades tingled as he presented his back to Mike, but he couldn't see any other way to play this. He shuffled into the kitchen and leant against a counter by Dave Black. There was a small table carelessly pushed to one side. This hadn't made much space as the room was small and lined with cupboards. Jonah tried to steady his breathing.

Jonah had his back to the front of the house and looked

out of the window. To his right was the door to the garden and behind him to the left was another doorway that he guessed led to the rest of the house. The kitchen was tidy enough, but dated. The doors were plain white with faded red handles, the work surfaces cheap and thin.

Dave, unable to move, flicked his eyes between Mike and Jonah. There was a strip of tape over his mouth but his eyes were speaking volumes. He was confused and scared and maybe just a little hopeful that someone had interrupted his torture. Certainly whatever happened next had to be better than dying on his own.

"Right so, now we have a problem, don't we?" Mike said. Jonah noted that he had no trace of accent, either foreign or from Birmingham. He sounded pure home counties or London. "Who are you? And don't mess me around." He stopped to think. "Actually, chuck your wallet and phone on the table there."

Jonah moved to his pocket but was brought up short by Mike "Slowly! Fingertips!"

Held between thumb and forefinger, he put his phone on the table. Reaching back into his pocket, he took out his wallet, separating it from his warrant card which he left behind.

But Mike saw the attempted deception and stepped right up to Jonah. He laid the sword on Jonah's right shoulder, sharp side against his neck. With his left hand he reached into Jonah's pocket. "Let's see what you're holding back."

Mike retreated to the other side of the small kitchen. Smart move, thought Jonah, remembering his self-defence training. The sword gives him an advantage in reach, and being close to me he'd given that away.

He flipped open the case and his eyes widened. "Right.

Detective Sergeant Jonah Greene of the South Wales Police. Nice to meet you." He picked up Jonah's phone and turned it over in his hands. "Can't remove the battery," he said to himself. "Pity." And then he threw it into an empty ready meal foil container in the sink. He ran the tap and the phone went underwater, with bits of breadcrumb floating around in the scummy water. Jonah watched it go and could have sworn he saw the screen flash before slowly fading out.

The two men looked at each other. The awkward silence was broken by Mike. "Tell me, are you looking for me particularly?"

"No," Jonah said. "I don't even know who you are. I was just making routine enquiries."

"Routine enquiries? I didn't know the police routinely crawled around people's back gardens late at night!" One eyebrow was raised to emphasise the comic nature of his comment, but his eyes remained cold and calculating.

Jonah felt as if he were outside his body. He could feel the ribbon of fear in his stomach, his heart beating too fast as he was breathing too shallowly. Worse, he could sense his thoughts shutting down. The pressure of making the decision of what to say next was too much, his brain couldn't handle it. The only thing he had left was to speak. Everything else was forbidden by Mike. Yet, now he had to choose from innumerable sentences, words, approaches, strategies.

Simple steps, he thought. He forced himself to breathe in slowly and deeply. He pretended he'd been winded on the rugby pitch, and held the breath, letting the oxygen spread through his body. Finally, he blew out slowly. When he opened his eyes again, Mike was staring at him quizzically.

"Sorry, just, you know, it's a bit stressful," Jonah found himself saying. Mike chuckled.

"So, you came here looking for me, I wonder how you knew?"

"Not you, particularly. Everyone in the area heard about what happened in Aberdare," Jonah stopped to take another breath. "The last thing any of us want to do is see a kicked-in door and blunder straight into," he paused, and waved around the kitchen, "well, walk in on a scene like this."

Mike nodded slowly to himself.

Jonah meanwhile was thinking about what his therapist had said. He'd been warned against compartmentalising his thoughts. But now, he seized on this idea. He thought about his family and if they'd miss him. Then he took that thought, shoved it into its own room and locked the door. He wondered how much the sword would hurt and what would happen next, then shut the door on that too. One by one, he shut down all the possibilities until he was just left with his training, with rational thought.

"We both want the same thing," Jonah said experimentally. Mike nodded slightly to indicate he should continue. "We want to get out of here, in my case in one piece, in your case with your freedom."

Mike looked as if he was considering these words. Then, without warning, he took a step and flicked the sword upwards towards Jonah. He pressed himself back into the worktop, but the blade still sliced through his sweatshirt and nicked the zips on his jacket. He felt a slight breeze where holes had been made in his polo shirt but couldn't feel any blood.

"That was for the hopelessly clumsy attempt to bond with me," he said, "straight out of the surviving a hostage situation handbook."

The sword flicked again, and Jonah jerked his head back. This time he felt a sting on his cheek and a trickle of blood reaching down to his chin. He reached out for a tea towel and pressed it to his face.

"And that was for lying to me. I could see it in your face, my height, my size, you've heard about me haven't you." He frowned at Jonah. "I don't know of many photographs of me around, and I don't recognise you, so this might be the first time you've seen me?"

Jonah nodded miserably, aware that he was conceding control to Mike.

"And you know who I am?" Mike asked and was answered with another nod. "Why don't you say my name, so we all know what's going on."

With a sinking feeling he mumbled, "Mike Khan." Dave Black looked from one to the other, aware now that he was in deep trouble. The terrifying stranger who had broken into his home and assaulted him had already let him see his face. But now he also knew his name, so he did not expect to see the next morning.

"Where did I go wrong?" Mike asked conversationally. "I need to know what the slip-up was."

Jonah considered for a second. He would protect the living but not the dead he decided. Every minute he kept Mike talking was another minute of life. "Patrick had a list. It had your name on it," he said simply.

"A list? I specifically said anything written, any note-books, anything like that was to be brought to me once he was dead."

" Patrick gave the list to another down-and-out before he died, and that person brought it to me once he found out Patrick was dead."

Mike shook his head. "My fault then. I underestimated him because he was a homeless drunk. I thought he was washed up. But that was clever. He must've set that up once he'd contacted Andrew and tried to blackmail him. What was on the list?"

"Seven names," Jonah said, watching Mike's face closely. "You, Elizabeth Barry and Andrew McRae, and Peter Calne." There was the slightest tremor in Mike's face at that name, just a tiny narrowing of the eyes, a small pursing of the lips. "I spoke to him about his time at university. And Emma Walters, Justin Day and Bill Wormslea were also on the list, but they're all dead."

"Hmmm, nothing else?" Jonah shook his head. "And when you went through his effects, there wasn't a folder, a pile of paperwork, notebook, nothing like that?" For the first time, Mike looked nervous or expectant.

"No," said Jonah, and Mike relaxed again. Jonah was left wondering what Mike was on about. He removed the tea towel and inspected the brown stain his own blood had made. He gingerly dabbed at his cheek with a clean part and found it had stopped bleeding. He didn't dare challenge Mike any further.

"And you got here from there? A list of seven names?" Mike sounded impressed. "That's quite some detective work."

"And it's on the system, you know." Jonah attempted to sound brave. "If I die, it won't die with me."

Mike weighed the sword in his hand. He swung it experimentally as if it was new and he was feeling the heft of it. "Are you really threatening me?" he asked, incredulous.

"No, just pointing out some facts." Jonah weighed his next words carefully. "Have you heard of a criminal called Kenneth Noye?" Mike waved the sword as if to say, carry on. "Well he was one of the Brink's-Mat robbers. Had a big old place out in the country, plenty of grounds to melt the gold down into fresh ingots, to sell them on. One night, his dogs start going nuts, so he goes to investigate, with a knife. Long story short, he stabs and kills a police officer who was crawling through the garden." Mike gave him a long hard look at this point. "When it comes to court, he has a good lawyer and claims that the policeman was all in black, no identification and didn't announce that he was police. Against all the odds he gets off. He thinks he's scot free but a few years down the line, he's in a road rage incident and kills another guy. This time there's an off-duty copper, just watching him from a parked car and he gets sent down for life." Jonah pauses for effect. "We always get people who kill police officers. They haven't yet closed the case on Yvonne Fletcher and she was shot by a Libyan diplomat through an embassy window."

Mike picked up the warrant card and turned it over in his left hand. "So, what you are saying is, this makes you invulnerable. Because of this card I can't kill you?"

"Not unless you want to live the rest of your life looking over your shoulder. And prison won't be a picnic either, once the screws learn what you've done. Another guy, Harry Roberts, spent the best part of fifty years behind bars for killing three police officers."

Mike pretended to consider. "So, really all I've got to do is mess you up badly enough that you won't be able to rat me out until the morning? But not kill you? That way I can make my escape and be out of the country before the ports and everything are closed. Maybe something that requires surgery..." It seemed as if he was talking to himself. "...so that when the ambulance turns up, they'll sedate you straight away. I could, of course, tape you to a chair too, but I think you're too resourceful. I wouldn't rest easy."

Jonah went white, his wound standing out lividly on his

cheek. If I'm about to get seriously injured, he thought, I'm going down fighting. Rush in close and grab his sword hand in both hands. Then try to land a lucky knee in his privates? Elbow in the pressure point behind the ear? His plan didn't extend much beyond that. Mike might be about his age, but he certainly had the advantage in terms of height and weight and weaponry.

Jonah needed an advantage and suddenly realised he was in a kitchen. Mike had probably overpowered Dave in the hallway before dragging him into the kitchen and taping him to a chair. He might not have got all the knives out of the way; it wouldn't have been a priority. He started to look around with quick darts of his eyes, cataloguing drawers, looking for a knife block. He glanced at the ashen figure of Dave, still taped to his chair, and wondered where he kept his knives.

"There is no escape," Mike said. He was right; he was leaning against the far wall. To his right was an archway into the rest of the house. The kitchen was tiny and if Jonah made a dash for the back door, the sword would be in his back before he touched the handle.

Jonah thought he heard a noise in the hall. He pushed himself upright to cover it, just in case anyone else was in the house. Mike suddenly stood upright, alert.

"It's okay!" Jonah held his hands out to calm the big man. "Just getting comfortable."

"Well, don't get too comfy," Mike said. "I've got to be going soon. Once I've figured out what to do with the pair of you."

"You know, if you kill a second of the guards, they'll make the link much more quickly. At the moment we're investigating all of Harris's life."

"Believe it or not," Mike said condescendingly, "I had

thought of that. I was going to kill sonny boy here, then clean up. It'd look like he'd disappeared. I'll dump the body in Southern Ireland. Should throw some doubt on the crew again." He paused with a smile on his face. "It was so funny, watching the police run around chasing their tails. And when you started blaming the guards." He shook his head, nearly laughing. "Priceless!"

Jonah kept flicking his eyes around the room. Still no knives. But he did see something that made his heart leap. A tiny dot of red flicked off the milk bottle on the windowsill. Please don't follow procedure, he prayed, please just shoot the bastard.

The red dot, flicked away from the window, searching for its target. Jonah turned his head and stared out at the back garden. "Nothing out there either," Mike said, walking to the window. "Nothing and nobody but us three in the whole world. No help... gaa, gaa, gaa!" he stopped speaking and started gurgling, his head thrown back. He gripped the sword tighter than ever and it beat a tattoo on the cupboard under the sink.

Sticking out of the middle of his back were two tiny spikes, with curly wires leading out of the archway. Farida carefully stepped into the room, leading with the taser unit in her hand. She was dressed in loose, dark blue trousers and a black hoodie worn with the hood up and a police baseball cap under it.

A large uniformed officer squeezed past her, and she released the trigger on the taser. When she did so, Mike collapsed to his knees, the sword slipping harmlessly from his hand. As he went down, the uniformed officer immediately grabbed his wrists and pulled them sharply together before snapping on the cuffs.

Mike was still kneeling on the floor, shaking from head to foot, unable to move.

Farida stepped into the kitchen. "What happened to your face?"

"I AM GRATEFUL," Jonah said. "But what the hell, I mean." As always Farida gave a small frown at religious swear words. "Well, what are you doing here?"

The kitchen was crowded. One of the uniformed officers was tending to Dave Black – he had slit the tape with a knife he found and was administering basic first aid. He had already radioed in for an ambulance.

The other uniform was grabbing Mike and checking him over. The kitchen was so small they could hardly move. There was also the crackle of radios, along with reassuring words for Dave and complaints from Mike.

"Can we move him outside?" Jonah asked.

"Come on, buddy," Farida said to Mike, as she loaded a fresh cartridge into her taser. "And don't think of headbutting someone or anything." He squirmed his shoulder away from the hand on it. "I'm meant to aim for a big muscle group, but if you squirm..." She lit up the red dot and let it hover over his crotch for a second. Mike paled and meekly joined the procession out of the kitchen. The corridor meant they were in single file, with Farida walking backwards to cover Mike.

"I know we argued," she explained as she walked, "but I also knew you were onto something." She looked slightly shifty. "I sweettalked a couple of the guys who were manning the MIT twenty-four hours a day, and they kept an eye on your computer activity. When I saw you'd added an action to visit a witness at gone eleven at night, well, I knew you'd..." She glanced round at the uniformed officer who was close enough to hear. "I figured you were on to something."

"And you just thought you'd come out here with a couple of prop forwards and a taser?"

Farida shrugged. "It seemed sensible. Especially when you didn't answer your phone. Although you won't believe how much paperwork I've generated. Just checking out a taser is bad enough, but discharging one in the course of duty? And when we get back, he'll have to be checked over by the FME as well!" Although she was complaining, Jonah could tell it was light-hearted banter laced with relief that it had worked out well. "How's your face? Was that the sword?"

"Yep. It's okay, I think, stopped bleeding." The first one outside, Jonah stepped sideways onto the pavement to let Farida out.

"Let the paramedics have a look when they've dealt with Mr Black. You've got a job to do," Farida said, nodding her head towards Mike who was being led out to the street. Jonah looked as if he was going to protest. "No, you earned this. You did the legwork, didn't let it go. Get the arrest on your record, do your career no end of good."

Jonah turned to face Mike as the uniform followed them out of the door. The other was still in the house with Dave Black. All three police made a semicircle around the towering figure of Mike.

"Michael Khan, I am arresting you for assaulting a police officer. You do not have to say anything, but..." there was a sharp crack that echoed off the houses. All three police officers immediately dropped to a crouch – the sound of a gunshot was unmistakable.

Mike remained standing for a fraction of a second. Jonah was aware that he'd been showered in blood. He felt it on his skin like a light rain. Still crouching, he saw Mike drop to his knees and then keel over sideways. Working on instinct the officers converged on Mike but there was no way to help. The shot had gone in below one ear and come out through the opposite temple. Blood was pooling under his head as his eyes stared glassily across the pavement. His chest was still – he was dead.

"Where did that come from?" The uniformed police officer looked all around without rising from a crouch as he spoke.

As if in response, a door slammed up the street, an engine started, and a car pulled away.

"I've got my car!" Farida stood up and started moving. But Jonah was already jogging down the road, past his own car. The end of the road was closed off with a kerb, pavement and bollards. When he reached this blockage, his side was already hurting from a stitch and he could feel the icy night air through the cuts in his clothing. His knee complained and he could feel the blood throbbing in his wounded cheek.

He looked both ways, hoping for brake lights or indicators but no cars were moving anywhere. This road wasn't blocked and there were junctions in both directions. "Damn it! Goddamn it!" he shouted.

He saw lights coming on and doors starting to open, so he forced himself to calm down and started the slow walk back to the crime scene. By the time he got back, the ambulance was there, strobing the scene with blue light.

He was intercepted by a short, stout woman with hair that was actually red, not ginger. She was one of the paramedics. "What are you doing running around?" she demanded. "You should be on your way to hospital."

"I'm not hurt," Jonah insisted. "The main victim is in there, kitchen at the back."

"Brilliant!" she said with heavy sarcasm, "another hero cop." She seized his chin in a painful grip before shining a small torch at his face as she turned his head one way, then the other. "It's a clean cut, but not sterile. You've got blood and grime all over you and no idea how clean the weapon was. And we can get some stitches in that and a dressing and minimise the scarring."

Jonah stared at her uncomprehendingly – his brain was now in overload. He had locked away every thought to enable him to cope. All that was left was procedure, and there was nothing in the book to help him cope with this situation. Jonah felt empty; everything had been washed out of him.

With a withering glance, the paramedic turned and took Farida to one side. When their discussion was concluded, she went into the house to help her colleague while Farida came over to join him.

"I've told her that I'll take you to the hospital in the next ten minutes," she said. "In fact, I had to promise. That way we can free up the ambulance for the poor sod in there." She tilted her head towards the door. "I've already called it in. We've agreed it's the same MIT as it's the same case as the one in Aberdare. As you were investigating that, it all links together. SOCO are on their way and an authorised firearms officer to make sure the scene is safe." She looked doubtful. "I've got in touch with the coroner's office to deal with Mike."

"We don't need an AFO," Jonah said. "The shooter's cleared off. I've been down there and it's deserted. Be halfway to the M4 by now if they've got any sense."

"Still, shots fired at police officers, there's a procedure for that."

"Yeah, gotta follow procedure," Jonah said bleakly.

CHAPTER 27

THE NEXT AFTERNOON, following a trip to the hospital, a shower and a few hours' sleep, Jonah found himself in the deputy chief constable's office. This was an office unlike any other he'd been in. The carpet was deep and the room large enough for both an impressive desk and an informal meeting area. Tasteful pictures adorned the walls, and a personal assistant had admitted him.

For this meeting, the DCC had chosen to use the informal area so people were grouped around a low table, sitting on a mix of chairs and sofas. He was the lowest ranked officer there, together with Farida. His direct boss, Linwood was there, as was DS Castle. More worryingly, the icy faced Ms Cross was present, along with a dour man in a suit who was introduced as 'Davies from the IPCC'.

"Right, so, I'm not entirely sure whether I should put a commendation on your records or a written warning." The representatives from HR remained poker faced, giving him no clue how to proceed. "It appears you've found the beheading suspect, arrested him and then he's been shot. Is that right?"

There were nods around the room. Jonah's story was full of holes, so he and Farida were saying as little as possible. He explained that he'd gone to interview the security guard on the off chance that he was returned home from the pub. The splintered door frame reminded him of the Aberdare crime scene, so he'd checked round the back before calling for backup.

"Was that wise?" Superintendent Castle interrupted.

"Well, sir, I didn't want to call in full tactical support for a simple burglary. I couldn't be sure at the time it was related to the other murder."

From there on, his account had been roughly true to events. Farida swore that she'd agreed to meet Jonah in the pub for a last-orders drink, had failed to raise him on the phone, and finally checked his actions on the computer.

"And you just happened to have a taser and two uniforms with you?" Castle asked.

"Well," Farida had the decency to look embarrassed, "I had a hunch. And Aberdare had spooked all of us, especially the women, we feel vulnerable." And from there the tale had once again proceeded much closer to the truth.

"So," the DCC continued, "we have one major crime solved, and then before you've read him his rights, he's become a death in custody, and we have the IPCC involved as well. Do we think the public will be reassured that we have replaced a beheading criminal with a shooting one?"

Jonah knew the truth, but he didn't want to admit to his many misdemeanours here in front of his boss, HR and the IPCC so he kept quiet.

"Well, unfortunately, shootings on the streets of Cardiff, while rare are not unheard of. So, we can manage the PR aspects of this one. But what we need, more than anything, to restore public confidence, is a swift resolution." He turned to Linwood, Farida and Jonah. "Are you still convinced the cases are linked?" All three nodded, not daring to speak. "We need to quickly establish that the dead man, ah," a quick glance at his notes, "Michael Khan did indeed commit the murder up in Aberdare. Then we need to investigate his murder. It might look like the suspect in that case has done us a favour in getting rid of Mr Khan, but I will not have vigilantes roaming the streets of Cardiff taking potshots at suspects. No one gets to fire towards my officers without facing the full weight of the law.

"Ms Cross, where do we stand in respect of allowing DS Greene and Philips back to work?"

She leaned forward, obviously keen to impress. "They've clearly been involved in a traumatic incident, and one in which one officer was held captive and an ECD was discharged by the other officer at a suspect. Further, they are involved in a case where we've got the death of a suspect in custody. Usually this would be more than enough to put them on suspension with full pay while we get an outside force in to investigate the circumstances." She looked at the dour man, Davies, who gave her the merest of nods to indicate that he agreed. "However, there is no indication at this stage that the officers were in any way involved with the death in custody."

Jonah had spoken to Linwood earlier and now prayed that he would rise to the occasion. He leaned forward to offer his opinion. "Ah, well, yes, from an operational point of view, DS Greene and Philips may well have a lot to offer. We need to find out how they came to be, er, involved with the suspect before he was shot. It is possible, indeed likely, that these very insights might bring us closer to the second killer." He glanced nervously at Ms Cross and Mr Davies. "Although a formal investigation hasn't yet begun, it is apparent that Mr Khan was shot from quite a distance. I've, ah, taken the liberty of speaking, informally of course, to the firearms officer who attended the scene. He told me that both bullet and cartridge have been recovered and we appear to be looking for a hunting rifle. Needless to say, its calibre and type don't match any firearms in use by South Wales Police, and none of our firearms officers were active that night. But I think we can all be quite certain that, while this was a regrettable death in custody, it was in no way as a result of any failings by my officers. It does appear to be an unforeseeable action by a third party."

The DCC looked at Davies from the IPCC who spoke for the first time in this meeting. "This is clearly a complex case," he said in a low, careful voice. "Ordinarily we would remove the officers from front line duties while we assembled an investigation to establish the facts of the case. However," he inclined his head towards Linwood, "I can see that there may be operational reasons to retain the officers involved in a more active role in the case. Certainly, I wouldn't want any of the actions of the IPCC to stand in the way of debriefing them more thoroughly so that the investigation of the MIT can continue unimpeded."

"So," the DCC said brightly, "it would appear the final decision rests with me. It does seem that you two have some unique insight that enabled you to catch the Aberdare sword killer. I'd like you, as soon as you feel able, to return to work with the MIT. But, you should keep to your desks, put everything you know into the computer and not been seen out and about in public. I think that about covers all the bases?" There were nods and agreements around the room.

As they all stood to leave, Jonah deliberately hung back. He caught Linwood by the arm and motioned for him to stay too. The DCC went over to sit by his desk and started looking through some paperwork.

"Sir?" Jonah said, standing in front of the desk.

"What? Oh, Greene? What is it?" He hadn't expected anyone else to still be there. His eyes flicked to Linwood as well.

"I believe I know who the shooter is, sir."

"Good! Good! Off you go and put it into the computer then."

"It's a bit complicated," Jonah confessed. "I think I know where she is, but if I'm right, she'll only confess to me. I've built up something of a rapport, you see. If I'm the one who confronts her, I'm sure I can get her to come in quietly."

"You think this was a woman? And you've built up a rapport with her? And now she's taking potshots at my officers?" He was incredulous.

"Well, I obviously never thought she'd go this far," Jonah said defensively.

"What are you on about Greene?" Linwood asked angrily. "If you know the shooter, let us know and we can arrest them! And you must come clean, tell us how you know her."

"No, no, please don't explain!" The DCC broke in, "I think this is one of those cases where I really don't need to know. Why are you telling me this? Why can't I just send in a firearms squad to arrest her."

"If I'm right, she's over the border in Gloucestershire. With clearance, I could go and arrest her, bring her back calmly. No publicity, no shots fired, all quiet and away from the press." Jonah looked imploringly from Linwood to the DCC. "I'm sure she'd confess to me, we could close the whole case, find out why Mike Khan did it and why she shot him. Have the whole thing put to bed within forty-eight hours."

"You have just been through a very traumatic experience," the DCC said. "Can your commanding officer confirm that you're fit to undertake another high stress job?"

"I have read the initial report from the witness who was held hostage before DS Greene got there," Linwood said. "I have to say that he kept his cool and played for time. He followed the procedure to keep the suspect talking and he attempted to establish a rapport. Even when he was injured, he still kept working to keep the public safe."

The DCC furrowed his brow and rubbed the bridge of his nose. Linwood shifted his weight from one foot to another, but he was waiting on his superior before announcing his decision. "You'd have to be supported by a tactical firearms squad, from Gloucestershire constabulary," he said finally.

"I'd be meeting her in a convent," Jonah explained.

"A convent? With nuns?" He looked shocked. "All the same, you're not going to meet a woman that you suspect of shooting at officers without firearms support. I'll order them to hang back, but you'll be able to call them in if needed." He gave stern look to both Linwood and Greene. "I'm trusting that you're not going to get us involved in a gunfight in a convent. Do you think he's up to it?"

Linwood considered his response. Finally he said, "If he can cope with a sword wielding maniac then I think we can trust him in a convent full of nuns!"

Jonah nodded, even though he wasn't sure if he'd just been complimented or not.

"It goes against procedure, interviewing a suspect one-on-one," the DCC said, "so you just go in, arrest her, and hand her over for a formal interview. Anything she says to you without a witness will be useless in court. You follow PACE guidelines to the letter. Do you understand?"

"Yes, sir, I believe it will all go quite smoothly."

"It had better." He glowered at Jonah. "If this blows up in my face, you won't have a career any more, DS Greene." He looked over at Linwood who nodded, enthusiastic at the prospect of firing Jonah. "I've seen your personnel record, and this is your last chance. Do I make myself clear?"

JONAH PULLED up outside the two-storey white building. It was wide and beautifully proportioned. A low stone wall stood to one side of the door with a cream sign announcing in tasteful gold script 'The Ministry of Capernaum and Bethesda'. The lawn was well kept and even the car park was clean and tidy.

He approached the wide steps and large door with trepidation. He wasn't sure of the rules. He knocked and waited. A slight woman answered, in a simple grey dress with a white blouse and a white wimple over her hair. She looked to be in her early fifties. Jonah was so used to talking to Farida, that he just accepted the wimple as another sort of hijab.

"Yes?" She frowned at him, making it clear that just by being here and being a man, he was in the wrong.

"I'm here to see a guest of yours, Elizabeth?" He decided to act as if it was an appointment. Behind him the drive stretched a short distance across the lawn to the edge of the grounds. Luckily, this was bounded by a high hedge which served to hide the van full of armed officers that were a condition of his coming. He imagined them back there, eating crisps and larking about. Waiting was one of the main parts of a policeman's job.

"Elizabeth? Yes, she did say that someone might call for her." She appraised Jonah a second time. He felt self-conscious of the dressing on his cheek, his general run-down appearance, and again, that he was a man. "We haven't had a man cross the threshold for several centuries, and we're not going to start now. You may meet our guest in the garden. Come around the side of the house, while I send someone for her. You'll find there are plenty of benches. You can wait there."

She went back inside for a moment, then reappeared to lead Jonah around the house. Through a small gate in a fence, he was shown into the gardens at the rear of the house. These were immaculately kept and set in lawns that descended from the house in a series of wide terraces. The whole was linked by paths of white gravel which led to low wide sets of steps. There were mature trees and flowerbeds bounded by low walls. Here and there were placed benches, summer houses and bowers, all angled to give a view to the west.

Jonah was led to a simple bench that was set back from the path on a small area of patio, its back to a low wall where the terrace rose above it. Like all the other seats, it was well located. As Jonah sat down, he looked west, across a valley, towards ever rising mountains in the distance.

It was a perfect spring day, with small white clouds being chased across the sky. The flower beds and tree branches had small buds of green standing out against the deep brown. Jonah felt a sense of unreality as he sat in rural splendour, preparing to wrap up a mystery that spanned twenty years and six murders.

He waited, nervously turning over the radio in his

pocket. Then he remembered it had a panic button and if he pressed it, then the convent would be presented not with one inoffensive man in a crumpled suit, but with a squad of heavily armed officers. He took his hand out of his pocket and clasped it with his other one.

Elizabeth came and sat next to him, clutching a dark red folder to her chest. She was more relaxed and happier than Jonah had ever seen her, and this made her strikingly beautiful. Her skin was clear and her blue eyes sparkled.

"This is a lovely place, and you're looking well," Jonah said.

"Thank you," Elizabeth said, "it is my sanctuary. Well, it was, I don't suppose I'll be coming back, will I?"

Jonah shook his head. "Maybe, when you're released? Who knows?"

Elizabeth nodded. "I could take my vows then I suppose. Once I've atoned."

"Why did you shoot him?" The question came out before Jonah had a chance to think.

"Who? Mike?"

"Yes, we had him. We had direct witness to kidnapping, assaulting a police officer, at least GBH, although we could have made attempted murder stick. And we would have got him then for Aberdare and lord knows what else. He would have died in prison."

"I did think about it. I really did. I was sat out there in the car. Waiting to see who would come out. Whether you'd succeed or if Mike would. But while I was waiting, I was remembering what sort of person Mike was, what we had made him. A life in prison, he would have risen to the top. He'd have been that inmate that even the guards were afraid of, the one who killed a nurse or injured a guard or another inmate." She stopped and stared at the mountains. "He was a rabid dog, better to put him down."

"You do know what you've just--"

"Yes, yes! That's why you're here, isn't it? To hear my confession, take me away?" She held out her wrists as if waiting for him to slap the cuffs on.

Jonah nodded.

"Did they let you come here on your own?" Elizabeth asked. When Jonah hesitated, unsure of how to answer, she said, "I didn't think they would let you."

"Why did you ask?"

"There's one more job to do, before you arrest me," Elizabeth explained. "And it needs to be watertight so he can't wriggle off the hook over chain of custody or evidence or whatever."

"Andrew McRae," Jonah said.

Elizabeth nodded. "There's only a couple of days left before nominations for the election close. We need to get this right, get him arrested and then get his name off the ballot. Could you bring another policeman here?" she asked.

"Give me a minute," Jonah said, gingerly getting the radio out of his pocket.

"DS Greene here, do you have a, er," he was going to say WPC but they hadn't existed since before he joined the force. He searched his mind for a politically correct term. "...female officer there?"

"Yes. Is there a problem?"

"No, sir."

"Are you under threat?" This was a code word.

"No, sir," this was the correct response. If he had said, 'there is no threat', then the troops would have come rolling in. "Could you send your female officer in here, please? No weapons though."

"Are you sure, sir? Are those your orders?"

"Yes, send her in."

"Okay, PC Baine will be with you shortly."

"There you go," Jonah said to Elizabeth. For a couple of minutes, they sat in the spring sunshine.

"That's Wales over there, you know," Elizabeth said, pointing to the mountains in the distance.

"The Black Mountains," Jonah confirmed. "It is nice here," he repeated. "Is this where you spent all the money?"

"Yes," Elizabeth answered. "I mean at first I spent a bit on myself, but once I had Jonathon, I saw how shallow it all was and well, I know I'll never fix things, but it helps a bit with the people who've been hurt."

PC Baine turned out to be a tall woman with blonde hair. Jonah had no idea of her figure as she was wearing uniform trousers and a bulletproof vest over a blue shirt. Her hair was held back with a flat clip and tucked under a baseball cap. Despite the no weapons request her belt still had an impressive array of equipment hanging from it.

"DS Greene?" she asked. "Constable Baine, as requested." She stood at ease in front of him. Jonah could hear a question in her voice.

"Thank you, I thought it might be easier with the nuns, to get a woman in here. I'm Jonah by the way and this is Elizabeth Gardner. Please sit down."

"Siobhan," she responded, taking a seat next to Jonah. "What do you need me for?"

"I need to confess, and make a proper job of it," Elizabeth said. She frowned at all the equipment and asked, "Do you still have a notebook with you?"

"Of course." Siobhan produced her police pocketbook and pen.

"Right, this might come to court, so I need you to take

notes," Elizabeth said, and Siobhan leaned forward to make sure she could see both of them.

"Hold on," Jonah said, aware of the loopholes that a defendant could climb through after the event. "Do you want a solicitor? And are you aware that what you say could be used in court against you?"

Elizabeth laughed. "I bloody well hope so!" Turning to PC Baines, she said solemnly, "I am aware of my right to a solicitor and am declining. I am making my confession in sound mind, and full knowledge that it's incriminating me." She looked at Jonah who nodded. It wasn't a proper caution, but it would have to do.

"Two nights ago, Friday, no, Thursday," she said, then stopped. She stifled a sob, then gathered her wits a little. "Damn! I'm sorry. I've looked forward to this moment for more than fifteen years and now I've messed it up." She sniffed and scrubbed hard at her eyes with the heels of her hands. "Right, two nights ago on Thursday the twenty-third of April, at about eleven forty," she frowned at Jonah who nodded to confirm the time, "I shot and killed Mr Michael Khan with my rifle." She paused again, then restarted. "Oh dear! That does sound awfully cold! But I suppose that's what you need for evidence and all that. Anyway, you had just led him outside that house in Robb Street in Cardiff. You were there with two other officers, a woman and a uniformed man." There was stunned silence from both officers as PC Baine calmly wrote down every word.

"I also took part in an armed robbery on the twenty-sixth of July 1996 somewhere in the countryside north of Cardiff. During that robbery, I shot and wounded a guard, and accidentally shot one of my fellow robbers, Andrew McRae." She looked at Jonah. "Have you got that far?" When Jonah nodded, she continued, "So, did we leave any

DNA behind? It was a mess; I'll tell you that much. I lay awake at night, thinking about it, and I'm sure we didn't get all the cash bags that we used on Andrew's leg."

"No, you didn't," Jonah said in amazement. Next to him Siobhan was wide eyed but was dutifully still taking notes. He glanced down and saw they were all done correctly. "We have a sample, enough to run a comparison, that's for sure."

"Where was I? Oh yes, for completeness, the other two robbers were Mike Khan and Patrick Kinsale both now deceased." She stopped to draw another long shuddering breath. "And finally, on the thirteenth of April 1996 at around eight thirty in the morning, I shot Bill Wormslea on the seafront just outside Bournemouth." She looked a little lost. "My gun, my beautiful rifle – a Steyr SSG 69. It is in the garage of my home in the Cotswolds. High up on the left at the back is a line of boxes on a shelf, and it's behind there, all oiled and in its case. I don't wear gloves so there'll be my fingerprints on there and nobody else's. And I know I lost the cartridge the other night, so I'm sure you can do all sorts of ballistics and things." She produced a set of keys from her pocket and Siobhan stunned Jonah by producing an evidence bag. She held the bag open as Elizabeth dropped the keys in. "Those are my keys to the cottage. You have my permission to go and get the rifle." She stopped and thought. "Though I suppose you can search it when you arrest me anyway?" Jonah nodded, still struck dumb.

He looked at PC Baine who simply shrugged. This was outside all of their experience.

"I haven't read you your rights properly you know," Jonah said. "You should have done all this with a solicitor present, in a police station with the tapes running ideally."

"Oh, but that would be so dull." Elizabeth brushed away his concerns with another wave of her hand. "It's lovely here. And I am of sound mind and I am resolved to confess. It's been weighing on me for years, decades even. I need this," she searched for the word, "absolution."

"Why did you it?" Jonah finally asked. "I can understand the robbery but why the murders?"

"That has also kept me awake at night, that question. The only answer is in this folder. I can't go over it again." She looked at Siobhan. "I did get this is information legitimately from the parties involved. It's all above board. There was no coercion involved. And I've had this folder in my possession for over twenty years. This is the first that DS Greene knows of it." She handed the folder over to Jonah. "Start with the handwritten sheets. They're like a diary I wrote a few years after the events. They explain what the affidavits are."

Jonah turned to PC Baine. "Gloves?" She produced a pair of latex gloves for him. Once he was not going to contaminate the evidence, he took the folder.

He slid out the papers inside. There was a stack of handwritten sheets on top of a few typed and signed pages. At a brief glance, Jonah thought they looked like affidavits. The signed sheets were each enclosed in their own see-through plastic wallets, and some had newspaper cuttings with them.

As he was instructed, Jonah turned first to a handwritten sheet. The writing was neat and rounded in blue biro on A4 lined paper. It looked like a dissertation from university – Elizabeth had even written her name, and the date at the top.

Imagining that forensic experts would examine it shortly, Jonah began to read; the first person to do so since it was written.

CHAPTER 28

Elizabeth Gardner 23rd May 2001

I'm putting this down in writing now, before my memory fades. Sometimes the medicines my doctor gives me make my mind go fuzzy, my memories indistinct. But I'm okay now, so I'll write this down before it all fades again, maybe forever.

I first met Andrew McRae in April 1995. We were both at university and he was magnetic, even back then. As this diary is to be unflinchingly honest, I'll admit now that I was attracted to him. I hoped that something might happen between us. He was a step above most other students, always in ironed shirts, clean shaven, never a hair out of place. On campus, this made him quite different, and I wanted someone of his class.

"Have you seen the latest figures?" he asked me, showing me a copy of the Financial Times. I'd deliberately sat next to him, hoping for a conversation. I'd noticed him looking at me several times over the last few weeks. I'd been trying to engineer this meeting for days.

I glanced down at the paper, rising graduate unemployment the headlines. "Yes, what about it?" My heart sank a bit – this wasn't classic chat-up material.

"Well, does it seem, you know right? I mean, what's the point of us studying hard, for three years, living in poverty, for what? To join the dole queue?"

"Is there an alternative though?"

"Do you think we're better than most people?" Andrew answered my question with one of his own. "I mean, it used to be that universities were for the best, the cream of the crop, future leaders of men. I mean, look at this." He tapped the paper again. "Now they're planning to turn all polytechnics into de-facto universities. That just means more graduates chasing fewer jobs."

I nodded sadly, unable to think of anything to say. Finally, I said, "This is the same discussion that's being had in bars on campuses up and down the country. It's all talk, nothing ever changes!" I was angry with his maudlin complaining when I'd been expecting so much more.

"What if it wasn't all talk?" Andrew asked with a quiet intensity. There was a hint of steel in his glance. He'd always had charisma, but now he was revealing something deeper in his soul. A willingness to go further, to whatever ends were necessary. "What if there was a way to guarantee that you'd be set up for life by the time you left this place?"

"I'm guessing it's not going to be legal?" My desire had ebbed but was now building again, tinged with curiosity. Despite the dry subject, Andrew was passionate.

"Laws are for the guidance of sages and the obedience of fools. Didn't we just agree that we're a step above people like that?"

I nodded, then said, "Yes, but there are always risks with breaking laws."

Now Andrew smiled, full wattage. "I'll have to introduce you to Mike. He's studying law, focusing on criminal at the moment. Between us we've found the loophole, the way around it." He paused to stare into my eyes again, to compel me with the power of his character. "But it requires boldness. Massive boldness, to set aside all the laws and conventions of society."

"But without laws won't we just become savages?" I was nearly breathless now.

"No! That's the beauty of it, we just have to commit two crimes over one summer, and then we'll be free for ever. In fact, afterwards, I'd actively encourage you to live a legal life, under the radar, never attracting any attention."

Now my curiosity was piqued. "What exactly are you planning?"

"No!" Andrew held up a hand. "As I said, it's illegal, so before we go any further, we have to have confidentiality. So, if you're in, you're totally in. If you walk away now, then you must never speak of this again." He paused and smiled at me and my insides melted at his approval. "But I think you're the right kind of person, I think you're just who we need. And I don't think you'll let us down."

"What do you want me to do?"

"We're meeting in the college bar, the Hub, tomorrow night at eight. Me, Mike and Patrick – you haven't met them yet. If you turn up there, you're in, no matter what. If you don't, I'll deny we've ever met." With this, he turned away with a flourish and strode off.

Who could resist such a suave, mysterious man? Certainly not my twenty-year-old self. Most of the other men and boys on campus were either sweaty sporty types, swotty nerds or stoned losers. Andrew was at the top of my very short list of eligible men.

By eight o'clock the next night, I was in pieces. If I

walked into the bar, I'd be guilty, a criminal. I was a nice girl, from a good family in a nice neighbourhood. Sevenoaks wasn't known for producing hardened criminals. I hated to admit it, but I was afraid. As well as fear, I felt that life was picking up, that I was on the threshold of something extraordinary, a chance to really live.

At five past eight, I walked into the bar. It was noisy, with music and comings and goings and chatter. The lights were low, and I was already late. I thought I'd look around, pretend I hadn't seen anyone and leave with my dignity, and liberty, intact.

"Elizabeth!" Andrew called out and raised his hand. Some invisible force pulled me through the bar to his table. As always, he was immaculate, side parted dark hair, pressed shirt, the whole works. Next to him was a giant of a man, in plain black T-shirt and jeans. He was overweight, but not hugely so, and, I later learned, around six foot six tall. This was Mike Khan, his dark round face betraying his Asian origins, his hair shaved down to a fuzz. The final member was Patrick, the most ordinary looking of the lot. Slightly nervous, wearing glasses, but above all, average in almost all things. Looking closer, I could see he lacked the sophistication of Andrew – frayed cuffs on his sweatshirt, faded patches on his jeans.

When I was sat down, Andrew nodded to Mike, who spoke. "Most of the big robberies get busted apart because they are done by career criminals who work in gangs and commit lots of crimes. They, in effect, form a closed community within larger society and once one member of the community is pressured to confess by the police it starts a domino effect of confession after confession. Of course, once they have the names, they can then pursue or fabricate the evidence to make the conviction." All of us were second or third year students and trained in a Pavlovian response to attend to a seminar, so we listened without interrupting. "What I'm proposing is that we start at the top. Instead of petty crimes working up to a big robbery, we start big, from cold. No links, no previous, no names known to the police for them to lean on. Just one big robbery, split the money, then leave. Once it's done, we then never contact each other again and try our best to live honest lives so that the police never even know our names."

Patrick looked up from the beer mat he'd been studying. "Where would we get enough money to make something like that worthwhile?"

Mike nodded at Andrew, who picked up the thread. "There are centres around the country that collate cash for the National Mint and the banks. All the cash that's handled, goes from tills into banks, and then needs to go to depots to be counted, checked and sent back out. I'm studying economics and it's all there in textbooks if you know where to look. My favourite is a depot in the hills outside Cardiff. It's not too far from here but also in quite a remote area. It's where they collect the cash, check it for wear, and sort it into denominations ready to go back out and fill up cash machines. If we pick our moment, we could hit one van on its way out of the depot and walk away with between ten and fifteen million pounds to split between us. Unmarked notes, already in circulation, completely untraceable. Enough for each of us to start a whole new life."

There was stunned silence around the table. Mike and Andrew carefully watched the other two. Patrick nodded slowly, as the impact of somewhere between two and a half and four million pounds dawned on him.

I was still paralysed and a myriad of emotions swirled

through me. Fear of course, but that was soon eclipsed by excitement. I'd come to university with high hopes of balls and fancy restaurants with eligible men. But towards the end of my second year, I'd settled into a life of trying to make a meagre grant last and drinking in cheap pubs. And now, as Andrew had said, life wasn't going to get any better even after graduation. The graduate jobs fair where you'd have your pick of golden opportunities was now a hollow joke.

But could I go the other way and become a bank robber? Wield a gun and demand money? As I tried to make this new vision of myself fit, Mike was talking again.

"Obviously the old system wouldn't have existed for so long if there wasn't an advantage to it. It survived because it means you can trust your compatriots. An armed robbery will be a perilous task, any number of things could go wrong. It will put all of us under immense stress and we've no idea how we'll all react. Some of us might freeze, or panic or anything. So, I've devised a slightly artificial, yet I believe efficient solution to this problem." He paused to look round, to make sure he still had us. He'd reached the crux of his plan, and his tension was palpable. "When we're carrying out the robbery, we might need to shoot people, maybe kill them. We need to know that we're all solid. Further, we can't have someone losing their bottle when the robbery is over and we've all split with the money." He produced a sheaf of paper. "I have here a form I've produced. I propose that, between now, and the robbery, we all kill one person." Andrew nodded while Patrick and I stared down at the table. "Doesn't matter who, doesn't matter how but it must be in a different county, another police force area, a long way away. And, before you do, you write a statement of intent, saying what you're going to do, signed and dated.

And, after the event, you update it with a confession, and a newspaper cutting. Each document will be copied, and we'll all have copies of each other's."

Patrick and I looked at each other. The pieces turned over slowly in my head. "So, if one of us goes down," I said slowly as Mike nodded encouragingly, "then we all go down."

"And we all know that we can trust each other at the sharp end," Patrick said.

"But," I started, "killing..."

Mike leaned forward, a lawyer in training. "If you've agreed to go into a situation with a loaded gun, then you have to accept the possibility that you'll have to fire it." I nodded, as did Patrick. "And if you fire it, then you also have to accept the possibility that you might kill someone. If you can't accept that, you may as well stay at home, wait til you get your degree and join the dole queue. Sit in some crummy flat drinking cheap coffee and smoking roll-ups. But it seems to me that you've already accepted that taking someone's life is worth the bigger goal, the bigger picture?" Dumbly we nodded. "So, we're good to go?"

"Yes," I said, feeling disconnection between my brain and my feelings. I had crossed the line, made agreements with a group of killers. All three of us now looked at Patrick, the one man who could betray us all.

"Wait a minute, are we suggesting murder? Killing an innocent?" He stood to leave and Mike reached out to grab his arm. I saw those big fingers digging right into the pale flesh of his forearm.

"No one's suggesting anything," Mike said in a low growl. "We've agreed. You've come here. You know the plan. You can't leave now." There was ice in his voice. He looked straight at Patrick, his meaning clear. "I've got to kill someone; I just haven't chosen who."

"Okay. Okay!" Andrew half stood and reached out to calm Mike. He released Patrick who sat down, rubbing his arm. "It's fine. It'll be a transition, adapting to the new morality. If it was easy, everyone would do it. But we must leave the herd behind, strike out in new directions. By coming here, you've already agreed. You just need to let your conscious mind catch up. This is a big opportunity, and you've all been chosen for it."

I looked between Mike and Andrew. I could feel the tension between them, one a bright shining star, the other dark and dangerous. I promised myself that this diary would be honest, so I won't write that I did it only because I was scared of Mike. Meeting Andrew was like meeting a prime minister or a rock star. At that point I wasn't even trying to get him to bed. I just wanted to please him, to do something so he'd think I was great. I could sense that he would accomplish great things and I wanted to tag along for the ride. And on the other side, I was scared of Mike, he was not someone you'd want for an enemy.

"No, no," Patrick said hastily. "Of course, yes. Thank you for bringing me in." The words were rushing out now. "I was brought up poor, coming to uni was the last chance for someone from my family to make it, and now I'm going to seize this!"

Mike slammed his huge hand down on the table. "That's it!" He looked around the table. "We've all seen the majority of humanity; they drift from being the school bullies into meaningless manual jobs. Friday night down the pub and home to spawn more children to fill the council estates and comprehensives. So what if one of them gets killed a bit early? To be honest I could give you a list of ten from my old school alone who are just a waste of oxygen!"

Now he had us in the palm of his hand. We'd been the outsiders, the dreamers, the ones who thought too deeply about things, and now we were the ones who would dare, who would act, who would go further than all the sheep around us.

"Just think about the money." Andrew now leaned forward. "If you ever waver, just remember why. When your classmates will be settling down and getting starter homes and wondering why their pay check never lasts, you'll be like a trust fund kid, managing investments, choosing sports cars, going on holidays!"

He didn't really need to say anything more. I could see a brighter future, a better class of people, moving in the circles I was entitled to.

That's when Mike produced his master stroke. Without a word, he handed out pieces of paper to each of us. They were all identical and outlined that in the next twenty-four hours he would pitch someone off the walkway outside college, straight to their death below. There were four boxes underneath, waiting for signature, name and date. Mike's was already filled in. There was a bit of shuffling as we each signed one and passed it on. Eventually we each had a document, signed by all of us.

"This is now like an affidavit," Mike explained. "Once my victim is dead, then you'll all be accessories to murder as you have proved you had prior knowledge. I suggest that Patrick goes next, then Andrew and finally Elizabeth. Also, I reiterate you must spread out around the country, then it'll all be different police forces and they won't tie anything together. Also, we shouldn't all meet together after this night. I'll pass on my signed confession and newspaper clipping in the next few days, and we'll go from there."

Several days later there was another meeting. This time furtive and hidden. We were all in one of the hall of residence rooms, having skulked in singly making sure we weren't followed. There was a damning newspaper on the table in front of us. The headline told us that Mike's victim looked likely to survive, albeit paralysed. The discussion swirled around the four of us. I was sat on the bed, knees primly together. Patrick at the other end of the bed, half turned and leaning against the wall. Andrew had the only proper chair and Mike just loomed, as always, too large for the room. Writing this all these years later, I can't believe it, but we tried to reassure Mike, tried to stop any more killing.

"Attempted murder is as serious as murder," Andrew said reasonably. "You proved that you were willing to risk a life, you took bold decisive action. It's not your fault a nurse stumbled along. One hour lying in the rain, with his blood loss, and he'd have been finished. The more crimes we commit on the run-up, the more risk. The original plan was that we go in cold – no previous records. I vote that Mike has fulfilled his obligation."

Patrick nodded grimly. "If any of us turned in the statement of intent and confession, you wouldn't see the light of day for a long time. Maybe even life. So you're as bound to us as if you killed him. I vote yes too."

All eyes turned to me. I thought then, naively, that we could restrain him. I was totally unaware of the monster we were creating. Now, having followed him through his career I'm aware that he's spent the rest of his life trying to make up for that first botched attempt. But, back then, mired in the mid-nineties, I raised my hand. "Yes, he has fulfilled his obligation."

After that, we all proceeded according to the plan. You can tell our grisly course from the papers with this diary – in case they're separated I can tell you that we all killed our victims. Mine was a nice clean shot which left a gaping wound in people's lives. I did learn from Mike's mistake and made sure no one could come along to save Bill Wormslea.

And then we came to the armed robbery. I won't bore you with the details, but the few days we spent at a self-catering holiday cottage afterwards were the most surreal of my life.

We had to bandage up Andrew's leg and finally take him to A&E with some cock and bull story about falling off a mountain bike onto a metal fence post. The rest of the time we had literally boxes of cash, piled up everywhere. We labelled the boxes and split the money, in bricks of one, two or five thousand at a time.

Andrew of course had a plan to ditch the cars and buy us one each, something small and second-hand so as not to attract attention. And then, we all went our own ways. I think this was the flaw in the master plan. We were left alone with stacks of money and an instruction not to contact each other.

There were exactly three people in the world who understood what I was going through, and I couldn't talk to any of them. With my share of the money I am resolved to try to undo the damage I have done. I have already started to donate to the Ministry of Capernaum and Bethesda and asked them to help the guard that I shot during the robbery. I will continue to live a good life and try my hardest to redress the evil I have done in this life.

CHAPTER 29

JONAH LAID ASIDE the handwritten diary and looked at the other contents of the folder. As promised, there were eight sheets of paper. Four proposals for murder, four confessions. All were signed by every member of the original group.

He had never trained as a lawyer, but he had enough experience of trying to get the CPS to prosecute based on evidence. He looked again and realised that prosecution wasn't the game here. There was ample evidence now to arrest Andrew McRae. Once he was arrested, his DNA would be taken as a matter of course. He wondered how quickly it could be matched to the sample on the cash sack.

Elizabeth and PC Baine were both watching Jonah expectantly. He gathered his thoughts and turned towards Elizabeth.

"Elizabeth Gardner, I am arresting you for two counts of murder, three of conspiracy to murder and one of armed robbery. You do not have to say anything, but it may harm your defence if you do not mention when questioned something which you later rely on in court. Anything you do say may be given in evidence. Do you understand?"

Elizabeth nodded, then remembered. "Yes," she said quietly. Tears started trickling down her cheeks. "I can't believe it's all over. What happens now? I'm not going to go over everything again and again in court. You can submit that diary, I'll attest that I've written it and it's all true. But that's it."

"I'll take you into custody in Cardiff now." Jonah turned to PC Baine. "Can you do me one last favour? Take Elizabeth in and let her collect her things. She won't be coming back here. I'll go and tell your team leader to stand down."

JONAH PUSHED BACK in his chair and stared at the screen. He'd known this day was coming but had still been unprepared. In typical fashion he has been scheduled for a meeting in DI Linwood's office at nine on a Monday morning. Nice, he thought, no time to prepare.

He climbed the stairs from the sanctuary of the Coroners Suite to CID with trepidation. He flashed back to months ago when he had left the department under a cloud. Would he still get the silent treatment? He had no doubt the grapevine was alive with rumours of his exploits, and they would all know that he had this meeting.

He reached the top of the stairs and stopped. Took a deep breath. Tried to find a spot to focus on to steady himself. The worn stair treads, industrial pale green paint, and fire doors of the stairwell did nothing to help.

Bite the bullet, he thought, and thrust the door open. Trying to appear nonchalant, he instantly took in the scene. As before, the desks were pale beech, the carpet blue. Here and there were filing cabinets and shelves occupied by printers, kettles, files and other boxes. The geography of a shared space that arises when a group of individuals were forced to work together. He kept putting one foot in front of the other and forced himself not to look for his old desk.

Slowly, impressions filtered into his consciousness. Unlike the morning of his departure, the place had its normal level of activity. Phones were answered, forms filled out, keyboards clacked, and conversations hummed.

He was already halfway to Linwood's office. The office hadn't been deserted, there was no silent treatment. He was being ignored and treated to business as usual.

To him, it felt like a standing ovation. Whatever was waiting for him in Linwood's office, it felt good to have made up ground with the rank and file CID officers.

Jonah sat down opposite his DI and tried to gauge his mood. Linwood looked back at him like a headmaster who had summoned a naughty schoolboy.

Jonah steadied himself by noting that his appearance hadn't changed. His shirt still strained to contain his stomach and his jacket was still sprinkled with dandruff.

"I thought we ought to get together after all the dust has settled from your little, um, jaunt. Expedition? Journey outside our boundaries anyway. How are things progressing with the CPS?"

Not read the paperwork, Jonah thought. "Well, they were a bit jumpy on the historic murders. Because they were twenty years ago, and there wasn't any evidence left at any of the scenes, they are not sure how safe the convictions would be."

"But I thought, ah," DI Linwood reached for some papers on his desk, "Mrs Gardner and Mr McRae were both pleading guilty?"

"Yes. But with a single confession from each, I think they're worried that they could be nutters who confess to cold cases. But I think the circumstantial evidence bears out their accounts. Also, we sent all the affidavits and the diary off to forensics. They confirmed that there's nothing to suggest they weren't written twenty years ago, and the signatures all check out too. That should help convince the CPS."

"The diary? Has Mrs Gardner said any more about that?"

"No. She's going down the written statement route. She swears under oath that it's a true record of events and that's all she's prepared to say. It does mean that she's pleading guilty to everything. She wants to go to prison as long as she can take the rest of the gang with her."

Linwood turned to stare at a calendar hung to Jonah's right. It was turned to a page that showed an operational police headquarters outside Reading. "She, um, she manipulated you? Us? Used the police to her own ends?" He appeared to be asking this question to a photo of an anonymous modern brick building.

"I don't think so, sir. I was aware she had an agenda and she might have thought she was playing us." Jonah paused for a second to work out how exactly to varnish the truth. "I was always aware that she was unstable and, in my opinion, dealt with her appropriately to achieve the best outcome all round."

"Hmmm. Well, I suppose. Yes. If that's how you see it." He turned to look at Jonah again. "However, you did ruffle some feathers, especially over at West Midlands." He scratched his ear.

"Sir? I got Mike Khan bang to rights." Jonah struggled to remain calm. He reminded himself that DI Linwood had been on his side and without his help he wouldn't have caught Elizabeth Gardner and wrapped up the whole case.

"That would be bad enough. They've been running an operation for years and then we swoop in and catch their main suspect. No one likes being made to look foolish, never mind the waste of resources. Then, worse than that, he gets killed while in our custody."

What the hell, Jonah thought. His previous good feelings towards Linwood evaporated. Out loud he said, "Sir, I had absolutely no idea that would happen. I would never expose my fellow officers to gunfire!" Jonah tried and failed to keep the annoyance from his voice.

"Well, that's as maybe, but it does, ah, look bad." Linwood sounded hurt. "Especially as earlier in the investigation, you were, erm, conducting enquiries on West Midlands turf without a formal approach."

"They were never formal enquiries," Jonah said through gritted teeth. "Khan's name came up in the case, and I had a couple of informal, off the record conversations. No Miranda, no records, just a friendly chat." There was an awkward pause. "All that aside, I have cleared up all those cold cases." Jonah swallowed his pride and prepared to play the game the way it needed to be played. "I couldn't have done that without your support." Linwood blinked twice, then realised that he could get some credit from this mess. He nodded slowly, and Jonah took this as a sign to keep on playing. "And we handed the McRae case over to West Mercia to keep them onside."

Again silence fell as Jonah recalled exactly how awkward that had been. Andrew McRae had been friendly with pretty much every ACPO level officer on the force. That had made his arrest rather embarrassing and a very quiet internal enquiry was under way.

"And, McRae is co-operating?"

"Yes, he's spent his whole life seeking power. With DNA linking him to an armed robbery, plus the two surviving guards' testimony, along with Elizabeth's diary, he knows he's going to prison. Now he's just negotiating how long before parole and at which category. That's why he's co-operating now."

"Hmph!" Linwood grunted to show that he was only interested in catching criminals and not speculating on their motives once they were caught. "And have you informed all the relevant parties in the cold cases?"

"Yeah, although CPS are dragging their heels, the cold case officers in the relevant forces are satisfied that we have found the killers and the cases will be closed."

"And I believe you had one survivor?" More papers rustled. "A Mr Peter Calne."

Jonah paled. He replayed the scene in his head. How do you tell someone that you've solved the puzzle they spent the last twenty years working on? That the entire course of their life was altered because someone was trying to prove a point. There was no conspiracy, no grudge. Just an evil man who needed a victim, any victim.

"Yeah," he said flatly. "Yeah, I let him know. As a courtesy."

"And you, are you, ummm, Okay?" Linwood asked the calendar.

Here we go, Jonah thought, the real point of the interview. "Yes, sir. Fit and ready for duty. Given all the circumstances I made myself an appointment with the duty psych and got a clean bill of health." One hour with a professional and he snowed him properly. No mention of the dreams, or the drinking, or the overwhelming fear that he wasn't strong enough.

"Yes, yes, I've got the report here." Linwood searched for the piece of paper without making eye contact with Jonah. Finally he found it and laid a big hand on top to stop it escaping. "So, you're sure you don't need any, ah, time off?"

"No, sir. If I could go back to my job, that would be best for me." He had been very careful not to take any time off. Not even annual leave.

"Hmph." Linwood scratched his ear again, adding to the dandruff on his shoulder. "Maybe that would be for the best. You went a long way off piste, caused a fuss with several other forces. Can't be seen to be rewarding you." He took a deep breath. "But, I suppose we have to admit that you did close out some cold cases as well. Yes, maybe you could carry on as before." He nodded to himself. "Best all round."

Jonah closed his eyes and exhaled, unaware that he'd been holding his breath. He had kept his job. Now all he had to do was keep his demons at bay.

ACKNOWLEDGEMENTS

Thank you for reading this book, especially if we've never met. As a writer, selling my books to strangers, is the best feeling. (Obviously, if you're friends or family, thank you for supporting me!) This was my first book to be published so it always holds a special place in my heart. As well as my readers, I have other people to thank who turn a first draft into a published book.

Melanie Underwood is my editor who finds and fixes my mistakes with endless grace and patience. The beautiful cover was designed by the talented team at Ebook Launch. Thank you to my wife Ellie who has always supported me and believed in my work, especially when I didn't. And Barry Blackmore and Anne Miller checked over the text for accuracy and typos. All surviving mistakes are mine.

Please consider leaving a review on Amazon. You can also sign up for my newsletter and learn about my other books by visiting my website GrahamHMiller.com. If you want to continue reading Jonah Greene's story, turn the page for the first chapter of the next book in the series, Buzzard House.

BUZZARD HOUSE - CHAPTER 1

Jonah Greene picked up his mobile – 6:37 in the morning – this call was not going to be good news. He got some small reassurance from seeing a work number rather than a family one.

"Uh? Hello?"

"Is this DS Greene? Jonah?" The voice sounded familiar and Jonah scrambled in his memory for a name.

"Yes. Dave Jones? What's up?" He nearly added that it had been over six months since they last spoke but bit it back. Even in his hung-over state he knew he didn't want to go back over that history.

"Yeah." There was a pause. "Thing is, we need a hand. CID, I mean."

"OK, what's up?" He checked to see if his wife, Alex, was being disturbed by the call. She pulled the duvet closer and rolled away so Jonah stayed where he was.

"Well, I pulled the overnight duty manning the phones, and we had someone fall under a train at Pontyclun this morning. Dozy 999 operator put it through to us."

"Isn't that a British Transport Police matter though?"

"Yeah, it should be. Is there any way you could swing it as a matter that the coroner needs to investigate?" There was a pause as Dave got to the point. "Last time we got into a head to head with the BTP we lost out. We'd like to even the score."

Jonah tried to swallow but his mouth was dry and tasted horrible. His head throbbed, and his eyes felt gritty. Slowly he marshalled his thoughts and tried to work through the logic of what David Jones, DC Jones in fact, was saying.

"Pontyclun is definitely in our area. And it counts as a sudden death." His thoughts were sluggish, so he felt his way along, thinking as he spoke. "So, I can certainly start my investigation before the BTP call me in."

"Definitely. And, of course, if it is complex you can always call in CID for extra support."

Jonah's emotions were slower than his thoughts, but they caught up. CID and BTP were fighting. He was a way round the problem, a way to get CID onto BTP turf. But the important thing wasn't the politics – it was that they'd called on him. For so long he had been a pariah but now he had a way to mend fences with his old team. He was even able to overlook the fact that DC Jones was treating him as an equal even though Jonah now out-ranked him as sergeant. As his head cleared, he knew he had to find a way to call in CID support. He didn't want to waste this chance to prove to his former colleagues that he could be trusted again.

"So, you'll do it?"

"Yeah, sorry, yeah. Of course. I'll call ahead and tell them not to move anything until I get there. It's the other side of Cardiff but I should only be thirty minutes or so at this time of morning."

"And you'll keep CID in the loop?" And show BTP who's in charge, was the unsaid message.

"Of course," Jonah said with a smile. Usually he hated all the politics but the chance to get one up on another force and win points with CID lifted his mood.

The fog of Jonah's headache was lifting, and a quick shower got him back into work mode. When he had finished, Alex had given up trying to sleep and was waking up for work.

"You're not normally up before me?" Alex frowned at Jonah.

"Yeah, sudden death. But it'll get me back in CID's good books so I'm willing to help."

With that, he got dressed, and within forty minutes of getting the phone call from CID, Jonah was on the platform of Pontyclun Station. It was a small, commuter station, and was more or less deserted. It had just two platforms, a bridge connecting them, and two basic shelters. Everyone who was there was official: station employees, rail workers, British Transport Police. Jonah looked around and couldn't see any passengers.

On the Cardiff bound side of the tracks was the standard white scene of crimes tent. Further back, just off the platform, the train was parked. Everything was eerily quiet – no train noise, announcements, or passengers talking. Jonah moved towards the tent, trying to work out who to ask if it was safe to go onto the tracks.

A short man in glasses approached, wearing what looked at first glance to be a regular police hi-vis vest. But Jonah knew better – he saw the chequered stripes and the words 'British Transport' above the police patch.

He held his hands out and attempted to shoo Jonah back down the platform. "I don't know how much you bribed that plod who's meant to be stopping journalists, but I'll have his job and you won't get your story! There's nothing to see here, we haven't even informed the relatives, so scuttle back ..." His monologue stopped when Jonah refused to move. Slowly the other man looked at his warrant card.

"Police, here to have a quick look over the scene."

"South Wales? CID?" He shook his head. "Fuck's sake! How many times do I have to tell them? This isn't your jurisdiction." He gestured around, then spoke slowly as if Jonah was deaf or stupid. "This is a railway. Tracks. Platform. Train. Buildings. All of it's legally railway. That means it's British Transport Police jurisdiction. If this place had sidings and sheds, then they would be mine too. Now piss off back to your station!"

"You have a dead body?"

"You know we do."

"Right. I'm DS Greene, the coroner's officer. This is a sudden death. So, I'm investigating on the coroner's behalf, under his jurisdiction."

The man gave a grim laugh. "It was sudden all right! Have you looked in the tent?" When Jonah shook his head, he continued. "Well I wouldn't if you want to keep your breakfast." There was an awkward pause. "You're the coroner's what? Which station?"

"Officer, from Cardiff Central." Jonah decided he'd pushed the other man far enough and adopted a more conciliatory tone. "I'm not CID – I answer direct to the coroner."

There was a pause as the two men stared at each other. Jonah felt a sudden twinge of doubt. What if this was a careful set-up by CID to make him look stupid?

But no, he thought, Dave had sounded like he didn't

want to talk to Jonah. He knew from his CID days that Dave didn't have any great imagination or flair for practical jokes. He felt sure that calling him had been a last resort.

He was also certain that cases like this should be cooperative between BTP and South Wales Police, but he knew it wouldn't be. Whoever this officer was, he clearly wanted to be in charge and had upset CID at some point in the past.

"Wait here while I phone my boss." This sounded like an admission of weakness from the BTP man, who turned his back to make the phone call.

With nothing better to do, Jonah looked around. He saw the white forensic tent. He had no desire to look inside, even before the warning from Mr BTP. He could only imagine what happened when hundreds of tons of moving train hit a human body.

He looked past it to the train which was stationary. He wondered if there were flecks of blood on the cab, but from this distance he couldn't tell which marks were dirt, rust, or evidence.

It was warm, even early in the morning. The combination of feeling gritty and tired at a station in the building heat cast Jonah's mind back to when he'd been a commuter. He imagined all those people packed onto trains, the different deodorants and body odours overlapping. He was glad he'd left it all behind, nearly twenty years ago now.

One of the train workers, in grubby overalls and hi-vis jacket waved to him. "You can come down if you want. It's not electric yet. They keep promising, but ..." He shrugged.

Jonah jumped down awkwardly. It was further than he realised. He had an uneasy feeling. Since his school days the message 'stay off the tracks' had been drilled into him.

He walked slowly towards the tent, allowing his eyes to sweep left and right across the tracks.

"Hey! What you doing down there?" BTP was back.

"The maintenance guy said I could," Jonah said.

"Well I didn't authorise it. I told you to wait while I phoned my boss."

"And, what did he say?"

"Apparently, we're to cooperate and share our findings," he said grudgingly.

"There you are, this is me, co-operating," Jonah said. As there seemed to be nothing else to say, he turned around and continued walking up the tracks, still scanning for anything that the BTP had missed.

At first, there was nothing of interest, just the usual litter of cigarette packets and fast food wrappers, all covered with a thin film of grease and dirt. Then something brighter caught his eye.

Trapped under one edge of the scene-of-crime tent was a crumpled photograph. Jonah pulled on a latex glove and carefully picked it up by one corner. It was still bright, not dirty like everything else down on the tracks. The subject was a boy, grinning awkwardly into the camera, slightly out of focus, and badly framed. It looked faded as if it was an old photo.

Jonah flipped it over and sagged. On the back was written 'Cofiwch Tŷ Bwncath'. Welsh. He hadn't been taught the language at school and had only learnt the basics since to get by. In this part of Wales, it wasn't necessary. With a sense of resignation, he slipped it into an evidence bag.

"Oi!" Jonah looked up to the platform, BTP was glaring at him. "What are you doing down there?"

The man was short but being on the platform he loomed over Jonah.

"I'm just doing my job, checking for evidence. Second pair of eyes and all that."

BTP man moved down the platform to get closer to Jonah. "What did you pick up?"

"Just an old photo," Jonah admitted, holding it up in its bag.

"Hmmm, well, like I said, cooperate and share," he said grudgingly. "Make sure you let us know if it's significant. There's so much crap on the tracks though, it's going to be nothing." He looked awkward as if making a confession. "I suppose with a high-profile case like this we'll have to bring in some CID officers to help us. When they're on board, I'll tell them to set up an evidence officer and you can show him your photo."

Jonah smiled to himself and nodded curtly. He had to turn away before the other man saw him smiling. He was imagining the reaction when the BTP officer tried issuing orders to CID.

"How high profile exactly?" Jonah asked. "Have you identified the body?"

The BTP officer looked around as if seeking a way out. He couldn't find one. "According to his driving license he was one Leo Davidson, aged fifty-seven." Jonah got his pocketbook out to make his own notes. "He lived near here, so he was probably commuting up to London. Obviously, we can't check if he looks like his photo but there's nothing to indicate he's not."

"Occupation?"

"He was a big name in sport, football and stuff, then he sat on committees. Probably lived near here because it's close to Ninian Park. He was on the board of directors for Cardiff FC and various charities."

Jonah looked around again. "Any witnesses, did you take names?"

"No, as soon as it happened most of the commuters bolted for the car park. We cleared the train, got buses to take them onward. They won't have seen anything either."

"So, no witnesses then? What about CCTV?" Jonah looked up and down the platform for cameras.

"Only in the ticket office and the car park." He jerked a thumb at the end of the platform. "That one was busted last week. Kids messing around."

"Kids? Are you sure?" Jonah looked up at the camera. It was a good ten meters above the platform on a thin pole. "What happened to it?"

"Plastic cover over the lens shattered. Like I said, it'll be kids with catapults or an air rifle or something. It's down on a list to be repaired."

"You don't think it's odd? The week before our victim goes under a train?"

"No." There was a firmness in his voice. "This is a railway. Kids always vandalise railways, it's what they do. We have thousands of miles of track, buildings, bridges, tunnels, machinery. You name it, they'll have a go. It's like they know we can't watch it all at once. If you went up and down here, you'd find graffiti, broken windows, stuff chucked on the tracks anything, and everything. And none of it would be connected with this case, it happens all the time."

Jonah thought around the problem. He came to one uncomfortable conclusion. "The driver, he must've seen what happened?"

"He'll be in the system now. We have a process to follow, some time off and mandatory counselling. When or if he feels able to tell his counsellor what happened, we have an arrangement. The details of what he saw, whatever he feels able to say, will get passed to me." He stopped there, and Jonah waited for the rest of the process.

"You'll let me know when that happens." Jonah filled in the gap. "I'll need to determine whether it's suicide, accident, or murder."

The BTP officer stomped off without a word. Jonah would've preferred a chance to interview the driver himself, but he knew he would get no further with the BTP officer. He also thought that the driver had witnessed something terrible and should be dealt with professionally.

Jonah shrugged and slipped the photograph into his pocket. As he left the scene, he phoned in to CID to let them know that he'd done what they wanted. Now, he would have to start a full investigation into the life of Leo Davidson and determine how he came to die under a train.

Later that morning, Jonah sifted through a folder full of paper and tried to put together a picture of Leo Davidson's life. In the past he'd tended to pigeon-hole people and define them by their occupation, such as a librarian, or a retired property developer, but Leo's life was more complicated. He had been a football player in his youth – he'd never broken into the higher leagues of the sport as a player, but after he left the pitch, he'd moved first to coaching, then to management. Recently his time had been split between sitting on the boards of several local teams, and various charity committees, all of them based around promoting sport among the young. Jonah picked up a brochure and phrases leapt out at him. 'Legacy of the Olympics', 'obesity time bomb', and 'timely intervention to create a lifelong passion for sport'.

The door opened, and DS Farida Philips came in, holding two coffees. She was wearing her official dark blue hijab. They had become friends over the last few months and she'd saved his life earlier in the year. "I brought coffee." She looked closely at him. "Looks like you need it."

"I'm fine, just got woken up early by this case. The victim was a commuter on an early start."

Farida's eyes narrowed. "Still looks like you're not sleeping."

Jonah took the coffee and pointedly didn't answer.

"So, what have we got then?" Farida changed tack.

"Well, a lot of passengers who may or may not be witnesses left the station as soon as they realised they wouldn't be able to get the train into work that morning."

"Brilliant," Farida said sarcastically.

"And as soon as the track was closed, station staff set up a replacement bus service which took the remaining passengers off to the next station."

"So, no witnesses?"

"Well the driver should make a statement in the next couple of days. But that'll be made to a counsellor and funnelled through the BTP, so God only knows when we'll see it."

Farida frowned and reached for a folder. "So, what are you doing here then?"

"Well, he was some big shot in the world of sport. Professional footballer when he was young, moved on to various boards and charities. Ate lunches on expenses and drank champagne with councillors, Assembly Members, and MPs. So, however he died, it's going to be high profile.

"What we need to do is look into our victim's life. What was he like, what happened to him? Was there any event recently that might lead him to commit suicide? Was he depressed? Or did he have enemies?"

"Even you can't be thinking murder at this early stage?"

"I don't know. I can't see why he would have simply fallen off a flat platform, so it's either murder or suicide."

"He could've had another problem, like a stroke or something."

"That is possible, but it'd be a one in a million chance if he had an event like that at precisely the moment the train was coming in." Jonah stopped to think. "I really doubt the post-mortem would pick it up."

"So," Farida said, "murder or suicide, with no witnesses?"

"It's not as if we can't track down the witnesses. He was waiting for the six twenty-two into Cardiff Central, where you can change for a train to London, stopping at Bristol." When Farida looked blank, he continued. "That's a commuter train. I can go down there tomorrow at the same time, and most of the same people will be there. They'll be waiting at the same spot on the platform so they can get on their usual seat on the train, every day."

"You'd better catch up on sleep then. It looks like the next early morning will finish you off!" Farida's tone was light, but Jonah ignored the jibe again. "Is there any CCTV?"

"Yes, but only the ticket office and car park. Should be emailed through later today. If you have time, you could help me go through it? We can see who was on the platform this morning. Then tick them off and see who doesn't turn up again tomorrow."

"Anyway, what am I doing here?" Farida asked. Jonah frowned at her. "I mean, no disrespect, but you could do this. It's your bread and butter now to go through the details and build a profile. And he's a public figure so there's plenty of information out there."

Jonah gave a wry smile. "I think this is part of my rehabilitation back into the murky world of CID office politics. At some point, BTP stood on South Wales Police's toes and they've been at odds ever since. Because I answer to the coroner, I have a foot in the door of this investigation which will upset the BTP and therefore make CID happy."

"So, I'm your reward then?" Farida had an amused half-smile.

"Kind of. Also, you're in CID, so you can report straight back to them and keep tabs on what me and the BTP are up to."

Farida shook her head despairingly.

"Damn! I almost forgot, what do you make of this?" Jonah took the photo out of his pocket and passed it over to Farida.

She took the evidence bag and turned it over to study both sides. "Don't know. Looks old. It's a proper photo, not a digital one. No website address or anything on the back. Is it from the scene?"

"Yes. But no way of telling how long it was there. That on the back looks like a blood spot."

"And it's fairly clean and dry." She frowned for a minute. "It rained last week so at most it's been on the tracks a few days. Have you translated the Welsh yet?"

"No." Jonah shook his head. "I didn't do it in school, and I haven't picked up that much since."

"It means, 'remember house something'. Hold on, there's an app you can get." She fished out her mobile phone. "Remember Buzzard House," she said triumphantly after a few seconds.

Jonah frowned. "Buzzard House? Where is that?"

"No idea. But I do have Google." They fell silent as she tapped away on her phone. Then she pushed the phone away from her as if she'd been burned.

"Shit!"

Now Jonah was worried – Farida hardly ever swore.

He looked at the screen and saw the result. It was a site for survivors of child abuse to tell their stories. And there was a whole page just for Tŷ Bwncath. He read the first paragraph out loud.

"From 1981 to 1994 Tŷ Bwncath operated as an outdoor activity centre. Specialising in giving holidays in the countryside to looked after children from inner-city areas, thousands of children stayed there on residential courses. However, rumours have circulated for decades about the abuse some of them allegedly suffered." Jonah frowned at the screen. "What are looked after children?"

"Children in care," Farida explained. "It's the new term for it, but official bodies use both."

Jonah nodded and handed the phone back to Farida. They looked at each other, unsure of what to say.

"This is not good," Farida finally said. "This could end our careers."

"What do you mean? Surely if this man was involved, people should know?"

"Not necessarily. It closed twenty-four years ago. At the moment, the only link we've got between Leo Davidson and that place is this one photograph." She stopped and rubbed her eyes, then got up to stand by the window. "How did you collect the photo, has it been logged yet?"

"I did it properly," Jonah said, hurt. "Rubber glove, by the edges, into the bag."

"Good. This is a nightmare. I say we get it a full work over from documents. We need to know the age, subject, everything. Is that Leo's blood? How long was it on the tracks? Are there any fingerprints?"

Jonah came over to stand next to her. "Are you sure? It's only one photo?"

"After Savile and Operation Yewtree there is only one way forward, and that's by the book. Actually, it wasn't Operation Yewtree, it's what happened beforehand. People reported Jimmy Savile several times. Reports were made, police forces opened cases, and nothing happened."

"Nothing?"

"No, the reports all just disappeared. Savile was canny and had friends in high places who could make all the trouble go away." Farida stopped to make sure that Jonah was listening. "Now that's happened once, we need to be super careful. There's only two ways this can go – either we ruin the reputation of someone who was innocent but had political connections, or we prove that he was a paedophile. I'm not sure which would be worse."

Jonah went back to the desk and opened a file. "You're right. The thing about Savile was that he was a loner. And everyone thought he was a creep. I mean no one heard the news and said, 'What him? I don't believe it!' Everyone kind of expected it. The reports must have been floating around for decades. It was only when he died that the victims came forward."

"Is there any family for Davidson?"

"We haven't had a chance to work out anything detailed yet. Next of kin was his wife, now his widow, so we'll need to be careful."

Farida left the window and walked to the board. Miraculously she found a pen that worked. "Right. We have one photo that may or may not be linked to Leo." She wrote 'photo' and 'Davidson' on the board with a dotted line between them. "That photo itself may or may not be linked to a place called Tŷ Bwncath. Which in turn may or may not have been the site of historic child abuse." She added these to the board.

"Can you do the document forensics?" Jonah asked, looking at the square of dotted lines that Farida had now drawn on the board.

"Yes. If I tell them it's sticking it to BTP, then the budget will be okay."

"Great, and I'll tackle Tŷ Bwncath." He picked up her phone and scrolled down a bit. "It says here it's north of Merthyr, so the first thing is to see if it's in our area or Dyfed Powys. Then I'll go through this website, see if it's real or not. Check for any outstanding investigations. I'll do it on the quiet, not raise any expenses. I can also check and see if there's any legitimate connection between Davidson and Tŷ Bwncath."

"Legitimate?"

"Well, he was a professional footballer, then he moved into management, and ended up getting onto the board of directors of several clubs. Tŷ Bwncath was an outdoor activity centre. It's just the sort of thing he'd have supported, been on the board of, or maybe coached at. That kind of thing. I have to build up a profile anyway, so I can keep an eye out to see if he had any connection to this place."

"And who do we tell?" Farida asked the one question that had hung in the room since that Google search.

"No one, yet. You're right – this is a time bomb. It could be nothing. Or mistaken identity."

"Or someone could've pushed a paedophile under a train," Farida said darkly.

"Which is still a crime," Jonah reminded her.

CONTINUE READING

You can buy Buzzard House on Amazon, available in all territories.

Made in the USA
Middletown, DE
14 February 2024

49751232R00209